APR 1 9 2007

DATE DUE

LEMONADE MOUTH

MARK PETER HUGHES

Delacorte Press
New York

Published by Delacorte Press
an imprint of Random House Children's Books
a division of Random House, Inc.
New York

This is a work of fiction. Names, characters, places, and incidents either are the
product of the author's imagination or are used fictitiously. Any resemblance to
actual persons, living or dead, events, or locales is entirely coincidental.

www.randomhouse.com/teens

Educators and librarians, for a variety of teaching tools,
visit us at www.randomhouse.com/teachers

Library of Congress Cataloging-in-Publication Data

Hughes, Mark Peter.
Lemonade Mouth / by Mark Peter Hughes.
p. cm.
Summary: A disparate group of high school students thrown together in deten-
tion form a band to play at a school talent show and end up competing with a
wildly popular local rock band.
ISBN: 978-0-385-73392-2 (trade ed.)
ISBN: 978-0-385-90404-9 (lib. ed.)
[1. Musicians—Fiction.   2. Interpersonal relations—Fiction.   3. High
schools—Fiction.   4. Schools—Fiction.]   I. Title.
PZ7.H8736113Lem 2007
[Fic]—dc22   2006020429

The text of this book is set in 11-point Galliard.

Book design by Trish Parcell Watts

Printed in the United States of America

10 9 8 7 6 5 4 3 2 1

First Edition

I'd like to thank my editor, Stephanie Lane, for her keen eye and sound advice, and my agent, Andy McNicol. Thanks also to all the folks at Random House who helped put this book together, especially Shameiza Ally; Anjulee Alvares; Lesley Krauss; Barbara Perris and her eagle-eyed cohorts; Tamar Schwartz; Trish Parcell Watts; and the fantastic Random House sales team. Special thanks to the following for their assistance and support: the Commando Writers (Michael A. Di Battista, Scott Fitts, Geoffrey H. Goodwin, Dalia Rabinovich and John Smith—go commando!), Suzanne Winnell Hughes, Peter Hughes, Susan Green, Hamilton Hackney, Ayesha Khanna, Raymonda Khoury, Shauna Leggat, Lauren McGovern, Kevin McGurn, Claudia Sorsby, Guru Swamy and Margarita Winnell. This book was made possible, in part, by a Society of Children's Book Writers & Illustrators Work-in-Progress Grant.

Last and most, I'd like to thank my wife, Karen. *Muchos besos, sandía de amor.*

For Evan, Lucía and Zoe—
mi tiburón, mi mariposa y mi frijol

PROLOGUE

Dear Reader,

As anyone can tell you, the facts surrounding the rise and fall of the late great Lemonade Mouth are steeped in legend and shrouded in mystery.

But I was there. I know the real scoop, the honest dish.

As a member of that historic Opequonsett High School freshman class and a close friend to the central players of the phenomenon, I have insights that future biographers will no doubt lack. Not that getting the full story out of each of those involved was easy. Stella, for example, had so much to say during my interviews that I ended up having to treat her to lunch three separate times—which cost a bundle. Olivia, on the other hand, left me only a small stack of photocopied letters with such faint handwriting that I had to hold them up to the light just to read them. Getting Charlie's part of the story should have been easy, since he was supposed to type it up for Mr. Levesque over the summer in order to avoid a failing grade in English Comp, but he ended up taking so long hunting and pecking at the keyboard that for a while it seemed like I'd see old age and death before I'd ever see his report.

But fear not, Dear Reader. My patience and efforts were well rewarded. And I'm pleased to be the only reporter with exclusive permission to tell the whole story, even the prickly, embarrassing parts.

At least the stuff they admitted to.

So it's fair to say that the document you hold in your hands is the definitive anthology of Lemonade Mouth, presenting a unique opportunity to peer inside the heads of each of the Fab Five. In keeping with the best practices of journalism, I have endeavored to report the facts in as truthful and unbiased a manner as possible.

Except when I didn't have all the facts.

In that case I just had to guess.

> *Naomi Fishmeier*
> *Scene Queen & Official Biographer*
> *of Lemonade Mouth*

CHAPTER 1

Misbehavior is a key attribute of true genius.
—Phineas Fletcher

WEN:
The Yungas Would Have to Wait

It all started when Sydney climbed out of the truck. Somehow, even though I didn't know it yet, what happened that autumn morning is what set everything else in motion. The second the passenger door banged shut, I turned to my dad.

"So tell me, is she living with us now or what?"

My dad kept us idling at the curb while she promenaded all the way to the bus stop, finally turning to blow him a kiss. "No, not at all," he said, snapping out of his trance. "She's just going through some roommate problems. It's not permanent."

Until August or so, my little brother George and I had hardly ever run into Sydney, my dad's girlfriend, even though they'd been seeing each other since the spring. Unfortunately, over the last month we'd started seeing a lot more of her.

Which, for me, was a real problem.

As we pulled away from the curb I snuck one last look in her direction. I tried to will myself not to, but I couldn't help it. Today, an early October morning as warm and humid as summer, she was wearing a revealing halter top and a pair of tight cutoff jeans that accentuated her butt perfectly. My God.

Dad was obviously going through some kind of midlife crisis.

At twenty-six, Sydney was sixteen years younger than he was. I sometimes caught myself fantasizing about her shiny black hair or her cartoon breasts. I felt terrible about it, *horrible*. After all, this was my *dad's* girlfriend.

I hated myself.

Still, my eyes couldn't help following her across the window until, mercifully, she slipped out of sight.

"You could've fooled me. She spends more time at our place than *I* do." I immediately regretted saying it. My dad wasn't about to let a comment like that go, and I had other worries at that moment. Not only had we wasted time dropping off Sydney, but before that we'd taken too long getting George to school, and before *that* we'd left our house late because Sydney took forever in the bathroom. So now I'd already missed homeroom and would probably arrive late for my social studies presentation. I was first on today's list.

"That's not true and you know it," Dad said, racing us through a yellow light.

I didn't answer. When he glanced over at me, I couldn't help thinking about how everybody was always saying how much we looked alike. And it was true that we had similar faces, both of us blond with glasses. My hair fell almost to

4

my eyes, though, while his was cropped short and starting to go gray over the ears. Our glasses were very different too. I wore black rectangular frames while he'd recently bought round wire-rims like John Lennon. Sydney's idea.

"Come on," he said. "Out with it."

I fiddled with the latch on my trumpet case. That afternoon I had freshman tryouts for Marching Band. "Well, for starters," I said, "she's a mooch. Practically every day I come home and she's loafing on our sofa watching our TV. Either that or she's helping herself to our food while she's parked at our kitchen table doing her little drawings." Sydney was studying part-time to be a graphic artist.

"She pulls her weight," he said, as if that had anything to do with it. "She cooks sometimes, and picks up around the house. Unlike somebody else I could name."

Right. She was like having our own nanny, the Sex Nanny Sent By Satan.

We shot past the line of orange cones in front of the school's new, state-of-the-art gymnasium, a construction project that was supposed to be finished over the summer but was still not quite complete because of money problems. Finally, my dad's truck screeched to a halt at the front entrance. That's when he turned to me and gave his I'm-opening-up-to-you-so-cut-me-some-slack look.

"Look, I know you're not sold on Sydney yet, but I happen to think she's terrific. She's smart and caring and a lot of fun. All I'm asking is that you hold your judgment, okay? Think about it? For your old man?"

I grabbed my backpack, my trumpet and the big manila envelope that held my presentation. I shoved the door open and hopped out of the truck.

"Okay?"

"Gotta go, Dad. I'm late."

I slammed the door and dashed up the steps. Once inside the school building, I knew from the empty hallway that the first-period bell had already rung.

I sprinted down the long central corridor. Up ahead I happened to pass Jonathan Meuse as he jogged toward one of the chemistry labs. A popular junior with a lot of friends, Jonathan was tall, redheaded and about as clean-cut as they came. He looked like a soap commercial with biceps. Most significantly, he was the student leader of the Marching Band trumpet section and would be at the tryouts that afternoon. I often ran into him in the hallways but he never acknowledged my existence because I was only a freshman. Like now. I'm positive he saw me wave but he ignored me.

I kept running.

Unfortunately, seeing Jonathan brought my mind back to this afternoon's tryouts again, which sent another jolt through my stomach. There was a lot on the line today. The way I saw it, getting into the high school Marching Band would be vital for my social life. I know, I know. You're probably thinking I'm nuts, that Marching Band kids are usually the opposite of popular. But I'd been studying it, and it was clear to me that Marching Band nerddom wasn't a firm rule. Just look at Jonathan—he'd figured out how to use it as a springboard to cool. And so would I.

Thing was, after two long years of living in middle school Nobodyland, I'd spent the beginning of ninth grade secretly observing the most popular kids—not just Jonathan, but also Seth Levine, Scott Pickett and guys like that—to see if I could learn anything that might improve my own social status. I figured if I emulated the coolest, after a while everybody would assume I was cool too. Like, right then I was wearing the same kind of Polo shirt and khaki pants I'd once seen on Seth Levine. When I'd waved to Jonathan, I did it in the same way I'd seen Scott Pickett wave to his friends—one motion, like a windshield wiper that suddenly stops midway. Yeah, I know this probably sounds stupid, but that was my strategy. If it looks like a duck and quacks likes a duck, it's a duck, right? It was all about attitude. Anyway, one other thing I'd noticed in my research was that pretty much all the popular guys were in at least one club or another. Usually it was sports, but *not always*.

Of course, sports were out of the question for me since I was about as coordinated as a jellyfish.

Which left me with Marching Band.

It might not be the football team, but it was all I had.

Finally I reached my classroom. By the time I burst through the door I was out of breath. Mr. Prichard, a stocky rooster of a guy, glanced significantly at the clock. "Well, well, well, Wendel. We were beginning to wonder if you were going to make it."

"Sorry I'm late," I panted, stepping past him and to my seat.

"We're just pleased that you deigned to grace us with your presence at *all* this morning."

I set my bag down.

"You do recall that today you're presenting, correct?"

"Uh, yes. I'm ready to do it now, if you are." I tried to grin confidently but was so frazzled that I think all I managed to communicate was panic.

"That would be nice."

Drew Baker and Jesse Rathbone, a couple of jokers I knew from middle school, leered at me.

I grabbed the envelope and headed to the front of the

room. On the way I took a deep breath and told myself to calm down. I was prepared for this. I knew everything about Bolivia. I'd memorized a speech about the Altiplano and the Yungas, I'd printed two five-color maps showing rainfall patterns and population density, and I'd even made handouts demonstrating the catastrophic effect the drought caused by El Niño in 1997 and 1998 had on the potato harvest. This would be a cinch.

But as I pulled the stack of papers from the envelope, my heart nearly stopped.

The top sheet was *not* one of my handouts. It was a charcoal sketch of a solemn-faced woman lying on a sofa. A completely naked, solemn-faced woman.

"Wendel?" asked Mr. Prichard. "Is there something wrong?"

I flipped to the next sheet. The same naked woman leaning forward with a pencil in her hand. In the one after that she sat on the floor. I was holding an entire stack of nude drawings of some lady.

Olivia Whitehead, a large, silent girl with shapeless hair that hung in a flat sheet around her head and often looked like it could use a good wash, gaped at me from the front row, her mouth hanging slightly open. I could hear her breathing.

I felt myself starting to sweat. How had this happened? Then I remembered Sydney asking my dad for an envelope to carry her most recent sketches to class. It was a drawing seminar called The Human Form. My dad had given her an identical envelope from the same stack as mine. Sitting next to me in the truck, she could easily have grabbed my envelope by mistake and left me hers.

That's when I looked more closely at the woman's face. It wasn't perfect, but she had the high, wide cheekbones, the tumble of unruly hair and far-apart eyes like a bird's. A wave of horror washed over me. It was *Sydney*. She must have sat in front of a mirror and used herself as a model.

I couldn't help staring down at Sydney's body, her big round breasts and secret hair. I flipped back and forth through the pictures. I suddenly realized that (a) there was no way I would be able to do my presentation, and (b) I was standing in front of my entire social studies class holding a stack of naked self-portraits of my father's girlfriend.

But that wasn't the worst of it. When I looked up again at the class I realized that everybody was staring at me like I was some kind of freak. Paul Cramer's eyes were wide. Elaine Wettenberg's lip curled in obvious disgust. I didn't understand at first. Surely they couldn't see the pictures.

But then somebody giggled.

And suddenly I knew.

I looked down and my worst suspicions were confirmed. There it was. A big, obvious triangle at the crotch of my jeans. A sideways teepee.

I don't remember swearing, but apparently I did. All I remember doing is dropping the stack of drawings to cover myself and then shooting out of the room. The Altiplano and the Yungas would have to wait for another day.

I staggered down the corridor. Even several doors away, the laughter from my classroom still echoed off the walls. My life was over. Even then I knew that this wasn't the kind of incident that got forgotten. Everyone had seen me standing there speechless at the front of the class, oblivious about Happy Roger saluting like a little soldier at full attention. Word would spread quickly. I was going to have to hear about this my whole freshman year, and then for the rest of high school. Decades from now, the story would still come up at reunions, with people buckling over with laughter at the memory.

Even then I understood that if I'd ever really had any chance of coolness, I could now kiss it goodbye. 🎐

STELLA:
Hail to You, My Evil Soul-Sista!

Once upon a time there were five little darlings named Charlie, Olivia, Wen, Mo and Stella, who sprang from the earth in a flash of light. For a while they stood around, ignoring each other and wondering who had put them together and why. All of a sudden a Kindly Old Fairy Godlady appeared before them and waved her wand saying, quote, "Thou shalt sprout Mouths of Lemonade!" And so they did, and, fortunately, they soon discovered that it was neither as sticky nor as uncomfortable as it had at first sounded. "Thank you, Kindly Old Fairy Godlady," they said, thanking her.

What can I tell you about Sista Stella that you haven't by now heard from those who already think they know everything?

Plenty.

I wear boxers. I like fruitcake. I've been a vegetarian since eighth grade. The summer after that, my mother got a new job heading a start-up development project at a lab in Rhode Island (something to do with saving the planet by making cheap biodegradable plastic out of plants), so a week before high school began, my family (my mom, my sister, Clea, and me, plus Leonard and the step-monkeys) had to pack our bags and load a U-Haul. If we hadn't left

Tempe, Arizona, would there still have been Lemonade Mouth? Who's to say?

If you want the story of *my* part in everything—and you want it to make *sense*—then I can't jump right into Lemonade Mouth. I'll need to begin a little earlier, explain a few things about my screwed-up life. There are a lot of misconceptions out there.

Let's start with my hair. As a lot of people know, since I was a little girl I'd always kept it all the way down to my waist. So why, two weeks into my freshman year, did I, in a fit of frustrated rage, hack it all off, leaving little more than short tufts?

Allow me to carry you back in time to that fateful Monday in late September when Stella, our incorrigible heroine, locked herself in the bathroom and went to work with a pair of scissors.

What on earth could have possessed her? What was going on in her head? At the time there were a number of theories.

My own mother, for instance, days later (after she'd gotten over her initial shock at seeing her formerly long-haired offspring in this new and strange state), would give a patronizing roll of her eyes and explain to anybody who asked that "Stella's still working through anger issues about moving." Which of course I *was*. It wasn't *my* idea to transplant my already sorry excuse for a life across the country to some nothing little town I'd never heard of. And did anybody act like I even mattered in the decision? Neither my mother nor Leonard had even asked for my thoughts before announcing that the move to Rhode Island was a done deal. Nobody *ever* asked my opinion. And after that, everything seemed to happen in a flash. Before I could even say *quahog*,

I found myself in New England at a cliquey new school that I hated, where I didn't know anyone and nobody talked to me.

"Thank you, O Mother Dear," gushes our smiling young protagonist, "for uprooting me from everything I'd ever known and loved!"

Of course I was angry. Who wouldn't have been?

Yes, the move may have been *part* of the reason why I ended up rifling through the kitchen drawers for a pair of scissors on that clear September evening. But it may surprise some of your readers to hear that it was *not* ultimately what pushed me over the edge.

My sister, Clea, who had recently started her freshman year at nearby Brown University but still often spent evenings stretched out on the family sofa in a self-absorbed fog, had a different theory. She thought it was all about a missed appointment.

"We all know Stella," she was overheard snorting to Leonard the next day. "She's immature and always has to have her own way. In her mind, just because she *finally* decides to get her hair styled, that means the whole world should stop in its tracks. So when my car breaks down and Mom has to pick me up instead of driving her into Seekonk for her all-important appointment, what's her natural reaction? Tizzy overdrive!"

As with many wrong theories, this one also wasn't completely devoid of truth. My mother *had* promised to drive me to get my hair cut, and in fact, this was the third appointment the distracted woman had made me cancel due to last-minute "emergencies." And I was indeed desperate to fix my appearance. It probably sounds strange, but after the move I started obsessing about things. I felt self-conscious about how much I'd grown over the summer—I'd always been on the tall side, but now I stood just over six feet in my socks. And my superlong hair was suddenly all wrong. *I* was all wrong. It didn't help matters that on my second day at my new school, as I ambled down the aisle to take my seat in Algebra, I passed a girl in a mohair cardigan and overheard her whisper, "Hippie Bigfoot," to the girl beside her, another mohair cardigan. I nearly died. Clearly, some drastic change was required if I was going to fit in around here. And since there was nothing I could do about my height, I suddenly felt my 'do was the obvious place to start. Something shorter, with more style, more oomph. Even though it would be a sacrifice, I was determined to make it happen as soon as possible.

But it wasn't my family's constant crises that led me to the radical mutilation of my coiffure.

Some people say it was because of Mr. Brenigan, the Vice Principal at Opequonsett High School. They point out that the very day I got busy with the scissors happened to be the same one in which the high school Powers That Be sent me home for wearing an allegedly obscene article of clothing. All it had been was a plain army-green T-shirt, albeit snug-fitting, onto which I'd added two handprints in yellow acrylic paint. But the small-minded autocrats in the front office felt that since the two handprints happened to fall on my breasts, the shirt was somehow inappropriate for a learning environment. The shirt was, of course, art. It was also the trademark look of Sista Slash, the famous activist and musical anarchist. I used to wear mine at my old school all the time, so when I picked it out that morning I honestly hadn't thought anything of it. But Mr. Brenigan insisted that I could return to school only after I'd changed into more appropriate attire.

Even now I can remember his exact words:

13

"Opequonsett High doesn't have a dress code, exactly. It's just that we have an unwritten line and that shirt crosses it." Mr. Brenigan, who looks like a tired Michelin Man with a receding hairline, leaned back in his chair and tapped his fingers together while he talked, as if what he was saying was deep.

"But . . . what about freedom of expression?" I asked, trying to hide the fact that I was nearly crapping in my jeans. It wasn't as if I'd ever been sent home from school when I lived in Tempe. Juvenile delinquency was new to me.

Mr. Brenigan gave me a steady gaze that went on and on. I began to wonder with growing alarm whether I'd missed something. That's another thing you ought to understand about me—I often found myself struggling to keep up, and it freaked me out a little. Maybe because every other member of my family was certifiably brilliant. My father, a biochemistry PhD like my mother, was working on a cure for pancreatic cancer in St. Louis. My sister was at Brown. My mother ran a lab that sounded like something straight out of science fiction, for godsakes! Even my step-family was impressive. Leonard had started his own software company and was a millionaire by age twenty-five, and the step-monkeys, at eight, were already demonstrating a surprising aptitude for taking apart their electronic toys and putting them back together again. My own apparent dumbness was a source of constant embarrassment. In biology class on my very first day, for example, instead of paying attention to Mrs. Birch's long, boring speech about some moth in England, I'd found myself staring at Mrs. Birch's belly, which stuck out from her otherwise-slender body like a beach ball. At the end of the lecture, when the teacher

14

asked if anybody had questions, I raised my hand and asked, "Are you pregnant?" At this, the boy next to me quipped, "No, Einstein, she just stuck a pillow under her shirt. It's the latest fashion." The class broke out in fits of laughter. I tried to shrink in my chair.

Anyway, during Mr. Brenigan's long silence I felt myself blush.

Eventually he half smiled. "You can't change the world. We run a tight ship here, Stella, and everybody's part of the same crew. I don't know what you were used to back in *Arizona*"—at this point he eyed me significantly as if he were studying an obvious bad egg from a scandalous part of the country—"but you'll soon learn that *here,* we respect the rules. Written and unwritten."

As you might imagine, that almost sent me into a frustrated conniption. So it does seem plausible that the T-shirt incident, together with Mr. Brenigan's speech, the memory of my stolen Arizona life, and the reality of finding myself an outcast in a new unfriendly school in a hostile new state, as well as my mother's obvious disregard for my feelings might, in combination, have been enough to set off the whirlwind of snapping scissors and flying hair that soon followed.

But it wasn't. Not quite.

Not to say that each of those points didn't weigh on my troubled mind. They absolutely did. But what ultimately sent me storming into the bathroom that night was something else.

So what was it? All right. I'll tell you.

The truth was, I didn't really know. All I understood was that I'd had a feeling welling up inside me for a while, a feeling I'd barely noticed at first but that now was growing

15

so fast it was practically taking over everything else. Like I was going to explode. Like all the atoms in my body were getting ready to burst and it was only a question of when.

I was a walking time bomb.

A piece of paper I received that day may also have contributed to The Hair Incident. In some other week, perhaps, the bad news delivered on this document might have rolled right off me instead of hitting me head-on like a renegade garbage truck. But given my volatile state in that monumentally crappy twenty-four-hour period, it's possible that this little spark might have been all that was needed to set me off.

So what was it?

It arrived in the mail. At home that afternoon, waiting for my mother to drive me to my appointment (still unaware that said appointment wasn't to be), I checked the mailbox. I noticed the envelope addressed to me right away—it was long and white and in the top left corner was the address of J. Edgar Hoover Middle School in Tempe, Arizona. There were several stickers eventually directing the letter to Rhode Island. I had a sudden idea what it was. Back in June, my old school had held a "Future Careers Fair" where a nurse, an insurance salesman, two artists and a veterinarian spoke to a crowd of eighth graders about their jobs. We could choose to take short written multiple-choice tests that were supposed to tell us about our personalities, aptitudes and the kinds of careers we might consider someday. Foolishly, I'd signed up and taken the tests. The results were apparently mailed late and, since my family had moved, had taken even more time to find their way to me. To be honest, by then I'd forgotten all about that fair.

But now here was the envelope. So I opened it.

Within seconds I felt like day-old crap.

Now, please forgive me if I don't detail everything the

16

letter said, except to say that it included an IQ score that confirmed my worst suspicions about myself. I knew something about IQ scores. My mother, a member of Mensa, the club for people with intelligence quotients in the top two percent of the general population, has an IQ of 164. I knew that 100 was average. So when I saw the number written by my name, that about-to-explode sensation I'd felt growing inside me for days quickly swelled until it was almost unbearable, until it literally throbbed through my body. Here was indisputable proof of why I so often found myself lost in class, why I was bad at math, bad at English, bad at everything.

Eighty-four.

In a family of geniuses, I was now a documented dummy.

I believe there are moments that can make you burst out of yourself, smash through the boundaries of your everyday life, the unhappy existence you have until then accepted without protest, and make a change that is dramatic, unexpected and right. And that, my friends, is the only explanation I can offer for what I did to my hair that night, why I apparently lost my mind.

Within minutes after my mother came home, I was at the bathroom sink with my hands gripping the porcelain so hard my knuckles were white. In the mirror my bangs covered my eyes, and shapeless turd-brown hair framed my grimacing face like limp drapes. *Eighty-four!* I wanted to scream but didn't. Instead, I held the scissors just above my left cheek and made the first cut. A long ribbon of hair fell to the floor. After hacking off the length from first one side, then the other, I reached behind my neck and bunched the remaining length in my fist.

It was gone in one vicious chop.

I was burning so hot that I wasn't thinking straight. I'd finally figured out why everybody else always seemed to make the decisions without asking me, why the universe was out of my control, run by the crappy ideas of other people. It was because I was stupid. I hated my life. And each slice of the scissors felt like a stab at my whole messed-up world.

Here's what I thought of Mr. Brenigan. Yank-snip!

Here's what I thought of natural selection and genetic variation. Yank-snip! Yank-snip!

It was only when I noticed the impressive piles of hair in the sink and on the floor that I came out of my trance. I balled my fists, each breath short and sharp. I blinked at the stranger who looked back at me from the mirror. My bangs were gone, and all that remained elsewhere on my head were short wisps that jutted out at harsh angles.

I'll admit it: I felt a brief moment of panic. What had I done? How was I going to face my mother? How would I get through the next day at school?

But then something unexpected happened. I stared hard at my reflection, truly studied myself. I could actually make out the shape of my head for the first time in forever. I leaned in closer. I couldn't remember having such a clear view of my ears. My neck either. It was thick and white and strong. I liked what I saw. Even my wide cheekbones, which I'd always thought made me look like a gorilla, now seemed almost regal.

And then, standing in the bathroom with most of my hair at my feet, I felt an unexpected adrenaline rush. The girl in the mirror was a different Stella that I barely recognized. Yet at the same time, she was like a long-lost friend, somebody I'd known all my life but didn't see a lot of.

I was looking at Sista Stella, my alter ego, my evil soul-sister.

The girl glaring back at me didn't need friends. She was a rock. She didn't care about geniuses or about Mr. Brenigan, or Mrs. Birch, or planet-saving Frankenstein plants, or her cliquey high school, or anything. She wasn't some frightened puppy, willing to sit down and obediently accept whatever crap the world dished out. She wasn't about to let other people make any more decisions for her.

In fact, Sista Stella was about to make a few decisions of her own.

CHARLIE:
The Ultimate Symbol for No Right Answer

I have to be honest English Comp is not my favorite subject. Which must be obvious to you since here I am having to do this extra paper just to squeak by with a C. But I'm terrible at writing. It takes me forever to get my thoughts organized. And I'm never sure how to begin either.

So I guess I'll just keep typing.

The 1st part of my story is kind of embarrassing I don't come off very well. In fact it kind of exposes the fact that I'm a big fat loser. You might even feel sorry for me. But I promise you it won't last.

The very very beginning part is also a little complicated. And kind of weird too. So bear with me.

I was in study hall minding my own business listening to my headphones. My eyes were closed and I was drifting in and out to Tito Puente. Do you know Mambo Diablo? Anyway that was the tune that was lulling me into a dream where I was playing my timbales and Mo Banerjee was getting into the rhythm she was dancing and it was a really good dream except I kept getting distracted by the voice of my dead brother Aaron. Right then he was saying things like *This is YOUR dream Charlie so why not make her dress shorter?* or *Get a grip! Stop playing your stupid drums and kiss her!*

Sometimes Aaron can be a pain in the ass.

OK so to shut him up I gave her a very very short red dress and high heels that I know she'd never really wear in real life. Anyway my sticks kept whizzing through the air like my hands were on fire. Like my body was only there to support my arms, you know? The ecstatic crowd jumped to its feet. Mo kept moving her Hips and gyrating to the music. She was a good dancer in my opinion. Then the next thing I knew she danced right up close and I felt her dark eyes on mine and my heart started hammering because I suddenly realized she was about to kiss me but even so I just knew that Aaron was going to say something obnoxious and ruin it.

That's when I felt the 1st spitball whack against my cheek.

I woke up with a lurch and yanked off my headphones. Gradually I remembered where I was. Mrs. Reznik the Music Teacher, a tiny scary old lady with a permanent cough, sat at a beat-up desk at the front of the room with her eyes closed like maybe she was having a dream too. The other kids sat quietly in their seats. Most of them were staring out the window looking bored out of their minds. Some of them were even doing homework. I touched my face. The wet wad of paper was dripping with someone else's spit. It trickled toward my mouth. It was really REALLY gross. I scooped it off and rubbed my cheek on my sleeve. Yuck.

An instant later a 2nd spitball hit my left ear. Somebody

stifled a laugh and when I turned to look, there were Scott Pickett and Ray Beech and Dean Eagler engrossed in their studies.

Yeah right Aaron said somewhere in my head. I wasn't surprised he was still there. He'd been making occasional appearances in my thoughts for days. *They're not fooling anybody.*

These guys were part of Mudslide Crush which as you know was a popular local rock band and everybody seemed to think they were the coolest kids ever to walk the hallways. They seemed convinced of it too. Ray especially enjoyed giving freshmen like me a hard time. He liked to call me Buffalo Boy. I guess because I have a lot of frizzy hair I keep kind of longish and I'm a little chubby. Not that Ray was exactly svelte. In fact he was a giant toad of a guy but that didn't seem to matter. He had a name for everybody. Earlier that week I saw him knock Lyle Dwarkin into a wall. Lyle's 14 but looks 10 and has to be the shortest kid in our grade. He was one of my few friends and he was ahead of me coming out of Metal Shop when Ray bumped into him and kept walking without even looking back. Like he didn't even notice.

Ray was a real bastard.

I wiped out my ear. I figured I had 2 options. On the 1 hand I could try for revenge on the other hand I could just ignore those guys. After all there were 3 of them plus I had a list of Irregular Verbs to review for 6th period Spanish and my Mother had been on my case about the 72 I got on the first quiz. It wasn't fair for them to get away with being such jerkoffs but what could I do? Everyone has to have their turn being freshmen I guess. Maybe if I studied quietly and didn't make a big deal of the spitballs Ray and his friends would leave me alone.

It was definitely the safer plan.

Go for it Aaron whispered. *Look at Scott's wet fingers. It was him! Hurl a fat one right at his head!*

Shut up I told him silently.

I want to stop right here and say that I'm not crazy in case that's what you're thinking. I knew perfectly well that Aaron's voice was only in my imagination and that he was really long gone. But my 14th birthday was only the previous weekend and my Mom and Dad and I went to visit his grave. After that I started thinking about him and what life might've been like if he was still here. Or if I'd of been the one stillborn with the umbilical cord wrapped around my neck instead of Aaron. It'd just been the luck of the draw, right? And people do say twins share a special connection. I read one time about a guy that fell in a deep hole and his twin who was miles away started getting these weird vibes until eventually he went out and saved him so the way I figured, it wasn't *completely* whacked for me to have these imaginary discussions with the brother I never knew.

Still, I know it's not normal, is what I'm saying. No need to send me to the guidance counselor, Mr. Levesque. Or lock me in a padded room or something.

My eyes fell on a drawing somebody made on my desk. A circle with a curved line down the middle, 1 side filled in with pencil. Yin and yang. Of course. With my cheek still warm from the spitball here I was staring at the ultimate Symbol for no right answer. The struggle between opposing forces. Action and Inaction. Success and failure. There was an uncomfortable balance in the Universe and who was I to try and tip it?

I couldn't make up my mind what to do so I pulled out a quarter and tossed it into the air. Heads I'd throw a spitball of my own, tails I wouldn't. When the coin landed I was staring at George Washington.

Decision made.

I slid down my chair and quietly tore half a page from my spiral notebook. I wadded it up and popped it into my mouth. As I chewed, Ray whispered something to Scott and then Scott looked over at me and grinned. I dropped my eyes and pretended I was studying my list of Spanish conjugations.

Yo tiro. Tú tiras. El tira. Nosotros tiramos. Ellos tiran.

A moment later I held the spitball under the table and rolled it between my fingers. When I judged that the moment was right I wound my arm back. I focused on the skin between Scott's ear and his annoying smirk. Then I let it fly. It whipped through the air and landed with a loud, soggy *thwack!*

That's when Mo Banerjee who was sitting right in front of Scott stood up and screamed.

"Aaaaaaaa!" she wailed, swatting the wad off her face and glaring in my direction. "So *gross* who was that aaaaaa!"

I cursed George Washington and my terrible luck. How had I managed to completely miss Scott and instead hit Mo right on the nose? I sank deeper into my chair. I wanted to disappear. Scott looked from Mo to me and back again. Then he laughed and so did Ray and Dean.

Oh man. You screwed up big this time.

Shut up.

With a violent cough Mrs. Reznik suddenly seemed to wake up. "Who did that?"

Since Mo was still screaming I worried I actually might of hurt her. Maybe even broken her nose or something. Was that even possible with a spitball? Oh God. Maybe.

"Mr. Hirsh" Mrs. Reznik said with her eyes boring a hole

right through me. "Did you throw something at Miss Banerjee tell me this instant!" I know I shouldn't say this but Mrs. Reznik always kind of freaked me out. Especially because she was really REALLY old and had this outrageous swirl of stiff brown hair like a giant chocolate cake on her head. It was lots more hair than I thought was natural and I was pretty sure it must be a wig because it never moved and never changed from day to day.

I felt my face heat up. I nodded. I knew this meant detention at the very least.

Behind me Leslie Dern and Kate Bates snickered.

"What was it?"

"A spitball!" Mo shouted. Her chin was out and her eyes narrowed at me. "Charlie you are a *pig*!"

I slipped further into my chair.

For once Aaron kept his mouth shut.

MOHINI:
Of Vampires and Victorian Ladies

"Need anything, Mo?" Mrs. Flynn asks from behind her computer screen. "Water?" From the way she's looking at me it's obvious she's as surprised to see me in trouble as I am.

I shake my head and stare at my knees.

It's Thursday afternoon and I'm fighting back panic on the long bench in the front of Mr. Brenigan's office, my double bass under my feet. I start to gnaw at one of my fingernails but then stop myself. I feel pressure building up behind my forehead—the first signs of a stress headache. I should've guessed this day would turn out to be a complete disaster. First I get whacked in the face with a spitball (that space cadet Charlie Hirsh apologized five times, but a ball of saliva-saturated paper is still a ball of saliva-saturated paper), and now this.

My eyes catch my reflection in the glass of Mr. Brenigan's office door. I scowl at my brown skin, dark eyebrows and straight black hair that I've always felt begins too high on my forehead. As the only Indian person in the whole school, sometimes I feel I stand out like a nigella seed in mayonnaise.

I want to scream at myself, *What were you thinking!?*

Thing is, I have kind of a grand plan, a complete vision of how my life is going to play out. First, I'm going to get straight A's for the next four years and then graduate high school at the top of my class, maybe even a semester early. Then I'll go to medical school, where I'll play classical bass in the student orchestra and, eventually, marry another Bengali doctor or maybe a college professor, somebody my parents will like. A couple of weeks ago I even started volunteering at the Opequonsett Medical Clinic, helping the triage nurses with paperwork and answering questions as people come in. It's the kind of experience that gives a person a leg up in her Ivy League applications. You have to think ahead like that when you come from a family with high expectations.

Anyway, everything about today's situation is horrible. What happened this afternoon definitely doesn't fit into my long-term strategy.

Since the previous winter I've been secretly mooning over Scott Pickett, high school soccer star and heartthrob drummer for Mudslide Crush, sure he doesn't know I exist. He's two years older than me, tall with blond spiky hair and a stare that leaves me prone to walking into walls. But he was never part of my grand plan. Still, at lunch on the second week of the new school year, out of the blue he pulled up a chair next to me and started chatting. After I revived from the initial shock, we ended up talking through my entire lamb curry and rice and his baloney and cheese pita roll. He told me about his band, his friends, and his record-breaking eight goals in a 13 to 0 victory against Bristol. By the end of lunch we'd shared his Twinkies.

In the library later that day, I told my best friend, Naomi Fishmeier. But her reaction wasn't what I'd expected.

"How come you never told me you liked Scott Pickett?" she whispered. She was putting the finishing touches on her first column for the weekly student-run newspaper, the *Barking Clam*. She was the self-appointed OHS Scene Queen. "You weren't worried I'd put it in the paper, were you?"

"No, I know you'd never do that to me," I said. "I just wasn't ready to talk about it with anybody. But you're the first I've told. Honestly." And she was.

"Mo! You should never hold back on your best friend!"

I apologized and all was quickly forgiven.

Naomi narrowed her eyes. "You better be careful about that boy. Don't you know he has a reputation?"

"No," I said. "I haven't heard a thing."

She leaned back and tapped her pencil thoughtfully on her glasses. She wore the thickest lenses I've ever seen. She was almost blind without them. "Well, a good journalist can't reveal her sources, even to a friend, but I have it on good authority that while he was going out with Lynn Westerberg, he was seeing two other girls on the side."

I felt my heart slow down. "Are you positive?"

She shrugged. "Well, I didn't personally catch him red-handed or anything, but I think it's true."

I stared at her for a moment, trying to decide what to do with this information. "No," I said finally. "I don't believe it. Not Scott. He's a good guy. He's sweet. And besides, it's not like we're going out or anything. We just talked."

And so, swayed by the afterglow of the Twinkie incident, I lived the next few days on a mission. Each morning I took gobs of time preparing for school, making sure to choose exactly the right outfit. Jeans and my red patterned oxford—too casual? Short black skirt with the pink satin blouse—too come-and-get-me?

To be honest, it was exhausting.

But it paid off. At first he'd speak to me as we passed in the hallways. Never for long, and just hello and what class do you have now, things like that. I tried to act like it was no big deal. But it was. After a lifetime of social obscurity, Scott Pickett was actually talking to me. The following Thursday he walked me almost the whole way home. After that, we were pretty much a couple.

It felt like Destiny.

Which is probably why I am now sitting here in front of the Vice Principal's office, feeling like I'm about to barf.

Here's what happened. I was lugging my bass down to the music room for my fifth-period lesson with Mrs. Reznik when I noticed a flyer on the lemonade machine announcing the dates for the Halloween Bash in October and the Holiday Talent Show in November. Even though it didn't say so on the poster, I knew from Scott that the band playing at this year's Bash would be Mudslide Crush. It was going to be a big deal to a lot of kids. Mudslide Crush had almost a religious following at Opequonsett High. Of course, seeing the announcement made me think of him again. Not that I need much prodding lately for Scott to interrupt my thoughts.

A few seconds later, still studying the flyer, I sensed movement near my left ear. When I turned, there he was. Scott. Out of the blue. Fate.

Suddenly I felt tongue-tied.

Looking back on it now, it's difficult to explain even to *myself* how what occurred next actually happened. But the facts are the facts:

Within moments of Scott's unexpected appearance, the two of us were making out in the bushes behind the new gym.

Keep in mind, sitting under a rhododendron with a double bass and a soccer star several minutes after the fifth-period bell had already sounded was an act of madness unlike anything I'd ever committed before. Certainly it wasn't part of my plan. Up until that moment I'd always pretty much thought of myself as a model of good behavior, a girl who never let her parents down. This little harlot with leaves in her hair was a stranger to me. In fact, other than one brief, hot moment at the end of my street the day Scott walked with me, I'd barely even let him kiss me. But something in the smoldering look in his eyes, the casual way he took my hand and gently tugged me toward the exit took me by surprise and swept me into a moment of pure insanity. In a way, I didn't feel like I had any choice.

I was like one of those helpless Victorian ladies unable to stop herself from meeting the vampire at the window.

Still, as I gasped for air in the bushes, a secret part of me was ecstatic about this new development. For that moment at least, it felt freeing to let go, to give in to my innermost passions. Plus, one of the undeniable side effects of being romantically connected with Scott Pickett is that it means you're *somebody*. Now, I've never exactly been at the center of everybody's radar screen. Being part of the trendy crowd was never my focus—I always had longer-term goals in mind. But now that I actually had a shot at joining the social elite, I was surprised at how thrilling it felt.

That is, until Mr. Yezzi, the Poli Sci teacher, happened to look out the window. When he saw us he started pounding on the glass.

So now here I am, summoned to the front office for the first time ever. Scott's in there with Mr. Brenigan now, but it's only a matter of time before it's my turn.

My headache is stronger now. I pick at a tiny woodchip lodged in the fabric of my Capris. With one unlucky spin of the Wheel of Fortune I've plummeted from perfect happiness to absolute despair. There I was, living my perfectly respectable under-the-radar life, but then I had to go and throw it away. Sure, establishing myself as a soccer tramp will probably catapult me into the popularity stratosphere, but at what cost?

And what about Mrs. Reznik? Odd as she is, I'm lucky she agreed to give me individual bass instructions as an independent study. What will she think when she hears that I skipped Antoniotti's Sonata No. 10 in G Minor for a smooch in the dirt? Will she change her mind about working with me? The school already cut the Orchestra program this year, and my parents certainly can't afford private lessons.

And my parents? I never told them anything about Scott, of course—a fact that sends a gush of guilt through my intestines whenever I think about it. Normally I don't keep secrets from my parents. But they grew up in Calcutta, the land of the arranged marriage, and they don't even want me *alone* with a boy, let alone *dating*. And as antiquated as their old-world views may sound, I respect my parents and hate to disappoint them. Telling them about Scott and me would break their hearts. So even though I feel sick about it, I've been keeping this whole thing a secret—what else can I do?

If they get wind of any of this, I'm dead.

The door eventually opens and Scott appears, his confident smile completely at odds with the knots in my gut. Mr. Brenigan waves me in. Scott passes me and whispers, "No big deal. Just detention."

Great. Another first.

I leave Mr. Brenigan's office about ten minutes later, my head pounding so hard I shoot straight to the bathroom and lock myself in one of the stalls until the feeling passes. After that, I calm down a little. I spend the final two periods of the day thinking about the silver linings: First, I was able to convince Mr. Brenigan not to call my parents. And second, even though we'll be in separate rooms, at least Scott and I will be in detention together.

Maybe I'll even see him again when it's over. 🌂

STELLA:
A Troupe of Clown-Faced Mimes
Dribbling Basketballs to Surf Music

It was the next day at school when I fully recognized what a terrible mistake I'd made.

Imagine the scene: There was our heroine, Sista Stella

30

the hopeless reprobate, newly sheared and wrapped in her stepfather's castaway snakeskin jacket. As she walked the school hallways the other kids drifted to the far side of the corridor as if terrified. Nobody even made eye contact. Our protagonist pretended not to notice, but even the teachers looked at her with suspicion. It occurred to her that when it comes to oversized girls with unconventional hair and snakeskin jackets, it wasn't as if this town had a corner on the market. But now she felt exposed and naked. What'd she been thinking, cutting her hair like that? Instead of fixing her problem, she made it much worse. Now she felt more out of place than ever.

Worst of all, there was no going back.

And now I can hear the cry from the rafters: *Tell us more, Sista! What happened next to the poor, misunderstood girl?*

All right, my devoted friends. I'll tell you.

Just because I knew I'd destroyed any chance I had of fitting in, didn't mean I'd changed my mind about taking action. For one thing, I was still furious with Mr. Brenigan. In fact, the previous evening I'd mapped out a strategy for exposing him as the thoughtless dictator he was. And as crappy as I felt that day, I decided I would still carry it out.

Why not? I had nothing to lose.

I knew that the ninth and tenth graders had an assembly on Personal Safety and Empowerment that afternoon. I made sure I was one of the first through the gym doors so I could take a front-and-center seat on the bleachers. As the freshmen and sophomores piled in, Mr. Brenigan leaned against the opposite wall looking bored. When he glanced in my direction I pretended to be interested in the palm of my hand.

For a long time nobody sat near me. Finally, having no other choice, a group of five girls, every one of them wearing hip-huggers, shuffled over. But when it looked like a tight fit for all of them, they tried to shove me to one side like they owned the place. "Find another seat, freak," barked one of them, a particularly beefy girl.

I didn't say anything. I just gave the girl the evil eye.

It wasn't long before the pompous princess looked a little less sure of herself and backed down. Soon, her friends exchanged worried looks, and a moment later, they squeezed into their seats without another unkind word. It occurred to me that there was at least one advantage to having crazy hair and a snakeskin jacket in the beehive of cliques and tyrants known as Opequonsett High School.

Eventually the principal, Mrs. Ledlow, an undersized woman with giant round glasses, appeared at one end of the room. She raised her hands and her voice boomed from four giant overhead speakers. "Boys and girls," she said, "I hope you're enjoying our brand-new, modern gym!"

During the applause that followed, I scanned the room. The gymnasium really was spectacular, with a glass cathedral ceiling, a shiny new floor, cushy bleachers, a mammoth sound system and even an impressive snarling quahog, the school's clammy mascot, painted in majestic gray and blue at center court. Everybody knew that building this new gym had ended up costing the town much more than they'd budgeted. Their solution was to cut back on other programs, like music.

Which spoke volumes about screwed-up priorities.

Finally Mrs. Ledlow asked everyone to show respect for our award-winning guest presenters by giving them complete silence. She went back to her chair and the lights dimmed. Then in a sudden torrent of sound, Dick Dale and

His Del-Tones came roaring through the overhead speakers. I was pleasantly surprised. For a few seconds everybody sat in the dark listening to delicious middle-eastern guitar riffs like the start of an Arabic surf adventure. It was "Miserlou," and my hands knew every twist and turn. But then, from unseen corners of the room, five or six wide-eyed men and women dressed in black overalls and white face paint wordlessly bounced, unicycled, danced, crawled and pretended to swim their way to the pyramid of sports equipment arranged at one end of the gym floor.

Apparently a troupe of clown-faced mimes dribbling basketballs to surf music had something to do with safety and empowerment.

By then my heart was pounding in my chest. What I was about to do was a risk, a bold act of defiance that would undoubtedly have repercussions. In my unhappiness and confusion, I admit I considered chickening out. But the moment passed. Within seconds, before the clowns got too far into their act, I stood up and strolled four or five paces onto the parquet floor, then turned around and threw off my jacket. I was wearing the very same T-shirt that had so traumatized the delicate sensibilities of the administration only the day before. Next I unfolded a cardboard sign I'd prepared, holding it up for everybody to see. In case there was anyone at the back with bad eyesight, I shouted the words over the music:

MY SHIRT, MY DECISION!
DON'T LET THE SCHOOL TAKE AWAY YOUR RIGHTS!

As I'd expected, there was an immediate uproar.

Some of the teachers jumped out of their seats and ran toward me. At first most of the kids in the bleachers just

33

looked surprised, but within seconds it seemed like the entire wall of them stood up and yelled. Some laughed, some waved their fists, and a few grinned and applauded.

"We're human beings, not cattle!" I called out, surprised at the pleasant rush I felt. I was enjoying the chaos.

The music stopped and the lights came on. Suddenly Ms. Stone, the algebra teacher, stood very close. "What do you think you're doing?" she spat up at me. "You're disturbing our assembly!"

I could feel the blood pulsing through my veins. In the excitement, it took a moment to focus my thoughts. What exactly *was* I doing? But then it came to me.

"I . . . I'm trying to change the world."

Mr. Brenigan, his face purple, appeared huffing and puffing behind her. Less than thirty seconds later, they walked me to the exit doors. I glanced over at the mimes as we passed them. They didn't seem overly concerned. They were just following my progress across the floor, apparently waiting for the anarchy to work itself out so they could start again. In fact, I could almost swear that one of them gave me the thumbs-up sign.

But my newfound boldness was short-lived.

Minutes later, I sat quietly in Mr. Brenigan's office while he read me the riot act. Away from the shouting crowds, I began to question the wisdom of my protest. What was I trying to prove, anyway? It wasn't as if the school rules were going to change. And when he sentenced me to a full *week* of detention, I felt all the fear and unhappiness I'd been wallowing in ever since school began well back up inside me. Plus, I hated to imagine how mad my mother would be when she learned how much trouble I'd gotten myself into. As Mr. Brenigan's stern voice droned on about disappointment and harsher punishments to come, I felt Sista Stella deflate inside me.

Soon after that, I was back in class just as friendless and alone as ever. Perhaps there was a little more whispering when I walked into the room, but other than that, nothing much had changed except that now I was a certified, publicly acknowledged freak. As I took my seat I could feel in my pocket the envelope that contained the documented proof of my own foolishness.

Eighty-four.

As if any more proof were needed.

WEN:
So Much for Sympathy

Mr. Prichard gave me detention for swearing in class. That meant I wouldn't be able to go to the band try-outs that afternoon unless I cut detention. And this wasn't even the worst of it. My problems were so much bigger now.

It wasn't long after the stiffy incident that I found out just how badly I'd screwed up my life.

During second period I tried to calm myself down. I could play it cool, act like Social Studies had never happened. I even managed to convince myself that maybe I'd been wrong, that nobody had actually noticed Happy Roger at full mast. This was just a normal day like any other, nothing to worry about.

It was a delusion that made me feel better.

But not for long.

By third-period Algebra my worst fears were confirmed. When I walked into the room there was a strange lull in the usual chatter, and as I strolled to my seat I could feel everyone watching me. I tried to ignore the strange vibe, and even pulled off a casual hi to Ted Papadopoulos, whose chair was next to mine, but he wouldn't look at me. He kept his eyes fixed on Ms. Stone, who was writing on the board. I opened my backpack and pulled out my notebook. That's when I heard giggling from the back corner of the room. I turned. Trisha Myers, Ashley Ducker and Georgia Cole were whispering and laughing—and, I thought, looking everywhere but at me.

"What?" I asked them, still holding onto the slim hope that this might have nothing to do with that morning.

Trisha shrugged and made a face as if she wasn't sure what was so hilarious. I scowled at them and turned back around. But that's when Georgia said, "Hey, Wen? How was Social Studies? I hear your presentation was . . . *stimulating*."

The three of them broke into fits. A few other kids started giggling too. Ted covered his face with his hand, but I could see he was shaking with laughter.

It took all my willpower to prevent myself from jumping out of the window.

After Algebra, it seemed like the whole school knew. Everywhere I went, people were snickering. In the hallway before American History, this junior, Ray Beech, bumped into me and shouted, "Hey! Watch where you're going Woody, you horndog!" And that was all it took for his buddies to fall over each other, laughing so hard they were practically in tears.

The humiliation was unbearable.

Thing was, last year I'd kind of screwed things up with my two closest buddies and now I was a little short on friends. That's why I'd been so determined to fit in this year. Until today I'd been imagining popularity, envisioning tables of kids turning to wave to me as I entered a room. But instead, kids were veering away from me like I was the plague. And I couldn't blame them. To be seen with me was committing social suicide. And it was all Sydney's fault. I knew I should just get over it, but I couldn't. I'd stuffed the envelope with the drawings under a pile in my locker, but even now when I closed my eyes I could still picture the delicious charcoal curves of her nakedness.

I know it sounds funny, but I was furious. It wasn't fair. It wasn't my fault that my penis had betrayed me. Sure, it was attached and everything, but it wasn't like I had any control of the little bastard. Could I help it if for some infuriating reason it had a thing for my dad's girlfriend?

I'd been damned to social purgatory by a dim-witted organ beyond my command.

After the seventh-period bell I stood in the hall halfway between the gym, where the Marching Band tryouts were about to start, and the stairway to the basement, where freshman detention was about to begin. I felt paralyzed with indecision.

Azra Quimby appeared from the crowd, her stuffed backpack over her shoulder. She came right up to me and just stood there, which kind of freaked me out. Finally she said, "Excuse me, Wen. You're standing in front of my locker."

"Oh." I stepped aside. "Sorry."

Azra and I had kind of a weird relationship. We used to be best friends. Along with another girl, Floey Packer, we'd been kind of a threesome, almost inseparable. But that all ended last year when I'd made the mistake of asking Azra

37

out. Now that we'd broken up, everything was uncomfortable between us.

A few seconds later she was crouched down, pulling things out of her backpack. Without looking up at me she said, "What are you doing here? Don't you have detention?"

"Oh, you heard about what happened?"

She nodded. "*Everybody* heard."

Another wave of shame washed over me. But I refused to let it show. "I'm trying to decide what to do. Today is Marching Band tryouts. Should I really forget about band and go to detention like I'm supposed to, or should I skip detention, accept whatever the consequences may be, and go to tryouts like I'd planned? What do you think?"

She stood up, her backpack restuffed and rearranged, and slammed her locker door shut.

"I don't know," she said, barely looking at me. "But I gotta get going or I'm going to miss my bus."

So much for sympathy.

Alone again, I realized I didn't have much time left. In less than four minutes the after-school activities bell would ring. So I took a deep breath, gripped hard on my trumpet case handle, and made my decision.

I ran toward the gym.

When I got to the open double doors, I could see a crowd of kids, each with instrument cases at their sides, standing around a table set up at one end of the gym floor. Jonathan Meuse stood in the thick of it like a scarlet-haired king holding court. He was already explaining how the Marching Band budget was smaller this year, so anyone who got in this year would be expected to sell a lot more chocolates than ever to pay expenses. But then he noticed me at the door.

"Oh, look who it is, folks!" he called. "Woody! Woody Gifford! You here for the tryouts, Wood-man?"

Everybody turned. A bunch of kids laughed.

Suddenly my legs turned to jelly. I felt every molecule in my body shrivel up. It occurred to me as I scanned the grinning faces that I might be better off spending my after-school time alone at home in front of the TV.

"No," I said, lamely, backing into the hallway. "I . . . uh . . . have detention."

As soon as I was out of sight I started running, my head as warm as a brick oven. I couldn't get away from there fast enough. When I came to my locker I stopped, yanked open the little metal door, shoved my trumpet and case violently inside, and then slammed the locker door shut again. For a few seconds I just stood there with my forehead pressed against the cold metal.

There's something incredibly humiliating about not being cool enough to try out for Marching Band.

A moment later I dragged myself toward the basement stairway. I figured I still had a half a minute or so before the bell.

OLIVIA:
An Introverted Virgo of the Worst Kind

Dear Naomi,

Let me start off by saying that I don't believe in accidents. I'd hate to think that whatever happens is simply the inadvertent outcome of a series of random events with no preordained purpose.

Anyway, there's too much evidence against it. I'm not saying that the future is already decided, only that each decision we make, however small, helps clear the path toward events that inevitably follow. For example, if I hadn't skipped American Lit, I wouldn't have had to show up to detention that afternoon. And if I hadn't gone to detention, everything would have been different.

But the fact was, Mr. Carr assigned _The Great Gatsby,_ a sad, beautiful story I'd already read at my old school. Plus, he liked to quiz us after each chapter and there's no better way than that to strip away all the fun of a good book. Which was why I chose to skip third period and spend the time curled up on a bench behind the janitor's equipment room finishing it for the third time. Which in turn was why, when the principal, Mrs. Ledlow, happened to make a rare visit to that corridor, she found me there. And _that_ was why, at 2:05 that afternoon, I had to show up to the basement for ninth-grade incarceration. Where Lemonade Mouth was born.

How could all that have been dumb luck?

I like to think that whatever happens was always meant to happen, like an unstoppable train that departed long ago and forever rolls toward an inevitable destination. Life seems so much more romantic that way, don't you think? Still, you asked me to tell my story so I guess I need to begin it somewhere. That afternoon in detention is as good a place as any.

It started like this:

Detention that day was downstairs with Mrs. Reznik, the music teacher. When I walked into the music room, a cluttered, windowless basement space near the A.V. closet and the school's boiler room, the little radio on Mrs. Reznik's desk was playing a commercial with a catchy jingle, that "Smile, Smile, Smile" one about teeth. It kind of stuck in my mind. That's not unusual for me. There's always some tune or other drifting around in my head.

Anyway, just as the bell rang I took a seat near the back. I was trying to concentrate on my breathing. I sometimes get panic attacks in stressful situations and right then I needed to keep calm. Nobody spoke. Mrs. Reznik sat at her desk, coughing and scowling as she leafed through a giant pile of paperwork. A tiny, narrow-faced lady with a body shaped like a piccolo, skin like worn shoe leather, and a startlingly large nest of lustrous brown hair, she was a sight to behold. I'd seen her reduce kids to tears with one look. There were rumors that the school administration had been trying to force her into retirement, but they couldn't get rid of her. I could understand why. The woman scared the pee out of me.

I studied the blackboard where she'd set down the law in sharp, spidery chalk letters.

Detention Rules:
1. No gum chewing, food or drink in the classroom.
2. You will remain seated.
3. You will not talk.
4. The first time you break a rule, your name will go on the board. The second time, you will receive another detention.

At my old school, St. Michael's in Pawtucket, they didn't even _have_ detention. St. Michael's is an alternative school, a place where they send kids who don't fit in somewhere else so they can get an education "without walls." But Brenda, my grandmother, told me back in July that we couldn't afford the tuition anymore so now I found myself back among the walls.

My chair squeaked and I almost jumped. Mrs. Reznik looked up. "Name please?"

The other detainees, two boys and two girls, turned to look. I tried to smile. I may have been an introverted Virgo of the worst kind, but at least I was working on it.

"Olivia," I reminded her. "Olivia Whitehead."

Mrs. Reznik frowned and scribbled something on a piece of paper. "You can all read the rules. I suggest you use this hour to work on something productive." Some pop song came on—Desirée Crane or Hot Flash Smash, somebody like that. Still, it was the "Smile, Smile, Smile" commercial that looped through my mind.

The other kids went back to staring into space. I only recognized two of them. Wendel Gifford, a kid who always seemed to dress in crisp, preppy clothes, was in my Social Studies class. We'd never actually spoken, but he'd embarrassed himself during a presentation that morning and I felt sorry for him. The Amazon girl with the leather skirt, savagely ripped tights, and short spiky hair was Stella Penn. After she'd pulled that crazy stunt at an assembly earlier that week, everybody knew who she was. The other two I didn't know. Tapping nervously on his desk at the far end of the front row sat a sullen, thick-necked boy with an overgrown mop of frizz. To my left fidgeted a skinny Indian-looking girl with long dark hair, big brown eyes and, at her feet, a huge, gray double bass case. She was biting her nails like a stress-fiend.

After a while, Mrs. Reznik went into a coughing fit. They were dark, rumbly coughs that seemed to come from deep in her chest. Everybody looked up. After a moment she stood and stepped toward the door. "I'll be back in one minute," she said, still coughing, and then left the room. When she came back she seemed better. In her hand was a green and yellow paper cup that said Mel's Organic Frozen Lemonade. It must have come from the machine I'd noticed at the top of the stairs. She set it on her desk and sat down.

I guessed the no-drinks rule didn't apply to Mrs. Reznik. Not that I was going to say anything.

Wen and Stella stared vacantly at the wall, the frizzy-haired boy tapped on his desk and the skinny girl absently fingered a pile of rubber bands. In a poster hanging near my chair, four old guys in short pants and feathered hats were playing accordions and tubas under this huge willow tree in the middle of what looked like some quaint, pastoral German village. I gazed at it and imagined myself into the picture. I'm pretty good at that, imagining myself somewhere I'm not. I find I can visit the nicest places that way. In my mind I was relaxing on the ground in front of the four guys, listening to their music and feeling the grass between my toes and a gentle breeze in my hair. Soon, the music transformed into the tooth song and I realized the commercial had come back on Mrs. Reznik's radio again.

Smile, smile, smile!
Would you like the perfect smile?
Don't you want your first impression
to be great?

I looked up. Every head in the room was nodding with each oomp-oomp-oomp of the tuba.

Bernbaum Associates, Bernbaum Associates,
Bernbaum Associates
Can fix your smile—<u>Don't Wait!</u>

Soon after that, Mrs. Reznik's cell phone rang. She put it to her ear and a second later she stepped out of the room again to take it, only this time she switched off the radio before she left. It took me a minute or so to adjust to the silence. My eyes drifted back to the rules again, and I found myself pondering Mrs. Reznik's skinny <u>D</u>'s and the steep slope of the tops of her <u>T</u>'s when I suddenly noticed that something felt wrong. I looked around.

Everybody in the room was looking at me.

That's when I realized I'd been singing the smile song. My face went warm. After a moment, Stella laughed. Wen shrugged kindly and turned back around, and then everybody else did too. I wanted to die.

There are different opinions about what happened next.

Mo, who of course I now know was the skinny girl, says it was Charlie, who at that time I only knew as the frizzy-haired boy, tapping on his desk that started it. Charlie says it was Mo. She picked

45

out a rubber band, stretched it between her thumbs and flicked it with her fingers. By changing the length she altered the pitch, making the same bouncing notes as the tuba in the commercial. I don't remember who was first, but it doesn't actually matter because before long they were doing it together. And it sounded good.

Boom tappa boom tappa boom.

Oomp-oomp-oomp.

Stella and Wen looked up. The next thing I knew, Stella shot out of her seat. She hopped over a row of desks to where Charlie sat.

"What are you _doing_?" he whispered, shrinking back from her. I wondered if he thought she was going to hit him. Big as he was, Stella looked like she could take him.

"Don't stop tapping!"

On the wall over his head hung a beaten-up ukulele. She reached across, grabbed it off the hanger and took it back to her seat. After adjusting the tuning pegs, Stella started strumming the chords of the jingle along with Mo and Charlie. The ukulele sounded tinny and crazy. But in a good way.

By that time I guess Wen wanted to get into the act. He went to the storage closet and rummaged around. Eventually, with a big silly grin, he held up a kazoo.

"Yes!" Stella whispered.

Still plucking her rubber band, Mo giggled. I kept glancing over my shoulder at the door, expecting Mrs. Reznik back any second. They played through the full song—the verse and even the Bernbaum part. Wen had the melody. It was a joke, but it still worked. The music from their makeshift instruments sounded so unusual, so exciting. My heart pounded. I suddenly didn't care if Mrs. Reznik showed up.

The next time the verse began, I sang the words.

Smile, smile, smile!
Would you like the perfect smile?
Don't you want your first impression
to be great?

Hearing myself sing in front of people felt weird. I'd never thought I had a very pretty voice. Instead of a pure, clear sound like the singers in, say, a Disney cartoon, mine is kind of low and scratchy, like a three-pack-a-day smoker. It's always been that way, even when I was little.

But Stella nodded, Wen winked and everybody was grinning.

Then dial, dial, dial!
Change your life, improve your style!
Call our dental experts 'fore it gets too late!

It felt like one of those perfect moments where everything comes together. But like I said, I don't believe in accidents. Even if this strange, musical moment, the final result of a long chain of seemingly unlikely events, never came to anything else, it was meant to be.

Something new had been born.

We were just starting over again when Charlie suddenly lost his grin and stopped tapping. I looked behind me.

Mrs. Reznik was standing in the doorway.

In the silence that followed, it was obvious she'd heard us. We waited for her to speak but she only stared, wide-eyed. Something important had just happened. Looking back, I could feel it even then. I think we all could. Only nobody knew what it was.

And none of us could have imagined it would change our lives forever. 🐾

CHAPTER 2

Apathy is for butt-wipes.
Get off your comfy sofas and do something!
—Sista Slash

MOHINI:
Baba

Naomi eyes me skeptically. "You're serious?"

"That's right," I say. "I can't keep lying to my parents like this. I'm losing sleep and I'm starting to hate myself. If being with Scott means I have to make up stories, sneak around and worry all the time about getting caught, then I can't be his girlfriend anymore. I have to drop him."

"Holy crap," she says. "That's huge."

It's Thursday afternoon, less than an hour after detention let out, and Naomi and I are sitting in the storage room at the back of my family's store. We own the only Indian grocery in the area. We're surrounded by several large sacks of basmati rice, an unopened case of Nirav Kesar canned mango pulp and a stack of Glucose Biscuits. My father is playing Indian music through the stereo. He's also burning incense at the front counter, and that along with the combined smell of chili powder, garlic, cilantro and dry curry powder, gives the air the familiar, pungent odor of home. When I'm not helping behind the register or stacking the shelves, my parents like me to study here too. They like to know where I am.

Naomi and I have an American History essay due on Wednesday and neither of us has even started. The topic is *Why Do Revolutions Happen?* But Naomi has mostly been flipping through one of her *Rolling Stone* magazines. We have to keep our voices down. My dad is at the register only a few steps beyond the doorway behind me. I can hear him speaking Hindi with a customer. I didn't tell him about detention, of course. I had to make up a story. I said I stayed late today because of a project. Another lie.

Naomi peers at me sympathetically over her glasses. I know she always had her doubts about Scott, but from the first day I started going out with him she tried to be supportive—and I love her for that. She also knows about my parents' no-dating rule. She's heard the story of my uncle Ramesh and aunt Anita back in Calcutta, who practically disowned my sixteen-year-old cousin, Sashmita, a couple years ago when they found out she went out to a movie with a boy.

She knows me. She knows what a mess I am.

"Plus," I continue, "I don't have time for distractions. I'm barely keeping up with my schoolwork. Not only do I have to hand in this essay next week but I also have to read chapters four through six of *The Great Gatsby,* and on Tuesday we have a Trig test, remember? Not to mention Debate and working here at the store. And did I tell you I'm increasing my volunteering at the clinic to twice a week?"

Her forehead wrinkles. "Don't get sick, Mo. Everybody

knows that people who work at those clinics are always catching something. Those places are swarming with germs."

I roll my eyes. "The point is, I can't let myself lose my focus. On top of everything else, Mrs. Reznik wants me ready to play Rabbath's Ode d'Espagne by the talent show. It's a killer. I'm already freaking out about it."

"If it makes you so nervous, why don't you tell her you'd rather play something easier? Why do this to yourself?" After a pause she says, "Look at your fingers. Are you biting your nails again?"

I curl my hand so she can't see. "This isn't middle school anymore, Naomi," I say, looking back down at my notebook. "When we apply to colleges, our grades and everything we do now, it all *counts*."

I feel her puzzled eyes on me. She's heard all about my grand plan, of course. She thinks I'm crazy. "Don't you think you might be taking things a little too seriously, Mo? You don't have to be Supergirl."

I sigh. Naomi means well, but she obviously doesn't understand. "I'm not Supergirl. Supergirl doesn't end up with a bunch of losers in detention. Supergirl doesn't get caught in the bushes in a lip lock with Scott Pickett."

That's when I hear a voice from behind me. "Monu, how is your essay going?"

My heart nearly stops. I spin around. My father is standing at the door, a clipboard in his hand, his gaze locked on me. My dad is a big man. He fills the doorway. With his dark, grizzly beard, intense eyes and accent, I can see why my friends used to be scared of him when I was a little girl. I feel my stomach rise into my throat because I'm not sure how long he was standing there.

"Uh . . . ," I stammer. "Fine, Baba . . ."

When he nods, pleased, I relax. He asks, "Will Naomi be coming home for dinner?"

Fortunately, Naomi is more composed than I am. "No, Mr. Banerjee, but thanks. My mom wants me home early tonight."

"Too bad," he says. "Maach Curry tonight. Plus I got a video for afterwards. It's an Amitabh Bachchan."

"You're kidding! *Muqaddar Ka Sikandar?*" she asks, pronouncing the name completely wrong, saying *Muhk-AY-dar Kay Sick-AND-ar* instead of *MOOK-uh-dar Ka SEEK-and-ar.*

"No. *Mr. Natwarlal.* We haven't seen this one."

I force a smile. Thank God my parents love Naomi and she loves them. She often comes over to our house to watch Bollywood movies with us. She doesn't always know what's going on, but she likes all the music and dancing. She can even name a lot of the big stars: Amitabh Bachchan, Shahrukh Khan, Preity Zinta, Isha Sharvani. She knows more about them than I do.

"Well, another time then." And then to both of us he says, "Keep at the books like your future depends on it. Because it does."

We nod.

The bell on the door jingles. My dad smiles again and then leaves to greet the new customer. After he's gone, Naomi and I exchange guilty looks.

A few seconds later she whispers, "So you're honestly going to do it? Break up with him?"

I nod.

She studies my face. "Really?"

I'm about to nod again, but then my eye catches an ad for zit cream in Naomi's magazine. The photograph shows a crowd of laughing teenagers chasing each other on a beach in their bathing suits. At the front are a beautiful blond guy and a grinning redhead girl in a pink bikini. They're running hand in hand and laughing like they just shared the funniest joke ever. Everybody looks so happy, but all I feel is frustration. I can never have a normal relationship—with Scott or anybody else. Unlike a *real* American girl, I'm going to end up in an arranged marriage, so if I find somebody I really care about, I'll always have to hide it from my parents and eventually I'll have to break it off.

To be honest, it makes the whole dating idea kind of depressing.

But now I try to picture myself breaking up with Scott and I can't help thinking about his olive green sweater, how it smells so good when I rest my head on his shoulder, or the way his soft hand felt in mine that time he walked me almost the whole way home. And I think Naomi can see that this is what's going through my mind. She doesn't say a word. She's known me since kindergarten. She knows I love my parents and I respect the sacrifices they've made, moving us here from Calcutta when I was two, getting used to a new language and working hard every day just to give my sister Madhu and me a better life than they had. She knows I want to meet their high expectations and that I hate the idea of disrespecting our family's traditions.

But she also knows that even though my family is Indian, the fact is I grew up here in America and deep down I want the same things every American girl wants.

Which is why I can tell she doesn't believe I'll really drop Scott.

And to be honest I'm not sure I believe it either.

It's first thing Friday morning and Naomi and I are heading to our lockers, which are across the hallway from each other. There's a note taped to mine. Even before I'm close enough to read it I recognize the handwriting and feel a faint throb in my forehead. I'm not sure why, but somehow I know this isn't good.

It says:

Meet me in my office right away. We need to talk.
—Mrs. Reznik

"Oh my God," I say to Naomi, showing her the note. "She's going to make me drop my independent study. I just know it."

"What are you talking about?" she says, squinting at the piece of paper. "Will you relax? There's no way Mrs. Reznik is going to drop you. Why would she do that?"

"First I skip her lesson, then I break her detention rules. You don't know what she's like, Naomi. She's kind of a musical drill sergeant. I always suspected she'd drop me at the first sign of weakness."

Naomi studies my face, concerned. "I believe you're losing your grip, Mo. Think about it. Before the school cut the budget, running the student orchestra was probably Mrs. Reznik's life. Now that it's gone you're like the closest thing she's got. She'll never drop you. I bet giving you lessons is the part of her day she looks forward to most. You even play her favorite instrument for godsakes."

It's true. Mrs. Reznik used to be a bassist with the Newport Philharmonic. She traveled around the world. On her desk are photographs of her standing with famous musicians like James Levine and Placido Domingo. But she stopped touring a few years ago and has led the OHS Orchestra ever since. It's not surprising she's furious that the school cut the program. She's a very serious musician. But *that*, I think, is the real reason she agreed to give me private lessons—she believed I was going to take them as seriously as she did.

At least she did until yesterday. Before I ruined everything.

"Go," she says, handing me the note back. "She probably has some new sheet music for you or something like that."

But I'm not so sure. I can feel the panic rising. 🎵

CHARLIE:
A Stupendous Challenge of Celestial Significance

I had no idea why Mrs. Reznik wanted to see me but to be honest when I read the note I was kind of happy. Because I was already late for homeroom and this meant I could get a late pass. I'd already gotten 3 warnings so far this year and Mr. Finnerty said next time he would send a note home. But now I wouldn't have to see Mr. Finnerty at all. Now instead of having to hurry I could take it easy.

The morning announcements were already droning out of the classroom speakers. The A.V. room was at the bottom of the stairs and when I passed it Lyle Dwarkin was standing on a rickety-looking stepladder stretching for something on a high shelf.

"What are you doing down here it's homeroom" I said. "Didn't you hear the bell?"

He craned his freckled head around. "Searching for a laptop projector for Mrs. Abraham." Of all the extracurricular activities offered at Opequonsett High School the geekiest of all had to be the Audio Visual Club. But not only had Lyle joined, he'd been elected Treasurer. Which meant my buddy was practically High Priest of the Weirdos.

I glanced around. The A.V. room was actually just a glorified closet: a bunch of shelves, a couple of tables, heaps of loose cables and boxes and keyboards and junk everywhere. In the garbage can I noticed a pile of empty Mel's Organic Frozen Lemonade paper cups. I wondered if any of them were Lyle's. A lot of the kids from the basement clubs seemed to go for that stuff maybe because it was the only machine nearby. The soda dispensers were at the other end of the building.

"This place is a mess."

"Not for long. We're getting ready to organize." Lyle climbed another rung so I steadied the ladder for him and he pulled a cardboard box off the shelf. "What are *you* doing down here Charlie?"

With my free hand I showed him the note from Mrs. Reznik. He read it. "Good luck. People get lost down here and never come back."

Yuk yuk.

The announcements ended and I continued down the hallway. It was cluttered with filing cabinets and unused furniture. 1 of the lights was out and another blinked unsteadily. The doors on either side of the corridor led to other little rooms set aside for the school's less glamorous clubs: the Chess Club, the Debate Team, the French Club, even the school newspaper. It was creepy. I wondered what Mrs. Reznik did to get banished down here. Overhead somebody was banging on the floor. Probably something to do with the construction of the team locker rooms. Bang. A couple seconds of silence. Bang. A couple more seconds. Bang. The Music Room was at the end of the corridor near the Loading Dock. The noise stopped just as I got to the door. Mrs. Reznik was sitting at her desk hacking away. She always seemed to have this nasty cough. It was kind of gross to listen to. But when she stopped she noticed me standing in the doorway and narrowed her eyes.

"Charlie you're late."

"Yeah" I said. "Sorry."

I would of asked what this was all about but she pointed her finger and said "Have a seat" and to my surprise when I stepped into the room I saw a row of chairs in front of the desk and in them sat Wen Gifford, Olivia Whitehead, Stella Penn and Mo Banerjee. The kids from detention. All at once I realized we were probably about to get chewed out for breaking the detention rules. Mrs. Reznik hacked some more but I barely heard. I was fighting back a full-body blush and trying to think of something charming to say to Mo.

That's when the voice came into my head again.

Get a grip bro. You're killing me. You keep going like this and you'll never get a date. See, in my twisted imagination Aaron was the cool, smooth one, except, since he was dead, he was stuck living vicariously through me. And I was constantly letting him down. *Just because you have a secret thing for this girl doesn't mean you have to act like an idiot around her.*

He was right. I needed to control my natural impulse to make an ass out of myself. Still, it was hard to forget the rumor Lyle passed on to me when I'd called him the previous night. That Mo was supposedly going out now with Scott Pickett of all people. After that conversation I'd attacked my drums for 2 hours straight.

Relax, man. Be cool. For me.

OK. Enough pressure. I got it.

I forced myself to walk in as casually as I could. The other kids looked as confused as I felt. Wen nodded to me we weren't exactly friends but we knew each other. I nodded back but didn't sit near him. Yesterday I'd heard somebody call him "Woody the Horndog" and it didn't seem like a good idea to associate myself with that kind of bad PR. As I took the chair nearest the door I couldn't help noticing Mo's hair. It was tied back today, revealing her small, perfect ears.

Even though it was 1st thing in the morning Mrs. Reznik had another cup of Mel's on her desk. "I'm glad you finally made it Charlie. I was just talking with the others about the music you made yesterday afternoon. And I'm wondering what the 5 of you are planning to do next."

She stared at me like I was supposed to have the foggiest idea what she was talking about. Her eyes locked on mine and she kept waiting for an answer until eventually I said "Uh . . . what do you mean?"

"Well surely you're not going to let it all go to waste are you? That would be like throwing away a windfall! Some musicians spend their entire lives searching for artistic synergy like I witnessed yesterday. Many never find it. Do you know what kismet is?"

I shook my head.

"Divine circumstance. It's not every day that life just drops into your lap. You 5 have been sent a gift. A band like yours is like a flower demanding the opportunity to bloom."

Huh? She wanted us to bloom?

Eventually Wen spoke up. "But . . . we're not a band."

"Of course you are. You heard yourselves. Didn't you sense something?"

She looked at me again. I was beginning to feel pretty uncomfortable. The truth was I *did* know what she was talking about. I *had* sensed something when we'd played. It felt good. Natural, kind of. But that didn't mean we should quit school and plan a national tour or anything.

"Well . . . maybe we played well together" Wen admitted "but we were just goofing around."

She jabbed her finger onto her desk. "There. So it wasn't only me. Now you need to get serious you need to start practicing." She sat back in her chair and looked around at each of us. "That's why I asked everyone here this morning. You have a lot of work to do if you're going to win the talent show and I'm not going to help if you're not planning to *win.*"

I wasn't sure what to say. Was she kidding?

I scanned the faces. Stella was glaring at her desk. Mo chewed on her pinky nail. Wen eyed Mrs. Reznik as if her head might start spinning at any moment. And that strange Olivia girl just picked nervously at the frayed edges of the ancient-looking backpack she held on her lap. It was a tattered pinkish thing with a Scooby-Doo decal. It looked embarrassingly like she might of stolen it from some defenseless 3rd grader.

Suddenly the banging started up again. Only this time it was so loud it sounded like somebody hammering their way through the ceiling. Mrs. Reznik scowled up at the graying tiles. We sat there listening for a few seconds. When it didn't stop she stood and walked over to a filing cabinet and grabbed a broom from behind it. Then to my amazement she started whacking the broom handle against a metal pipe that ran up from the floor. *Whack! Whack! Whack!* I could hardly believe what I was seeing. As she swung her arm over and over again she glared at the ceiling.

Eventually the banging stopped and so did she. In the quiet that followed she set the broom gently back in its place and then took her seat again all dignified.

"They must be tearing something down directly above us. Either that or they're trying to drive us all out of our minds. Can you imagine allowing such a racket above a *music* classroom? Have you ever heard of anything so *uncivilized*?"

The 5 of us just sat there. That proved it. This old lady was certifiably nuts.

"Anyway" she said smiling again "what do you say about the talent show?"

I pretended to examine the top of my desk. The whole idea of playing at the talent show with these guys was ridiculous. Mrs. Reznik's wig was obviously on too tight. Did she honestly expect us to get up in front of the whole school and play kazoos and rubber bands? We'd get laughed off the stage. OK sure I often daydreamed about playing dance music, maybe bringing out the timbales like Tito. But this would never be the polished salsa combo I pictured. Even if we didn't end up making ourselves look like complete morons, I was sure I'd somehow embarrass myself in front of Mo.

There was no way I wanted any part of this stupid idea.

But I kept my mouth shut. Why should I be the 1st to tell the old lady she was a total moonbat?

It was Stella who finally broke the silence. She wasn't even looking at Mrs. Reznik. She stared at her knuckles like she was studying them. "I . . . uh . . . I don't think so. I'm not much of a joiner."

Mrs. Reznik frowned.

Mo was next. "I'm sorry too I think it's a really, uh, interesting idea and everything but I can't. I have a crazy schedule right now Mrs. Reznik I'm taking two extra courses and volunteering at the clinic. Not to mention working at my family's store. So I honestly don't have the time to squeeze in a single extra thing."

Not too busy for Scott though Aaron taunted silently.

A moment later I felt the old lady's intense eyes on me again. What was I supposed to say? In the end all I came up with was "Yeah I'm really busy too" but even as I said it I realized how pathetic I sounded. I could of kicked myself. Why didn't I dream up something better? Mo looked at me like I was an idiot.

"And Olivia?"

Olivia's face went pink. She seemed like a strange girl. I'd seen her walking alone in the hallways, her hands gripping the strap of her backpack as she crept around like some frightened ghost past rows and rows of lockers. She kept to herself and never seemed to say a word. It occurred to me that as low as I was on the social totem pole she was even lower.

It was a long time before she finally answered. But when she did her voice was deep and gravelly and so quiet I almost had to strain to hear her. "The problem is I'm not a real singer. And I'm not comfortable onstage. The biggest audience I've ever performed for was at home." She seemed to have more to say but she looked too anxious to go on. Her face got so red that I wondered if she was going to burst it was almost painful to watch. Finally she said "But singing to thirteen cats isn't the same as singing to a gymnasium full of people. I can't do that I get nervous."

Wen and I looked at each other. *Thirteen* cats? She *sings* to them?

"Oh but Olivia" Mrs. Reznik said in a gentle voice "everybody gets nervous onstage. You'll get over it."

"No you don't understand. Once when I was in the 4th grade musical I threw up all over the other kids. I was only in the chorus."

I tried to picture the 5 of us onstage, Scooby-Doo Girl vomiting all over Stella's ukulele.

Mrs. Reznik frowned again. "What about when you sang in detention?"

Olivia took so long to respond that I wasn't sure she'd even heard the question. Eventually she looked up from the frayed edges of her bag. "That was . . . different. I can't sing in a band."

After that everyone went quiet.

Until Wen said "Well I guess that counts me out too after all we can't exactly bloom if it's only me." I think he meant that to be funny but Mrs. Reznik gave him a withering glance and he looked down.

Mrs. Reznik didn't say anything right away. While everybody sat in yet another awkward silence she took a long thoughtful sip of her lemonade slush. To tell the truth I couldn't wait for the bell to ring so I could get the hell out of there.

"Reaching for greatness is never easy" she said finally. "And I understand that we all have our own obstacles to overcome. Still I can't help thinking that you're missing the point. This is a challenge worth taking. Something *happened* yesterday, something special. Call it luck call it celestial alignment, whatever you wish. Whatever it was, who knows when *or if* it'll happen to any of you ever again. And I'm sure each of you knows what I'm talking about. You heard yourselves."

My foot tapped nervously. I wouldn't of admitted it to anyone but part of me felt like maybe there was something to what she was saying. Glancing around the room though I wasn't so sure. Did I really want to associate myself with Olivia Whitehead the silent nutjob? Or Wendel Gifford who'd publicly shamed himself into social exile? Or Stella Penn the she-warrior with a fondness for starting riots in school assemblies? Not that I was exactly Mr. Popularity or anything, but that only made the problem worse. Except for Mo, we had to be the most hopeless bunch of high school rejects ever.

Sure, I always wanted to be in a band. But not this one.

"Wait a minute Mrs. Reznik" Wen said out of the blue. "Didn't Mudslide Crush win the talent show last year? Don't you think they'll enter it again this time?"

"I *know* they're going to" Mo said. "Scott told me."

And there it was. Scott told Mo stuff. This didn't exactly *prove* what Lyle said about them but it was pretty good evidence.

"So we *can't* win" said Wen. "Mudslide Crush is really REALLY good. They have a huge following. Even if we did pull something together and competed, we wouldn't have a snowball's chance."

Mrs. Reznik waved her hand like she didn't buy a word of it. "Nonsense. Look, I've been surrounded with music and musicians my entire life and believe me I can tell an ensemble onto something revolutionary from one that's merely competent."

I couldn't believe she said that. Merely competent? Mudslide Crush? She was talking about a band that everybody practically bowed down to. They had a huge following.

Mrs. Reznik set down her empty cup. "Consider this.

Music is a manifestation of ourselves. Of our unique voices, whether as individuals or groups. Think about that. Your collective voice is 1-of-a-kind. It's so strong, so extraordinarily honest. How can you stifle it? Don't you want to stand up and show everybody who you are?" She leaned forward. "Aren't you tired of letting others carry the day? Aren't you ready to be *heard*?"

I couldn't figure this lady out.

"Think about it" she said. And then in a voice that sounded like she was trying to be diplomatic she added "Mudslide Crush is *fine. You 5,* on the other hand, should aim higher. You could be"—she squinted her eyes like she was searching for the word—"*stupendous.* You're going to shake things up around here. I have a feeling about this."

WEN:
Honestly, I'm Not Hungry

I was lying across the sofa listening to "A Night in Tunisia," the bebop fighting it out with the explosions from George's video game. For appearance's sake, I'd set my American History textbook on the coffee table and my spiral notebook on my lap while my other hand fingered the valves of my trumpet and tried to keep up with Dizzy Gillespie. In my head I'd even worked out my own little staccato two-bar riff that contrasted with Dizzy's wandering melody.

My American History essay was due the next morning but, needless to say, I was having a hard time getting started.

Sydney wasn't exactly helping. Through the doorway I

could see her at the kitchen table constructing a sculpture out of an old boot, a jar of peanut butter and a pile of colored feathers. From the sofa I had a terrific view of her bare shoulders and her long, narrow neck. Plus, every now and then she'd get up from her work, shuffle into the living room, and hover over me until I looked up.

"How was school today?" she'd ask fake-casually, or, "Should I open a bag of chips?" This time she said, "It's a nice afternoon, want to go for a walk?"

I shook my head and immediately looked back down.

After a moment she backed away a couple steps. "If I make brownies, would either of you eat them with me?"

"No thanks." I kept my eyes on the blank page. When I'd returned her sketches last Thursday afternoon, I couldn't even look her in the face. She, on the other hand, had tried to laugh off the mix-up.

"Are you kidding?" George asked, his round, cherubic face glancing up sweetly from the massacre on the screen. He'd been defending the universe ever since he came home from school. "I'd eat them."

Sydney smiled at him before padding back out of the room. I couldn't stop myself from sneaking another look. Tight jeans today.

A moment later I laid back, closed my eyes and let the music distract me from my thoughts. Thank God for Dizzy. Now *there* was a player with *chops*. Sure, Miles was a genius, if you were in the mood, and Satchmo was everywhere, but if you were looking for a fearless, no-holds-barred improviser, an innovator who could take a melody to the highest registers and then completely change direction on a dime, nobody topped Diz. He was one of a kind.

That thought brought me back to what Mrs. Reznik

said on Friday morning. On the one hand, I kind of liked the idea of being a part of a new, experimental quintet, especially since there would be no Marching Band for me. On the other hand, I knew we would never actually win the talent show, and a part of me still wanted to hide under a rock until graduation. That day, nobody'd sat with me at lunch and as I'd stood in line, two senior girls glared at me like I was some kind of juvenile offender. Azra and Floey were nearby and they hadn't talked to me either. They were avoiding me.

I didn't blame them.

If high school was a garden, I was poison ivy.

Not that it really mattered if I wanted to try this band thing. I got the feeling that the other detention kids wanted to make music together about as much as they wanted to eat fertilizer. Still, I spoke with Olivia in class later that day and told her she really did have an amazing voice. I wondered if she changed her mind then maybe the others might consider changing theirs.

If we did end up going onstage, maybe I could hide behind Charlie or something.

Just as the album ended, Sydney walked in again from the kitchen. By then George had finally turned off the computer and gone to his room. "You have a lot of homework tonight, hun?"

Hun?

"No," I lied. "I'm almost done."

"Great. I need a break. Mind if I watch a little TV?"

I gave up on my essay for now. "Fine. Whatever."

She plopped herself down on the other end of the sofa and folded her legs. Not only could I smell her perfume, but the light from the window made her eye shadow sparkle. My mother, a high-flying executive who lived in Manhattan since the divorce seven years ago, hardly wore any makeup at all. What was my dad doing with a woman who painted her eyelids glittery blue?

Sydney picked up the clicker and turned on some afternoon talk show. A few seconds later she said, "Oh, I discovered a bag of Fig Newtons. Want one?"

"No, thanks."

"Sure?" She leaned toward me, raised an eyebrow and held out a cookie. "They're *reeaaally* good. . . ."

The way she was bending forward suddenly gave me a perfect view of her cleavage, like two oversized honeydew melons loosely wrapped in a cloth napkin. It was all I could do to maintain eye contact.

"Uh, no," I said. "Honestly, I'm not hungry."

"Okay." She pulled back the cookie and put it in her own mouth. "Suit yourself."

I decided to try and focus again on my essay but my eyes kept sneaking glances at her. After a few minutes, I got up and locked myself in the bathroom. When I went back out there, I decided, I'd be stronger. I wouldn't even look at her.

OLIVIA:
Wish You Were Here

Dear Ted,

I know it's only been a few days since my last letter, but I was in a used bookstore this morning and I saw this collection, Tomorrow's Castaways:

The Complete Essays of Phineas Fletcher. Do you remember reading me his Little Castaways stories when I was five? Remember "The Red Canoe"? I used to spend whole evenings imagining you and me in that canoe drifting merrily to wherever the river happened to carry us. I haven't thought about that in years, and suddenly here was this collection. It felt like a good omen (I know, I know—you don't believe in omens, but I _do_) so I grabbed it. Anyway, I thought it might brighten up your cell.

I'm concerned about Nancy. As I write she's purring like a lawnmower but lately she hasn't been mixing as much with Barbara, Hillary or Laura, who she used to adore. But then again she's about two decades older than them in cat years. I think she's feeling her age. Plus, I think the poor thing lost some weight. She's like a feather on my legs.

Brenda, on the other hand, is in a frantic mood. Not only did she agree to put up a table at the church fair this weekend (I went down to the beach and collected a bagful of quahog shells to paint and sell as ashtrays) but she's also working on four rush orders, including personalized announcements for a triple bar mitzvah in Michigan. It's a big job with all new artwork so I've hardly seen her in days. Last night she even worked through "I Love Lucy." But we're glad business is finally picking up.

You asked how many friends I have at my new school. Well, if you count the lunch ladies and the librarian I guess I'm up to three. Yup, I'm practically in the running for homecoming queen (ha ha). The truth is, it's pretty tough here. Seems like most of these kids have known each other since birth and, as you know, it's always been hard for me to open up. I want to make friends, of course—you have no idea how much. It's just that I feel like the only return item in a store full of happy customers. I'm trying to fit in but I keep freezing up. But I'm still on the lookout for a kindred spirit. Well, I guess there <u>is</u> this one boy. His name is Wen. Very serious, a Scorpio I think. For some reason I'm okay around him. Maybe because he kind of reminds me of you.

Oh, here's a good one—ready for a laugh? Mrs. Reznik, the music teacher, wants me and Wen and three other kids to perform in the school talent show. Can you imagine? Me, with <u>my</u> voice, singing onstage? Just the thought gives me the shakes. I told her no, of course. And the weirdest thing is, since then Wen has been showing up at my elbow a couple times a day asking if I'm thinking about doing it. He says he actually likes the way I sound.

Clearly, the boy must be out of his mind.

By the way, to preempt the question I know you'll ask: Yes, I like him. He's very cute. And funny. Okay? Satisfied? Not that anything's going to happen, of course, but at least now you don't have to bug me about him.

Anyway, gotta go. The girls are meowing at me so I guess it's feeding time. See you next Saturday. Miss you.

Your Diva Daughter (ha ha),
Olivia🐾

STELLA:
Lost in Translation

There I sat, wispy-headed and silent, barely listening to my sister tell a long, dull story. Wednesday was Family Night. My mother had recently discovered the idea in a discarded domestic bliss magazine, and this week she'd dragged the entire household to some chichi French restaurant on the East Side of Providence. As my mother and Leonard sat in rapt attention, Clea went into excruciating detail about a project she was working on for business class. It had something to do with bubble wrap, but her story was sprinkled with incomprehensible phrases like "supply chains," "activity based costing" and "price erosion," all of which flew completely over my head.

This wasn't a new phenomenon.

Perhaps I'd ended up in the wrong family. Had there been a mix-up at the hospital, maybe a botched adoption from Planet Stupid?

While Clea droned on, I was relieved to see that I wasn't

70

the only uninterested person at the table. For a while I amused myself watching the step-monkeys stuff straws up their noses and pretend to be walruses.

"Pull those out, Andrew!" my mother eventually snapped, practically leaping over her plate of half-devoured roasted duck to pull a plastic tube from the boy's nostril. "Tim, sit quietly in your chair! All right, tell me again Clea—what did your professor say about the destination-enhanced consolidation?"

Leonard wasn't talking much, typical for him. But he took this break in the story to cram a hunk of braised tuna into his mouth.

"Yuck," I said. "How can you eat that?"

Either he didn't hear or he was ignoring me. Still, I couldn't help picturing the poor fish with a hook in its mouth. Some people argue that fishes can't feel pain, but of course they can. Studies have proven it. Just because you can't see the agony doesn't mean it isn't there.

I picked at my dinner—asparagus with grilled goat cheese. Back when I first went veggie, my mother worried it would backfire, as if her foolish daughter was certain to give herself some nutritional deficiency or something. "She's always getting these ideas that don't work out," I overheard her saying to Leonard at the time. "Like when she was four and decided to put her hand on the hot stove to see what it would feel like. Or the time when she was ten and she got it into her head to stand up on her bicycle seat and ride downhill. She broke her arm in two places! Did you know that she once stuck a fork into an electric socket just to see if her hair would stand on end? Sometimes I don't know what to do with the girl. She can be so stubborn. She gets these crazy notions and doesn't think them through."

Wrong, mother dear. More than four months of no meat and so far I still had all my teeth.

I was surprised out of my reverie by a cold feeling on my arm. I looked down and realized that one of Tim's spastic moves had knocked over his water, which now was soaking into my sleeve. I jumped back from the table.

"Pissant! Look what you did!"

"Don't make a scene, Stella!" my mother hissed. She dove across the table, righted the cup, and hurled a linen napkin on the dark stripe that was expanding on the table-cloth. "It's not the end of the world. Just wipe your-self off!"

I clamped my mouth shut. Formerly easygoing, my maternal forebear had lately become the Queen of Stress.

Before long the step-monkeys were fooling around again and Clea's narrative had picked up right where it had left off. I once again found myself on my own, with the choice of watching the step-monkeys try to knock each other off their seats, listening to a seemingly endless story I couldn't follow or watching my mom and Leonard devour their cuisine of cruelty.

With this family, was it any wonder I'd hacked off my hair?

As Mom nodded in time to Clea's droning voice and Leonard stuffed his face, my thoughts crept back to the conversation with Mrs. Reznik.

Revolutionary. That was how the old lady described the music those kids and I had made in detention. It was a ridiculous word to use, of course. It was just a stupid commercial played on weird instruments. But still, the word had been turning around in my head all day. And even though at first I'd been appalled by the thought of doing the talent show, I now found myself toying with the idea. After all, playing that dumb song had probably been the most fun I'd had since arriving in this godforsaken part of the country. And it wasn't as if I had anything else to look forward to in my life at the moment.

Eventually, Clea put her monologue on pause so she could go to the bathroom. After a minute or so of silence my mother said, "What about you, Stella? Anything special going on at school?"

I was surprised at the question. It was the first time all week that my mom had expressed an interest in my life. But then again, I hardly ever saw her anymore now that she was busy being the big-shot biochemistry boss. Back in Arizona we used to do things together, just the two of us. We'd ride the Rio Salado bike path or go out to coffee and chat. Now everything was different. "Support me in this, Stella," she'd said as we'd packed our bags. "The timing might not be ideal, but this is an opportunity of a lifetime, a chance for me to do something I really believe in." But now that she'd dumped me into a new state and left me to fend for myself in an unfamiliar school, where was *her* support for *me*?

Just as I was about to open my mouth to answer the question, my mom's cell went off. "Sorry," she said, checking the screen, her forehead wrinkled with concern. "It's the lab. I have to take this." She put the receiver to her ear.

It was while watching my mother listen to the phone that I had a revelation. I may have chopped back my locks, but there was still something very, very wrong with my life. And if anybody was going to fix it, it wasn't my family. I was on my own.

For some reason a question occurred to me: *What*

would Sista Slash do? Surely that outspoken crusader for human rights, personal dignity and self-reliance wouldn't take this wholesale relegation to the backseat of life without a fight.

And that's when I made my decision.

Revolutionary. It meant causing a shift or change in the status quo. And that was exactly what I needed right then.

After my mom finally folded her phone shut I said, "Mother, in answer to your question, as a matter of fact there *is* something special going on at school. Or at least there's about to be." For dramatic effect, I speared an asparagus with my fork and brought it thoughtfully to my mouth.

"And? So what is it?"

Everybody was looking at me now. I let them wait. "I'm going to join a revolution."

My mom looked puzzled. Tim and Andy glanced at each other and rolled their eyes. After a long quiet moment, Leonard, his mouth still full of dead tuna, said, "Well, good for you, Stella."

I got the distinct impression that they all thought I was nuts. But just as I was about to explain about the band, Clea appeared at her chair again. Even before she sat down she plunged right back into her story and everyone's attention returned to her as if there hadn't been any break at all.

On the outside, I kept calm. On the inside, I felt like the fish on Leonard's plate.

MOHINI:
Mysteries and Moonbeams

Thursday afternoon I find another mysterious note, this one tucked between the strings of my bass, a folded piece of neon-yellow paper with my name on it.

> *FLUKE OR DESTINY?*
> *WHICHEVER IT WAS, WE NEED TO TALK.*
> *COME TO BRUNO'S PIZZA PLANET TODAY*
> *AFTER SCHOOL.*
> *—S*

"Weird," says Naomi. "It's from Scott?"

"I don't think so," I say. "Doesn't look like his handwriting."

"No? So who's 'S' then? And what's this about fluke or destiny?"

"I don't know."

I can practically hear Naomi's imagination whirring into overdrive. "Hmmm . . ." she says. "A mystery. Okay, let's consider the possibilities. Sarah Obinsky? Sabina Boch? How about Seth Levine. Maybe he likes you and thinks you're *destined* to be together?"

"Seth Levine does *not* like me," I say, fighting a smile. Seth is the senior class president. He doesn't even know I exist.

"How can you act so nonchalant about this? Somebody sent you a secret message and you have no idea what it means or who it's from. Aren't you intrigued?"

I nod. Of course I am. I just can't figure it out.

"So are you going to show up to Bruno's?" Bruno's

75

Pizza Planet is a popular hangout a block from the high school.

"I'm not sure," I say, still staring at the message. And that's when an idea hits me. "You don't think . . . 'S' could be Stella Penn, do you?"

Naomi's forehead wrinkles. "Stella? I don't know. Anything's possible, I guess."

I hope not. I don't think I want anything to do with that giant, scowling girl. With her freaky hair, towering height and that bizarre jacket she always wears around the school, she blends in about as well as a chainsaw in a chamber orchestra. Even worse, she seems like some kind of political fanatic.

"That's all I'd need. What if Stella has some crazy idea like maybe we should play that song until they stop killing whales or something?" I crumple up the note and shove it into my pocket. "That's it, I've decided. It's too weird. I'm not going."

But of course I do go. Even though I have Trig homework, even though I ought to be doing the pre-lab questions for Biology tomorrow, and even though I've been planning to go to the library to research the Battle of Brandywine Creek (I'm doing a four-page extra-credit essay for Mr. Dewonka), I'm too curious to keep away. After my last class ends I stay late to talk with Mr. Prichard because my Social Studies presentation is coming up at the end of next week and I'm completely flipping out about it. But after that I hurry over to Bruno's. Five minutes later I'm rushing through the front door.

For midafternoon, the place is pretty busy. I scan row after row of tables that look like flying saucers, more than half of them full. With a star-painted sky, giant papier-mâché craters and aliens and weird lights that glow in ghostly neon, Bruno's is decorated to feel like you're eating in outer space. Even the little stage area where Bruno sometimes features local musicians—mostly acoustic guitarists playing quiet, eerie chords—is decked out to look like the moon. Bruno's Pizza Planet is a junk food joint with extraterrestrial ambitions.

It takes me a moment to spot anybody I know, but then, under the Milky Way, I see her waving me over.

S for Stella. Mystery solved.

I almost spin around and head back outside, not only because I figure that anything to do with Stella Penn means trouble but also because sitting with her at the circular booth in the corner are all the other kids from detention.

But Stella calls to me before I get a chance. "Mo!" she shouts across the room. "We're all signed up!"

I'm not sure what she means, but her piercing screech temporarily halts the conversations at the other space ships.

"For the *talent show*!" Stella calls, as if it should have been obvious. That's when I notice that there's something different about her appearance today. Then I realize what it is. Her short, spiky hair is no longer black. It's green. I also notice the Patties sitting at a booth at the opposite end of the room. Patty Norris and Patty Keane are juniors, Ray Beech and Dean Eagler's girlfriends. They turn and I'm sure they see me but they don't say hi, even after I wave. It bothers me but I don't let it show.

I approach Stella's table as calmly as I can, like meeting up with this unlikely crew is something I do all the time. Sitting next to Stella on one end of the rounded bench is Wen. He's nodding his head and I'm wondering if he's in on this with her. Aware that the Patties are probably watching me, I set my backpack by the table but I don't sit.

"But, Stella," I say. "We already talked about this. It's not going to happen."

"Sure it is. I wrote our names down on the sheet. It's official." She takes a sip from a paper cup of what looks like frozen lemonade. "That's why I asked everyone to come here today. Mrs. Reznik is right. If we're going to win, we have a lot of work to do."

I'm not sure how to react. She's obviously out of her mind.

I glance around the table. Wen is still smiling, but it's kind of a nervous smile. Charlie is eyeing Stella uneasily as if her head might start spinning at any moment. Olivia just stares at the table like she's imagining she's somewhere else.

Stella curls her lip at all the silent faces. "Look, this is our cosmic shot at immortality. The winner of the talent show wins respect, right? Don't you want that?"

For a few seconds nobody answers. "Well okay, maybe . . . ," Charlie says finally, as if he's worried that this green-haired oddity might bite him, "but even if that's true—and I'm not saying it is or it isn't—we won't win. We're not polished enough."

"No problem," says Stella. "All we need is a little experience. Which is why I *also* signed us up for the Halloween Bash."

This is getting weirder and weirder. "But . . . how did you pull *that* off?" he asks. "How did you get anybody to even *consider* us for the Bash?"

She grins. "It's amazing what a vice principal will agree to if he thinks his biggest problem student is finally working on something productive. Why don't you sit?" She levels her gaze at me and points to the empty seat. "Join us."

After a moment's hesitation, I do as I'm told. When I'm seated I notice the Patties aren't there anymore. Their stuff is gone too. They must have packed up and left. "Let me get this straight," I say. "You *lied* to Mr. Brenigan and now he thinks we're some kind of rock band or something?"

"To quote Sista Slash, 'To make good stuff happen, you sometimes gotta finesse your way around the system.' " I can see it in her face now. She is completely serious.

"But Stella," says Charlie quietly, "playing rubber bands and banging on desks in detention isn't exactly the same thing as having a band. Other than Mrs. Reznik, nobody thinks we can actually perform in front of an *audience,* right?"

"I'm not saying we should play rubber bands and bang on a desk. We'll use our real instruments. You have real drums, right?"

I turn to him. To tell the truth, I have no idea if he does or not. But he nods.

"Okay then," she says as if she just proved a point, "so why shouldn't you play them in front of an audience?"

That's when I jump in again. "For starters," I say, looking around the table for support, "what would we play? The smile song over and over?"

Nobody says anything. Finally, Wen shifts in his seat and opens his mouth for the first time. "I don't know. Maybe it isn't such a crazy thought. We could *learn* other songs, right?"

I can't believe I'm hearing this. Are Charlie and I the only sane people at the table? "Hold on, Wen. You actually think this is a good idea? How can we possibly come up with enough music to perform at the Bash? Halloween is less than a month away! I, for one, don't have a lot of time to spare right now. I'm taking eight courses this semester!"

"I'm just saying it's an interesting thought," Wen says. "That's all."

Stella doesn't seem fazed by anything we've said. She picks at a scab on her elbow. "Sure, we'll learn plenty of other songs. I have a bunch of ideas. I was talking with Mrs. Reznik about this. We're not going to be just some throwaway pop band. We won't play any trash. No Desirée Crane–type sellout crap for us, only music that makes a difference. Our stuff will need to be"—she pauses for a moment, deep in thought—"*important*. Know what I mean?"

I don't, but Wen nods.

Olivia still hasn't said a word. I look over at her, wondering what she's thinking. Trying to interpret her expressionless face, though, is like trying to read a blank wall.

I realize I'm biting my nails again so I stop myself.

But then it hits me. In all the excitement, I forgot the most obvious reason in the world why we can't do this. The details of the Bash aren't public knowledge yet, but I happen to have inside information. "Wait a minute. Hold on. How can we play the Halloween Bash when I know for a fact that this year's band has already been chosen, and it's going to be Mudslide Crush, same as last year?"

I turn to Charlie to get his reaction. My guess is he'll recognize this as an injection of indisputable reality into this otherwise crazy conversation. But he looks away. His face reddens and he suddenly seems focused on a satellite hanging on the wall.

Across from me, though, Stella hardly bats an eye. "Mudslide Crush is going to play at the Bash. But Mr. Brenigan agreed that we will too. We're splitting the night." She grins again. "We play first."

I open my mouth to answer, but I can't think of what to say. I'm amazed.

Suddenly I'm looking at Stella in a new light. In her short time at our school I've seen her stalking the hallways, always alone, a supersized girl with an attitude as big as New England. She's always seemed like trouble, maybe even a little unstable—definitely a person to avoid. And yet, sitting with her now I can't help admiring her confidence. She really thinks we can pull this off. And the more I listen to her, the more I wonder.

Plus, I have to admit that the idea of sharing a stage with Scott and his friends wasn't completely unappealing.

"But I just can't," says a quiet, scratchy voice to my right. "For one thing, my voice isn't very strong. It doesn't take much straining for me to go hoarse."

"But you wouldn't have to strain, Olivia," says Wen. "We'll get microphones."

Olivia doesn't seem convinced. "I'll freeze up. I already told you, I get nervous. I'm not a real singer."

"Listen, Stella," Wen says, looking a little less optimistic than before, "maybe this idea just isn't realistic. We shouldn't do it unless all five of us are in."

Stella sits back in her chair, looking thoughtful. For a long time, nobody speaks.

"Okay," she says finally. "So like Mrs. Reznik said, it's not going to be easy. But tell me this, guys"—she scans our faces—"aren't you tired of living on the sidelines?"

No one answers. Stella looks directly at me but how am I supposed to answer a question like that?

"What's the biggest problem with our school? I'll tell you. It's that most kids don't step up. Why is it okay that only a chosen few are seen as important and everybody else is a nobody? Why do we accept the way things are? Are we afraid to make our own decisions?" She looks around the table. "I don't know about you, but after *I'm* gone I don't want to be remembered as just another face in the yearbook, another kid that people vaguely recall passing in the corridor." She presses her big hands on the table. "Don't you want to show the jocks, the popular kids, everybody you know, that you're not somebody to overlook, that you're exceptional? Aren't you guys tired of being nobodies?"

I think for sure somebody's going to protest but no one does.

Stella leans forward. "Look, Wen and I are in. Who's with us?"

I glance around. I realize that the near impossibility of getting our act together in only about three weeks actually excites me.

Even so, I'm still surprised when, after a long, painful silence, I hear my own voice say, "Okay. I'll give it a shot."

Everyone turns to me. I feel my face heat up. I know I'm probably making a terrible mistake so I quickly add, "But only if everyone else agrees. And I'm only committing to one practice, that's all. After that, if it feels like it's going to work out I'll keep going, but if it doesn't I'm out."

Wen is obviously surprised. Stella is beaming. After a moment Wen spins to his left. "Come on, Olivia. You can do this. I know you can. Say you'll give it a try."

Olivia looks up and takes a deep breath. For just an instant too long, her eyes linger on Wen. It's subtle, but I notice. And I recognize that look. "Okay," she says, practically whispering. "If everyone else wants to do this, I'll try. But I can't make any promises."

Now all eyes are on Charlie. After a while he says,

"Looks like it's up to me then." He laughs, but it's an un-easy kind of laugh. "On the one hand, I've always *wanted* to be in a real band. But on the other hand, I think this might just be the stupidest idea I ever heard." He laughs again, but everyone is still waiting. "Hey, guys, I don't know what to say. I'm the worst in the world at making de-cisions." Then an idea seems to come to him and I watch him reach into his pocket. "Tell you what," he says, pulling out something and holding it up. It's a quarter. "Let's do it this way. Heads we go for it. Tails we don't."

And believe it or not, that's how it happens. Charlie tosses the coin and we all watch it spin in the air. I hold my breath. By the time it lands in the center of the table all five of us are leaning forward, practically craning our necks to see what it says.

George Washington.

Everybody's in.

CHAPTER 3

Following the light of the sun,
we left the Old World.
—Christopher Columbus

WEN:
The Weirdest Music Ever Heard

One of the misconceptions about Lemonade Mouth is that we were a natural fit, like the individual parts of a five-piece puzzle. Not true. As a matter of fact, the way I remember our first practice we didn't even get along.

It started off all right. It was the Friday after our meeting at Bruno's, and Mrs. Reznik let us clear a space in the music room. To my surprise, Naomi Fishmeier and Lyle Dwarkin came to cheer us on. Lyle, a tiny kid with an acne problem, even hooked up some microphones from the A.V. room for Olivia and Mo. We ran through the smile song first, replacing the rubber band, kazoo and ukulele with Mo's stand-up bass, my trumpet and Stella's electric guitar. Instead of the standard drum set I'd expected Charlie to bring, he'd set up a wall of bongos, congas, timbales and a box of other noisemakers I couldn't even name. The song went okay. Listening from the long ledge over the room's noisy old radiator, Naomi and Lyle applauded even though I thought we sounded stiff and nervous.

After that we worked on Stella's ideas.

"No, no," she barked at Mo. "Can't you feel it in your bones? It's E then A then D for *two* bars, then back to the E, *then* a B-flat. Ready?"

Without waiting for an answer, Stella began bobbing her head up and down as she machine-gunned angry power chords through her amplifier. Mo and Charlie tried to follow, but were obviously having a hard time. I attempted to add a note here and there and Olivia hummed along a little but mostly we just watched.

Stella had handed out a long list of tunes she wanted us to learn, all hard-rocking protest songs by this neo-surf guitar slinger named Sista Slash. Stella played the original recordings for us but, to be honest, I didn't like them much. The one we were attempting right then was "Damn You Petty Tyrants." Lyle had his hands over his ears. I could hardly blame him. We sounded like an unruly mob at a discount music store.

"Come on, Charlie!" Stella called out over the noise. "It's a straight-ahead four-four beat! Stop trying to make it so complicated!"

His jaw tight, Charlie pulled back to a much simpler rhythm.

Mrs. Reznik was in the little adjoining room she used as an office. Every now and then I could hear her coughing. Before we started, she'd told us she was going to keep out of our way because she believed in giving creativity space to grow. "Never let an outside influence interfere with the creative process," she'd said. "You certainly don't need me butting in just as you're trying to work out your *process*. Don't worry, I'll let you know if I feel you've crossed the borders of artistic decency." Now she appeared at the doorway and frowned. A moment later she quietly shut the door.

Not long after, Mo, who had been struggling to pluck out a bass line the way Stella had instructed, stopped playing. Then, one by one, we all did.

"What's the matter?" Stella asked.

I didn't want to say anything. Stella was a big kid, and could be kind of intimidating. But finally it was Mo who spoke up.

"This isn't working," Mo said. "We're terrible."

"What do you mean? We'll get it. We just need to keep practicing. Maybe we should listen to the song one more time."

Stella went to turn on her little stereo again, but Mo waved her hand to stop her. "Wait, listen. . . . I know these songs are important to you, Stella, but did you ever consider that maybe they're not right for us? Let's think about this."

For some reason, Stella seemed insulted. Her face went all pink and she looked hurt. "Are you saying I didn't think about it? I thought about it plenty." She glared at Mo, but Mo stared right back. Nobody else spoke. I was thinking how funny it was that the smallest of us was the only one who didn't seem afraid to speak her mind. I suddenly had a new respect for Mo.

"And as far as these tunes not being right for us," Stella continued, "how can you say that when we haven't even given them a chance?"

That's when I jumped in. "I think I agree with Mo," I said. "These songs are okay, I guess, but they don't feel . . . comfortable to me."

"Me neither," Charlie said, setting down his sticks.

Stella scowled. "These tunes are a passionate call to arms. They're perfect for us!"

Over her shoulder I could see Naomi roll her eyes.

"All right," Stella said impatiently. "Let's see if everybody agrees. What do *you* say, Olivia? Should we give up on these songs already? And if so, do you have any better ideas?"

Olivia had been standing quietly in the corner, shifting her weight back and forth from one foot to the other. She almost wilted under Stella's gaze. "I don't know . . . I guess I can try to work on them some more. . . ."

"That's more like it. Look, it's going to be great. I think all we need to do is change our approach." Stella scanned the room and settled on Charlie's arrangement of congas and bongos. "Maybe you should try using a real drum set."

That's when Charlie's face went red. He stood up, set his hands on the bongos, and narrowed his eyes at her. "This *is* a real set. It's *my* set. It's what I play."

Lyle and Naomi exchanged glances.

"No need to get offended," Stella said. "I'm only trying to find a way to make this work. I, for one, am willing to be flexible. Okay, how about another idea. Mo, I don't think your acoustic bass is powerful enough. Now, I bet if you were to get an electric one it would be much more—"

"That's it," Mo said, setting down her instrument. "I'm out of here."

"What?" Stella asked. "Now you're going to stomp away?"

"Why shouldn't I? I obviously don't belong here."

"Wait," I said, feeling a sudden rising panic. I wanted this band to work and besides, Sydney had gone up to Boston so I'd given up a perfectly good Sydney-free Friday afternoon with George and my dad for this. "Don't just leave," I said. "Let's talk this through."

But Mo wasn't interested. "In case you never realized, Wendel, I play classical bass, not surfer grunge or whatever Stella calls this. And I'm going out tonight so I don't have time for this garbage." She glared at Stella and then spun back around to unlatch her case, her long black hair swinging.

Charlie followed her lead and began breaking down his set. Everything was suddenly falling apart. I was amazed at how quickly it had happened.

"Come on, guys," I pleaded. "We can work this out—"

But nobody was listening. Before long, there was a lot of yelling going on.

"You're quitting before we've even started!" Stella growled.

"If anybody's a petty tyrant, it's you, Stella!" Charlie shouted back.

It went like that for a while. Naomi and Lyle, still perched on the ledge, looked uncomfortable, probably wishing they hadn't come at all. It seemed obvious that this had been a complete waste of time. Any minute, Mrs. Reznik's face would appear at the door again—this time to send us home. Surely we'd crossed the borders of artistic decency by now. Worse, Olivia seemed to be working herself up into some sort of crisis. She was rocking back and forth, hugging her shoulders. Was I the only one to notice?

I felt a terrible sinking feeling. Everything was crumbling around me. As a high school pariah, and with Azra and Floey gone from my life, my only remaining chance at having any kind of social existence at all was riding on this group of kids—but now I was going to have to get used to being alone and friendless. But then I remembered that I was still holding my horn. I'd been thinking about the riff I'd been working on at home the other day, the two bars I'd come up with while listening to Dizzy Gillespie, and in all the commotion my fingers kept walking through the notes.

I'm not sure what made me do it, but just as Mrs. Reznik's door opened and her concerned face appeared, I put my trumpet to my mouth and played.

What happened next was what Naomi liked to call the First Lemonade Mouth Miracle.

After only a few notes everybody stopped shouting and Olivia stood still. At the end of my riff, I started all over again. Suddenly there was no other sound but my horn. Mo looked at me like I was crazy, but Charlie's eyes lit up. A moment later, he was scrambling to put back the conga he'd broken down. By the end of my fourth time through the little melody, he held his sticks in the air. With a mad grin, he attacked his drums like I'd never seen. It was a primal beat straight out of the jungle, with Charlie's hair whipping in all directions, his arms whacking at his congas like they were possessed.

Lyle smiled, Naomi's head started bobbing to the rhythm, and Mrs. Reznik, who only seconds before seemed about to send us packing, suddenly closed her mouth and leaned against the doorway.

A moment later I was thrilled to see Mo upright her instrument again. This time, though, she took out her bow, waited two bars and then pulled it gently across the strings.

What came out were four long notes, each one starting low but then sinking even lower, like a walrus slowly diving through deep water. It was hypnotic. Stella seemed to hesitate but after a moment she set down her electric guitar and went over to the ukulele, which still hung on the wall. She pulled it down and then stepped close to the microphone by Mo's bass. The next time Mo began her pattern the ukulele came to life, sending out a high-pitched, rapid-fire series of notes that, to my surprise, blended perfectly on top of the other instruments.

The total effect—Stella's Hawaiian gunfire merging over Mo's moaning bass, Charlie's chaotic percussion and my jazz-inspired riff—bizarre as it was, somehow worked. It was as if electricity shot through the room. I felt it and I could see it on everybody else's faces too. We were a wild party, a crazy, rhythmic riot. Lyle and Naomi sat up, their mouths hanging open. Mrs. Reznik stood like a statue in the doorway.

And Olivia hadn't even started singing yet.

I looked in her direction. She was staring at the microphone and taking deep breaths. After a moment she glanced over at me and nodded. I had no clue what she was about to sing, but to make room for her voice I dropped my horn back. At exactly the same moment, Stella simplified what she was doing on the ukulele. It was as if we'd been playing together forever.

After bracing herself with one more deep breath, Olivia put her mouth in front of the microphone.

> *I don't know where I'm going*
> *I don't know where I'd like to be*
> *I cannot see beyond this moment*
> *But let this moment swallow me*

And I—
I'm singing a new song—
I—
I'm singing a new song—

She'd found a slow meandering melody, completely different from my trumpet riff and yet just right. With the reverb from Lyle's speaker, Olivia's voice echoed and sounded more emotional than ever before. I could hardly believe she came up with words like that off the top of her head, this girl who hardly ever spoke.

My hair stood on end. The rush I'd felt in detention was back.

After that, Stella and I took turns playing short fills between verses, and then we gave a longer space for Mo to play a solo that sounded like Mozart on acid. Finally, Olivia sang the beginning part again. When I felt like the end was near I nodded to the others. They seemed to understand or maybe we all just felt it, but it worked out perfectly. The four of us stopped playing on exactly the same beat, leaving Olivia's vocal as the only sound for the final two lines.

I . . . I'm singing a new song.
I . . . I'm singing a new song.

We stood completely still as the echo of Olivia's voice faded. Even after that nobody moved or made a sound for a long time, as if doing so might break the spell.

That's when I noticed Naomi staring at us like we each had suddenly grown three heads. At first I thought maybe she didn't like what we'd played, but then she started clapping. Lyle joined her but it was slow and uncertain, like he wasn't sure that what he'd just heard was real.

"That," Naomi finally said in an awed voice, "was absolutely the weirdest music I've ever heard. Did you just

91

make that *up?* Oh my God, you guys are . . ." She didn't finish right away. She tilted her head as if seeing us for the first time. Finally she said, *". . .gigantic."*

Lyle nodded. "You guys are going to be *huge.*"

Mrs. Reznik seemed pleased too. "All right," she said. "I believe you've worked out a process. But don't let compliments make you overconfident. You still have a lot of work to do before you're ready for your audience."

As for Charlie, Mo, Stella, Olivia and me, we were as surprised as anybody else at what had just happened.

But we were all grinning. Even Stella.

MOHINI:
A Supernova of Irrational Thought

It's later that night and I'm on the Opequonsett town beach. A crowd of kids laugh and talk behind me while I gaze into the fire. The breeze from the ocean ruffles my hair like invisible fingers. Eventually, I feel a hand on my shoulder. Scott's back.

"Comfortable?" he whispers, easing himself into the sand beside me.

I smile as he wraps his arm around my shoulders. "Oh yes. Very."

I've been looking forward to this evening all week. Scott and his friends have made a small fire by the water. There are about twenty of us. I've never been invited to anything like this before—a party with the coolest of the cool. I should be at home practicing the Rabbath piece, of course, or the Dragonetti concerto. I promised my parents I'll perform at the temple on the last day of Durga Pooja, the ten-day festival of eating and celebrating that starts in only a week. Plus, I had to lie to them again this evening—I told them I'm with Naomi tonight. But right at this moment it all feels worth it. This evening is special. Scott and I have been seeing each other for twenty-three days, and now with the eyes of all his friends on us, I feel like he and I are more of a couple than ever.

Besides, what could be more romantic than sitting by a campfire with the guy you like, the ocean waves gently crashing nearby?

Ray Beech ambles by with a case of beer. God only knows how he got his hands on it. Ray is not exactly my favorite person, but he's Scott's friend so I've been trying my best to warm up to him. Scott takes a can so I do too. Another uncomfortable first. My family's Hindu so we never drink alcohol.

Somebody is playing Mudslide Crush's newest album, recorded in Dean Eagler's basement over the summer. Dean's dark, warbling voice drifts through the air as the Patties and a bunch of other girls I barely know nod their heads in time. It's a warm evening for October, but right then a cool autumn gust sends shivers through me. Immediately, Scott takes off his jacket and wraps it over my shoulders.

"There," he says. "Better?"

I nod and pull it tight. I can barely contain my happiness. All I can think as I lean my head on his shoulder is that Naomi was so wrong about him. I asked him about Lynn Westerberg and he assured me it'd all been a terrible misunderstanding. He swore he would never cheat on anybody, that he doesn't believe in dating more than one person at a time.

We sit together, just Scott and me, staring contentedly into the flames. After a while, he turns his head and starts nibbling my ear. More shivers. I can't help giggling.

Here we go again, I think.

Twenty minutes and half a beer later (swallowed in tentative, sour gulps that left me disappointed from the first sip—but since I've already broken a bunch of taboos, what's one more?) we're making out in the darkness behind a nearby dune. As I suck his upper lip into my mouth, I wonder exactly what it is about him that drives me wild? Why do I feel like a different person whenever he's around? It's actually a little scary. In fact, when I feel his hand start to reach under my shirt, a part of me goes into a panic. I worry just how far I'll let him go.

Maybe what happens next only happens because that part of me is desperately *searching* for a way out. Or maybe not—maybe it's only the breeze, which carries a part of Ray Beech's conversation from the other side of the dune to my ear.

". . . that's right," I hear him say. "I guess Mr. Brenigan, that butt-wipe, expects us to jump up and down for joy now. Lucky us, we still get to play *half* the gig."

Somebody snickers, a sound a little like a horse whinnying. Patty Norris. "Unless," she says, "she convinces him to cancel you guys altogether."

"Don't even get me started about that freak."

I freeze. "What's that?"

"What's what?" Scott's hand is still attempting to make its way north despite the gentle barricade I've set up with my arm.

"Were they talking about the Halloween Bash?"

"Who?"

"Listen," I whisper, pulling away a little and nodding in the direction of the campfire. "I just heard Ray and Patty say something about Mr. Brenigan and how he wants you guys to play half a gig. He sounded annoyed."

"I don't know, I didn't hear." He starts on my neck again. "Don't worry about it."

"Wait," I say, trying to disentangle my body from his. I haven't mentioned anything about our little band to Scott. I'm not entirely sure even now if I really intend to be a part of it. Still, I guess I've been expecting that if I *do* tell Scott, he'll be pleased. "I want to know what he's mad about."

"Why is it important right now? It's stupid."

"Not to me it isn't." I scoot away and sit up, both relieved and disappointed.

A moment later, Scott sits up too. In the moonlight I watch him rub his eyes. "Okay, okay," he sighs. "Brenigan told Dean today that we don't get to play the full night at the Bash."

"So?"

"So that's probably what Ray was pissed about. We all are. You know that girl Stella Penn? The one with the green buzz cut? Well, I guess she told Brenigan she has a band, and crazy old Mrs. Reznik is in on it. Anyway, the two of them got Mr. Brenigan to agree to give this so-called band half our time."

I nod slowly, trying to look sympathetic. I have to tread carefully. "Is that . . . really such a big deal?"

"Of course. He's a complete idiot."

"Why?"

"Well, because Stella's a freak. Haven't you noticed?" He scoots closer to me again and starts planting gentle kisses all over the side of my neck. It feels so good I don't try to stop him. Still, I can't help thinking about how only this afternoon Stella and I were hanging around together. Somebody left a fashion magazine under one of the desks, and while we waited for Charlie to pack his drums neatly away in the corner of the music room she and I took turns drawing facial hair on the models. By the time Charlie was done, the two of us were practically hysterical over a bikinied blonde we'd turned into a pirate, complete with a mustache, a goatee and an eye patch. The parrot that Stella drew on her shoulder was particularly hilarious.

"I don't know," I say. "I've talked to her. She may be a little different, but she seems all right to me."

"Yeah, sure."

By now he's been working on my neck so long that I worry he might leave a hickey. I wiggle away. "So anyway, have you heard who's in this band?"

"Not really," he says. "I only know about Stella and that loser Charlie Hirsh. Oh, and Olivia Whitehead. Now there's a real whack job."

I ignore that. "Nobody else?"

"Why do you care?" He slowly runs his finger down the back of my blouse, sending a wave of electricity through me. "Those kids are nothing. The guys and I are going to blow those freaks away. Come on, let's not talk about this anymore. We're wasting time." I feel his hand try to reach under my shirt again.

"Well," I say, twisting away, "I was waiting to surprise you with this but, the thing is . . ." He follows me across the sand and puts his face directly in front of mine, his smile betraying only a hint of impatience. ". . . *I'm* one of those freaks."

Even in the darkness I can see his eyebrows draw together. He stares at me for a second and then pulls back.

"We haven't agreed on a name yet or anything—but we're not bad, actually. You should hear us."

He keeps staring. "You're kidding, right?"

"It'll be fun. We get to share the same stage on the same night. Isn't that great?"

"Oh, yeah," he says. "That's just . . . wonderful."

"But I thought you'd be *happy*."

He shakes his head like he can't believe what he's hearing. "Look, Mo, it isn't that I care about you being in a band. It's just that I'm pissed off that *this* band is taking half our night from us."

I try to give him a playful smile. "So it's *your* night, is it?"

"Yes. Well, it was supposed to be anyway, until Brenigan carved it up. We had big plans for this year's Bash. I think you should tell Stella and the others to back off."

"I don't understand. Why should this be a problem?"

He shrugs. "I guess I'm just a competitive guy."

For a long, quiet moment I watch his silhouette watch me. This reaction is surprising. In fact, he seems so ruffled about the Halloween dance that I decide not to mention about the Holiday Talent Show. Let him warm up to the idea first. I move closer and snuggle next to him. "Did you ever consider that maybe I'm competitive too?"

"Okay, but Olivia Whitehead? Charlie Hirsh? Come on, Mo, you guys are way out of your league."

"What!" That's when, laughing, I pop him one on the shoulder. "Scott Pickett, don't be such an arrogant jerk!"

"Not *you*. I don't mean *that*." He laughs, but only a little. "It's just that I honestly have no idea what you're doing with those losers. Take my advice and tell them you're not interested." Then he comes in even closer. "Look, you're a special person, Mo. I really like you. A lot. You should know that."

I don't answer right away. How can I? He takes my hand and a supernova of excitement renders me temporarily incapable of rational thought. Eventually I manage, "I really like you too." I lean in and we kiss again.

A part of me realizes even now that he really *is* being a jerk about the band, but I decide that deep down he knows it and is going to feel bad about it later. Anyway, I don't want to argue. After another long kiss we sit quietly and stare up at the stars. Eventually, he stands and helps me to my feet so we can head back to the campfire.

"So?" he whispers as we round the dune. "What did you decide about the Bash?"

"Decide?" I give him my best mischievous smile. "Well, after considerable thought I decided *not* to dump you for what you said."

"What *I* said? About your friends?"

"About my band mates." I grin and take his hand again, leaning my head against his shoulder the whole way back to the fire. 🎸

OLIVIA:
Bikini-Clad Policemen on Old-fashioned Bicycles

Dear Ted,

I've been sitting here in the backyard for almost an hour gazing into the woods, listening to the crickets and thinking. I get some of my clearest thoughts down here in the grass. And today I have a lot to mull over. I spent most of the afternoon at Wen's house. Remember that talent show I wrote you about? Well, I decided to give it a shot after all. I figure it's time for drastic measures unless I want to stay friendless for the next four years. When the time comes to go onstage, I guess I'll just have to do whatever I can to stifle the panic. (She thinks, "Happy thoughts, happy thoughts, happy thoughts . . .") Very un-Virgo of me, I know. Impressed?

Anyway, Mrs. Reznik is helping us. We decided we're only going to play our own music because anything else we attempt sounds like crap (our ukulele player's word, not Mrs. Reznik's). So this morning in Social Studies Wen mentioned that he and I should maybe try and write some songs together. I guess I misunderstood because when I showed up at his house this afternoon he seemed surprised to see me. But it worked out fine. He introduced me to his father, Norman (Wen's clone—short, wiry, baseball cap, big smile), his little brother, George (Eddie Munster with freckles) and Norman's amazing girlfriend, Sydney. Sydney works in a used bookstore in Providence and loves to read so we had a lot to talk about. Plus she's an artist. Listen to this: she painted a whole case of soda cans, each with its own bikini-clad policeman on an old-fashioned bicycle. So cool.

Wen knows the words to every Wham Bam Racer song. He sang some of them even though (as he freely admits) he has the worst voice ever, even worse than mine—like a mountain goat in a death throe (his words, not mine)! He made me laugh so hard that for a few minutes I stopped obsessing about Nancy (who's doing better now). Wen's even a P. G. Wodehouse fanatic like me, can you believe it? The truth is, I believe I'm starting to have a crush on him. And that's a problem. After all, I'm sure he doesn't feel the same way about me. How do I know? Well, for one thing, he's obviously in lust with Sydney. All afternoon, whenever she was around he practically tripped over himself trying to look in the other direction.

Poor boy.

Anyway, the good news is that by the time I left Wen's house he and I had five new songs. I'd brought my accordion to help us, but we seemed to work best with Wen coming up with most of the music and me writing the lyrics. The songs are just outlines, really, skeletons of words and melody that the others can fill in next time we get together. Still, I think they're okay.

Stay tuned.

Your Biggest Fan,
Olivia

P.S.

*I lied when I told you Nancy is doing better. Sorry.
I wasn't going to get into this because I figured
there was no point in bringing you bad news,
especially when I'm not even sure about it. But
I was about to lick the envelope when I had a
change of heart. She was originally your cat, after
all, so withholding the truth wouldn't be right. The
fact is, she's still hardly eating. Brenda and I are
in a state about it. We've been trying everything:
hand feeding her warm tuna, even giving her
potassium supplements. So far nothing seems to
work. The earliest vet appointment we could get
was for this Wednesday. We've been putting on
brave faces for each other, trying to convince
ourselves it's a stomach flu or something, but in my
heart of hearts I'm not so sure. Needless to say, I'm
losing sleep over it. But of course, whatever Nancy
needs we'll get her. Apart from Brenda and you, my
girls are the closest friends I have in the world.*

    *I hope I'm doing the right thing by telling you.
I'll write when I know more.*

STELLA:
A Puzzling Interruption

Picture, if you will, your beloved Sista Stella, her short
locks now a blaze of glorious green, carrying her ukulele
everywhere she went. It wasn't exactly *her* ukulele, of

course, but Mrs. Reznik said she could use the one from the music room as long as she needed. And Stella wasn't carrying it around to show off or anything, it was just that she liked to keep it close. Imagine our musical maverick carefully removing the instrument from its case several times a day just to look at its shiny red finish, its perfect silver frets. Our former directionless loner suddenly felt like she had a purpose, a raison d'être, and she was determined to take good care of the beautiful instrument, to keep it protected, polish it and change the strings often.

Now picture a bunch of self-important juniors and seniors giving her the evil eye as she walked the hallways. Not that they didn't stare before, secretly studying her like she were a curious specimen, keeping their distance as if worried she might spontaneously burst into flames. But suddenly now it was even worse.

How did this baffling new heat from passing glances affect me?

Well, I won't lie. I found it all pretty freaky. Still, who could blame me, a naïve newcomer at the time, for assuming I was getting these dark stares only because kids thought I was some kind of music dork? According to Wen, though, that wasn't it at all. He told me it was because somebody had spread the word that I was responsible for cutting the Mudslide Crush show short. Naturally, I was surprised to hear it was that big a deal. Apparently this band had quite a following. Its fans even had a name for themselves: the Mudslide Crushers. Sure, I'd heard some of Mudslide Crush's music, and it really *was* a good band in a power-pop kind of way—but who *were* these people, some sort of suburban cult?

But I tried to ignore the looks. Just because Mudslide

Crush was popular didn't mean they couldn't share the stage for one solitary night.

That Tuesday afternoon my own neophyte band met again for our second practice.

"I see everybody brought their official underworld membership badges," Wen said as we were setting up.

I wasn't sure at first what he was talking about, but when I looked around I realized. Today, not only did Mrs. Reznik have her usual Mel's cup from the nearby machine, but each of us, myself included, had brought one too. Before moving to Rhode Island I'd never even heard of Mel's Organic Frozen Lemonade, but during my visits to the basement in recent days I'd developed a taste for it. The icy cold slush was a welcome change from soda. But in my short time at this school I'd also learned that drinking Mel's was something people around here usually associated with the oddball kids who hung out in the basement. If somebody was carrying the signature yellow and green paper cup, that usually meant they were in one of the school's less glamorous organizations.

Everybody seemed to recognize what Wen meant. Mo laughed. "I guess this means we're an official basement club now."

It suddenly struck me as strange that Mo would want to be down here with us. After all, unlike the rest of us, she had somewhere else to go. But then again, it seemed to me that Mo didn't really fit in with that crowd of Barbies and Kens I sometimes saw her with. There was something off-kilter about her. For starters, she was a human pressure cooker. You could see in her eyes that the girl was always on the verge of panic. And then there was the bullheaded way she did everything—like insisting on lugging that bass around with her all the time even though it was practically bigger than she was. Being the only Indian kid at school didn't help either. In any case, here she was—maybe not as obviously out of spec as the rest of us, but out of spec just the same.

I held up my cup, "We're subterranean and we're proud!"

Everybody grinned. They each grabbed their own cups and held them up, and then we all took a sip together.

The dark and windowless music room was not a particularly peaceful place to practice, though. Not only was it situated below the new locker rooms which were under construction, but it was also directly adjacent to the bathrooms so the pipes shook, loud as crap, every time somebody flushed—which always seemed to happen two or three times in a row.

"Down here, everybody's an underachiever," Wen quipped after the third or forth time it happened. "Even the toilets."

Wen was all right.

Still, I didn't care about the noise. To be honest, after everyone dissed my Sista Slash ideas at the last practice, leaving the group with only the one tune, I worried that we wouldn't be able to get our act together on time. Plus, we still didn't have a name. The subject had come up a few times already but nobody ever had any good ideas, and anyway, nothing seemed to fit. And this worried me. Mr. Brenigan had been pushing for a name to put on the fliers. The Bash was only in seventeen days.

But after practice got going, I realized that at least we had a handful of new songs thanks to Wen and Olivia. Who knew they had it in them? Olivia had even brought an ancient-looking accordion, which they hooked up to one of that Lyle kid's distortion effects. Freaky cool. Out of all the new songs, the one that especially bowled me over was one called "Skinny Nancy," a spooky tune with mysterious words:

> *Eat, Skinny Nancy, eat*
> *Before your time is done*
> *You are a fading flower, a setting sun*
> *Enjoy this moment, my lovely one*
> *Eat, Skinny Nancy, eat*

That blew me away.

I asked Olivia what it meant but she wouldn't say, only that it was personal. I kept pushing but the girl was a hard nut to crack. Finally, Charlie came to her defense:

"Leave her alone," he said. "Why should it even matter what she says it means? Can't everyone interpret the words whatever way makes sense to them?"

The first time I'd ever laid eyes on Charlie, all I'd seen was a big slow, disheveled kid with a monotone way of talking and an occasional psycho look in his eyes—a kid at the absolute bottom of the high school food chain. But now I recognized that he was actually a thoughtful, sensitive guy. He seemed to take everything seriously, and I liked that about him. I could understand why he and Olivia might see eye to eye.

I was also beginning to feel my own unlikely connection to our strange, taciturn singer. That very morning in Biology while everybody was supposed to be silently reading our textbooks, I, uninterested in chloroplasts or ribosomes, had instead been secretly reading an X-Men comic

I'd hidden inside the textbook pages. But when I looked up I noticed Olivia on the opposite side of the room staring directly at me. Caught, I'd felt my face heat up. But that's when Olivia quietly lowered her own textbook just enough to show what was inside. A paperback novel. A moment later, we were both having a difficult time holding back laughter.

In any case, after that fight during our first practice, I was determined not to let anything else threaten to split my fragile new band apart again.

"All right," I said, hoping to end the tension with a smile. "It's personal. As long as Olivia and Wen keep coming up with songs that good, I guess I don't have to know what they mean."

That's when somebody pounded hard against the door. It was three loud thumps so sudden and forceful that they made me jump. And immediately afterward I thought I could hear footsteps sprinting away down the hallway.

"What the heck was that?" Wen looked as startled as I felt.

By the time we got to the door and peered down the hallway, there was nobody there except a couple kids from the French Club. Just like us, they were checking to see what the commotion had been.

Charlie scratched his cheek. "That was weird. I wonder what that was all about."

Then Olivia said, "Look!" She was pointing up at the ceiling behind us.

Everyone turned. Hanging from a tile above the entranceway to the loading dock was what looked like one of those baby mobiles, those funny little circular arrangements of colored objects on strings that you hang above a newborn's crib—except this one was made of five empty Mel's cups.

"What is it?"

I wasn't sure, but I had a sinking feeling that it wasn't fan mail. When I looked closely, I noticed that underneath a layer of grime, each cup had a frowning face drawn on it in black marker. One of the faces had rectangular glasses. "I'm . . . pretty sure that's supposed to be *us*."

"Whoa," Charlie whispered. "Bizarre . . ."

Everyone crowded closer. At the top of the mobile was a folded piece of paper. I reached up and picked it off the string.

"Come on, Stella," said Wen impatiently. "What does it say?"

As I unfolded it, I felt a wave of dread. I didn't want any more problems. When I'd started at this school, all I'd wanted was to fit in. But it sure wasn't easy. I quickly read the note and then showed it to the others.

"Freaks Back Off the Bash."

CHARLIE:
Stella Shoots Her Mouth Off

Has music ever transported you to another place? Do you know that feeling when the bad stuff in your day fades and your body can't help moving to the sound? Do you? Maybe it's just me. Sometimes when I'm playing my timbales and everything feels just right I can close my eyes and the energy practically lifts me into the air like that Tornado in "The Wizard of Oz" it surrounds me and carries me up and away.

Anyway at our practices that's how I felt.

Mrs. Reznik didn't say much the first couple of afternoons but after that she wasn't shy about pointing out our screwups. I caught her tapping her foot in time to the rhythm though so I could tell we were at least OK. Even that strange mobile incident didn't bother me for long. Because at last the 5 of us were *jelling*. Musically anyway.

But soon I couldn't help recognizing that there was an unexpected downside. It's kind of funny but the 1 thing I wanted before any of this happened was to get close to Mo. Every day between Metal Shop and Spanish I used to watch her passing me in the hallway and I'd wrack my brain trying to come up with some pathetic excuse to speak with her. Now here we were walking together down the corridor. Like buddies.

The problem was that a lot of the time what she wanted to talk about was Scott Pickett.

"Want to know something hilarious Scott said?"

"Did you hear what happened to Scott at the game against Bristol yesterday?"

"If a boy doesn't call his girlfriend for a couple days should she be worried what do you think? You're a guy, right?"

Right.

You're pitiful Aaron would whisper. *If you don't either run for your life or set her straight about that jerk then you are a spineless loser of the saddest kind.*

By now, Mr. Levesque, you're probably thinking that Aaron was right. And maybe he was. But how could I tell Mo that I hated Scott's guts? That I thought he might even be involved in leaving that spooky mobile for us? For 1 thing she might suddenly realize that I liked her and then decide that was the only reason I was cutting him down. For another she seemed so in the clouds about him that probably she wouldn't listen to me anyway.

In the end I flipped another coin: heads I'd tell her the truth, tails I wouldn't. It came up tails.

That's why Thursday as Mo and I made our way along the main corridor I was keeping quiet. That was right before Stella got herself into trouble again. Mo was filling me in on all the drama behind how Scott repaired the ripped Upholstery in the old Honda his dad was letting him use I kept nodding and trying to be as supportive as I could while my eyes secretly scanned the crowd for Lyle.

As usual Aaron was exasperated with me. *Pathetic!*

We came to that short hallway near the Cafeteria and I happened to notice Olivia at the snack dispensers. I spotted Olivia between classes a lot. I'd see her walking alone in the hallways in that hunched-over way she had. I tried to say hi a couple times but I don't think she heard me. And now here she was again only this time she wasn't alone. Standing behind her at the machines were Ray Beech with Patty Norris and Patty Keane—2 stuck-up girls from Dean Eagler's crowd. I stopped walking.

"What's going on?" Mo asked.

I nodded in the direction of the machines.

Olivia slid her dollar bill into the slot. Patty Norris reached in front of Olivia and pressed the big soda button before Olivia had a chance to choose anything for herself. When the can dropped, Patty grabbed it.

"Thanks" she said. "My favorite."

They were maybe 15 yards away but still close enough that I could hear Patty Keane snicker.

Then Ray piped up. "Olivia Whitehead that's your name, right?" Except the way he said it didn't sound like a question.

Patty Norris poked the cartoon decal on Olivia's backpack. "God I just *adore* your bag. Where did you get it? It's so retro glam. That's what you're going for isn't it?"

I could practically see Olivia disappear into herself. Like a turtle retreating into her shell. Her face went blank and she stared at the floor.

Patty Keane reached out and stroked the back of Olivia's head. "And girl, how *do* you get these lovely locks to hang this way? I think the dead fish look is so *in,* don't you? What do you use? Crisco?"

Patty Norris pulled the tab from the soda. With her long red hair and perfect skin and spooky green eyes Patty was practically Opequonsett High School royalty. "What's the matter Olivia don't you want to share your secrets with us?"

Olivia didn't move.

Ray came in closer. "Word has it you're in that new freshman band. You're the singer, right? Well well. Why don't you belt 1 out for us right now?"

"Oh yes *please* do" Patty Keane said.

All this happened so fast that until then I wasn't sure what to do but now I started in their direction pushing my way through a crush of kids heading to class.

Mo was already a couple steps ahead of me. "What's going on here Ray?"

He didn't seem especially bothered to see us coming. "Oh look who it is. Our very own bass-playing Benedict Arnold."

Mo walked right up to them. "What's that supposed to mean?"

"Olivia" I said. "You OK?"

Patty Norris frowned like we were the ones causing the problem. "Relax we were only talking about shampoo it's not our fault that your girlfriend here doesn't want to hang out with us."

"Maybe she thinks we're not good enough for her." Ray pointed to the can in Patty Norris's hand. "Swig?"

"Certainly." Patty handed it over.

Olivia's face was so flushed that the acne across her forehead stood out like a neon relief map.

That's when I noticed Stella watching us from the end of the corridor, her book bag slung across her shoulder and a paper lemonade cup in her hand. She'd obviously seen what was going on. But there was no time to think about Stella just then with Ray looking like he might lash out at Olivia or Mo at any second. So before I thought better of it I blurted out the 1st thing that popped into my head.

"You'd better leave her alone."

Ray's lip curled. "What was that Buffalo Boy? A threat? And if we don't who's going to make us?" He put the can to his mouth. Patty snickered again.

OK I'm no runt or anything but Ray was probably the biggest kid at school. So what could I do? But all of a sudden I was tired of watching these guys act like they were better than everyone else. I couldn't see Olivia's face anymore but I could hear her breathing in short rapid breaths that pulsed like a heartbeat.

"Me" I said trying to sound confident. "I guess I'll have to be the one to make you."

With his free hand Ray grabbed my collar and yanked me toward him he laughed right in my face. A few droplets of soda sprayed onto my nose. Then he let go of me and shoved me back against the wall. "Sorry man" he said wiping his mouth and still chuckling. "I just couldn't help it you're so funny."

"What's the matter with you Ray!" Mo shouted. "You're acting like a complete creep! Were you the one who left that mobile thing for us downstairs? Wait until Scott finds out about this!"

"Look" I said "let's try and be reasonable. We can talk this through."

"Don't bother" said a calm voice right behind me. "This is just oppression plain and simple. You can't reason with people like these." Stella. She'd walked up when I hadn't noticed. When I turned she was setting her book bag on the floor. She took a long sip of her drink and eyed Ray and the Patties coolly.

Ray sneered. "Well if it isn't the ringleader of the freaks. How are you Stella?"

But Stella didn't say another word. She pushed past Mo and me and then planted herself directly between Ray and Olivia. She flashed Ray a grin.

Mo and I exchanged glances.

And that's when it happened. While everyone watched, Stella stood on her toes and blew a giant mouthful of lemonade slush all over Ray's face. My heart nearly stopped. Patty and Patty's jaws dropped. Ray put his arm up to block the spray but it was too late. Yellow goo dripped from his nose and ears and his skin was shiny with it. He cursed and looked ready to take a swing at Stella.

But I'm sure you remember what happened next, Mr. Levesque, because that's when you rushed over from the main corridor. I remember how your face was all red. "What exactly is going on here?"

"Nothing" Ray said, wiping his face on his sleeve. "We were just trying to purchase a soda when these freshmen came over and started threatening us. The next thing we knew, Lemonade Mouth over there let loose!"

112

Patty looked ready to explode. "She ought to be locked up!"

I watched you take in the scene: Ray looking every bit the Victim with his wet face and hair and a dark stain forming on the top of his shirt, and Stella still holding the lemonade with a satisfied grin. Suddenly I had new respect for this strange, fearless girl.

That's when the bell rang.

Everything ended quickly after that. Sure Stella ended up getting another detention but even at the time she said it was no big price to pay. I hear she didn't even put up a fight about it. Later, of course, everybody knew it'd been worth it.

After all, word got around about what happened.

And besides, our band finally had a name.

CHAPTER 4

*Lemonade Mouth wasn't that great. Everybody
talks about them like they were superheroes
or something. Well they weren't, all right?
They sucked.*
—Dean Eagler

MOHINI:
Suspicious Minds

It's Thursday night and I'm in my room on the phone
complaining to Charlie about the number of irregular Latin
verbs I have to learn. It's funny how before Lemonade
Mouth happened, Charlie was just another Metal Shop kid.
With his uncombed hair and his perpetually half-tucked
shirt, he was only some slob in my grade, probably not too
bright either. But lately we've had sort of an unofficial rou-
tine where we grab a Mel's together on our way to Spanish.
We also talk at lunch, at practice and sometimes even during study hall. Whatever's on my mind, Charlie always
seems to understand. He has a way of calming me down,
distracting me so I don't completely stress out.

Now he's telling me all about this theory he has about
universal balance. It's long and complicated, but what it

more or less boils down to is that, according to Charlie, everything that ever happens is bound to set off some equal and opposite cosmic reaction somewhere.

"I guess it makes sense," I say when he's done. "It's kind of like physics."

"Yeah, maybe. But it sure explains a lot, doesn't it? Like why, even as things change, some ultimate realities stay the same, you know? Maybe you find money lying on the ground, but then later somebody steals your bike. Maybe your TV breaks, but then you read a terrific book. Somebody cries and then they feel better. You see? Two sides to everything. Equilibrium."

I ponder this for a moment. "In a way, it's kind of like how the Hindu gods have two forces, a male and a female. Like, there's Shiva, the god of destruction, and he's paired with Parvati, the goddess of love? Two opposites forming a whole?"

"That's it!" he says. "You get it!"

After that he asks me about India and Hinduism, so I tell him how tomorrow is the first day of Durga Pooja, and that my mom is downstairs cooking like a maniac, and that right now the house reeks of fish. He wants to know all about my family, which is kind of nice. Scott never expresses an interest.

After I hang up, my dad knocks on the door and asks me what I've been doing. "I was on the phone," I tell him.

"Why weren't you studying? Don't you have your Latin exam tomorrow?" He's standing in the doorway in his kurta and flip-flops.

"Baba," I protest. "Cut me some slack. I took a break."

His eyebrows wrinkle with concern. "Who were you talking to?"

"Just Charlie."

For the tiniest of moments, a look of panic flickers across my dad's eyes. I've seen that look before, but not often. Like a tightrope walker momentarily losing his balance. I'm not sure why he would have a problem with Charlie. My dad met him yesterday afternoon and it went fine. There was no practice because I had to help out at the store. I hadn't expected to see anybody, but he and Olivia surprised me with a visit.

"What are you guys doing here?" I said from behind the register.

Charlie grinned. "Just dropping by to say hello. Plus, we've never been in your store before so we wanted to see what it was like."

I was surprised how glad I was to see them. Olivia went straight for my dad's ornate, fading poster of the elephant-headed Hindu god of prosperity. "This is Ganesh, right?" she asked me.

"That's right."

"He's . . . beautiful," she said in her quiet, earnest voice.

I wasn't sure what to say to that. But I was glad she liked the picture. "It's always been one of my favorite parts of the store. When I was little I used to stare at it for hours."

She stood there for at least a full minute taking in Ganesh's golden skin and the layers of complex jewelry he wore on his head and body. Finally she said, "This poster is absolutely the most breathtaking thing I've seen all day."

Olivia can be kind of spooky sometimes, but I like her.

My dad was in the back room but then he poked his head around the doorway. "Monu, are these friends of yours? Why don't you introduce me?"

So I made the introductions and everybody was super

polite. Charlie even bought some chai tea. At the time, my dad seemed pleased to meet them but now, with him standing in my bedroom doorway, I'm beginning to wonder. His eyebrows press even closer together and he eyes me like a crime suspect.

"Don't get any ideas with that boy."

This takes a moment to sink in. Suddenly I realize what my dad is saying, that he actually thinks there might be something going on between Charlie and me. *Charlie* and me! It's almost funny. Here I am drowning in an ocean of guilt about going out with *Scott,* and yet my dad is concerned about Charlie, of all people.

"Baba . . . ," I say, my face burning. "We're just friends."

The next day Naomi meets me at the clinic and we walk home together. I tell her what my dad said. As usual, her reaction surprises me. "Well," she says thoughtfully, "do you like Charlie?"

I'm so caught off guard by her question that at first I don't understand what she means. "Sure I like him," I say. "He's nice."

"Okay," she says, "but would you go out with him? If it weren't for Scott, I mean."

I roll my eyes at the suggestive gleam in Naomi's eyes. "Don't be ridiculous. Me and Charlie? It's not like that with us."

She shrugs. "I'm only asking. After all, you talk about him almost as much as you talk about Scott."

"No, I don't. You're exaggerating."

"I'm not."

But she is. Charlie and I like each other, but not that way. Plus, we're so different. "It wouldn't work out and we both know it. He's just great to talk with and get a guy's perspective. We're just friends."

She still looks skeptical. "So you're saying there's no chemistry at all?"

I shake my head.

"Whatever you say." She adjusts her backpack on her shoulder. "But I've seen you two together. There's chemistry there somewhere."

I really don't think so, but she seems so sure. Is it possible I can be attracted to someone and not even know it?

Still, I roll my eyes again. "If I want chemistry I have Scott."

But saying that brings on a fresh pang of unhappiness. The thing is, over the past few days I haven't been telling Naomi or Charlie the whole truth about Scott. I'm not sure why. Maybe a part of me thinks if I tell anybody about my unhappy suspicions it might make them come true. I would never say it out loud, but sometimes I wonder if Scott only asked me out because he saw me as exotic, his little Indian princess. And now the novelty has worn off. It isn't that Scott and I aren't talking anymore, but it definitely doesn't feel the same lately. We pass each other in the hallways and say hi, but hardly more than that. He's always in a rush to get somewhere else. I've been trying not to panic but to be honest I'm on an emotional rollercoaster. Like the last time I saw him at lunch—which happened even before the snack dispenser incident. Holding my tray, I searched the cafeteria crowd for him. Scott and I share the same lunch period only every other day because of the rotating schedule, so I always look forward to eating with him. Today he was sitting alone at his usual table, smiling and calling out to a passing buddy. But the moment I joined him he got all gloomy and quiet.

"What's the matter?" I said, setting my tray down. "Aren't you glad to see me?"

After that brief sullen moment he shrugged and managed a smile. "Sure I'm happy," he said, putting his hand briefly on mine. "Just a little distracted. State finals coming up and everything. It's not you."

"You sure?"

But that's when Dean and Ray joined us, crashing their trays onto the table. And then the conversation abruptly changed. After that, I tried to read on Scott's face whether he was telling the truth. A part of me felt sure that something was different, but another part of me didn't really want to know.

By now, Naomi and I have been walking silently for about half a block. I'm listening to the crunch, crunch, crunch of the leaves beneath our sneakers. Eventually I look over to try and read her expression. I feel the need to hear myself say it aloud again. "If I want chemistry," I say once more, this time trying to sound extra confident, "I have Scott."

Naomi shrugs again. "Whatever you say."

WEN:
The Freak Table

Even after a couple of weeks, kids wouldn't let the Social Studies incident drop. I tried to laugh it off, but being called Woody was getting old. The good news was that the Halloween Bash was only two weeks away. Plus, I now had my own little group of friends to hang out with. Whenever our schedules allowed, the five of us would sit together for lunch at a round table at the back of the cafeteria. We ignored the whispers from some of the kids who were already calling it the Freak Table. It was a lot easier for me to ignore everybody else when we were together.

Not that sitting at the Freak Table was always comfortable.

"Do you ever stop to think about what you're eating?" Stella demanded of all of us one day. "One minute a cow is grazing peacefully in the middle of a field, and then a few days later it's sliced up and served on your plate." She gave a meaningful glance at Olivia, who was working on a roast beef sandwich. "I have news for you people: meat is murder."

Olivia hardly seemed to notice her.

Stella looked around the circle for support. That was the thing about Stella, she acted like she didn't care what anybody thought, but she really did. I sometimes saw in her eyes that deep down she desperately wanted us to like her. And even though she could be tactless and stubborn, this vulnerability actually *did* make me like her.

Oblivious, Charlie shrugged. "I like Sloppy Joes." He bit off a hunk of his dripping sandwich, some of the juice dribbling down his chin. Stella looked pained.

Mo said, "My family doesn't eat beef or pork."

"But you eat fish," Stella said pointing to Mo's lunch, which looked like some kind of white fish and rice thing she was eating out of a plastic container.

That's when I said, "It's not so easy to make a big change like that, Stella. This cafeteria doesn't offer vegetarian meals."

"So? Can't you bring your own meat-free lunch?"

"I guess," I said. "But I'd have to convince my dad.

Whenever I bring a lunch from home, he's always the one to make it."

Stella blinked at me. "You're fourteen years old, Wen. When are you going to start making your own lunch?"

Everyone looked at me and I felt the blood rush into my face. "So my dad makes my lunch. What's the big deal?"

Mo came to my rescue. "My mom made mine," she said.

Stella rolled her eyes. "Well, that's no surprise. After all, you're a princess." I could tell by her expression that she meant it to be funny, but Mo didn't take it that way.

"I resent that!" she said. "And I doubt Wen and I are the only ones. I bet a lot of kids let their parents make their lunches. How about you, Charlie? When you bring a lunch, who makes it?"

"My mom," he said around another mouthful of meat.

Stella looked ready to reply, maybe even to apologize, but Mo wasn't done. She seemed determined to prove her point. She turned to Olivia, who was pulling a piece of yellow cake from her brown paper bag. "Who made yours? Your parents?"

Olivia didn't even look up. "No, my grandmother. I don't live with my parents."

Mo turned back to Stella, satisfied. I was pretty sure Stella was about to say something else, but that's when Mo's friend Naomi Fishmeier, who was also sitting with us, butted in.

"You don't?" she asked Olivia. "So where *are* your parents?" That was Naomi, ever the investigative journalist.

There was an uncomfortable silence, but I guess everyone was just as interested to hear more about Olivia because everybody waited. Olivia and I had written songs together but she never seemed to want to talk about herself. I was as curious as everybody else to hear what she had to say.

Olivia looked up. Her eyes moved from face to face around the table. Finally she said, "My mother left when I was little. I don't remember her. My dad's in prison."

Charlie and I glanced at each other. Nobody spoke for a few beats. In the end it was Stella who had the nerve to ask the obvious question.

"Umm . . . so what's your dad in prison for?"

She answered without flinching. "Armed robbery. Manslaughter too. He held up a 7-Eleven. The owner pulled a gun and my dad shot him. He died."

Then she went back to her sandwich.

Everybody was silent after that.

STELLA:
Picket Signs and Toxic Waste

Even with all the support Mrs. Reznik gave me and my little band of misfits, I was always careful not to cross her. She was still a formidable old lady with a quick temper and a heart-stopping glare. Even Mr. Brenigan seemed scared of her.

Even so, my new friends and I felt a growing bond with the bewigged old musician. Over lunch we would talk about her.

"It's complete crap that she's stuck down in that basement," I once observed over a lentil and fried-tofu sandwich. "Can you imagine spending your whole day in that depressing room? It sure seems like somebody doesn't like her."

Mo nodded. "Being down there is like practicing in a cave."

Olivia, who'd been stuffing her face on a turkey leg,

122

now said, "I hear the school board wanted to cut the whole music program this year to save money. They only kept the Marching Band because of the football games."

"That's what I heard too," Wen said.

Charlie grunted. "Yeah? So why is Mrs. Reznik still here then?"

Nobody seemed to know the answer, not even Mo.

"She must have put somebody in a wrestling hold," Wen said. It was a joke, of course, but for all anybody knew it might not have been too far from the truth. Mrs. Reznik was definitely a fighter.

In any case, the five of us felt a certain loyalty to her. Even if nobody ever said it aloud, I could tell that we all felt that the talent show was, among other things, a chance to show the administration that somebody at this school still cared about music.

And that loyalty seemed to be a two-way street. Mrs. Reznik was so determined to help us that on the last week of October with only six days to go until the Halloween Bash, she came in on a Saturday afternoon so we could practice in the music room. Unfortunately, that happened to be the same afternoon that my dear mother suddenly announced that I needed to stay home. Actually, to be honest it may not have been such a sudden announcement. It's *possible* that she mentioned a couple weeks earlier that there was a reception for some venture capital people who were paying for the development of the Frankenstein plants, but if she did, I'd forgotten all about it. In any case, I was still furious. With the Halloween Bash so close, how could anybody expect me to skip practice just to babysit the step-monkeys?

"Why can't Clea come home and do it?" I asked, suddenly frantic.

"You know why not. For once in your life, Stella, stop being so selfish! Why can't you take a little responsibility around here without making a fuss?" My mom flashed me the evil eye, cutting off all further discussion on the subject. Then she turned away and leaned back into the mirror to carefully apply some last-minute lipstick. "When you're try-ing to save the planet," she said, using her Voice of Wisdom, "you need to make the occasional sacrifice."

This, of course, was completely unfair. But I knew there was no point in arguing. My mom had always been some-thing of an environmental crusader. Back when she was still a lowly researcher at a nonprofit university lab, she had on more than one occasion dragged me out of school just so I could help carry picket signs in front of toxic waste sites. In my heart of hearts, I admired that about her—how she doggedly pursued her ideals no matter the odds against her.

Still, that didn't make it okay for her to preach to me or to stick me with the step-monkeys on a Saturday.

"Okay," I said, "but why does that sacrifice have to be me?"

"Oh, don't be so dramatic," she sighed. "I'm in a hurry and I'm getting tired of banging heads with you."

I felt myself deflate. After all, it didn't seem so long ago that my mother and I hardly ever fought. Before the move, we were practically best friends. Now I felt like we didn't even know each other. Didn't she see how important this new band was to me? Didn't she care?

I was about to open my mouth again when she said, "I don't want to talk about this anymore. I'm going and you're babysitting and it's not up for discussion."

And that was that. I could only sit at the kitchen table, furious. As my mother tarted herself up for her big after-noon, it seemed incredibly unfair that the whole reason I had to stay at home with the step-monkeys was just so she could rub elbows with other geniuses and venture capitalist fat cats. It certainly wasn't a good enough reason for me to have to blow off practice.

No way.

Luckily, I came up with a backup plan. As soon as my mother's Volvo left the house, I ran up to my stepbrothers' bedroom. They'd pulled apart the linen closet and had hung sheets and blankets over chairs to make a giant fort. I pulled up a quilt wall and stuck my head inside.

"Put on your jackets and come with me," I said. "We're going for a bike ride to the high school."

They looked at me and then each other. A moment later the boys were pedaling with me down the street, shouting and cheering like cowboys on a wild cattle run.

The step-monkeys were spazoids, but sometimes they were all right.

Problem solved.

While we practiced, the boys spent the afternoon running up and down the hallway, playing spies and banging on instruments Mrs. Reznik let them use.

Later, of course, my mother wasn't exactly a happy camper. Practice ended up going on later than we'd planned, so when I got back to my house my mom was already home. "I don't know what's come over you recently, Stella—you're out of control!" she said. "Who gave you permission to take the boys to run around practically unsupervised in the high school basement? You didn't leave a note either, and I was worried! Can't you ever take a moment to consider how your actions might affect anybody but you, you, *you*?"

Of course, even before I'd left the house I'd known my

mom wasn't going to be thrilled when she heard I'd brought Tim and Andy to practice, but at the time I hadn't mentioned my plan because I couldn't risk my mother saying no. I may not have been the brightest bulb in my family, but you don't have to be a genius to know that it's easier to get forgiveness than permission.

MOHINI:
Durga Pooja

My family arrives at the Sri Lakshmi Temple and we all pile out of our rusty old Subaru, my parents, my grandmother, my little sister Madhu and me. Madhu, who is nine, runs around in a tizzy of excitement.

"Hurry up!" she pleads. "Let's go, let's go!"

The last day of the Durga Pooja celebration is the biggest. It's kind of like a Hindu Christmas, where everybody gets together to celebrate and have fun. But I'm having a hard time getting into the spirit. My head's been throbbing off and on for days. Scott and I talked last night and things seem better, I guess, but this morning I still find myself worrying. His friends avoid me, and I get the feeling its not just lingering resentment about the Bash—it's that my new friends aren't cool enough. Sometimes I want to scream at Scott. Why doesn't he tell his buddies to lighten up? But of course I never say a word. I'm too afraid of rocking the boat in case he decides to dump me.

Part of me is furious at myself for feeling that way, or for even liking Scott at all. But the truth is, I can't help it.

I'm Jell-O around him.

Before we enter the temple we all leave our shoes

outside the door. Inside, the air smells of incense and there are crowds of people chatting and milling around, women in bright saris and children running and laughing. A few older men sit cross-legged on the floor, talking. We know lots of people here.

The Sinhas, a Bengali family we haven't seen in a while, wave at us. Smiling broadly, my mom and dad lead us in their direction. While my parents and Mr. and Mrs. Sinha catch up, Madhu runs off to join a bunch of other little kids. Selina Sinha rushes over and gives me a warm smile.

"How's high school, Monu?"

Selina is my age and one of the prettiest girls I've ever seen, with perfect skin and eyelashes as long as diving boards. She takes my hand and leads me away so we can talk privately. She just started at a new school too, and she's excited to compare notes. Plus, she whispers conspiratorially in my ear, she thinks she has a crush on Rajesh Harbhajan, a gangly boy who at this very moment is watching us from across the room. She wants to know what I think about him.

"I don't know," I say. "He's cute. Does he like you?"

She nods seriously. "He's head over heels."

"He is? How do you know?"

"Oh, he told me," she says matter-of-factly. "We went out to a movie together last week."

I stop walking. I study her face to see if she's serious. "You did? What if your mom and dad find out? Won't they freak?"

She tilts her head comically as if considering whether or not I'm crazy. "They know, Monu. My dad *drove* us." She gives me a wicked grin. "That's the advantage of being the last of five daughters brought up in this country. By now my parents have given up trying to turn any of us into perfect little Bengali women. They're just happy that I come with them to temple."

I suddenly wish I had older sisters.

Before long our two families are walking around the temple together. Unlike a church, which only has one altar, a Hindu temple has several. Ours has eight, each for a different god, each lit with oil lamps and adorned with fruits and flowers. Durga Pooja is a harvest festival, sort of a party celebrating Mother Nature. The service is informal. Uday Sharma, a skinny, gray-haired old man who loves to play checkers with my dad, is our pundit, our spiritual leader. He wears white and has long hair tied in a bun at the back. We follow him from altar to altar, folding our hands as we watch him perform the prayers, which are in Sanskrit. Behind me I occasionally hear my dad or my grandmother or Selina's mother say "Jai Durga Maa," which means Hail Mother Durga. As I listen, I'm feeling a little less anxious. Something about the rituals and the incense and the sound of the prayers is calming.

Afterwards we head downstairs for the buffet. While everybody chats and eats, various people stand at the front of the room to perform. Madhu and some of her friends do a dance, and an old lady I don't know sings some verses in Sanskrit. I don't understand a single word, but it's lovely to hear. Eventually my dad prods me.

"Go on, it's your turn."

So I get up and walk to the front of the room where my bass is already waiting. The chatting quiets a little as I take my bow in hand. I smile. I'm not nervous at all. The Dragonetti piece isn't especially difficult. I attack the opening three half notes and then the descending scale, and after that I can't help looking up and noticing the pride on my parents' faces.

A while later I'm back in my seat and, for a joke, my dad leaps up onto the stage and starts pounding on a dholak, a kind of drum, which prompts a bunch of little kids to jump up and dance. The thing is, my father has about as much rhythm as a drunken octopus and everybody knows it. But he's having fun.

"Sit down and stop playing the fool!" my mom calls over to him. But she's smiling as much as everybody else.

Everyone laughs, including Selina and me.

And now a sudden realization hits me: My headache is gone. All the stress weighing on me earlier seems to have evaporated. How long has it been since Scott or his friends even crossed my mind? Or my Latin exam—which I didn't do as well on as I'd hoped—how long since I fretted about that? Or even about Lemonade Mouth and how we still sound shaky, especially on the newest songs, even though the Bash is only a few days away? Instead I'm sitting at this long rowdy table clapping and cheering my dad on. And suddenly I feel a surge of gratitude.

Because I love my family. And because, for the first time in ages, I'm laughing like I don't have a care in the world.

OLIVIA:
A Queasy Feeling About Something Gigantic, Unambiguous and Personal

Dear Ted,

Nancy's the same. This morning she picked at some tuna and even ate part of an egg, but the vet still thinks it's only a matter of time. Got your card. I set it by her bowl. I'm glad you agree with Brenda and me about this. After all, she's not in any pain and seems happy so we didn't have the heart to have her put down just yet. (What a strange, cold phrase. "Put" seems so neutral, so everyday—like setting a cup on a table. And exactly what do we mean by "down"? The direction suggests something creepy. What a trivial, vague and detached way to describe something so gigantic, unambiguous and personal.) In any case, we're doing everything we can to make sure her final days are filled with the things she loves. We've been putting on her favorite videos, carrying her around in a basket and taking her on walks. Brenda's even letting her sleep on her pillow.

In the meantime, we're trying not to think too far into the future.

> You're always in my heart,
> Olivia

P.S.
On top of everything else, this Friday is the big night. In four days I'm supposed to sing in front of a huge crowd at the Halloween Bash. To hear Stella talk, she's already convinced we're going to blow everybody away, and she goes on about the Talent Show like we've already won it. Now

she's even suggesting that we sign up for Catch A RI-Zing Star, the battle of the bands WRIZ holds every winter. But she's way ahead of me. I'm still sweating about the Bash this weekend.

With all this anxiety, Nancy, the band, plus the pressure of constantly being around Wen while trying not to let him see that I like him, I feel like I'm about to lose my lunch practically all the time.

What was I thinking two and a half weeks ago? Joining this band was a horrible mistake. ☹

CHARLIE:
An Unexpected Goodbye

1 afternoon an odd thing happened in the basement it was Tuesday and we were practicing in the Music Room. All of us were worried because there were only 3 days left before the Bash and we still didn't have enough music and we were still making mistakes on the songs we had. Mrs. Reznik wasn't around. Maybe she went upstairs to the Office or outside to have a cigarette or something. I don't remember. Anyway we stopped for a break and Olivia went to get a lemonade and when she came back she just stood in the doorway looking red-faced and bothered.

"What's the matter?" I asked her.

"They're taking the Mel's machine away."

At 1st I wasn't sure what she meant. "What? Who?"

"2 guys in green uniforms" she said. "Some of the A.V. kids are there watching."

Why would anybody take away the lemonade machine? It

131

wasn't broken or anything. Wen and Stella were fiddling with their instruments and Mo was sitting on the floor squeezing in some homework during the break. But now everybody looked up. I had a sudden uncomfortable glimmer. Something didn't feel right about this. All at once the 4 of us set out into the corridor with Olivia to see for ourselves and sure enough when we got to the top of the stairs 2 muscle-guys in matching green outfits had the Mel's machine strapped to a trolley. They were wheeling it down the hallway toward the freight elevator. Lyle was there along with 2 other A.V. Club kids, Steve Gelnitz and Dawn Yunker. The 3 of them looked like they couldn't believe what was happening either.

"What's going on?" I asked Lyle.

"Don't know. They're taking away the lemonade machine."

"Yeah I can see that. But why?"

Lyle shrugged. "Don't know."

That's when David Bickenracker and Vic Toules, a couple of juniors from the basketball team, happened to walk by. When he saw us David snickered and I heard him whisper to Vic. "Freaks." I don't know if anybody else heard him but I did. I pretended I didn't.

By then the freight elevator doors were already open and the 2 men were on either side of the machine getting ready to move it inside. After a moment's hesitation Stella stepped in their direction and the rest of us followed behind.

"Hey!" she called out. "What are you doing?"

"What does it look like we're doing we're moving this out of here" the bigger of the 2 guys said. He had a barrel chest and a short black beard and kind of looked like that guy Bluto from *Popeye.*

"Yes but why?"

132

"No idea. Our job is just to bring it back to the warehouse."

"Is it . . . coming back again?" asked Lyle. "Or is this one getting replaced or something?"

The guy shrugged. "No idea. But there's no replacement in our truck." With a nod to the other guy the 2 of them pressed their shoulders against the metal and guided the big machine onto the elevator. A moment later the doors closed and we were left gawking at each other.

OK I know it was only a drink machine and this should of been no big deal. But for some reason it felt like a really crappy thing had just happened. I felt really bad. Betrayed almost. Only I didn't understand why. But when I noticed all the other glum faces I suspected I wasn't the only one.

"I don't get it" Wen said still staring at the elevator doors. "I liked having that machine around."

Olivia, Mo and the A.V. kids nodded but didn't say anything. Stella looked kind of pissed off. "Why didn't anybody let us know this was going to happen? Why didn't anybody ask us?"

There was a pause where everybody just kind of stared at her. "What do you mean?" Mo said finally. "Why would anyone ask *us?*"

Stella didn't answer because of course Mo was right. Who were we that anybody would need our approval? OK sure we spent loads of time in the basement and maybe we drank a lot of lemonade but that didn't make it realistic that anybody would of let us know before taking it away. I thought of the basement clubs and the piles of empty cups I always saw in the trashcans. I knew that Mrs. Reznik wasn't going to be thrilled about this either.

"It's not the end of the world it's only a stupid lemonade machine" I said just to say something.

Nobody answered. And even though I knew what I said was true I still couldn't help feeling like we'd been somehow wronged.

Without another word we all trudged downstairs. When we got there the guys were already moving the machine out of the elevator and into the hallway. Instead of going back to what we'd been doing, we followed a few paces behind as they rolled the big metal thing down the corridor and onto the Loading Dock and then we watched them load it into the back of a white truck. Even though I couldn't explain it, the heavy feeling in my chest was still there.

"It's funny" Mo said as the truck pulled away "but it's kind of weird to see it go."

Stella didn't say anything but her face was all red and her hands were shoved firmly into her pockets.

And then I remembered what Wen had said about the lemonade being like the official Underworld Membership Badge. At the time, he was joking but even so there was truth to it. The thing was, the lemonade machine had kind of been *ours*. Most other people got sodas from the dispensers by the Cafeteria. Even though I hadn't thought much about it before, I now realized that in the past 3 weeks that frozen slush had become for my friends and me sort of a connection, almost part of our group identity. And not only for my band either. For the A.V. Club too, and the French Club, the math team and the *Barking Clam*. And even for Mrs. Reznik. In a strange way, the lemonade really felt like a membership pass to an underground society that I hadn't truly realized I'd been part of.

I know that probably sounds kind of ridiculous but it was true. At least that's how it felt as I watched the truck pull around the street corner and out of sight.

STELLA:
The Craziest Explanation Ever

Burning with indignation, I decided the next morning to go straight to the Powers That Be to demand an explanation about the purloined lemonade machine. Why was it taken away? Who made the decision without even so much as a hint ahead of time to the people who used it? We had a right to know.

Charlie came with me. The front office was unusually crowded and chaotic. One of the busses had arrived late, so there was a line of kids waiting for passes. Ahead of us in line stood three Barbie dolls who kept glancing back at us and smirking at each other. Charlie didn't seem to even notice, but I did. As it happened, I was already feeling like twice-fried crap that morning because of a rash of pimples I'd discovered on my forehead that morning. What's more, with a sideways glance at Charlie I noticed that he was looking even more disheveled than usual. There was a troubling eggish stain near the pocket of his half-tucked shirt, and his chaotic hair jutted out at all kinds of improbable angles as if he'd combed it with a towel. As far as the Mattel triplets, even though I didn't know any of these perfect specimens of rosy-cheeked girlhood, their obvious disdain made me want to shrivel into a ball.

But I didn't. Instead I gave them the iciest glare I could muster until all three of them turned white and looked away.

Eventually, most of the crowd got sorted through and then it was our turn at the counter. Mrs. Flynn, the pretty secretary with the church lady hairdo, looked overwhelmed. "Can I help you?"

I leaned on the counter. "Yes. We want to find out what happened with the lemonade machine."

"Lemonade machine?"

"That's right. The big yellow and green Mel's Organic one that used to be at the top of the stairs near the A.V. room? Two guys hauled it away yesterday afternoon."

Mrs. Flynn frowned. "There was a lemonade machine over there? Hmmm. I never even knew that." She didn't seem to have anything else to say.

I felt a wave of frustration. "Um . . . yeah," I said with maybe a little more sarcasm in my voice than I meant. "Like I said, there *was* one. But now it's gone and we're trying to find out why. We deserve an explanation."

That's when Charlie, perhaps the more tactful of us, stepped in. "We were wondering why it had to be taken away and whether it's coming back. Is there a way to find that out? We're just curious." He grinned sheepishly and then added. "We, uh . . . we liked that machine."

Mrs. Flynn seemed to consider. She looked over her shoulder and spoke to the other secretary, Mrs. Silvestro, a big-haired middle-aged lady with permanent dark circles under her eyes, who was typing into a keyboard. "Faye, do you know anything about somebody taking away a lemonade machine?"

Mrs. Silvestro didn't look up from her screen. "Uh-huh," she said. "It was part of the deal for the scoreboard."

"Scoreboard?" Charlie asked, his forehead wrinkling. "What do you mean? What deal?"

"To finish the gym. A soda company agreed to donate the money and all we had to do was get rid of any competing machines."

"What?" I asked. "What does a soda company have to

do with anything? And how does frozen lemonade compete with soda, anyway? That's the craziest explanation I ever heard!"

At this, Mrs. Silvestro finally stopped typing and turned in our direction, glowering over her glasses like I was an idiot. "I don't like your tone, young lady," she snipped. "The money had to come from *somewhere*. Now, if you have any other questions I think you'd best bring them directly to Mrs. Ledlow or Mr. Brenigan, who aren't here at the moment. If you have a complaint, you can ask your parents to take it up with the town finance committee. Anything else?"

By then, my face was burning. "No," I said more quietly. "I think that's it." There was no point in arguing further. I wasn't going to get any more information from this woman.

And so we left the office in silence, feeling no better than when we'd entered. I wasn't sure why, but I felt more shaken now, even cheated. As we trudged down the corridor, my earlier indignation swelled. Charlie and I agreed—there was something wrong here, something that definitely didn't sit right.

And I, your Sista Stella, wasn't about to let this mystery pass without further investigation.

WEN:
A Volcanic Eruption

Thursday afternoon started off badly, then got worse.

I was already in a foul mood as I pedaled up the steep hill toward my house. That afternoon had been our last practice before the Bash, but it was a complete disaster. Mo hadn't shown up. No note, no explanation. Charlie tried to call her but she wasn't home. It was weird.

With no other choice, we decided to practice without her. But Stella and I kept forgetting the breaks and Olivia seemed to have a hard time remembering the words. In the end we'd cut the afternoon short. We didn't want Olivia to strain her voice, and nothing was working out anyway. It wasn't just Mo's absence. I think the pressure was getting to us. It felt like there was a lot riding on this performance.

"Don't worry," Stella had tried to assure us. "It's just last minute nerves. We've gone over these songs so many times that we could play them in our sleep."

But judging by today, I wasn't so sure anymore.

I kept pedaling. It was a chilly, late October evening and even though it was only dinnertime, it was almost dark. At least I'd thought to pull on my winter jacket. Still, my fingers were cold. To make matters worse, before I reached the top of the hill it started to rain. I could already feel the drops splashing up to the bottom of my jeans.

After I reached my house, I had to struggle to get into the little shed where George and I stored our bikes. Somebody had planted a table right smack in the doorway, blocking my space. It wasn't a regular table; it was ancient-looking and heavy with a flat concrete disk at the top and a metal foot-pedal. A pottery wheel, maybe? In any case, I didn't need to be a detective to guess whose it was.

I could practically feel the heat rise in me, like a volcano about to erupt. What was Sydney doing storing her stuff in our shed? What right did she have?

I managed to shove the contraption aside just enough to make a narrow space for my bike. Then I stormed toward the house, dripping, sure I'd find Sydney inside. The woman was practically a permanent fixture. Each of the last three nights I'd come home to find her parked at our kitchen table playing backgammon with George, a plate of munchies within arm's reach. Now I'd had enough.

But as I approached the front steps the screen door swung open and my dad stepped out, his keys in his hand. "There you are, kiddo. I thought you said you were practicing late tonight."

"We're not," I said through my teeth. "Where's Sydney?"

"In the shower." He chuckled. "We went on a nature walk and she slipped in some mud. She's fine, she's just cleaning herself up."

For a second, that threw me off. A nature walk? Since when did my father go on nature walks? Even worse, for a second I couldn't help picturing Sydney in our bathroom, slowly peeling the muddy clothes off her body.

I quickly forced that image out of my head.

Before I could say anything else my dad said, "We ordered Thai. I'm heading out to pick it up. Keep me company?"

At first I was going to say no, but then I reconsidered. I probably wasn't in the best state of mind to confront Sydney. In fact, I was liable to say or do something I might regret. A quick ride would give me a chance to cool down and collect my thoughts. She'd still be home when we got back. Besides, I couldn't exactly have it out with her while she was in the shower.

"Sure," I said. "Let's go."

For the first couple of minutes of our trip neither of us said much. Against the sound of country music and the windshield wipers sloshing back and forth I fumed, trying to decide the best way to point out to my dad how wrong Sydney was for him—and for our family. It wouldn't be easy. He didn't seem to see it at all. Still, somebody had to tell him.

In the end, he was the first to speak. "Big day for you tomorrow."

I grunted. I didn't want to talk about that.

He turned down the radio a little. "I know you already said you don't want any of us to come see you play, but if you change your mind I'd really like to stop by."

"It's not that kind of event, Dad."

It was cool of him to want to go, and a part of me would have been happy to have him there. But I didn't want to be the only kid who brought his dad to the Bash. As if he'd read my thoughts, he smiled and said, "We could hide in the back where nobody would see us."

I didn't answer. I had a hard time imagining my dad and George crouching under the bleachers. But he was kidding. At least I was pretty sure he was.

And then an uncomfortable question hit me. "When you say 'we,' who exactly do you mean? You're not talking about bringing Sydney, too, are you?"

"Of course. She wants to see your band. We've all been hearing about it for weeks."

I felt the lava rushing back into my chest. The idea that my dad would actually consider parading Sydney in front of my *school,* displaying his way-too-young-for-him girlfriend to everyone I knew—well, that was just infuriating. What was he thinking? Didn't he have any idea about boundaries?

"Okay, Wen. Out with it. What's the matter this time?"

So I turned to him with a hard stare. "Sydney," I said. "That's what the matter is. She's taking over our lives."

He glanced over at me but then looked back at the street, his face darkening. "Now don't start that again. You're being unreasonable."

But I wasn't about to stop. "Unreasonable? She's always hanging around, even when you're not there. She uses our house like her own personal art studio. And now she's even storing her furniture in our shed! Did you know that, Dad?"

"Yes," he said quietly, his eyes still glued to the road. "I knew that. I suggested it."

It took me a moment to soak that in. "You did? Oh. Well, then. I guess I shouldn't be surprised. And I guess that makes it all right for her to shove everybody else's stuff into a corner, doesn't it?" I glared at him.

He didn't answer. Even in the evening shadows I could see his white-knuckled fingers gripping the wheel. His jaw was stiff too—stiff in the way that meant he was about to blow up.

But I didn't care. I was on a roll.

"I gotta be honest with you, Dad. Sydney has you wrapped around her little finger and you don't even see it. I don't think you realize how oblivious you've been."

Finally, he spoke. "If anybody's being oblivious around here it's you."

But that was crazy. "Me? What are you talking about?"

That's when, out of the blue, he suddenly spun the wheel, pulled the truck over to the side of the road and slammed on the brakes. There was nobody else on the street so it didn't matter, but we came to a sudden halt and it made my heart practically stop in my chest.

"Dad, what are you doing!"

He stopped the engine. Without the sound of the radio and the wipers it seemed as if the rain tapping on the roof got louder. For a few moments my dad just sat there staring at the dashboard. I expected him to shout at me but he didn't. After a moment his grip on the wheel seemed to relax a little. When he spoke his voice was cool and level.

"What am I talking about? Well, I guess I'll have to spell it out for you. The reason I say it's *you* who's being oblivious is that you don't seem to see how wonderful Sydney is. Or what effect your attitude is having." He took a deep breath and then turned to me. "Do you have any idea that she's scared of you? Well, she is. She tiptoes around you. You've made it perfectly clear how you feel about her. In fact, you've been such a cold fish that I'm amazed she sticks around at all."

I crossed my arms on my chest. "That's ridiculous."

"No, it's not, Wen. It's the truth. Look, whatever issue you have with Sydney I really need you to figure it out, kiddo, because in case you haven't noticed, I'm crazy about her. And she's crazy about me. That's the way it is. And if for some reason that makes you unhappy right now then I'm sorry, I really am, especially since—" But then he stopped.

I waited, but he looked away.

"Since what, Dad?"

He leaned back on the seat and closed his eyes. Obviously there was something else he'd stopped himself from telling me. My mind reeled to think what it might be. One thing was sure, I wasn't about to let him hold back now that he'd started.

"Come on, tell me. What were you about to say?"

He took in a deep breath and then blew it out again. "Okay. I wanted to wait until you came around a little, but I guess now's the time." He turned to me again. Hard as my heart was already beating, it suddenly sped up a notch. "Wen, the thing is, Sydney and I have decided to get married."

I wasn't sure I'd heard him right. I think I just blinked at him for a couple of seconds. Finally I said, "You're kidding."

"No, I'm not kidding. I asked her and she said yes. I'm in love with her, Wen. And she's in love with me. I know she's a little younger than I am, but she's an amazing person. The kindest, most generous I've ever met. She makes me happy. Besides, I'm not exactly an old man and it's not like you boys are little children anymore." He studied my face. "Come on. Tell me you're glad for me."

I couldn't speak. In love? Married? The news was hitting me in waves. This couldn't be true, could it? If so, then Sydney would never move back to her apartment. She'd live with us for real. Whenever I came home, she'd be there. Whenever I got up in the morning, whenever I came back from school, whenever I did anything at all around my family, I'd see her relaxing on the sofa, or bending over to pick up a magazine, or maybe arching up to grab a cereal box.

I'd never be able to get rid of Sydney. Ever.

Without thinking, I reached for the door handle. The next thing I knew I was standing in the rain.

"What are you doing, Wen?"

"Going for a walk." I slammed the door, then turned and started in the opposite direction. Cold rain dripped

143

from my hair. My brain felt numb. I wasn't sure where I was headed, only that I had to get away.

From behind I heard my dad's door open. "Hey, don't do this—"

I spun back around.

"I'm not getting back in!" I roared. A fat raindrop hit my forehead and started trickling toward my ear. "I said I'm going for a walk! And don't even think about following me!"

My dad had one leg out of the truck, but I guess he saw on my face that I was serious because he stopped. I glared at him. After a moment, I spun away again, dug my hands deep in my jacket pockets, and kept walking.

CHARLIE:
A Wrecking Ball to the Stomach

Thursday afternoon after our final rehearsal before the show everyone went straight home. Practice had been a disaster. On top of barely getting through our newest songs and our panic about the Bash everybody was worried about Mo and where she was and why hadn't she at least called? I phoned her house a couple of times but got no answer I tried Naomi but then I remembered that Mo had told me she was interviewing some local Folk Musician at Bruno's that afternoon. Before Stella left to go home she wondered aloud if Mo was backing out but I was pretty sure that wasn't it. Mo wouldn't do that to us. Especially not with the Bash only a day away. Still, this was way weird for her.

After everyone left, my mom decided the 2 of us should go out for Chinese. My dad would be home late from work as usual and she didn't want to cook. But I could barely sit still at the Restaurant and I ended up rushing us through the meal.

It was raining when we drove back. The minute we got home I ran to check the messages. The light was on. I pressed the button.

"Hi Charlie it's me." Mo. She was almost whispering. There were a few seconds of sharp breathing. "I hope you get this tonight. Call me I need to talk."

Something *had* happened.

"Hello?" Mo had picked up on the 2nd ring. Her voice sounded normal enough at 1st but when she realized it was me she started crying. "I hate him! He's an absolute bastard!"

"Who?" I asked, really really worried now.

"Scott!"

That's when Aaron whispered *So tell me something we didn't already know.* It's also when Mo started bawling.

"It's OK it's OK" I said trying to sound calm. "Tell me what happened."

It took a little more coaxing but eventually I got the story: Immediately after school she'd headed to Scott's locker to say hi. When she got there she found him with Lynn Westerberg, his old Girlfriend. Scott and Lynn were facing each other too busy making out to notice anybody else. Mo said she'd stood frozen, unable at 1st to believe what she was seeing. But then Lynn finally saw her. Her eyes went wide and she whispered in Scott's ear and unfortunately Mo was close enough to hear.

"Oh God Scotty it's *her.*"

There was a long pause where Scott stood perfectly still. Eventually he turned around. "Hi Mo" he said with that stupid half grin he always has, his voice calm. "You remember Lynn. Right?"

"You should of seen his expression" Mo sobbed over the phone. "He thought it was funny! The bastard!"

I sighed. No doubt about that.

Still in shock Mo staggered a couple of steps backward and then spun around and ran away she said she was so hurt that she was having a hard time breathing but even then she half-hoped Scott would follow her. And maybe try to explain himself. Maybe it had all been a misunderstanding.

But of course he didn't.

"Now I know why he wasn't talking with me like he used to" she said still sobbing. "I was just a novelty to him something new to try. I wouldn't mind so much but why did the truth have to come out like *this?* If he didn't want to go out with me anymore then why couldn't he at least have the courtesy to break up with me?"

I didn't have an answer.

"But that's it we're over! Done! I hate him!"

I'm not proud to admit that a selfish part of me did somersaults at the news. In my mind Aaron almost shrieked with happiness. *That's it, bro! You're in!* But after a brief moment of mental high fives with my long-dead brother I felt like an ass. All this time I'd been imagining Aaron as the coarser, more self-centered twin and me as more evolved. Yet here I was sinking to his level. Mo was in pain after all and I really did care about her. Right now I needed to help her through this.

She and I ended up talking for about an hour and a half. Even as I tried to comfort her Aaron made me feel bad about it. *This is good, buddy. VERY good. Play the sensitive friend while she's vulnerable and in no time she'll be putty in your hands.*

Aaron could be quite a bastard himself.

Even after all that time talking on the phone I don't think the breakup had completely settled in Mo's mind. One minute she'd say "Oh I was so stupid! Naomi warned me this would happen!" or "I can't believe I actually *lied* to my parents for that jerk!" But a moment later she'd go the other way. "Tell me the truth Charlie do you think there's any chance that someday he'll realize what he did and we'll get back together?" How was I supposed to answer that? I only came up with variations on "I don't know but anybody who would treat you this way doesn't deserve you."

By the end she seemed to feel a little better. "I'm so sorry I didn't show up at practice tonight" she said finally a little calmer. "I just couldn't."

"Don't worry about it. No big deal. Everybody will understand."

There was a long silence. Then she said "I'm so glad we're friends Charlie. I really needed you tonight and you were there for me. Thanks."

"No problem." I couldn't stop that selfish part of me from doing one more cartwheel.

There was another pause. Finally she said "Want to hear something funny? Naomi actually told me she thought you and I liked each other. I mean in a romantic way."

I could hardly believe my ears. *Here you go stud! This is your moment! Tell her you DO like her!* But I guess my brain was still absorbing this amazing statement and my mouth was stuck closed. OK sure at the back of my mind it'd occurred to me that with Scott out of the picture it wouldn't be long before I could make my move. But I didn't think she would be the one to do it instead of me! Or so soon!

Come on! shouted Aaron. *What are you waiting for?*

147

But I was too slow. And that's when she dropped the bomb that ruined everything.

"I love Naomi but sometimes she just doesn't get it" she said. "It's obvious that you and I are too different to ever be more than just friends. But it's our differences that make us such *good* friends, don't you think? For me it's just wonderful to have a guy friend I can talk to. With no strings attached."

I felt like a Wrecking Ball had just hit me in the gut. Even Aaron was speechless.

But she kept going. "I'm telling you right now Charlie that in the future if I ever feel like I'm falling for somebody else I've learned my lesson. I'm going to RUN in the opposite direction. My parents are right—I shouldn't be dating. I'm never going to sneak around or lie to them for some guy ever again you don't know how much I hated myself for letting them down because of Scott. What was I thinking?" She laughed but it wasn't a real laugh it was more like she was putting herself down. "I'm so glad Naomi was wrong about you and me. The idea of us together . . . I just don't see it fitting into the grand plan. I mean for *either* of us. Could you just imagine how weird that would be? The 2 of us? A <u>couple</u>?"

Even though my heart was in my throat I forced a chuckle. "Right" I said. "That would be weird."

That night I lay curled up in bed trying to block Aaron's moaning. He sounded like an injured buffalo. *Oh man Charlie I can't believe you why didn't you listen to me? Why didn't you tell her when you had the chance? You're useless you know that? I can't believe this crap just my luck I'm the one that dies and gets stuck living through a bonehead who just sits there like a jackass when the girl of his dreams says she*

only ever wants to be just friends. Good work! You're pitiful,
bro. Pitiful.

Which is why on Friday I showed up for the Halloween Bash exhausted. Instead of sleeping that Thursday evening I spent the whole night wide awake trying to stop myself from banging my head against the wall.

CHAPTER 5

Sorrowful and great is the artist's destiny.
—Franz Liszt

LYLE DWARKIN:
Scrambling Under the Gaze
of a Sadistic Behemoth

Halloween is a big deal in Opequonsett. On the Friday closest to October 31st, the high school always throws a dance and just about everybody goes. The school sets up a wooden stage at one end of the gym and kids deck the place out with pumpkins, fake cobwebs, spooky lights and stuff like that. Everyone dresses up in funny costumes and gets ready to go wild to live music. The next night there's a smaller party at the middle school, the one I'd attended the previous two Octobers, but I was much more excited this year. Everybody knew that the Halloween Bash at the high school was the big one. Most of all, this year my buddy Charlie and his band were playing and I got to work the soundboard. I was sure it was going to be a fantastic night.

But it certainly didn't start off that way.

I arrived early with the rest of the A.V. Club so we could set up the cables and microphones for Lemonade Mouth and figure out the best volume and effects settings. It was a job that should have taken us an hour or so. But by 7:30, only thirty minutes before the party was supposed to begin, Mudslide Crush still hadn't let us near the stage. Dean and his friends were taking their sweet time setting up, each one of them playing a long solo and spending ages testing each microphone while their sound guy adjusted the levels. And then they'd insisted on running through a bunch of songs—I don't know, maybe seven or eight of them. They were making us wait on purpose. It was infuriating.

While Dawn Yunker and I sweated it out by the sound-board, Lemonade Mouth, most of it anyway, sat stony-faced on fold up chairs underneath the giant new scoreboard. Wen looked sullen and seemed to have a cold, Charlie had dark circles around his eyes, and Mo, who'd only just arrived, kept biting her nails and wouldn't even look up at the stage. Stella was quieter than I'd ever seen her, hugging that ukulele to her body almost like she expected somebody to try to smash it. The worst part was that we were still waiting for Olivia to show up. No one had even heard from her since school ended.

"I don't know what happened," I heard Wen say. "She told me she was definitely coming."

"She must be on her way," whispered Charlie uncertainly. "Maybe she got held up."

But I didn't have time to worry about that. When Mudslide Crush finally cleared out, we only had twenty minutes or so to set up. The A.V. Club sprang into action. While Charlie and the others set up their instruments, we worked fast. I grabbed the board as Dawn and the others scrambled onto the platform. We'd learned to be wizards at repairing old cables and microphones with electrical tape, gum and whatever we had lying around. The trickiest part would be miking Charlie's drums. There were so many of them.

One by one, each musician stood on the platform and rushed through a few notes so I could find the right levels and write them down. Ray Beech didn't make it any easier. He appeared next to me and hovered close while I scrambled, watching my every move but not saying a word. And let me tell you, when a sadistic behemoth is glaring at you, it's hard to concentrate. Soon somebody dimmed the lights and the first crowd of costumed kids started wandering in. But I wasn't done figuring out where to set some of the levels.

In the end I just had to take my best guess.

DAWN YUNKER:
Guys Are Pigs

At 8:15, Olivia still hadn't arrived. I was fighting the butterflies in my stomach, so to kill time I went back onto the stage and fiddled with the pickup on Mo's bass. I thought I'd heard it pop a little during the sound check. It wouldn't hurt to add an extra piece of tape to be sure it held in place. Mo was nowhere in sight. After Scott Pickett came off the stage, she'd bolted from the gym and closed herself inside the *Barking Clam* office with Naomi. It was no mystery why. By then it was common knowledge what had happened between Mo and Scott. But it was a good thing that she wasn't around just then to see what I saw: Scott standing in the middle of the gym with Lynn Westerberg hanging all over him.

Guys are pigs.

The place was filling up. While the sound system pumped out music from one of Lyle's dance mixes, kids in costumes greeted each other with shrieks of laughter. There were some wild outfits this year. I saw the usual witches and ghosts and things like that, but there were also a bunch of funny ones: a tube of toothpaste, two giant purple aliens, a Ping-Pong table. The entire basketball team had dressed themselves like babies in diapers. I planned to change into my costume as soon as I was done with Mo's bass. I was going to be a toaster.

I finished with the tape. I hoped Charlie and his friends were as good as Lyle said. Especially since that ass Dean Eagler and his buddies had made such a big fuss, as if Lemonade Mouth was going to ruin the whole evening.

Then a couple seniors dressed as plants called up to me. "What's the deal with the band? When are they starting?"

"I'm not sure," I said, trying to sound calmer than I felt. "Soon, I hope." I couldn't help glancing toward Charlie, who was talking frantically with Lyle near the soundboard. What would they do if Olivia never showed?

But just as I left the stage, Stella came rushing over to me. "Where did she go?" she said, her face red and frantic.

"Who?"

"Olivia. Wen just said someone told him they'd seen her run through here. Did you notice where she went?"

I shook my head. "No. I didn't see a thing."

LESLIE DERN:
I Am Not Going to Throw Up

So I was standing at the sink in the girls' bathroom with Kate Bates, adding the final touches to our makeup. I'd convinced Kate to come as a French waitress like me even though she complained that the miniskirt made her butt look big. It did, but I didn't say so.

Just as I was leaning in to darken my eyeliner, the door behind us burst open so loud I jumped, which totally made me smear my eyelid. And then in the mirror I caught a glimpse of that Olivia Whitehead girl rushing toward the first stall. She looked as pale as aspirin and she was holding her hand over her mouth. She was talking to herself too. It wasn't loud, but Kate and I both agree on what we heard. She repeated it a few times:

"I'm *not* going to throw up! I'm *not* going to throw up!"

And she didn't.

At least not until just before she reached the toilet, anyway. But then, from the sound of it, up came everything she'd eaten all week.

MR. BRENIGAN:
A Terrible Mistake

I wasn't sure what the problem was. Stella Penn and I had agreed that her band would begin playing at 8:00 on the dot and now it was 8:15 and we were still waiting. I had Dean Eagler and a few other seniors and juniors on my back about getting started with the live music. I told them to relax, that Stella's band would come out soon. But I kept checking backstage to try to find out what was going wrong. Every time, Stella would assure me that everything was fine and they were almost ready. From the beginning, from that very first afternoon when she'd walked into my office and asked me to allow her band to perform at this year's Halloween Bash, she'd promised me there wouldn't be any problems. I'd admired her confidence. She told me in no uncertain terms that after playing at the Bash, she and her band planned to win the Holiday Talent Show. Despite reservations, I'd decided to give her the go-ahead.

But what a headache it turned out to be.

It's amazing how a little thing like a high school band can cause an uproar in a town like Opequonsett.

Still, the thing was, and I want this completely understood and in the record: I started off rooting for her. It's not easy being the new kid in a place like this, and even though Stella had a bumpy start to the year, after our initial talk she had me honestly convinced that she wanted to turn herself around. Anyone could see she was a girl with a great deal of potential. I hoped allowing her this opportunity would give her a constructive place to focus her energy.

But now as I checked my watch again, I began to realize I'd made a terrible mistake.

RAY BEECH:
One Final Tonguer

It was hilarious! Twenty minutes after they were supposed to start, the gym is swarming with people, and the freshman freaks still aren't ready! So Dean slides back up to Butt-Wipe Brenigan and in his best suck-up voice he reminds him that we're planning on doing two sets and maybe since everyone is waiting we should just start our first one. A couple of minutes later Butt-Wipe says okay. Yes! So then just as we're about to get up on stage, I see Mo Banerjee wander in from her hiding place like the Last of the Bummed-Out Princesses. At that exact same moment, Lynn pulls Scott's face to hers so she can give him one final tonguer before the show. Mo sees the whole thing! Her eyes completely bug out and then I watch her scurry away again, her face in her hands. It was great!

So we start our set, and I can't hold back a huge grin. We really got those freaks good!

CYNTHIA STENMAN:
Eavesdropping with Marilyn Monroe

I was sitting on the toilet in the girls' bathroom while Olivia was barfing her guts out in the next stall. So gross! A minute later the main door slammed open again.

"Olivia? You in there?" I knew the voice. It was Stella Penn.

"I'm here," Olivia groaned. Then there was this completely revolting dry-heave sound like she was some kind of sea otter or something.

Then I heard Stella say, "Please leave!" Obviously, she was talking to Leslie Dern and Kate Bates, who I'd been eavesdropping on until Olivia showed up.

It didn't take them long to scurry away.

After the door swung shut again I heard Stella step closer. She waited a few seconds and then asked Olivia if she was okay. "Yeah," Olivia's voice said. "I mean I'm not going to die or anything."

"Can I open the door?"

Long pause. "Okay."

There was more shuffling from the hallway and then a guy's voice called in. "She here?"

"Yep," said Stella. "She threw up. But she looks fine and says she's okay."

I heard some whispering and then the guy said, "We're coming in."

I nearly freaked but I kept quiet. From the footsteps I realized that two people, not just one, had joined Stella and Olivia.

"How you doing, Olivia?" I recognized this voice, too. Charlie Hirsh.

Olivia took a while to answer. "I can't go out there."

After a moment Stella said, "Why not?"

"I just can't."

That's when the door opened again and somebody else tried to come in. Whoever it was, Stella took care of it. *"We're in here!"*

"But I have to use the bathroom!"

"Use the one by the cafeteria! Can't you see we're having a *conversation?*"

Whoever it was, they went away.

I quietly pulled up my legs. Thank God I'd come as Marilyn Monroe. If I'd worn a scarecrow costume, my original idea, the leaves probably would have crackled and given me away. I didn't want to miss this.

"But you *can* do it," said somebody else, another guy. "I know you can. We rehearsed everything. We're good. Your voice is great. Besides, you and I put everything we have into writing this music. And the words you wrote, they're wonderful."

Olivia took a deep breath. I thought she was going to spew again but she didn't. "I'm so sorry, Wen. I didn't want to let you down, any of you. But I can't do it. I just can't."

"Won't you tell us why?"

"I'm just . . . I don't know. I'm scared."

There was a long silence before anybody spoke. It was so quiet I could hear the sound of water dripping from one of the faucets. Finally Wen said, "I know what you mean. I'm scared too."

"Me too," Charlie said.

Stella didn't say anything right away. Something was happening out in the gym. I heard the crowd suddenly cheer and then Mr. Brenigan said something through the microphone but I couldn't make it out. A moment later the audience screamed even louder and the music started up. I recognized the opening guitar chords. It was Mudslide Crush.

That's when Stella finally spoke.

"Please, you can't quit," she said in a voice quieter than I'd ever heard coming from her mouth. "This is really important to me. I haven't told any of you this but the truth is, everything I do I screw up. My mother thinks I'm out of control and I need to make this work to prove to myself that I'm not a complete idiot." In the space underneath the door, two spike-buckled combat boots (who else's could they be but Stella's?) moved even closer to Olivia's stall. "I'm scared too, but please, Olivia, don't back out now."

SETH LEVINE:
Waiting for a Mudslide

This year would be my last Bash, and I intended to make it a great one.

Through almost the entire Mudslide Crush set I danced

158

with Wendy Davis, who came as a witch, and Jane Seiseki, who'd sewn up a sheet, a string and a big piece of cardboard to look like a giant teabag. Me, I was Abraham Lincoln. We were laughing and working up a sweat, but after a while my beard itched and my ears were pounding so I decided to get some fresh air. On my way out I ran into Kyle Reeves and a bunch of the Student Council crowd getting rowdy at the back of the gym. Somebody offered me a Jell-O shot. After that I needed to hit the john so I slipped out the double doors. A few kids milling around in the main foyer gave me high fives and shouted things like "Abe! Dude!" or "Way to go, Mr. Prez!" It was a laugh.

Anyway, while I was on my way to the john I stumbled across a handful of kids speaking in hushed tones at the entrance to that little hallway near the janitor's equipment room. There's a bench in that hallway, and over their shoulders I could see it. There sat five glum-faced kids, none of them talking—just staring into space. The whole scene struck me as weird.

"What's going on?" I asked one of the guys at the front of the hallway.

"Lemonade Mouth," he said quietly, like it was a funeral.

Curious, I looked over his shoulder again. I didn't know any of them by name at the time, but I'd heard about this band, of course. Some of my friends were disappointed because a bunch of freshmen were going to cut into the Mudslide Crush show. They made a big deal out of it. In my opinion, it was all kind of ridiculous. Mudslide Crush had played the Halloween Bash the previous two years. Their songs were okay and all, but I thought they all sounded the same after a while. I was glad to have some variety this year.

But then earlier tonight somebody told me the fresh-man band had backed out at the last minute.

Now, I asked the guy, "They gonna play?"

"I think so. They're waiting for Mudslide Crush's set to end."

That's when Azra Quimby, a freshman I knew from the student council, pushed past me with her friend Floey Packer, that girl who takes pictures for the school paper. Azra smiled at me but then she followed her friend down the hallway. That's when Floey took a shot of them. You know the one—I think everyone does: the five of them sitting on that bench looking intense, their faces drawn and pale. Stella is the only one looking at the camera. I think she did that on purpose, making her eyes all wide and kind of crazy for dramatic effect. Everyone else is staring in different directions, like they're deep in thought. The truth was—and I know this because I was there—they were just waiting for the other band to finish so they could have their turn to play.

Right after that I heard everyone in the gym cheer as Mudslide Crush ended their last song. Then I heard Dean Eagler say something like, "We'll be right back after a short break. Oh, that is, unless the other band finally got their act together. Which is kind of unlikely, don't you think?"

The laughter echoed all the way down the corridor.

AZRA QUIMBY:
The Crowd Goes Quiet

Everybody heard what Dean said. I glanced over at Floey and she looked mad. She didn't like Dean. Ever since he'd treated her like dirt at a party about a year before she'd kept away from him.

I touched Wen's arm and whispered in his ear. "You all right?" I had to admit, I felt bad for him. Plus, I'd already been feeling guilty for giving him the cold shoulder for so long. Even though things had changed between us, there was a time when he and Floey and I used to be inseparable.

He grinned. "Fine. Perfectly relaxed."

But I could tell he was lying.

Stella had insisted that everybody in the band stay backstage until Lyle came back and gave them the signal. That would mean everything was all set for them to come out. When he did, they all stood up and went to the door nearest the platform. Just before opening it, Stella stopped.

"Everybody ready?"

Nobody spoke, but they all nodded.

Then they pushed through the double doors and walked over to the stage. It was a strange moment. As soon as the kids in the audience saw them, the whole place went quiet.

MRS. REZNIK:
A Bloodthirsty Medieval Mob About to Witness a Hanging

The show didn't start off well.

The five of them walked out and I still couldn't help wondering why none one of them had thought to wear a costume. It never even occurred to me to remind them, I just assumed they would. The impression they gave was that they hadn't put any thought into this being a Halloween

161

event and had shown up in whatever they happened to have on, which for most of them meant T-shirts and jeans.

Olivia Whitehead approached the microphone like a frightened deer. She stood frozen while the others played the opening bars of their first song. She clearly missed her cue, and then the others had to stop playing to start the song over again.

"Pitiful," I heard some little twerp whisper. If I'd seen who'd said it I would have given them a piece of my mind, I can assure you.

Olivia was obviously terrified. I couldn't help feeling sorry for the girl, especially after all the trouble I knew she'd already had in her young life.

I braced myself. From the beginning I'd set expectations high. Maybe too high. Mohini was a gifted bassist, of course, when she applied herself. And after overhearing the music they'd made at my detention a few weeks earlier I really believed they had something unusual going for them. When some of the students started pressuring Elliott Brenigan about his decision to give these freshmen a chance I'd stood by him—and them. But now here they were, all five looking scared and unsure.

I have to admit, I was secretly concerned.

I crossed my fingers. From a group of juniors standing near me I heard whispering and laughter. There was an anticipatory feeling in the room, like a bloodthirsty medieval mob about to witness a hanging. I was aware that there was a contingent of students looking for any reason they could find to make the lives of these kids miserable.

But that's when Olivia took a deep breath and seemed to pull herself together. Then her voice rang out full and strong and seemed to emanate from the depths of her soul. After that, the atmosphere changed.

JANE SEISEKI:
Exactly How She Felt

I was confused and hurt and thinking about going home. Why did Seth leave me stranded on the dance floor right in the middle of a song? Why didn't he come back? He just walked away. He didn't even tell me where he was going. Was I nothing to him? I'd thought tonight would finally be our night, but obviously I was wrong. Why did I do this to myself? When would I listen to Wendy and accept that he just didn't like me the way I liked him? Nobody ever does.

And then Lemonade Mouth came out, looking all geeky and cool with their weird instruments and their serious faces. The music was slow and strange and beautiful. Everybody went quiet. It was like they cast a spell over the room. I found myself swaying back and forth. And then that fat girl opened her mouth and floored me. I leaned forward to catch every word:

> *I hear people say . . .*
> *These are the best days of our lives*
> *But they don't know, they don't know*
> *I like to think . . .*
> *That when we're older we'll laugh so hard*
> *That today's tears will fade like old*
>   *photographs*
> *I'm not the same since I met you*
> *I'm not the same since I met you*

I suddenly felt my throat tighten up. These were *my* exact feelings, emotions I'd been having for a long time but never talked to anybody about. She was speaking for *me*. It sounds weird, I know, but even that first time I heard the song it made me feel like I wasn't alone. And that voice! How could a sound so grizzled and worldly come from such a chubby, innocent-looking face? Who *were* these guys? I'd seen the girl with the buzz cut and the long plaid shirt skulking around the hallways—she was kind of hard to forget, but I didn't even recognize the others.

> *From the first time you swept past, I knew . . .*
> *You changed my life but I don't dare tell you*
> *And now I feel your breath in every breeze*
> *Your whisper in the rustle of the leaves*
> *I'm not the same since I met you*
> *I'm not the same since I met you*

My breath caught in my throat again. I closed my eyes and thought of Seth. I knew exactly how she felt.

ANDREA BECKHAM:
Slow Dance

Before they came out I was alone at the side of the gym. Rodney, my best friend, had spent most of the Mudslide Crush set trying to get me to dance but I wouldn't.

"This is a good one, Andrea," he'd say, grabbing my hand at the beginning of just about every song. "Come on, let's go!"

"No," I kept insisting. "But you go ahead if you want to."

"What's the matter?" he asked finally. "Don't you want to have fun?"

I shrugged and smiled, but inside I was annoyed at him for even asking a question like that. He of all people should understand that I wouldn't feel comfortable in front of all these kids. What was I supposed to do? But I was here, wasn't I? I'd converted my wheelchair into a throne by wrapping the back and armrests with gold paper. A red velvet cape and a paper crown later and *voilà!* I was a queen. Just because I didn't want to make a spectacle of myself rolling around bumping into people on the dance floor didn't mean I don't like to have a good time.

Rodney looked disappointed. Finally he squeezed my hand one last time and left me to join the others in front of the stage, which is why for the final few Mudslide Crush songs I sat alone and watched him dance. Even though a part of me burned to get out there and join him, another part wouldn't let me. Instead I smiled, occasionally waved, and did my best to hide the fact that sitting by myself was making me feel like crap.

But then Lemonade Mouth played.

Their music gripped me in a way I can't even describe. It was like five space aliens had taken over the stage. I was mesmerized. And from the moment they appeared I felt a connection. I knew Wen Gifford and Charlie Hirsh—these guys weren't part of any in-crowd, they were outsiders like me. And yet there they were onstage making this weird, emotional music that, even from the very first notes, stirred something inside me. And everybody I could see seemed as awestruck as I was.

That night was the first time I ever heard "Skinny Nancy." Now I have the poster on my wall where I see it every morning when I wake up. It's a black-and-white shot of the five of them alone on a beach. Olivia Whitehead is the closest to the camera and her face takes up the biggest part of the picture. She's sitting in the sand and facing the ocean, eyes closed, her hair blowing across her face. She looks so peaceful. At the bottom of the poster in thick yellow letters is a quote from that song:

Enjoy this moment, my lovely one.
—LEMONADE MOUTH

Oh, and that night I did. "Skinny Nancy" was my first-ever slow dance.

That night changed everything.

SCOTT PICKETT:
A Bolt Out of the Blue

I couldn't take my eyes off Mo, nodding in time and looking so intense as she gripped her bass. Lemonade Mouth was a bolt out of the blue. First they grabbed everybody's attention with a couple of slower tunes with killer hooks, and then they kicked it up with four or five rockers that got the place on its feet. I hated to admit it even to myself, but those freshmen were good. Looking around at everyone's faces, I could tell I wasn't the only one who was surprised. Kids rushed to get closer to the stage, others climbed onto each other's shoulders. At these dances there are always a few hanging out in the lobby where the music isn't so loud, but now people crowded back into the gym to check out what the fuss was about.

The music was a storm, and not like anything I was used to hearing. One minute they sounded kind of classical (even the ukulele, if you can imagine it), other times it felt like straight-ahead rock but with a Latin beat. Still other times the music was just weird and wild. That kid on the trumpet could play. And Olivia—that girl had a voice on her. It was crazy. That messed-up freak who looked like a drowned rat—who would have guessed? There was one slower song with a chorus that went something like, "I'm Back Among the Walls." Amazing. Made me shiver.

Worst of all, I couldn't help being impressed by Charlie Hirsh and his crazy jumble of drums. He seemed to know each one up and down and he worked them like a master, his long, spiraling hair flying in all directions. As a drummer myself, it was a little humbling.

The first hint of worry flashed through my mind. I'd thought the Holiday Talent Show was going to be a cake-walk for Mudslide Crush. Now I wasn't so sure.

It was during that "Singing a New Song" tune that I felt a pull at my shirt. "What do you say, Scotty. Want to find a dark corner somewhere?" Lynn had been hanging off me and clutching at my arm all night. It was like she couldn't bear to be separated. Which, to be honest, reminded me of why I'd broken up with her the first time.

But before I could answer, Ray, who was dressed as a giant rubber ducky—complete with a beak, a sailor's hat and webbed feet—caught my eye. Standing there in his yellow suit he rolled his eyes at me and then stuck his fingers in his ears. A bunch of my friends slouched along the wall nearby. Dean, Patty and a crowd of the hardest-core Mudslide Crushers were glaring up at the stage.

And that's when my competitive streak kicked back in. What was the matter with me? Okay, so these freshmen were good, but my buddies and I were better. We were the headliners around here, not them. I grinned back at Ray and stuck my finger in my mouth like I wanted to barf. Halfway across the gym from each other, we both laughed.

"Come on, babe," Lynn said. "Let's go. . . ."

Unfortunately, right over Lynn's shoulder I had a clear shot of Mo, her eyebrows pulled together in concentration. All at once I had a harder time caring whether or not Mudslide Crush was better than Lemonade Mouth. And I didn't want to go. I couldn't stop looking at Mo. I suddenly realized that if Ray hadn't kept telling me I could do better, I probably would still have been with her. She wasn't like the girls I usually dated, quiet and agreeable but clingy. Mo was a lot of fun and she spoke her mind. We had long discussions and whenever we disagreed it was okay to say so. I liked that about her. Mo was special.

The truth was, I really liked her. And apparently I hadn't stopped.

"Scottyyyy—!" Lynn said, rising up on her toes to come closer. "Aren't you *listening* to me?"

But it was too late now for Mo and me. As I felt Lynn's tongue slip into my ear, I couldn't help thinking that I'd already gone and blown it.

PATTY NORRIS:
Aloha

Ray and I couldn't stop laughing. The whole thing was a joke.

For starters you had that Stella kid up there playing this tiny little Hawaiian guitar. I was like, "Where's her hula skirt?" Know what I mean? And then behind her the dumb-looking fern-haired guy had this crazy wall of drums that he went around whacking at like a spaz. The fat chick even broke out an accordion for a couple of the tunes. An accordion! Were they kidding? Yeah, maybe they had two or three okay songs, but come *on!* What was the big deal?

If you ask me, those freshmen weren't that great.

DELILA CZERWINSKI: Charlie! Charlie! Charlie!

I'll never forget that night. Dina, Veronica and I were dressed to kill and having a fantastic time. It'd been Dina's idea to come as cats. She said the Halloween Bash was the perfect excuse to wear something sexy, so we painted our faces and put on cute kitten ears and, most importantly, low-cut black leotards. We spent the whole Lemonade Mouth show near the front of the stage making up weird dances and flicking our tails at each other in time to the crazy rhythm. It was a blast. After each song we screamed at the tops of our lungs and checked out the drummer. I'd never seen anybody play like that. He was amazing. Somebody told me that everyone in the band was from our school but I didn't ever remember seeing him before. The three of us decided he looked like that movie star—the one with the scruffy dreadlocks and those incredible blue eyes, what's his name? Anyway, he kind of reminded me of him. At one point, Veronica tried to climb onto the stage but somebody pulled her back down, thank God. What was she planning to do, throw herself at the boy? Veronica pretended to be such a tramp sometimes. She was a riot. Eventually one of us found out his name so after each song we'd scream it over and over. *"Charlie, Charlie, Charlie!"* It was one of the best times my friends and I ever had together.

MANNY VALDEZ:
Of Life and Love and Yearning
and Regret and Hope and Loss
and Being Alone and Waiting

By midway through the set, kids stood all around the gym making up freaky dances to go with the freaky music. I joined in too, which is saying something since I'm not normally much of a party person. I usually hang back at stuff like this. In fact, I only showed up that night because my friend Digby nagged me down so hard.

At one point Digby and I climbed up onto a table to get a better view. It was a wild scene, lights flashing, all these kids dressed up in costumes and letting loose. At the end of each song we all screamed our heads off. It felt like the music tapped something in me that I never realized was there. I felt weird energy in my legs, my fingers. It was crazy. The words were about life and love and yearning and regret and hope and loss and being alone and waiting—it was like they were talking directly to me.

NAOMI FISHMEIER:
A Line in the Sand

Yes, Dear Reader, I was there too.

From where I stood in the audience, I can tell you that Mo looked completely focused on playing her bass. Which was a good thing. I was relieved that at least for now she seemed to be feeling better.

Finally Olivia announced that their next song would be their last, and that it was something written by Stella.

Stella? Mo never mentioned to me that Stella had written a song. I didn't know what to expect, but I figured it was going to be memorable.

I was right.

It started off with Charlie banging his drums in a steady, regular beat, kind of like a march. That went on for quite a while and soon everyone was either clapping or stomping their feet in time. Meanwhile Stella, who'd stepped away from her place, pulled away a cloth that had been draped over something at the side of the stage. It turned out to be three oversized coolers. She opened the first one and pulled out a little paper cup, which she handed to somebody near the front of the stage.

"Pass them back!" she shouted. "They're for everyone!"

Without any further instruction the kids at the front started handing the little cups to the kids behind them, who also handed them back, like an assembly line. In the middle of the crowd, where I stood mesmerized, everybody crushed forward. I craned my neck to see if I could figure out what she was handing out. But even before I got mine and sipped the sweet slush inside I recognized the logo on the cup.

Mel's Organic Frozen Lemonade.

At that point somebody—Lyle, probably—must have flicked the switch to lower the movie screen because it rolled down from the ceiling.

That's when Olivia stood back and Stella took the microphone.

"Friends, lend us your ears," Stella said, her voice echoing over the hypnotic drumbeat. "We'd like to take a moment to shine a light on a recent event, a change at our school that may have seemed inconsequential to you at the

171

time, that in fact you may not have even noticed, but one that nevertheless affects us all in ways both large and small."

The drumming abruptly stopped. Stella's eyes moved significantly across the audience.

"We'd like to talk about lemonade."

I exchanged glances with Floey Packer, the girl I was standing with. Where was Stella going with this?

By now the screen had completely unrolled, and suddenly there appeared behind them a giant image of a Mel's Organic machine. That's when the drumbeat picked up again, but now Mo's bass joined it with a series of sharp, low notes that made the moment feel urgent.

"As many of you may know," Stella continued, "there used to be a Mel's Organic machine by the east stairway next to the basement club corridor and the music room. It was there for a long time."

The image on the screen changed to a shot of the club hallway in the school basement, including the *Barking Clam* office. In black and white, the corridor looked even more shabby and depressing than usual. "As everybody knows, it was mostly the kids from the basement clubs that drank the lemonade from that machine. That's why the lemonade has come to symbolize the kind of kid who joins the A.V. Club, the Chess Club, the math team, the school paper."

I heard giggles from various places in the audience. Stella acted like she didn't notice.

Now the dreary hallway image was replaced with a shot of a younger Mrs. Reznik. Seeing her with long hair and in an evening gown was kind of startling. She looked beautiful and dignified. Not only that, but she was standing between Yo-Yo Ma, the world-famous cellist, and Elton John, the pop star.

"This year," Stella went on, "as many of you are aware, the budget for the music program was cut way back and Mrs. Reznik, our illustrious and beloved music teacher and fellow Mel's Organic enthusiast, was banished to the same dingy, drafty catacombs as the basement clubs."

There was some uncomfortable fidgeting in the crowd around me. I don't know about anybody else, but I felt bad for Mrs. Reznik. I never really thought about how she was down there in that gloomy room all day. But now it didn't seem fair.

"As any of the basement club kids can tell you, spending time in one of those noisy, cramped basement rooms is not exactly living in luxury, certainly not as comfortable as, for example, the cushy new locker rooms recently built for the exclusive use of the sports teams. Still, Mrs. Reznik and the kids downstairs made the best of it. And the best part of being in that basement was the lemonade machine. It was sort of a consolation prize for the outsiders, the second-tier kids."

She paused and let the driving beat pound for a measure or two.

"But then came earlier this week. While most of us were unaware, two guys in green uniforms came and hauled the machine away in a truck. And do you know why?"

Nobody made a sound. The picture on the screen changed to a black-and-white shot of an old, grizzly guy in a suit sitting at the end of what looked like a corporate boardroom.

"This is Mr. Harold Barkley, president of the Barkley Bottling Company in Detroit, Michigan. When he heard that the taxpayers of Opequonsett didn't want to pay for a new scoreboard . . ." she pointed to the new electronic scoreboard, which was boxy and green and, in my humble opinion, kind of ugly, ". . . he had an idea. He called the town and offered to donate the money as long as the school agreed to remove any machines that weren't owned by Mr. Barkley's company. Which meant taking away"—she held up one of the little cups—"the Mel's Organic Frozen Lemonade."

There was a murmur of surprise from the crowd.

She kind of half-smiled. "Now, before okaying this deal, you might have thought somebody would have at least asked the opinion of those of us who used and loved that machine, right? Wrong. Now, I like soda as much as the next person, but I don't appreciate it when somebody decides that it's okay to use me as a corporate pawn."

The growing rumble of voices around me steadily increased. I heard indignant calls of agreement from all over the gym.

I couldn't help grinning. She was crazy, but she was brilliant.

"Why am I telling you this?" she asked, the rhythm suddenly getting even louder. "Fellow travelers, this isn't really just about a lemonade machine. It seems to us that there is a pervasive attitude at this school that certain people are better or more important than others. Ask yourself: Why did the school decide to build a state-of-the-art gym while slashing the music program? Why wasn't the basement included in any of the renovation plans? Are the kids in the Chess Club and the French Club and the A.V. Club less important than the sports teams? And why did the school feel like it was okay to trade our beloved lemonade machine for a new scoreboard, lovely as it may be, without even asking any of the basement kids what they thought? Well, my friends, we're here to tell you that some of us think that music is pretty important too! And that the basement clubs are cool—and no less important than any other club!"

By then, the buzz of the crowd was pretty noisy. Stella had to talk loudly into the microphone to be heard.

"And it's not only the administration that has this attitude! We've noticed that certain people around here, certain kids, like to put you down if you're a little different, if you have your own style that doesn't quite match up with the norm."

I happened to be standing close to Richie Benedetti, a skinny, pimple-faced sophomore who hardly ever said much. He and two of his friends, all in jeans and black concert T-shirts, had already been nodding in agreement with Stella, but now their eyes grew even more excited and they started shouting their approval.

"Well, I have a question," she said. "Just because you're not part of a particular trendy crowd, does that really make you a geek? A loser? Does it make you a *freak?*" Suddenly, she had to shout over the commotion. *"Because if it does, then there certainly are a lot of us freaks around here!"*

The sudden roar of the crowd took me by surprise. Richie and his friends shook their fists in the air and started jumping up and down, wide grins across their faces. The cheering went on for a while. Eventually the giant picture on the screen changed to a huge cup of lemonade. Wen came in with a trumpet line that reminded me of a military call. Over the noise Stella called out, "We're tired of being treated like we're second-tier! We're tired of letting other people make our decisions and set the rules! To some of us, basement kid or not, the sweet slush that the lemonade machine offered was more than just a drink—it was a freak badge of honor! *And we want it back!*"

That's when Stella stepped back from the microphone and Olivia started singing:

> *I want lemonade In my cup!*
> *Hmmmmm, Hmmmmmm*
> *Hold it high! Raise it up!*
> *Hmmmmm, Hmmmmmm*

It was catchy. It felt like an anthem, almost a battle cry. Olivia repeated it and soon everybody joined in. While we sang, Stella held up her lemonade and called out, "Freaks unite! Raise your voices! Take a stand! Don't let anyone treat us like second class anything! This is *our* school! Never let them forget!"

There was an explosion of swirling colored lights and it seemed like the entire gym was full of excited kids stomping, cheering and holding up little cups. I have to admit, jaded concert-veteran though I was, she had even my heart pounding. Even Olivia smiled. A moment later Stella led us all in a chant. "Bring back Mel's! Bring back Mel's!"

That's when I felt someone push rudely by me. I turned. Mr. Brenigan was pressing his way through the crowd to get to the stage. At the end of the previous song I'd noticed him wandering out of the gym, probably to go to the bathroom or something. Now he was back, and he didn't look happy at all.

RICHIE BENEDETTI:
Flying Buttons

Mr. Brenigan seemed hell-bent on shutting them down. And that's exactly what he did in the end, but not before

Stella moved to the edge of the stage and started ripping off that long shirt she was wearing. Drew, Pete and I started screaming even louder then. We got so excited we nearly bugged out.

Pete called over to me. "What the hell is that crazy chick doing?!"

But I had no idea. I just stood there holding up my little cup of lemonade slush and watching her buttons fly off, one by one. Turned out, underneath she was wearing that T-shirt, the same one she got busted for wearing at that assembly at the start of the year. It had two big hands, one on each of her boobs—which, I don't mind pointing out, were *choice!* Sweet! I'm sure my eyes nearly popped out of my head!

A couple seconds later the lights went out. The entire place went nuts.

It felt like a revolution.

CHAPTER 6

Children say that people are hung sometimes
for speaking the truth.
—Joan of Arc

OLIVIA:
Nancy

Dear Ted,

It's 3 a.m. I can't sleep. Nancy's gone.

*It happened this morning (actually, yesterday
morning now) sometime before dawn. I know that
because she was purring in my arms on Friday
night before I went to bed, but on Saturday
morning Brenda and I found her curled up cold on
her pillow. The other cats spent most of the day
hiding behind the sofas. Brenda and I could hardly
look at each other without tearing up. We laid poor
Nancy in a shoebox but couldn't bring ourselves to*

take her outside and bury her right away. Brenda cooked all morning. Breads, pastries, a gigantic pot of chili—far more than the two of us could possibly eat in a month. Which was all right, because I think all that cooking helped distract her.

The whole morning all I could think was that I wanted to call Wen. The truth is, I think about him all the time and just then I felt like hearing his voice might make me feel better. I kept reaching for the phone but I always stopped myself. Even though Nancy is in one of our songs, I'd never mentioned she was a cat to anybody, not even Wen. It just felt funny having to explain it now. But then in the early afternoon the phone rang. It was Wen. After that, everything came gushing out of me. I must have sounded a little hysterical because the next thing I knew he insisted on coming over. A few minutes after he arrived, Stella, Charlie and Mo showed up too. Nobody pushed for any long explanations. All they said was that they wanted to be here with me. Can you believe that?

At first it felt strange having so many people over since, as you know, Brenda and I usually keep to ourselves. But everybody was nice to Brenda and kind to me and eventually I felt comfortable—calm even. We went out to the yard and buried Nancy under the crabapple tree, the one she always liked to climb. We even picked wildflowers from the back garden and laid them on her grave. We held hands and I said a prayer. I wish you could have been there. It was beautiful.

Afterward everybody came in and ate, which seemed to cheer Brenda up. Plus I think she was glad to see I really do have friends, that I wasn't making them up. They even got her talking and laughing a little. Anyway, I'm a bit better now. As Brenda keeps saying, Nancy was never in any pain and we did everything we could for her. Still, I can't help thinking about what's precious in my life. Which is why I wish I could be with you right now.

I'll come up next weekend. I promise.

Love always,
Olivia

P.S.
Almost forgot to mention—I got through the school dance without passing out. Thank God it's over. The vice principal shut us down before we finished our last song, but Stella says not to worry. She and the others are even more excited now about the Holiday Talent Show. Stella says there's no stopping us.

Which is what I'm worried about.

On the bright side, at least I don't have to get in

front of an audience again for another month and a half.

And yes, I know you want me to bring my friends up so you can meet them. (Not exactly Mr. Subtle, are you?) But I hope you understand that I couldn't possibly. I'm sorry. And it's not _you_—you know that, right? I'll never be ashamed of you, Daddy. Never. It's just that I'm not comfortable. True, they're all smart kids with kind hearts, but you never know how people can be. And yes, I know you always think I have trouble trusting, and maybe it's true. But I'm just not ready.

Please understand. 🌸

WEN:
Of Clouds and Confessions

"How about that one up there?" I asked. "A person, maybe? A giant old woman with a skirt and an umbrella?"

"No, that's not it," Charlie said. "Think bigger."

"Skip me," Olivia said. "I'm not ready."

Mo took her time. "Hmmmm. An upside-down hand. A khamsa. That's good luck."

Stella sighed. "I don't know," she said. "I don't see either of those."

Saturday afternoon turned out to be unusually warm. The five of us had climbed out of Olivia's bedroom window and were lying comfortably on the flat part of her roof. We'd arranged ourselves like bicycle spokes, our heads close together in a circle. We were staring up at the clouds.

181

"I don't believe in luck," Olivia said. And then after a pause she said, "A dandelion. In a flat gray vase."

Olivia's house was tiny. It stood in a small clearing in the woods so it was hard to see from the road. Earlier that afternoon, when I'd finally found the long dirt path that she called her driveway, I realized that I must have passed it hundreds of times without ever noticing it. I set my bike against a garage that leaned a little to one side, and then I took in the walkway, which was overgrown with weeds. The paint flaked from every wall I could see. I wasn't convinced that I'd come to the right place. Or that anybody lived there at all. But then Olivia had appeared at the door, looking paler than usual with dark shadows under her eyes. Inside, the air smelled sweet, a little chocolaty maybe, like somebody was baking. The place was cluttered with stuff. Tattered armchairs, mismatched end tables, cat furniture, music boxes—there was barely enough room to move around. Jumbled onto shelves and piled onto coffee tables were stacks of old books, magazines, newspapers, photograph albums and box after box of what looked like dusty trophies, porcelain figurines, letters and other stuff I couldn't even guess at. But the clutter somehow felt comfortable, like you just wanted to pull up one of the chairs, grab a box and spend the afternoon going through it.

Olivia introduced me to her grandmother, a square-jawed turtle of a lady with a walking stick. I told them both how sorry I was about Nancy. Eventually Stella, Mo and Charlie joined us. We went outside and held a little ceremony for the cat, and after that we came back in and sat around on ancient sofas. It wasn't long before Charlie and I got Brenda (Olivia's grandmother insisted we use her first name) laughing with our stories about the Halloween Bash, which already seemed longer ago than just the previous night. Olivia even smiled, which made me glad I'd come—that all of us had.

More than three hours later, none of us felt ready to break up our little gathering. Now on the roof, I think we were all feeling relaxed, peaceful even. Charlie's voice broke the long silence. "You guys are way off," he said. "It's a one-eyed zombie pushing a baby carriage."

Mo chuckled. "How do you figure?"

"Isn't it obvious? Look, see the head? The monster's shoving hard like the wheel is stuck or something."

I squinted but I didn't see that at all.

"Maybe it's just me," Stella said. "But once again all I see is a blob. A giant white, fluffy blob."

Nobody spoke for a couple seconds, but then we all laughed, including Stella.

I think that was the moment when it first struck me that something had happened. With the five of us up on Olivia's roof gazing at the sky, I suddenly realized that everything felt different now. And I was sure I wasn't the only one who sensed it. I didn't know exactly when it'd happened, but hanging out after Nancy's funeral that Halloween afternoon, Lemonade Mouth felt almost like a family.

And as weird as this family was, with everything that was going on with my messed up family at home, I was grateful to have this new one to fall back on.

Olivia's voice pulled me out of my thoughts. "How bad did we mess up last night?" she asked nobody in particular as far as I could tell. "I mean, what do you think they're going to do to us on Monday?" It was a question that had probably been on all our minds but which until now none of us had actually asked aloud.

"Detention," I guessed. "At least. Worse, maybe. Mr. Brenigan was pretty unhappy."

"You don't think they'd actually suspend us, do you?" It was Mo's voice. "My parents would disown me."

"Who knows?" I imagined having to explain it all to my Dad. My stomach sank at the thought. With the whole Sydney thing going on, I'd already fallen off his A list. "It's possible."

But that's when Charlie chimed in. "Come on, guys. You gotta stop thinking that way. Yeah, sure, we might get in a little trouble—and just so you know, *my* mother wouldn't exactly be thrilled about that either—but we all talked about this last week and decided it was important to make a statement. Remember?"

Nobody argued. It was true.

"So we need to keep reminding ourselves that we did the right thing. And there's nothing anybody can do to us now that would take that away. Plus, didn't we pull it off with style? Weren't we everything we wanted to be? Unconventional? Fearless? And even if some kids tried to stop us, didn't we make it happen anyway, without compromises? I have no regrets. None."

I didn't know what to think. Even if we did the right thing, I still felt like we'd made big trouble for ourselves. And that Mr. Brenigan wasn't going to let us off without any punishment at all.

"I guess you're right," Mo said, even though she didn't exactly sound convinced. "Maybe we did okay."

"Okay? Are you kidding? We were *great*! We *blew them away*!"

An airplane came into sight from behind one of the branches that framed our view of the sky. We watched quietly as it crept along, trailing a white line across an otherwise clear patch of blue. Eventually it sank behind another tree and disappeared.

That's when Stella finally spoke up again, but there was a lot less confidence in her voice than in Charlie's. "Sometimes I feel like I'm just too stupid for anything I do to ever work out."

"How come?" asked Olivia. Like me, she was probably remembering what Stella had said through the bathroom stall at the Bash. "Why do you say that?"

"Look what happened last night. If only I'd thought it through ahead of time, I would have realized they were going to shut us down."

I hoped she was joking. "Stella," I said, "you could say the same thing about any of us. And in any case, who was it that got us all over to Bruno's and convinced us to form a band even though not everybody wanted to? Who persuaded Mr. Brenigan to let us play the Bash? As far as I'm concerned, you're an absolute genius."

The others chimed in, but Stella was too stubborn to listen.

"Well, as long as we're confessing," Mo said after a while. "I guess I'll go next. Sometimes I feel like the biggest fraud in the world."

Her words seemed to drift up into the sky. At first I didn't understand, but then she started telling us about her Indian family, and how no matter what she did she never felt like either a genuine American or a genuine Indian. I never really thought about that before, but it made sense. How could you ever feel comfortable if no matter where you went you felt like you belonged someplace else? It made me see Mo in a new way.

"Okay, I have one," Charlie said. "Sometimes I'm convinced that the only reason I'm alive is because of some gigantic cosmic mix-up."

It was a strange thing to say, but then he told us all about his twin brother who died at birth, and how he thought about him a lot. This was all news to me. "It makes you think," he said. "It's like, why was I the one who lived? What if it was supposed to be my brother but for whatever reason there was some screw-up, some major celestial mistake? You know what I mean? I wonder about that sometimes."

I didn't know what to say. I had no idea he had this cloud hanging over his head. I could only imagine how sad it would feel to know I had a twin who was gone forever. And I wondered what else I didn't know about him, or about the secret lives of any of my friends.

Suddenly I felt like it was my turn and everyone was waiting for me. Now, normally I don't get into conversations like this. When there's tough stuff to talk about, I'm more likely to make a joke and laugh it off than to really discuss it. Which is why I was so surprised when I heard myself say:

"Sometimes I wish I had a time machine."

To be honest, I wasn't exactly sure what I meant by that. But it wasn't long before I figured it out. I told my friends about my dad, about how Sydney was taking over our lives, and how sucky it was that they were getting married. I didn't say anything about how I lusted after her, of course, but I did tell them how I wished everything could go back to the way it used to be, before it all got so complicated. And everybody listened and nobody said I was crazy. It's weird, but that afternoon as I lay staring up at the branches, it was almost as if there was something in the air that made me want to open up. Maybe it was because we were looking at the sky and not at each other, I don't know, but I was surprised how easy it was. And talking out loud about this stuff actually made me feel a little better.

"How about you, Olivia?" asked Mo. "Anything to confess?"

There was a long silence. Finally I heard Olivia say, "No. Only that I'm glad you guys came. Thank you."

It was a nice thing to say, but I couldn't help feeling a little disappointed. After all, I suspected there was so much she could have shared with us but didn't. About her life, about how she ended up living in this spooky little house in the woods with her grandmother and, most of all, about her dad. I was sure I wasn't the only one who wanted to know. But none of us pushed her. Not today of all days. But all the same, I wondered why she wouldn't trust us enough to let us further into her world.

After that, nobody spoke. As we stared quietly into the sky, a bird swooped into view, diving from out of nowhere, rising above the trees and finally gliding in a wide, slow circle. A cool breeze passed over us, shaking the branches and making me shiver. A moment later, a shower of orange and brown leaves fell all around us like confetti.

I was the last to leave. Olivia and I were both quiet as she walked me to my bike.

"What are you thinking about?" she asked finally, her hand on my elbow.

I shrugged. "I'm thinking about how fitting it is that on Halloween I'm headed back home where I'm pretty much guaranteed to run into the Demonic Deadbeat of Decoupage."

Olivia frowned. "Maybe you should give Sydney more of a chance. She's really not so bad."

"That's easy for you to say. She's not marrying *your* dad." The words popped out of my mouth before I realized what I was saying. And then it was too late to take them back. I felt about two inches tall. But if I'd upset her, her face didn't give it away. She looked as calm and unreadable as ever.

The leaves crackled under my feet as I wheeled my bike around. Darkness was already seeping into the woods. I hadn't meant to stay here this late. I wondered vaguely if Olivia's house ever saw any trick-or-treaters. Were there any kids brave enough to venture through these trees?

And then I realized how close Olivia's face was to mine. She was watching me.

"What are *you* thinking about?" I asked her.

"Clouds," she said almost at a whisper. "How, if you're in one, it can make you blind to what's right in front of you."

"Okay . . . ," I said, not sure what she meant. That often happened with Olivia. Then, looking into her solemn, brown eyes, I suddenly felt something else I didn't understand. It was a weird, dizzy feeling. I didn't know what it was, but it scared me a little.

But then she looked away. In the late afternoon shadows, her face seemed especially long and tired. She took a couple steps into the clearing and then, her back to me, she gazed up again at the sky. "And another thing about clouds is that they never disappoint you. They can be anything you imagine them to be. . . ."

I still didn't understand, but she obviously had more to say so I waited. She seemed deep in thought again. I couldn't help thinking that even though Olivia knew so much about me and my life, she had a whole set of experiences that I couldn't even begin to guess about. What would it be like to have a dad in prison for killing someone? I figured it must eat you up inside. I asked her once, but she just shrugged it off. Olivia seemed to keep a lot of things locked behind a door she never opened.

And now the sudden empty feeling in my gut made me realize how much I wished she would let me in.

Watching her on her front walkway in the dimming light, I also realized two more things: First, that she wasn't going to say anything else after all. And second, that with Olivia, silence could say a lot.

CHARLIE:
Mozart's Banjo

Somebody left yet another note on my locker. It was 1st thing Monday morning and I'd already missed the home-room bell which is why the school corridors were empty. As usual I was running late and out of breath. But when I spotted the big white piece of paper taped above my combination lock I slowed down. Even from twenty feet away I could just about make out the letters written in thick black marker. I considered. Could it just be a message from 1 of my friends? Lyle asking me to meet him after class maybe? Stella announcing she'd come up with another crazy idea?

Somehow I didn't think so.

Finally I was close enough to read it:

COME TO MY OFFICE <u>IMMEDIATELY.</u>
—MR. BRENIGAN

My breakfast sank. I pulled the note off the metal door and studied it again. Oh no. Here it comes. It didn't take a genius to guess what this was about.

The heavy feeling didn't go away when I got to the Front Office and saw Mo, Wen, Stella and Olivia already waiting on the long bench in front of Mr. Brenigan's doorway like death row convicts. Mo gnawing at her pinky nail. Mrs. Flynn the secretary offered me a sympathetic smile but then before I could even sit down Mr. Brenigan's scowling head appeared.

"All here? Good. Everybody into my office."

The 5 of us filed in. There were only 3 chairs for us so Stella and I stood. Mr. Brenigan stepped around his desk and settled into his humungous cushioned seat. For a few seconds he glared at us and tapped his finger on his lip. He looked angry enough to burst. "I suppose you know why you're here?"

Nobody answered.

"That was quite a performance on Friday I imagine you kids think you're very clever?"

Olivia shuffled in her seat.

"I have to tell you, I'm disappointed. A school dance is no place for a"—he seemed to search for the right word—"political *tirade*. What you did was uncalled for and completely disruptive. And *you*—" he pointed at Stella "—you let me down. Didn't you promise you weren't planning anything funny? Didn't you assure me there wouldn't be any problems?"

"But it *wasn't* funny Mr. Brenigan. And there weren't any problems" Stella said. "We just spoke our minds. Nothing dangerous or disruptive happened! So you didn't have to shut us—"

But he held up his hand. "I don't need to hear it I heard enough on Friday night. What you kids pulled, inciting people like that—it was inappropriate. Even subversive. Especially that speech about the soda machines. Frankly the financial decisions of the school board are none of your business." Stella opened her mouth to speak again but Mr. Brenigan didn't let her. "Mohini aren't you planning on applying to medical school? Didn't it even occur to you to consider the effect of having an incident like this on your record?"

Mo's face turned an odd color.

"Olivia. Charlie. Wen" he said, taking in each of us 1 at a time. "I hope this isn't going to be the start of an unfortunate trend. This is only the beginning of your 1st year here and I wouldn't say any of you are getting off to a particularly auspicious start."

After a long pause I heard Olivia's husky whisper. "So what are you going to do to us?"

"Excellent question. What to do?" He sat back and tapped his lip again. "I consulted with Mrs. Ledlow and we considered our options. On the 1 hand there's detention. But somehow that doesn't feel sufficient. After all, we've tried that a number of times with Stella but it obviously didn't have much effect."

Stella was leaning tight-lipped against a bookshelf.

"We talked about suspension but that seems a little overboard. Especially considering that 4 out of 5 of you don't have much of a history of troublemaking." Mo kept chewing absently on her fingernail but even as she did I could see a hint of relief on her face. "In the end she left the decision up to me."

I caught a worried glance from Wen. Here it comes.

"My decision" Mr. Brenigan said finally "is to take a combined approach. 1st you will all have 1 week of detention starting today. And since I'm in charge of freshman detention this week I expect to see each of you *promptly* at 2:05 this afternoon."

Nobody spoke. To be honest I was too scared. Mr. Brenigan could be pretty intense when he wanted. I braced myself for 2nd of all.

"In addition" he looked directly at Stella now "to prevent any further grandstanding I'm disqualifying all 5 of you from participating in the Holiday Talent Show."

Stella's eyes went wide. "You can't do that! We have a right to—"

But he held up his hand again. "No Stella this is not up for discussion I've already spoken with Mrs. Reznik and we've already removed your names from the list."

Mrs. Reznik agreed to remove our names from the Talent Show list? Really? I had a hard time believing it.

"As you know, we run a tight ship around here. And I won't have you kids turning another school event into a circus. You should be thankful I'm letting you off so easy." Again Stella started to speak but he cut her off. "But if you try to pull anything like that again—any disruption of school activities, any provocation of the students to cause any kind of trouble at all—I promise you I won't be so lenient next time do you understand?" His eyes scanned our faces 1 more time. "As of this moment, Lemonade Mouth is finished."

I just gaped at him. He was serious.

Mr. Brenigan stood up and pointed to the door. "Alright we're done. Back to class."

He herded us out of his Office. We were all too stunned to argue. Besides, it was obvious he wasn't going to listen to anything we had to say.

After he shut the door we stood there blinking at each other. Then we wandered into the Lobby outside the Front Office just as the bell sounded for the end of homeroom. Kids started pouring into the hallways. None of us could talk. I felt like I'd been punched hard. It wasn't the detention—I didn't care about that so much—but to be kicked out of the Holiday Talent Show was *big*. I couldn't help glancing at Stella her jaw looked really tight now and for the 1st time ever she didn't seem able to speak. I knew how much she wanted us to win the Talent Show so I felt especially awful for her. And for Mrs. Reznik too. I still didn't believe she wanted us to stop playing. Lemonade Mouth was sort of her baby after all.

But then I glanced around at the 4 faces of my friends and realized that everybody looked just as bummed out as I felt. And that's when it occurred to me that Lemonade Mouth hadn't been Mrs. Reznik's or Stella's or mine or any one person's. It'd belonged to all of us.

And I could tell I wasn't the only one surprised at how bad it hurt now that it was gone.

But soon after that a strange thing started to happen.

All day kids I barely knew kept coming over to talk to me. It was weird. I'd been walking those hallways since the beginning of the year and apart from my friends and the occasional run-in with Ray Beech, most kids had pretty much ignored me. But not anymore. Suddenly everybody had something to say about Lemonade Mouth. Not that all of it was *positive*. The cooler juniors and seniors would sometimes roll their eyes when I walked by, but there were a bunch of kids who gushed about the show they'd tell me which of our songs was their favorite and ask how long I'd been playing my drums.

And when the school paper came out, the whole front page was about us:

193

LEMONADE MOUTH A SENSATION

By Naomi Fishmeier, Scene Queen

More than anything else, this year's Halloween Bash will surely be remembered for the unexpectedly powerful performance of the freshman band Lemonade Mouth. Made up of Mohini Banerjee, Wen Gifford, Charlie Hirsh, Stella Penn and Olivia Whitehead, the group defies musical categorization.

With its unlikely hodgepodge of instruments including a ukulele, an accordion and what can only be described as a bewildering wall of assorted percussion instruments from another galaxy, Lemonade Mouth is surely the weirdest, freshest new direction in music since Mozart's mother threw out his banjo. Add to that the mournful, soul-shaking lyrics and vocals of Olivia Whitehead (who knew?) and an attitude that champions the rights of students and the sidelined against the privileged and empowered and you have the makings of a giant new musical phenomenon unlike anything this writer has ever seen.

The article went on and on about how great we were. According to Naomi we "opened up a new and vital musical landscape" and "provided a missing voice for the struggles of the less than glorified among us, a battle cry for underdogs everywhere." Yikes! She even had quotes from kids who said our music had "touched their souls and opened

their eyes to a whole new way of looking at themselves."
Which was crazy of course. OK sure I felt like we were a
good band and everything. But come on.

The story ended by questioning why the administration
shut us down just for challenging the social order of the
school and for "shining a light on a shadowy, elitist decision
regarding the soda machines—a subject the *Barking Clam*
promises to investigate in full detail." Mudslide Crush was
mentioned only once. In the last paragraph.

There was even a picture of us from when we were sitting
on that bench waiting to go on. At the time, I'd been in such a
state that I barely remembered anyone taking that shot but
now as I stared at the black and white image I couldn't help
being surprised. We looked good. In a moody kind of way.
Cool even.

That's when I felt a tap on my shoulder.

"Hey you're Charlie, right? The drummer in that freshman band?"

I turned and there was this tall swanlike girl with feathery
hair and a neck that went on forever. I'd seen her around. I
was pretty sure she was a junior. I almost looked behind me
to see if she was speaking to somebody else. But she wasn't.
She even knew my name.

"Uh . . . yeah?"

She brushed a plume of hair from her eyes. "How did you
learn to do that? You're *amazing*! I've never seen anybody
play like you before!"

That woke Aaron up. *Oh. My. God.*

I had to agree. In fact, I had a hard time getting my mouth
to answer it was like I suddenly had shrink-wrap around my
brain.

"Your band is so . . . *wild*!" she gushed. "I'm a *huge* fan!"

All I could think to say was "Thanks."

"I'm Veronica" she said.

"I know." It wasn't true. Only 2 seconds earlier I had no idea what her name was but like I said I wasn't thinking straight. Plus the way she was smiling at me was flooding my bloodstream with distracting Chemicals.

Even weirder, a part of me felt guilty because of Mo. Which I realized was ridiculous. When I'd called Mo Sunday morning to make sure she was doing OK with the whole Scott thing, she'd sounded kind of annoyed. All of a sudden I felt like she didn't want to talk with me anymore. Besides, she'd pretty much spelled it out on Thursday that going out with me would be like betraying her *grand plan*—that ridiculous road map she'd set out for her life. Even when she 1st told me about it I'd said it was kind of crazy. "A plan like that doesn't leave much room for the unexpected, Mo" I'd said. "Don't you ever do anything impulsive? Anything reckless just because you're dying to know what it feels like?" But it obviously didn't have any effect on her. The girl was not about surprises.

I needed to give up on her and face reality. There really was balance in the world. Good with the bad. So now that Mo and I were finally friends of course she *couldn't* feel the same way about me as I felt about her. Yin and yang, right? Anything else would've thrown off the symmetry of the Universe. Just like if people were excited about my band then it only made sense that Mr. Brenigan would *have* to take it away. Equilibrium.

Earth to Charlie! Earth to Charlie! The goddess Veronica waits! Don't just stare at her say something!

I wanted to. I really did. But I was overwhelmed so I stood there like a moron. Eventually she said "See ya around" and left. A moment later I just raised my hand and waved.

Holy crap! You really are hopeless, you know that?

But it wasn't as if I was used to beautiful girls throwing spontaneous compliments at me. This kind of thing never happened before.

And the shockers didn't stop there. As I sat down at the beginning of Spanish class (I arrived late as usual), Lyle casually reached over and set a little square plastic CD box in front of me.

"What's this?" I whispered.

"It's you" he said. "Surprise."

I took a closer look. Somebody had taken the picture of us on the bench and turned it into cover art. Over our heads was the title: "Lemonade Mouth: Live at the Bash."

"It's your show" he said speaking softly and keeping his eyes on the board. "We recorded it."

"You did?"

"Yes don't you remember I told you we would?" He grinned. "And I don't mean to brag, but the sound quality came out killer."

I could hardly believe it. I was looking at a Lemonade Mouth CD.

"Wow" was all I could think to say. "Thanks."

But it got even weirder. "Listen, a bunch of kids already asked if they could buy them." He shot me a guilty look. "I hope you don't mind but I went ahead and sold 5 copies for $10 each. I figure they each cost less than a buck to make so that's over $45 profit. But I also figure the A.V. Club should take 20% for doing the recording and packaging and distribution. That OK with you?"

I could only blink at my friend.

Finally I could see why the A.V. Club elected him Treasurer.

Over the next few days kids started walking around with

our music in their headphones. I would hear people humming our songs. They even knew the words. It was bizarre.

Another big moment happened around that same time. 1 day Olivia and Wen and I were leaving the Cafeteria talking about how strange it all was when we suddenly came across Ray Beech outside the bathrooms. He was with Terry Cabeleira, this short nervous kid from the Drama Club, who had his back to the wall and looked terrified. Ray was leering down at him. But before we could push our way closer an amazing thing happened. 7 or 8 kids stepped out of the passing crowd and gathered around Ray. None of them was particularly big, but like a sudden swarm of angry bees they managed to move him to 1 side so Terry picked up his books and got away. Ray tried to push back but there were too many of them. "You're a freak!" he shouted as they scattered off. "You're all freaks!"

The 3 of us looked at each other. Other than Stella, we'd never seen anybody else even *try* to stand up to Ray before.

After that, lemonade seemed to replace soda as the drink of choice. Since you couldn't buy Mel's at school, people must of picked it up at Bruno's. I saw Terry Cabeleira in the hallway a few days later. When he saw me he grinned and lifted a cup into the air. "Hey Charlie!" he called out. "Look! I'm holding it high! I'm raising it up!"

It was a strange feeling. I guess I was a celebrity, sort of. All because of a band that didn't exist anymore.

MOHINI:
The Parking Lot Fleas

After that meeting in Mr. Brenigan's office, I feel like my whole world is falling apart. Scott's gone and Lemonade Mouth is dead. Being banned from the talent show means I won't even be able to play my solo, the Ode d'Espagne that I've been working so hard to learn.

First period today happens to be my bass instruction with Mrs. Reznik and she's in a bad mood. Her face is all pinched and she hardly says a word as I play. Eventually I put down my bow right in the middle. I can't even look at her.

"What is it?" she growls. "Why did you stop?"

That's when I tell her what Mr. Brenigan said. She doesn't look particularly surprised. She coughs and it sounds even worse than usual. That's when I realize she doesn't look well. Her face is grayer than normal, and even her wig, if that's what it is, seems a little off kilter. Finally, she looks at me with just a hint of sympathy. Her normally critical eyes turn unexpectedly soft.

"Never mind about him," she says. "The thing for you and your friends to remember is that you are artists. There will always be those who don't appreciate the work of true visionaries. It doesn't matter. To an artist, beauty and honesty are everything. The fact that music has the power to stir up controversy should neither direct nor impede the pure creative impulse. Be proud," she finishes with a wink. "You played beautifully and honestly."

Which is a nice thing to say, but it certainly doesn't help me feel any better when I run into the Patties and a pack of the other Mudslide Crusher girls on my way to my second period class. They're coming in the opposite direction, talking and snickering. Their chatter quiets when they notice me. As we pass, one of them says, "Nice going, Drama Queen. Feel better now? Lynn says hi."

Suddenly I feel more dumped than ever.

But that afternoon my mood takes an unexpected turn for the better and I realize that not only is word out about what happened with Mr. Brenigan, but there's even a small faction of kids in the school who seem to think my friends and I are heroes. I realize this after a handmade sign mysteriously appears in the main first-floor hallway:

LET LEMONADE MOUTH PLAY THE HOLIDAY SHOW!

Of course, students aren't allowed to post anything without permission, so the teachers pull the sign down almost as soon as it goes up. But soon another, with the same message, appears near the gym. It happens again and again. And word gets around about that too. The first day of the signs, the five of us get called to the office half an hour before my monster Trig exam. I'm not happy about having to see Mr. Brenigan again. That's all I need—more stress.

"What are you trying to pull here?" he demands. "What's the purpose of these messages? Do you *want* to make trouble for yourselves?"

The five of us just look at each other. "It's not us," Stella says. "We're not putting them up."

He gives us a hard stare. "You kids are playing a dangerous game and you're going to lose."

He doesn't keep us there long, thank God, probably because he doesn't have any proof that we did anything wrong. He lets us go with a warning. But I can tell he doesn't

200

believe us. To be honest, I have my doubts too. Alone in the corridor outside his office, I ask the others if it was any of them. Everyone shakes their heads. Even Stella.

"No, I swear," she whispers. "I honestly have no idea who's putting those things up."

I study her face. She's telling the truth.

On the second day, even more signs appear. I start seeing them everywhere, sometimes two or three on a wall. I know it isn't all the same person now because different signs have different writing. And there are more messages now: "Raise your voices!," "Bring Back Mel's—This Is *Our* School!" and even, "Don't Stop the Revolution!"

I'm in biology when Mrs. Ledlow makes an announcement over the intercom. "I wish to remind everyone that school rules limit the posting of student notices to the message board by the lobby restrooms. Any students found breaking this rule will receive disciplinary action."

I'm sitting at my lab bench at the time. There's stifled laughter all around. Everyone knows what she was talking about. It's a weird feeling, knowing that some unknown kids are fighting for my friends and me. I can't help glancing over at Wen, who's at a bench across the room. He's staring back at me.

And I can feel everybody else looking at us.

Somebody calls out from the other end of the hallway. "Hey, Mohini!"

I turn. Richie Benedetti and Pete Boucher are at the other end of the corridor grinning at me. I don't know those guys very well. They're part of a sullen crowd that mostly keeps to themselves. I sometimes see them hanging out near the busses after school. Ray Beech has a name for them: The Parking Lot Fleas. Anyway, Richie and Pete don't look too sullen now.

"Hold it high!" they call out in unison. "Raise it up!" They give me thumbs-up signs and then disappear around the corner.

Everything feels different now.

While some kids treat me like I'm a star or something, Scott acts like I don't exist. I rarely see him in the hallways anymore and on the few times I do, he pretends I'm not there. He even ignores me in study hall, which is tough since our assigned seats are so close. All I can do is keep my nose pressed in my book and act like I don't care. But it feels like there's a clamp on my forehead. Sometimes it gets so bad I have to hide in a bathroom stall until the feeling passes.

But it's a funny thing about those headaches. After a few days, I stop getting them. In fact, it's a surprise to me how *quickly* I feel better.

It isn't just that the Lemonade Mouth signs are a distraction. Not eating with Scott anymore means I end up spending lunches at the Freak Table more often, which I start to look forward to. I also feel more focused now. I've recommitted myself to my grand plan, studying harder than ever and increasing my hours at the clinic.

Most of all, I'm relieved that the lying and sneaking around is over. I guess I never realized just how badly it was eating me up inside.

All in all, I'm astonished how easy it is to get used to no longer being Scott's girlfriend. It's weird. Being with him used to mean so much to me, but now I spend my time with my new friends and Scott doesn't feel so important. I guess I finally recognized that one of the big reasons I liked

Scott was that it meant being part of the in-crowd. And now I know what that's worth, I don't want it anymore.

And that's what I'm mulling over on my way to study hall when I happen to pass the open gym doors and see two janitors setting up a ladder near the far wall. They're about to take down another mystery sign. Tied to the metal bars high above one of the basketball nets hangs a giant bed sheet with painted purple letters.

MY SPIRIT IS A LION THAT WILL NOT BE CAGED

I wonder how somebody got it up there without being seen. But I can't help smiling. The line is Olivia's from our song "Better Places." It's one of my favorites.

It's been more than two weeks now, and the mysterious messages haven't stopped appearing. A week ago somebody filled an entire wall in the girls' bathroom near the cafeteria. The next morning it was the boys' locker room. So far nobody's been caught. Now, just before the janitors can pull the sheet down, it's a nice feeling to see our words hanging in the new gym high above the shiny parquet floor. It really feels like I'm still part of something. Something even bigger now than before.

Even though I'm not sure what it is, exactly.

Suddenly I sense movement near my ear. I spin around in a panic, because for some reason I have a flash that it might be Scott. Thankfully, it isn't.

It's only Charlie.

"You think Brenigan's ever going to change his mind?"

"No way," I say. "Not a chance."

He smiles in that cool, sleepy-eyed way he has. "Me neither. Walk together?"

"Sure." I adjust my book bag on my shoulder and continue down the hall with him.

Things have been different with Charlie, too. For starters, since the Bash I've found it hard not to notice how girls hover around him. To be honest, it's annoying. Sure, all five of us are suddenly getting attention we aren't used to, but my God!

"How's Veronica?" I ask, unable to stop myself.

He shrugs. "I don't know. Fine I guess."

I study his expression, but if there's any sign of hidden feelings I don't catch it.

"Just curious." Now I feel stupid for bringing it up. In the two weeks since the Bash, Charlie and I have stopped having our regular heart to heart chats. He hardly ever seems to want to walk to class with me anymore. He's always in a rush to see a teacher, maybe meet with Lyle or whatever. When I try to meet him at the Metal Shop he's always gone before I get there. It's almost as if he's trying to avoid me. Anyway, even though we see each other in crowds, like at the Freak Table, it isn't the same as before.

And I have to admit, I miss him.

"Listen, I have news," he says, changing the subject. "What would you say if I told you we could play another show?"

I don't answer. Surely he isn't serious.

"Come on, what would you say?"

"I'd say you're nuts. Didn't we just agree that Mr. Brenigan's never going back on his decision?"

We turn the corner and start up the stairs toward the study hall. "I'm not talking about playing here at school. Listen, Lyle told me he talked to Bruno. From the Pizza Planet? Well, Lyle gave him a CD and Bruno liked it. He says he'll let us play there sometime."

I gape at him. Lemonade Mouth at a pizza place? Is this a joke?

"It's not so weird. Mudslide Crush played there a few times. It's not like he'd pay us much, either, or put us on a great night. Lyle says Bruno won't let us play a Friday or Saturday because we haven't proven we bring in a big enough crowd. Even Mudslide Crush never played there on a weekend. But something's better than nothing."

I'm having a hard time taking this in. He really is serious. And even though part of me feels excited about this unexpected news, another part of me is worrying about turning the pressure back up in my life. That's been the silver lining of Lemonade Mouth being over: managing my time has been a little easier.

"Just think," he continues, "depending on how it goes, this could even lead to a regular gig."

"A regular gig?" I stop walking, suddenly aware of the pressure already growing in my forehead. "I don't know. Isn't it enough that we didn't get suspended already?"

"Mo, Mr. Brenigan said we couldn't play at school events, but he can't tell us not to play anywhere at all."

"What does Olivia say? Have you asked her?"

He looks at his shoes. "She says she doesn't want to do it," he admits finally. "I guess singing in public, even just the one time—well, it really was hard for her. So far she's saying no." To me, this comes as no surprise. When Mr. Brenigan pulled us from the Talent Show, I think we all suspected that deep down Olivia probably felt a little relieved. "But if everybody else is up for it don't you think we can convince her to change her mind? Think of it. Bruno's."

I'm prevented from answering because just as I open my mouth to respond, Hilary Levanthal, a freckled, pointy-nosed sophomore who seems determined to cram herself into a miniskirt every day even now that the weather is colder, appears between us. "What? Are you *kidding*? Lemonade Mouth at Bruno's? You *gotta* do it! So many kids would come!"

My cheeks grow warm. This is a private conversation! How long has she been listening?

But Hilary's rudeness doesn't seem to faze Charlie at all. "Wow, thanks Hilary. That's really nice to hear."

"Well, you guys are the best!" She gives him a wide, toothy smile, and then for an uncomfortable moment the two of them stand there grinning at each other while I seethe. Finally, she puts her hand on his arm. "See you later, Charlie."

Then something inside me, something irrational and completely out of my control, makes me spin around and stomp away. I drop my head and keep marching, pushing my way through the crowd.

"What's the matter, Mo?" Charlie calls, catching up with me.

"Nothing." I keep moving. I don't look at him.

As we round the final corner I can almost feel his eyes studying the side of my face. "Really, tell me what's going on."

But I *can't* explain, not even to myself. Still, the bell is about to ring and he's waiting for me to say something.

"Charlie," I say, still walking fast and not looking at him, "in case you haven't noticed, Olivia isn't the only one feeling stressed around here. It's everything I can do to keep my grades up in Trigonometry and Latin. And that's on top of the rest of my classes, bass lessons with Mrs. Reznik, volunteering at the clinic and working at the store.

I'm already pushing the limits of what I can take. Sure, I agreed to do the Halloween Bash and even the talent show, two *school* events, but now you're talking about an even bigger commitment." We're near the door now, so I spin around to face him. "Plus, did you know that after Trig this semester I'm considering filling the space with another elective?"

He shakes his head.

"Well I am. Pre-calc." And then I can't help adding, "If you and I ever got a chance to talk anymore you'd know that."

His expression changes. I can't be sure because the lighting in the hallway isn't great, but I almost think his face is turning pink.

Suddenly I feel like a jerk. It isn't that anything I told him is a lie, it's just that something inside my chest is pulling at me, like I'm not telling the whole truth—even though I'm not exactly sure myself of what the whole truth is.

But suddenly it dawns on me.

All at once I realize that I'm gazing into his eyes like a desperate puppy. And finally it hits me, the awful truth. It practically bowls me over like a hot bucket of obvious. Suddenly I feel like the dumbest girl that ever was.

I'm *crazy* about him.

Why didn't I see this before?

And then, still gaping at his face, I make a decision: I have to stay away from Charlie. I'm not going to make the same mistake twice, sneaking around like a thief and lying to my parents like I did with Scott. No way. Not again.

"Mo," he says, "maybe you don't realize how big a deal Lemonade Mouth is to a lot of kids around here. We're not just a band to them. It's weird, but somehow they've made us . . . I don't know . . . *more*. It's almost like they've put us at the center of a *movement,* you know what I mean?"

But I'm not capable of speaking at the moment. And as I gaze mush-headed over Charlie's shoulder, I happen to notice Andrea Beckham rolling around the corner in her wheelchair. Seth Levine is with her, and Jane Seiseki too. In a way, it's strange that I have the clarity of mind to even notice them, considering what's going on in my head. But like Richie and Pete, Andrea is another quiet kid who rarely ever smiles and seems to exist in the margins. And yet here she is rushing toward us from the direction of the Speech and Language lab with two of the most popular kids in school. Jane is pushing her fast, with Seth running alongside. All three of them are giggling. They've obviously been up to something. But when they notice us, they slow down.

"Look who it is," Seth says in a low voice. "Two of the instigators themselves."

Andrea gives me a conspiratorial look. "Did you guys hear about the gym?"

Not sure what to say, I just nod.

"That wasn't you three, was it?" asks Charlie.

They look at each other and laugh. And then Jane whispers, "Nope. But whoever did it, it was a good one, don't you think?"

Andrea leans forward and speaks in an even quieter voice. "It's just terrible what the school is doing to you. You guys deserve to be treated better." I realize that I've never seen her looking so happy. I take in her face, her soft features, her cheekbones that stand out when she smiles. Andrea normally wears her hair so that it covers her features, but now she has it tied back. I realize that she's beautiful. I've never noticed that before.

Seth glances over his shoulder. "Guys, we can't stop. We gotta get away from here fast."

Even as Jane starts to turn the wheelchair, Andrea is still beaming at us. A moment later Charlie and I watch them vanish down the hallway. Then the bell rings. Now, it isn't like me to show up late to any class, even if it's only study hall. But Charlie and I take one look at each other and then we both sprint in the direction Seth, Jane and Andrea just came from. Whatever they've been up to, we want to find out.

The Speech and Language lab isn't far; it's just around the corner all on its own in a little dead-end corridor. When we round the bend we both stop, frozen.

The signs are hung everywhere. Lemon yellow paper arranged in a checkerboard pattern across all three walls. The effect is impressive, even pretty. Most are the usual messages like JUSTICE FOR LEMONADE MOUTH and MEL'S IS MARVELOUS but I especially notice the ones near the bottom.

JUST BECAUSE YOU NEVER LOOK AT ME DOESN'T MEAN I'M NOT HERE

Another of Olivia's lyrics. And I think again of quiet Andrea Beckham, the last person I would have expected to make a big statement about anything. But then I remember with growing pride the word Mr. Brenigan used for us.

Subversive.

When Charlie speaks, he doesn't look at me. "So you really can't play another show?" But words won't come. And the truth is, I'm not sure what I want anymore.

STELLA:
Lemon Gags

My friends, it certainly was a turbulent time for our embattled ukulele-toting maverick and her ragtag gang of malcontents. Suddenly they found themselves at the center of controversy, both vilified and idolized, depending on who you asked. So it was no wonder why, as our down-trodden diva trudged home from school one cold after-noon not long after Thanksgiving, her head was weighed down with troubles. She felt herself slipping back into that deep funk she'd fallen into at the beginning of the school year. The Holiday Talent Show had happened only the night before and, depressingly, Mudslide Crush had won. Her own aborted band, formerly the sole happy diversion in her otherwise gloomy new life, would never play another show.

Worst of all, she was still feeling guilty about Olivia.

Okay, here's the thing. Since the Bash I'd felt like a real jackass for pressuring Olivia into going onstage. That night, after Mr. Brenigan shut off the music and everybody else was taking down the equipment, I'd noticed her sitting alone on a stool in the corner, her shoulders hunched and her eyes closed.

"Are you all right?" I'd asked her.

"Fine," Olivia had said after a moment. "I'm . . . just fine."

But I could have sworn her whole body had been shaking.

Now, as I trudged up the front steps to my house, I wondered if I really *had* gone too far that night. Maybe my mother was right—I was selfish and irresponsible, an immature kid who never considered how my actions might affect anybody else.

Once inside the house, something felt different than normal. Where was the noise? Usually when I came home in the afternoons the TV would be blaring and the step-monkeys would be up to something chaotic, perhaps sliding down the stairs or pretending to swordfight in the kitchen. It was normally my job to make sure they didn't maim themselves until my mother came home from the lab. But today the house was strangely calm.

And then I noticed my mother. She was on the sofa, her jacket on.

"Hi," I said, confused. "What are you doing home so early?"

"I thought we'd go out," she said, grinning. She explained that Tim and Andy were at a friend's house and that she'd decided to duck out of the lab early. "We have an hour or so to ourselves before they're back. It's time we restarted our tradition. Want to grab a coffee somewhere?"

For a second or two I didn't answer. The woman had been MIA for practically the whole three and a half months since we moved, and now all of a sudden she wanted to spend time together? Why should I let her off so easy? Why not let *her* feel the silence for a while? I almost said no.

But I didn't. A part of me still wanted to believe that my mother and I could be friends again. So fifteen minutes later the two of us were seated at a table in Paperback Joe's, the little bookstore café next to the photo place in the center of town, me with my usual decaf mint mochachino and my mother with a caramel latte. Back in Arizona we used to go out and talk over coffee all the time, just the two of us. But it'd been a while.

To my shock, my mom asked, "So, how goes the lemonade crusade?"

This was the first time she had ever brought up the subject—even though I'd been clipping Naomi's articles about the lemonade controversy and leaving them in obvious places. There were rumors that the town was even thinking about expanding the bottling company deal to the middle school in order to make improvements to the school grounds. But my mother, so self-absorbed lately, had never said a word about it. Not even once.

"Great," I lied. I was trying to fight back my growing pessimism, but it was hard. After all, what did hallway signs matter now that the Talent Show was over? "Sarah Beth Adams got into an argument with Mr. Dewonka in class yesterday. A bunch of kids are boycotting the soda machines now, but Mr. Dewonka says the whole thing is ridiculous. He thinks everybody should stop complaining and just be thankful that we have the new scoreboard. He also says that as part of the deal, a small percentage of the money we spend on soda is going to come back to the school to buy new sports equipment. So he says we should all be happy."

"This is Mr. Dewonka?" my mother asked. "The history teacher?"

"Right. Anyway, Sarah Beth, this mousey little girl with a voice like a fairy princess, stood up to him. She told him that since the students were never included in the decision-making process, taking the machine away was kind of like taxation without representation. You should've heard her."

My mom raised an eyebrow. "Sounds like you're causing quite a stir in your new school. Be careful, Stella. Don't get yourself in any more trouble. I'm concerned about you."

"Don't worry about me. I'll be fine." I felt my resentment thaw a little. I could see that, in her own way, my mother really *was* trying to make things okay again. "How about you? How are things going with the Frankenstein plants?"

My mom took a thoughtful sip from her steamy mug. "Not so well, actually," she said finally. "One of the investors we were counting on is thinking of backing out. If we don't see real progress soon, I'm worried the whole project might be scrapped."

"Scrapped? But . . . how can that be, Mom? You just started."

"Well, I knew when I took this position that there were no guarantees." She shrugged as if she was trying to be philosophical about it, but it was obvious that this was eating her up inside. I felt sorry for her, but at the same time I couldn't help feeling secretly excited. If the plant thing didn't work out, would that mean we might move back to Arizona?

That's when, out of the blue, my mom came out with an unexpected peace offering. "I'm sorry I haven't been around for you much since we moved. It can't be easy for you to start again in a new place, and I know you've been mad at me about it. It's just that right now I feel like I have my big chance to do something really important with my life, to make a real difference. And I feel like I have to give it everything I have for a while." She watched me from over her cup. "But it won't last forever. I promise."

From across the table, I felt her eyes searching my own until finally I had to look away. "It's okay," I said. "Don't worry about it."

The truth was, as hard as it'd been for me, I really did

understand how much the monster ferns, or whatever they were, meant to my mother. Ever since I was a little kid, she'd talked about making the world a better place. Imagine finding a way to make plastic that doesn't hang around as trash in our ecosystems for thousands of years. For a genius biochemical environmentalist like my mom, this project must have felt like the Holy Grail.

"I'm so glad you understand," she said with a grateful smile. "Thanks for bearing with me."

I took a sip of my coffee. It was delicious and warm. And suddenly, sitting in that shop, I felt a little better. In fact, for one misguided moment I actually believed things with my mother might be back to the way they used to be. We were friends again. We could talk without getting mad at each other—*would* talk, in fact, whenever we had the chance. I even felt excited that we still had more than half an hour left before we had to head back home. I had so much to say. I wanted to tell her about my new friends and my new school, about the A.V. Club and the Patties and so much else. I wanted to let her know how hard it was to fit in, and how depressed I felt about Lemonade Mouth ending. For one crazy moment I even decided I would show her the envelope that I still carried in my pocket, maybe ask if she thought there was a chance that the IQ results could be wrong.

But that was when my mother's cell rang—and brought me crashing back to reality.

When the call ended my mother said, "Oh, I'm so sorry, Stella, but that was the lab." All at once I felt my excitement fizzle away. I knew what was coming. My mom sighed. "I know this is incredibly bad timing . . . but there's a problem and I absolutely *have* to go back. I'll make it up to you, I promise."

A moment later we were back in the car, our coffees abandoned in the shop not even half-finished. "Listen, I'll drop you off at home so you can meet the boys when they get back," my mother was saying as she sped out of the parking lot. "Leonard won't be home until late tonight. I'll leave you money so you can order a pizza for dinner."

But I wasn't really listening. I felt like a fool.

As far as I knew, nobody even tried to change Olivia's mind about playing at Bruno's. *I* certainly didn't. I wasn't going to pressure her again, and anyway, I was sure she wouldn't do it. But then one chilly Tuesday morning as I got off the bus at school, I noticed a bunch of kids crowded on the asphalt near the side entrance. At first I wasn't going to bother finding out what the fuss was about. My breath billowed out in a thick fog, and my fingers were so cold I wondered if they were going to fall off. I wanted to get my freezing butt inside as fast as possible. But then I noticed Wen, Mo and Charlie gathered together at the back of the crowd, so I shoved my hands into my jacket pockets and walked over.

"What's up?" I called.

They didn't answer, exactly. In fact, nobody in the crowd was saying much, which seemed kind of strange. Wen just nodded toward the wall, which I still couldn't see because I hadn't made it around the corner yet. "Check it out," he said.

As I walked through the crowd, kids stepped aside. And then I saw what everyone was looking at.

Drawn in chalk across the brick windowless wall were five gigantic faces. *Our* faces.

"Do you *believe* this?" Charlie asked quietly.

All I could do was stare.

Whoever had drawn it was pretty good. Sure, Wen's glasses were a little too rectangular, Olivia's face a little too long and the green of my hair a little too fluorescent, but it was definitely us. And there was a lemon stuffed into each of our mouths—gags preventing us from talking. In thick purple lettering across the top of the wall was a long quote from someone I'd never heard of:

WE ARE ALL, EACH AND EVERY ONE OF US,
MISUNDERSTOOD. AND EVERY INDIVIDUAL IS ABNORMAL.
BUT I ASK YOU, WHERE'S THE FUN IN NORMAL?
—PHINEAS FLETCHER

Scribbled below that in yellow chalk was:

I'M A FREAK AND I'M PROUD!
LEMONADE MOUTH—DON'T STOP THE REVOLUTION!

I didn't know what to say.

And then I noticed Olivia, the real-life Olivia, standing beside me. As I'd walked up to the wall, she must have been only a few steps behind. I watched her face as she took in the giant picture. Her eyes lingered on the words.

She stayed quiet for a long time.

It was at the end of that day that Olivia came up to Wen and me as we got ready to walk home. Without any explanation, she told us she'd decided to sing at Bruno's after all. When she walked away, we turned to each other, speechless. We couldn't help grinning.

Lemonade Mouth was back.

CHAPTER 7

Only the pure in heart can make a good soup.
—Ludwig Van Beethoven

OLIVIA:
Houseplants, T-Shirts and Unrequited Desire

Dear Ted,

Happy New Year! It's study hall so I thought I'd write. Sorry it's been so long. I have so much to tell you.

First, I'm resting my voice. Want to know why? Bruno asked us back again this Thursday because our first gig was packed. Half the crowd was in costume too. Most of the football team came as potted plants. Stella called them up onstage and they line-danced behind us. The audience went nuts. And remember I told you about those guys that don't like us, the ones in that other band,

Mudslide Crush? Well, even _they_ showed up, although they mostly just stood quietly at the back with Bruno. We made a point to welcome them, though, and everybody cheered. Anyway, I'm doing a little better now. I figure if I stare at the back wall and don't think about the people, I'll get through it. I'm not saying it's _easy_, just okay.

I'm glad you received the extra CDs you asked for. Want to hear something bizarre? So many kids have been walking around listening to our music that Mr. Brenigan said nobody could play it anymore. Can you believe that? He banned it! Nobody is allowed to listen to anything in the hallways anymore. Personally, I think the rule has more to do with the soda machines than anything else. I think Mr. Brenigan is tired of people asking about them. Anyway, you can probably imagine how effective the rule is. It's easy to sneak an earphone in when you want to. My guess is, more people are listening to us in the corridors now than ever before.

My horoscope today: "Take unexpected changes in stride. Don't lose faith. Get ready for a startling new experience." They got that right. Charlie's friend Lyle is selling Lemonade Mouth posters and T-shirts. I can't tell you how strange it feels walking around the hallways and seeing your own face on other people's chests. But not to worry. It's only a matter of time before Mr. Brenigan outlaws the T-shirts too.

Here's another crazy update: Remember I told you about Catch A RI-Zing Star, the annual WRIZ battle of the bands with the most popular local groups from all over the state? I don't know if you've heard of it, but Desirée Crane won two years ago, and this year the winner gets a one-album deal with Epiphany Records. Anyway, Naomi Fishmeier started a call-in campaign to get us on the band list. We're not even signed up, but just the idea of it gives me stomach cramps. Performing at the Providence Civic Center wouldn't be like playing at a pizza place. It holds over <u>fourteen thousand seats</u>. And the Catch A RI-Zing Star finals are shown on TV, so who knows how many other eyes would be watching?

You asked about Wen . . . well, he's pretty much the same as ever. Still oblivious around me and weird around Sydney. But I'm getting used to it. After all, do I have any choice? And no, I'm <u>not</u> going to tell him how I feel, because if I do it might drive him away, and then I really would be miserable. I guess some people are meant to find connections and others aren't, and I'm obviously in the latter category and that's just the way it is. I'm okay with it, so stop worrying about me. All right, sometimes I get secretly furious at the boy. A couple nights ago I stopped by his place (it's stuffed with Sydney's furniture now—his living room is almost as chaotic as ours!) to write some new songs. When I got there, Sydney told me Wen was out with his dad and would be a little late so she suggested we paint our toenails. When Wen finally came back and found us laughing on the sofa, our bare feet in the air, cotton balls between our toes, his face went all glum. Unfortunately, Sydney and I had a hard time fighting back the giggles. We weren't laughing at <u>him,</u> it was just the situation. But Wen left the room without saying a word. He went back to his usual easygoing self as soon as we were writing upstairs, away from Sydney. Still, I couldn't help fuming at how clueless he is.

But I felt sorry for him too. Poor, sweet, confused kid.

Miss you,
Olivia

P.S.
Oh my God. It's 11 p.m. and I'd already sealed and stamped your envelope but I had to rip it open so I could add this note.

Are you ready for this?

Believe it or not, I just heard "Skinny Nancy" <u>on the radio.</u>

Let me set the scene: Brenda and I were sitting at the kitchen table playing a quiet game of gin rummy with the cats flopping around our feet and on our laps. Suddenly the phone rang so I picked it up and Wen's voice said, "Turn on WRIZ right now." And then he hung up. It was a weird message, but I did what he said and flipped on the radio. And there we were. I couldn't believe my ears. Turns out, WRIZ has a local music show and somehow they got our CD. Brenda and I threw our cards into the air and screamed. Which sent the cats fleeing in all directions. But we didn't care—Lemonade Mouth was on the airwaves!

WEN:
Have You Hugged Your Radio Today?

I rushed down to the kitchen to tell my dad we were on the radio but when I got there I found him and Sydney standing really close to each other, Sydney's arms over my dad's shoulders and his hands on her waist. I felt like maybe I was interrupting something, and I expected them to pull apart, maybe act uncomfortable, but they didn't. My dad just turned his head a little in my direction with this dopey grin.

"What's going on, kiddo?"

"Uh . . . we're on the radio," I said, muffling the excitement in my voice because I suddenly felt embarrassed. "Right now. WRIZ."

After a brief hesitation, his expression changed. "You're kidding."

I shook my head.

He and Sydney suddenly let go of each other and my dad switched on the kitchen radio. Sydney shrieked. While my dad cranked up the music, she grabbed my shoulder and squeezed. George came pounding down the stairs in his pajamas to find out what the fuss was about. When I pointed to the radio it didn't take him long to understand what was happening. It was a weird feeling, the three of us staring at the speakers, grinning from ear to ear, and George hopping all over the place like a Mexican jumping bean.

My dad wrapped his arm around my neck. "That's it, kiddo. The big time. You're a star!"

"Yeah right," I said. I knew it wasn't true, of course. But still, I couldn't help feeling lightheaded.

Then everybody started hugging each other and I guess I got caught up in it because a few seconds later I realized too late that I had my arms around Sydney and she had hers around me. It wasn't a long hug or anything, but it was long enough. The moment after she gave me a quick congratulatory peck on the cheek and then moved on to George, I stood there frozen. I realized to my horror that for a brief instant I'd sensed her breasts, under her sweater, actually brushing up against my shirt. It was an awful realization. I forced myself not to think about it.

When the song was over the DJ said, "That's brand new from a band called Lemonade Mouth off their CD *Live at the Bash*. Call and let us know if you like it as much as we do."

After that the phone started ringing one call after another. "How much did you hear?" I asked Mo.

"Almost all of it. I was studying right by my radio when you phoned. Can you believe this? My dad's bursting to call Calcutta."

Stella whooped so loud I had to hold the phone away from my ear.

But I couldn't blame anybody for being excited.

I had a hard time keeping my eyes closed that night. After all, who in their right mind would have predicted in September that the five of us would get this far? I wondered if this was how Dizzy felt the first time he heard himself on the radio. I know it was just some late-night exposure on a local radio show, but it felt like a big deal. Like we'd made it to the next step.

But even as those exciting thoughts bounced around in my head, my alarming brush with Sydney's breasts refused to stay blocked from my mind. It was a disturbing memory, not just because it was so unforgivable to think about the touch of your dad's fiancée's boobs, but also because I realized that the experience had left me feeling completely different than I would have imagined. I guess I wouldn't have been surprised if I'd felt some terrible, secret thrill, but that wasn't what happened, exactly. It was weird. I don't know if I could even explain the emotion I'd felt, but whatever it was, it hadn't been what I'd expected.

As I lay in bed that night it took me forever to get to sleep.

MOHINI:
A Surprise Visit

One morning I show up for my regular every-other-day session with Mrs. Reznik and discover that she's out sick. At the front office they tell me it's just a cold. I don't think anything of it. But she's not back four lessons later, so by then I'm concerned.

"She's *still* out?" Charlie asks around a mouthful of PB&J. It's lunchtime and as usual my friends and I are sitting together at the Freak Table. "Wow. How long has it been now? A week and a half?"

"Almost two," Stella corrects him.

Wen frowns. "It's hard to picture Mrs. Reznik getting sidelined by just a cold."

It's true. She's such a Rottweiler of a personality that it's easy to forget she's actually just a little old lady. Until now I think part of me doubted anything could ever hold her back—I figured she was too stubborn to allow it.

Late that afternoon the five of us are assembled on the front steps of Mrs. Reznik's duplex apartment. Her address was easy to look up because she lives right in town. In my arms is a big plastic container of chicken soup we made ourselves at Olivia's. Stella knocks.

We wait for a long time. Nobody answers. Stella tries again.

Olivia eventually shrugs. "Maybe she's not home."

More time passes and still nobody comes. And it's only then that it occurs to me how our idea of surprising Mrs. Reznik might have been a mistake. Maybe we should have called first. And then disturbing questions start to form in my head. When was the last time anybody actually heard

224

from her? What if Mrs. Reznik is lying dead on the floor in there?

Wen shifts his weight from one foot to another. "Should we knock one last time or just give up?"

But that's when we finally hear something. Somebody shuffling. A throat clearing. "Hello? Is someone there?"

I'm so relieved to hear that familiar cough. "It's us, Mrs. Reznik. Lemonade Mouth. We heard you're sick so we made you some chicken soup."

After a pause, I hear the lock unlatch and then the door opens, but only as far as the inside chain allows. Mrs. Reznik's eye and nose appear in the crack. "Oh, it *is* you," she says, her voice raspy. There's an uncomfortable moment where everybody's just standing there not saying anything. It's hard to tell if she's happy to see us or if she wishes we'd leave her alone.

"We don't mean to disturb you," says Olivia. "You're probably feeling too sick for company. We can just leave the soup and go."

"No, no. I'm a little better today. Let me undo the chain." The door closes and then after a brief moment it opens again, this time wide.

And what I see nearly makes me drop the soup.

It's Mrs. Reznik all right, but not like I'd ever seen her. And it isn't just that she's wearing a bathrobe and slippers. What catches my attention the most is her head. Her elaborate brown wig is gone. Her real hair, I now see, begins startlingly high on her forehead, and is short, wispy and gray.

I think she senses that we're all staring because she seems to straighten her back and hold her head higher, like she's determined to maintain her dignity.

"Are you sure this is all right?" I ask, absolutely mortified now.

But Mrs. Reznik remains composed. "Yes, please come in," she says calmly. "Just give me a few seconds to make myself presentable. I'll be right with you."

After that she disappears through a doorway while we wander inside. The apartment is small and smells of cigarettes. I find a little, tidy kitchen and leave the soup on the counter. Embarrassed, everyone drifts into the living room. It's modest but cheerfully and neatly decorated. There's an armchair, a sofa, a TV and lots of pictures, most of them photographs of people I don't recognize. There's a button pinned to one of the lampshades that says, "I'm Pro-Accordion, and I Vote!"

Nobody looks comfortable, but we're here now so what can we do?

"Check this out," whispers Charlie, nodding his head toward an enormous bookshelf that completely covers one wall. It's filled top to bottom with CD's and old vinyl LPs. I scan the titles. Lots of classical, but an impressive mix of other stuff too. Amy Beach, John Cage, Patsy Cline, Tommy Dorsey, Ella Fitzgerald, The Gypsy Kings, Gary Karr, Edgar Meyer, Leontyne Price, Jonathan Richman, Michelle Shocked and even a whole row devoted just to the Beatles. Everything's in alphabetical order.

"I'm sorry I don't have much to offer you," Mrs. Reznik says, finally joining us after what seems like forever. "Would you like something to drink? Tea?" She has her wig on now so she looks more like how we're used to seeing her. Instead of the robe, she's now wearing penny loafers, slacks and a silk blouse with a scarf. There's even a little makeup around her eyes.

226

"You're not supposed to offer us anything," I say. "You're sick."

She waves her hand dismissively. "Oh, I'll live. It's just a really bad cold. Honestly, I'm practically over it."

She takes a seat. In the oversized, winged armchair she looks tiny. She gestures for us to sit. Wen and I settle on the rug. Charlie, Stella and Olivia take the sofa.

The conversation starts out pretty stiff. Even though she was the one who brought us together, none of us really knows her very well—even me, after all the individual lessons. She isn't an especially easy person to get close to. She thanks us for the soup. We talk a little about how we were about to play our third Bruno's show. Soon, though, we sort of run out of things to say. Mrs. Reznik's hands stay rigid in her lap. She seems unsettled at having company and I wonder if we're the first visitors she's had in a long time. After a silence that seems to last forever, she reaches for a pack of cigarettes on the little table beside her. She puts one in her mouth, lights it and takes a deep drag.

"I don't mean to be rude," Olivia says. "And I know it's none of my business, but did you ever think of quitting smoking?"

I'm surprised and even a little embarrassed that Olivia actually said this, but Mrs. Reznik seems to take the question in stride. "My doctor keeps telling me to," she says, slowly exhaling a giant fog of smoke. "But I tell him that when I die I want to be buried with my lighter in my hand and a menthol ultramild in my mouth."

She says it so seriously that at first I don't realize she's kidding. But then a wry smile appears on her wrinkled face. Wen starts laughing and she does too, and I realize it was just a joke, her way of telling us that, for better or worse,

227

she's comfortable with who she is and doesn't plan to change. On the one hand it's kind of sad because I think smoking is such a nasty habit, but on the other hand, who am I to make another person's decisions for them?

Pretty soon everyone else is laughing too and I have to admit, it *is* pretty funny.

After that, we all seem to relax a little. We end up drinking tea after all (I make it) and gabbing about a lot of things: the school, how crazy it is that they keep playing "Skinny Nancy" on the radio, Mrs. Reznik's life growing up in Philadelphia, her time in the Newport Philharmonic. I ask her about a black-and-white shot on the mantel where she's sitting at a table full of handsome looking people in fancy dresses and tuxedos. Turns out, one of them was Prince Albert of Monaco. I'm amazed. I try to imagine what it must feel like to be in the company of royalty.

"Oh, don't be too impressed with titles," she says. "Still, though, you don't eat with a prince every day."

Wen asks about a serious-faced young woman who appears in several of the photographs.

"That's Gina, my daughter. She lives down in Florida."

"Do you see her often?"

"Once or twice a year, depending."

Funny, I had no idea she even *had* a daughter.

As usual, even as the rest of us are chatting and laughing, Olivia doesn't say much. But I notice that she seems to spend more time watching Stella, Charlie, Wen and me than she does watching Mrs. Reznik. I wonder what's going on in her head, but I've already resigned myself to the fact that Olivia will forever remain a mystery.

My eyes are drawn again to the picture on the mantel, the one with Mrs. Reznik and Prince Albert, and I wonder once more about being in the presence of royalty. But then I turn back to see the current Mrs. Reznik, older and even more dignified, listening with an amused smile as Stella tells a funny story. She really is an impressive person—accomplished, kind, oddly charming, uncompromising in her views but generous with her time. In her giant winged chair, she even looks like she's holding court.

And suddenly I no longer wonder what it would feel like to be in the presence of royalty. Because I realize I already am. 🖋

CHARLIE:
Upside-Down Universe

A lot of surprising things were happening around that time it seemed like my whole life was turned on its head and everything suddenly felt like it was moving incredibly fast.

After WRIZ began to play our songs in their regular rotation even more people started showing up to see us at Bruno's. After only 3 packed shows Bruno agreed to let us play on a weekend.

I was actually feeling ambition for the 1st time ever. Even offstage. I watched a lot less TV and started working harder at school. So my grades improved. Which got my Mother off my back. I even began paying attention to how I looked in the morning I picked out a clean shirt every day and combed my hair. OK so I still didn't have Mo, the 1 girl I thought about all the time, but at least there were a bunch of other girls talking to me now. And sure, without Lemonade Mouth most of them would never have looked at me twice but who was I to complain?

The biggest bombshell came when I found out that Naomi's campaign to sign us up for Catch A RI-Zing Star actually worked. Another band on the original list had to drop out so WRIZ called us only 2 weeks before they were supposed to tape the Show. The news that we got a spot took a lot of people by surprise. Especially Ray Beech and Dean Eagler. Mudslide Crush had been trying for years but had never been selected. Of course most of that crowd had been badmouthing us for a long time but now it got even worse. The day after we found out about the Competition, Ray and Dean and their friends showed up to school in handmade T-shirts that said stupid stuff like

LEMONADE MOUTH KILLED MY PUPPY

or

GOT LEMONADE MOUTH? USE MOUTHWASH!

"What's the matter with everybody?" I overheard Ray grumbling to Scott Pickett. "They act like those freshmen are God's Gift to Losers or something what a scam! Damn freaks are just too stupid to see through it."

But it didn't really bother me. By now the fact that our success bugged those guys so much was beginning to feel kind of like a compliment.

It was all an incredible rush.

And even though I knew we were a long shot at best I still couldn't help thinking about what might happen if we actually won Catch A RI-Zing Star. Look at Desirée Crane. OK sure she was pretty much a 1-hit wonder but "Call a Doctor, I Bin Infected (by Your Love)" had been all over the radio for a whole summer. And this was the Competition that started it all.

After our 4th Bruno's show I was breaking down my set when I sensed somebody walk up behind me. "Not bad

Charlie." A guy's voice. "You really know how to play." I turned and almost fell over when I saw who it was.

Scott Pickett.

I wasn't sure if he was serious or if this was just an opening line before some kind of slam. But I said "Thanks."

"I'm happy for you." With his thumb he gestured over his shoulder to the big crowd that'd come to see us. "This whole Lemonade Mouth thing. Mo told me you guys were pretty good. I didn't believe her at 1st but she was right. I'm a fan."

I think my jaw might of hit the floor. For a few seconds we stayed frozen with me crouched on the ground and him just standing there looking uncomfortable until he finally said "See you 'round" and walked away. I felt completely weirded-out.

But then I had a thought. What if this was just him trying to inch closer to Mo? I'd seen the hangdog face he had whenever she was nearby. Maybe he figured that if he sucked up to me then I would tell her what a great guy he was and eventually it'd help him get her back?

But maybe that was too cynical. Something Aaron would come up with.

In any case, Scott acting friendly to me at *all* was weird. But like I said there were a lot of surprising things going on around that time.

WEN:
Tamworth Rules

Olivia was waiting at the bus stop at the corner of County Road and Massasoit just like she promised, her Scooby-Doo backpack over her shoulder. Mo arrived soon after, followed by Charlie and Stella. Each of us was bundled for the cold. Once more I tried to get Olivia to tell us what this was all about but she still wasn't talking. And once more all she said was, "Do you trust me?"

Everybody looked exasperated. "Of course we do."

But she still didn't seem sure. "Wait then. You'll see."

It was a weird feeling, not knowing where we were going. And dragging myself out of bed at 7 a.m. wasn't something I usually did on a weekend. But the invitation was so strange. Olivia had asked us one at a time, pulling me aside one Friday afternoon at the end of January. Her face had been flushed and her voice unnaturally timid, even for her. She wanted me to go with her somewhere but she wouldn't say where. Except that it was going to take most of the day and that we wouldn't be back until late afternoon. She also asked if I had a passport or a birth certificate.

"Sure, I got a passport two years ago when we went to Mexico. But what do I need that for? You planning on taking us out of the country?"

"No," she'd said, her face serious. "But make sure you bring it, okay?"

The whole thing was a mystery. An adventure. How could any of us help being curious? Besides, I had nothing better to do. If I stayed home I'd probably end up helping my dad move more of Sydney's furniture into the house. Seemed like there was something new every day. She was always rearranging things, dragging strange-looking desks and tables in or out of storage, even finding new stuff at antique stores. Or else I'd end up spending yet another Saturday listening to the two of them make wedding decisions. If I was asked to comment on one more doily pattern my head was going to explode.

Eventually the shuttle to Providence pulled up and we

got on. The bus had that certain plastic smell, one I was familiar with from my occasional trips into the city, sometimes to catch a concert at Club Babyhead or maybe just to go to the used record store. The seats were half full. I took the spot next to Olivia, Charlie grabbed the seat across the aisle, and Stella and Mo sat behind us.

Olivia was barely visible inside her giant gray parka and a wool cap that looked like her grandmother might have knitted it for her. She wouldn't look up. Her foot kept tapping on the floor.

"What's the matter? You all right?"

"I'm fine," she said.

But there was definitely something weird going on. She was usually pretty quiet, but I'd never seen her like this.

"Oh, I almost forgot. I brought you something." I fished around in my pocket until I found the tiny plastic compass I'd pulled out of my desk drawer at home. I reached across and gave it to her. "In case we get lost on the way to wherever we're going."

Mo, who was leaning over the back of our seat, laughed. For the first time that morning, Olivia smiled. I couldn't help studying her face. Something had seemed different about Olivia lately, only I couldn't put my finger on exactly what it was. It wasn't just that her hair was looking better now, softer, like she'd started taking care of it. It was something more basic than that. So what was it? I searched for clues in her eyes, but that just confused me even more. Until that moment, I would have said they were brown, but now I saw that they weren't—at least not completely. On the edges they were lighter, almost yellow. They were amazing.

She pulled me out of my thoughts when she suddenly said, "I'm glad we're doing this, guys."

But doing what? At the station in Providence Olivia led

us to a booth where we bought tickets for the Greyhound to Boston. An hour and a half later we were on yet another bus, this one heading up toward New Hampshire. But the time flew. We had a lot to talk about. WRIZ was playing us regularly by then, not just "Skinny Nancy," but "Back Among the Walls" and "Singing a New Song" too. We were call-in favorites. And our first weekend show at Bruno's had been an even bigger success than the first three midweek ones. The place had been jammed to the legal limit, there were people lined up outside, and almost everyone was in costume—since our first performance was Halloween night, it'd sort of become the thing to do at our shows. At the end of the night Bruno told us he wanted to book us for Saturday nights twice a month at least through the spring. We were still getting over the shock.

As we left Massachusetts Stella finally asked. "Are you going to tell us where we're headed or what?"

"Soon." The farther north we traveled, the faster Olivia's foot tapped. After we passed through Manchester she closed her eyes and started taking long deliberate breaths and exhaling slowly.

"Relax," I whispered into her ear. "Everything's going to be all right." I put my hand on her arm to try to calm her.

But then as we passed the first exit off I-93 into Concord, a change came over her. She gripped the arm of the chair, sat up straight and opened her eyes. "Okay," she said. "I'm ready for my confession."

Charlie shifted in his seat. Mo and Stella's heads appeared above us again. We waited.

She took a deep breath. "Fifteen years ago there was this boy, a seventeen-year-old high-school dropout, a troublemaker, who met this girl at a party. She was sixteen.

A few months later he got her pregnant. At the time, she was living with her mother and the boy was staying with friends because he didn't get along with his own father. They were both terrified about this news, but they decided he would move in with the girl and her mother, and they'd have the baby."

I watched Olivia's face. Her eyes were focused on the back of the seat in front of her, her fingers picking absently at the fabric on the arm of her chair.

"Finally, the baby came. It was a girl. Even with three of them taking care of her, life wasn't easy. The boy and the girl started fighting. It didn't help that when the baby was a year old the boy had to serve a three-month jail term for stealing stereo equipment from a department store. It wasn't his first offense. And then one day soon after he got out, the girl packed her bags, called a cab and never came back."

Charlie was leaning forward to hear her. "She just . . . left?"

Olivia nodded. "It wasn't her first time. She had problems even before she met the boy. Fights. Drugs. Her mother said she'd already disappeared four or five times in two years, once for three whole months." For the first time, Olivia looked around at us. "The girl had issues."

I nodded.

But she quickly added, "Not that I'm saying the boy was any saint either. He wasn't. But the thing is, with the girl suddenly gone and him the only parent for the baby—well, it seemed to have an effect on him."

"Olivia, who are we talking about?" I said finally. "Your parents?"

"Please, just listen okay? This isn't easy for me. I don't usually . . . do this."

From the sound of her voice, I got the feeling that was an understatement.

"Okay, yes," she said after a moment. "I'm talking about my dad. But it's important for you to understand that he was a good father to me. Really. I remember. A lot of guys in that situation get scared, they run off and leave the kid for somebody else to deal with. But he didn't. He bought me dresses, sang to me. He was always reading me stories. He was a big reader, still is. And no dummy either." Her face got a little softer. "Did you know I'm named after a character from Shakespeare?"

We all shook our heads.

"Twelfth Night," she said, with the faintest of smiles. She sat back again. "Anyway, he got a job driving a cab, earned his high school equivalency, and when I was six he even started taking night courses at Rhode Island College. He was going to be an English teacher."

"So what happened?"

"Well," she said after a pause, "when I was eight the cab company had cutbacks and they laid him off. And then nobody would hire him because of his prison record. Anyway, my grandmother says he started drinking again. And one night he got so desperate he decided to hold up a store."

I realized her face had gone pale and she was sweating.

"Listen, Olivia," Stella said. "If you don't want to say any more you don't have to."

"No, I want to," she said slowly, still pulling at the threads of her armrest. She closed her eyes. When she spoke next her voice was almost a whisper. "My dad didn't even own a gun. What he pointed at the old man behind the counter, the storeowner, was a fake, a plastic toy. But it looked real enough. Enough to scare the storeowner, anyway. His name was Gustavo Costa. The thing was, he'd prepared himself for this. He'd been robbed before and he wasn't going to let it happen again if he could help it. So he reached under the counter and pulled out a Smith & Wesson .38 revolver. His wasn't a fake."

That's when the bus turned onto an exit ramp and somewhere at the far edge of my consciousness I heard the driver announce our arrival at the next stop. But I didn't catch a word of it. All my concentration was on Olivia.

She kept talking. "My dad dropped the toy and put his hands in the air. But then Gustavo moved closer and my dad lost his head. He jumped him and they struggled. The gun went off in the old man's leg." She opened her eyes and looked at me. "He died in the hospital later that night. The irony is that the doctors said it wasn't actually the bullet that killed him, it was a heart attack."

The doors swung open and other passengers stood up and made their way down the aisle. Some of them gave us curious glances.

"This is our stop," she said. But without making any move to gather her things she added, "I'm not making any excuses for what my father did. That man, Mr. Costa, he was a real person with a real life of his own. He grew up in Portugal in a little town called Sintra. He didn't have any family, but he collected pottery. He was sixty-three. I *know* my father did a terrible, awful thing. And he knows it too. But he's still my dad and I love him. You guys have to understand that he isn't a monster or anything. I need you to tell me that you believe me about that. And that you'll give him a chance."

I felt a strange jumble of emotions. First, a terrible sadness—not only about what had happened but also that she'd carried all this inside her for so long. But at the same time I was grateful she'd told us, that she'd finally let us in. I suddenly wanted to touch her again.

"You will, won't you?" she asked. "Do you trust me?"

"Yes, Olivia," I said, taking her hand. "We're your friends. We trust you."

The lady behind the desk at the Tamworth State Penitentiary greeted Olivia by name. She asked us to empty our pockets while another guard checked bags and took copies of our paperwork. Everybody seemed to know Olivia. And they appeared to be expecting us, like everything was arranged in advance. Eventually we were led into a large visiting room, and then to a table where a small, neatly combed man sat with his hands folded in front of him. As soon as Olivia was close enough, he stood up and wrapped his arms around her while the guard watched.

"Everybody," she said, smiling nervously over his shoulder. "This is my dad." I was surprised. He didn't look anything like her.

"You must be Stella," he said, turning around. "And Charlie, and Mo. And *you*," he said, giving me what seemed like an especially warm grin, "you must be Wendel." His voice was surprisingly soft and gravelly, and I couldn't help smiling too. It felt somehow comforting that he and Olivia had that voice in common. I held out my hand to shake his, but he stepped away, glancing at the guard. "Sorry, can't do that. The rules. No physical contact except with family members, and even then only twice each visit, once at the beginning and again at the end. But it's a pleasure finally to meet you all."

We sat down, him on one side of the table, all of us on the other. At first the conversation was polite and stilted. He asked us about ourselves and about school and as we answered his questions I could almost feel the guards' eyes watching. But that passed. Eventually I forgot about them, and the six of us were gabbing and smiling like we were sitting at somebody's kitchen table. Soon, of course, the topic turned to Lemonade Mouth. Olivia's father, whose name was Ted, was interested in hearing all about our recent shows. He wanted to know everything. And every now and then I watched him beam at Olivia. He obviously adored her. And I realized that meeting her father made me look at Olivia differently. She was somebody's little girl.

At one point, Charlie made some joke about the spare decorations in the room—there were only a couple of official looking documents taped onto otherwise blank walls—and everybody laughed. And that's when I saw it, the family resemblance. Their faces lit up in exactly the same way. They had the same eyes. And then she smiled at me and I realized something else—that she finally looked happy, maybe the happiest I'd ever seen her.

It was only then that I fully appreciated what this meeting meant to her. To them both. And for that moment at least, I really did suddenly feel like everything was going to be all right. 🎤

CHARLIE:
Welcome to Our Freak Show

Just when the future looked bright for Lemonade Mouth everything started to fall apart. 1 disaster at a time.

Some people say it was Destiny. Like maybe our band was doomed from the start. Others think it was the Competition. That getting into Catch A RI-Zing Star jinxed us somehow. And of course there's always the lingering rumor—a joke really—that some of the Mudslide Crushers put a hex on us. OK it *was* weird how the bad breaks kept coming 1 after another. The disasters piled up so quickly and made such a mess of everything that some people even gave them a name:

"The Curse of Ray Beech."

But any rational person could tell you that was a ridiculous idea. The things that happened next were only the Universe keeping its natural balance. Things were getting too good. It was time to knock us down a few notches. Yin and yang.

Anyway whatever you believe the reason was, the tide started to turn on us the night before Catch a RI-Zing Star. In retrospect we probably should of cancelled that last Bruno's show since it was so close to the big day. Plus all of us were already way tired. Being in a band was a lot more work than I'd ever imagined. But Fridays were always big nights for Bruno and we'd already made the commitment to him.

Even before we started playing I had an uneasy feeling. While we set up our instruments, Ray Beech and Dean Eagler strolled in. They'd come to our 1st show of course but they'd kept quiet and stony-faced at the back. Tonight they wore tight, suspicious grins while they sauntered over to shoot the breeze with Bruno. Bruno was a middle-aged guy with beefy arms and Elvis sideburns and a loud laugh. I already knew he was friendly with Dean and Ray from the times Mudslide Crush played the restaurant. Still, it made me nervous to see him yucking it up with them.

And then just as we began our 1st song, Dean and Ray parked themselves at a table right by the stage. It wasn't like they were doing anything wrong exactly but the way they were smirking made me uncomfortable. I tried not to let them bother me too much though. To be honest, by the middle of our set I was kind of distracted anyway. Something was wrong with Mo. She kept slipping up. Which was way weird for her.

"You OK?" I whispered at the end of "Back Among the Walls." She'd missed the start of her solo by 2 whole beats which was a mistake she'd never made before her eyes looked kind of droopy too. "You don't look so great are you sick?"

"It's just allergies" she whispered back. And then almost more to herself than to me she said "I can't afford to be sick." Then she sneezed for about the 3rd time in maybe 30 seconds.

For a brief moment the red rims around her eyes made her look like she'd been crying it reminded me of that awful telephone conversation we'd had the night before the Bash. Even after all this time her comment that I didn't fit into her stupid grand plan still bothered me. I felt a sudden flash of frustration. With her and with myself.

Right then and there I decided that as soon as the show was over I would flip a coin. Heads I'd ignore everything inside me that said I should keep my stupid mouth shut and let her know how I really felt. That I thought about her all the time and cared about her in a way I'd never cared about anybody else before. Tails I wouldn't.

Stella started the opening chords for "Everyday Monsters." All over the big room kids in bizarre outfits sprang from their UFO tables and began dancing and jumping around. But Ray and Dean still looked like Cheshire Cats—you know, like in that Disney cartoon. All smiles. By the end of the song while everybody else was applauding I heard Ray say "Losers!" He was pretending to cough but his table was close enough that I distinctly heard the word. It made Dean laugh so Ray did it again and again. "Losers! Freaks! Losers!"

I looked over at Wen. He shrugged and mouthed the words "Ignore them." He started playing the opening riff to "I'm Singing a New Song."

But Ray and Dean didn't stop. By the end of the song they were both coughing out words and giggling like idiots. Unfortunately that's when a flock of new arrivals like Patty Norris and Beth Blanchard and a bunch of the other Mudslide Crushers wandered in from the cold. Dean and Ray called out to them and everybody greeted each other.

That's when Mo started up "Anywhere But Here." That song had an extended moody beginning with no words. As the bass moaned and Wen's trumpet came in I couldn't help watching Ray and Dean whispering and smirking they were definitely up to something. Stella and I exchanged glances but what could we do?

After that, everything happened pretty quickly. About a minute into the music Ray stood up, grinned at his friends and then stepped casually onto the stage.

"Good evening ladies and gentlemen" he said grabbing the mike "and welcome to our freak show!"

I couldn't see Olivia because she was standing behind us waiting for the vocals to begin but Mo and Wen and I nearly jumped out of our skins. Stella glanced over at me obviously unsure what to do but when I almost stopped drumming she shot me a look and her mouth formed silent words. *"Keep playing!"*

I did as she said.

My eyes searched the crowd for Bruno but I couldn't see him. He must of gone into his Office or something.

Dean gave Ray the thumbs-up sign. Ray leered back at his friends. Some of them were still standing and others had taken seats at the last empty booth at the back. At 1st they seemed surprised to see Ray onstage but now they sat up and started clapping and hooting.

"I'd like to take this moment to introduce the band" Ray said like some twisted Master of Ceremonies. "Over here with the green hair, biker duds and toy guitar we have that bright bulb known as Stella Penn. Don't get too close she bites!"

Dean and the kids at the back laughed. Most of the others just looked confused but some of them joined in the clapping. I guess a lot of them probably weren't sure if this was supposed to be part of the show or not. After all, it wasn't the 1st time other people had joined us onstage.

By then Stella had moved in closer. Her face had reddened a little but she kept her cool I heard her say "Come on, Ray, knock it off."

But Ray ignored her. "And on my left are Charlie 'Buffalo Boy' Hirsh—a kid with a personality so electrifying that he's been known to fall asleep in the middle of his own sentences—and Wendel Gifford aka the one, the only . . . Woody the Horndog!"

There was more hooting and laughter. Wen glared at Ray like he could of socked him a part of me wanted to throw down my sticks and lunge at him too. But neither of us stopped playing. I guess we all had the crazy idea we could still salvage this somehow.

"Ray" Stella said a little louder "you're making a complete ass out of yourself."

"And finally" he said, gesturing with a sneer toward the other side of the stage "let's not forget that psycho of song, fresh from the insane asylum, Miss Olivia Whitehead . . . or of course my very own buddy's Hindu-honey ex, his former dark-skinned delight . . . Mo 'Hot Curry' Banerjee!"

I couldn't believe he actually said that. The ass! When I looked, Olivia was shrinking against the wall and Mo was leveling a glare at him like I'd never seen. I searched for Bruno again. Still nowhere in sight.

Back in the audience some of the kids started to sense what was going on. A few of them began calling out "Off the stage! Get him off!" Others banged on the tables or stomped on the floor.

Boom! Boom! Boom! Boom!

Ray spread his arms. "Ladies and Gentlemen, I give you . . . *Loser Mouth*!"

Dean and his other friends howled with laughter. Other people shouted or shook their fists.

And then Ray started singing.

"Eeeeat, Freaky Freshmen, eeeeat . . . before your tiiiiiime is done . . ." He was using a fake raspy voice that I guess was supposed to sound like Olivia but just sounded ridiculous. "You are pathetic looooosers, you weeeeigh a tonnnnn . . . enjoy this buuuurger, have anooooother one . . . Eeeeat, Freaky Freshmen, eeeeat!"

The muscles in my jaw went tight. By the end of his chorus all of us had finally stopped playing. Ray kept going, though, following the rhythm of the table-pounding and foot-stomping. Finally a couple guys stepped onto the stage and tried to pull him away. And then Ray took a swing at them.

That's when everything went crazy.

Even more crazy I mean.

In all the Chaos it was impossible for me to see everything or to tell exactly what happened when. Dean jumped into the mess then the next thing I knew a bigger fight broke out. The crowd pushed forward. I finally saw Bruno his face was all flushed and he was pressing his way through the mess but he was too far away to stop it. Pretty soon the entire place was going nuts with kids grabbing each other and knocking over tables and others screaming and shouting somebody stepped toward Olivia but Stella shoved him away. I tried to call out for everyone to calm down but it was no use there was nothing I could do but stand back. I looked desperately around at Mo and the others but they looked as stunned as I felt. I don't think any of us could believe what was happening.

Before our eyes our peaceful night of music had morphed into anarchy.

MOHINI:
Death Warmed Over

"You sure you're well enough to do this, Mo?" my dad asks tentatively. "You look a little pallid."

It's the next morning and I'm slouching quietly in the passenger seat of my dad's Subaru. Finally we pull to a stop at the corner near the medical clinic. The world outside looks bitter and gray, with fat, dime-sized flakes of snow just starting to drift onto the windshield. It's only eight-thirty but the clinic parking lot is already full. There's a nasty flu going around. For almost two weeks the drop-in waiting area has been jammed with bleary-eyed people blowing their noses.

I gather my strength and pull the door handle. "I'm fine, Baba. I'm just having a hard time waking up."

The truth is, my head is pounding and I feel like there's a golf ball lodged in my throat. I dragged myself out of bed, though, because I'm scheduled to volunteer until 11:00 and I can't afford to pull out at the last minute. I'm counting on a good recommendation from this place.

Standing in the cold as the Subaru pulls around the corner and out of sight, I wave and even manage an upbeat smile. But after the previous night's fiasco, I actually feel anything but upbeat. Okay, so the riot at Bruno's fizzled out about as quickly as it started and, amazingly, nobody got hurt, but Bruno was clear that Lemonade Mouth would never play there again. And the fact that he banned Mudslide Crush too was no consolation.

What a disaster.

And that wasn't even the worst of it. At home after the show I got into a big argument with my father, which is why we hardly said anything to each other in the car this morning. Last night, Charlie's mom ended up giving me a ride in her van and Charlie insisted on walking me to my door, so when my dad met me at our front porch he found the two of us together. Even before the Hirsh's van pulled out of the driveway I knew from the suspicious look on my father's face that something was up. He didn't waste any time getting to it, either. He didn't even ask me how the show went. He just said, "I want you to stop spending so much time with that boy."

"Wh-what?" I didn't understand right away. My head was still reeling from what happened at Bruno's.

"You know exactly what I mean, Monu. He seems a little too comfortable around you."

Now, this was maybe the third or fourth time my dad had brought up Charlie so by now I understood what he wanted. All he was really looking for was a little reassurance. He seemed to need that every now and then. Normally I would have said something like, "Baba, you really don't need to worry. There's nothing going on between Charlie and me. We're only *friends*. I promise. Okay?" And I'm sure if I'd said that then everything would have been all right.

But last night I was in no mood to go through the same old script again. It had already been a tough evening, I wasn't feeling well and I could barely think straight. Plus, over the past few weeks I've been mulling over what Selina Sinha said in temple about her dad, and I've been getting frustrated about having to constantly assure my own father what a good girl I am. It's ridiculous. Am I really so wild?

Besides, deep down I knew that my dad's concerns were well founded. For weeks I've been careful to avoid being alone with Charlie. I'm almost always the last to arrive at our practices, and the first to leave. I never linger at the Freak Table. I avoid walking with him to class. But I never stop thinking about him.

That's the frustrating truth.

Of course, last night I didn't tell my dad any of that. Instead I kind of lost my temper. "Leave me alone, Baba! I'm not a little kid!"

He was obviously surprised. I don't normally talk back to my father. Briefly I saw that panic again, that tightrope look. But then almost immediately the shadows on his face darkened. "You're too young to know what's right for you! Certainly too young to have ideas about this boy!"

I didn't answer. I could feel my pulse booming in my temples.

"Oh, you think I'm blind?" he continued. "You don't think I see the way he looks at you? Or how you look at him?"

I glared at him. This felt like the last straw at the end of a long day full of last straws. "Well, what if I *do* like him!" I snapped. "Is that really so wrong? Don't you know me well enough to trust me to make my own decisions? I'm fourteen, you know, and perfectly capable of making good choices, but you just want me to keep being your little girl, don't you? Well, I'm not a little girl anymore, Baba, and this isn't Calcutta!"

His eyes went wide. He wasn't used to me talking this way to him, and to be honest, neither was I. When he spoke next, his voice was quiet and his teeth were clenched.

"While you are living under this roof, child, you will respect your family's wishes."

His words were certain but his eyes still looked frightened. And then it hit me what my dad's been scared of all this time. He's scared of *me*. He's afraid of what might happen if he loses control.

And what's more, I realized that I've been just as frightened of that as he's been.

All at once I felt like a jerk for putting him through this. My dad doesn't always come off that way, but he's actually a real softy and he's only doing what he thinks is best for me. I was so confused I didn't know what to say.

"What's the matter here?" asked my mother from the stairs.

Finally, still locking eyes with him, I said, "I guess I don't really have much choice, do I?" Then I marched upstairs, brushing past my mother in a frustrated huff. I didn't even end up telling them about what happened at Bruno's.

Anyway, last night left me a little rattled.

Now, in front of the clinic, I fight back a shiver and

trudge up the walkway to the building, ignoring the dizziness in my head and the ache in my bones. I don't have the flu. I have a big Pre-calc exam to study for this weekend and even though the class is killing me, I had to get special permission to get into it as a freshman so I'm determined not to blow it. Plus I have a Social Studies paper due on Tuesday, and a debate tournament on Thursday. Not to mention Catch A RI-Zing Star in just a few hours.

I can't be sick. I refuse.

The world spins slightly as I lumber through the front entrance. I guess I'm not paying enough attention to where I'm going, because in that little decompression area between the two sets of automatic doors I walk right into a raggedy blue dough-boy jacket.

"Oops, I'm so sorry," I say. I look up. It's a heavyset guy in one of those fuzzy caps with earflaps. It's a couple of seconds before I recognize him.

"Charlie . . . ? What are you doing here?"

"Waiting for you."

This is strange. I feel my heart quicken. Waiting for me? Why? And why this morning, of all mornings?

"I'm a little late," I say. "I have to sign in."

"Just a second." He pulls off his cap. "I . . . I have something I need to say to you. It won't take any time, I promise."

I feel the blood rush into my face. But I wait.

"Mo, I . . ." He blinks and then looks away, first at the ceiling and then his feet. "I'm sorry. This isn't easy for me."

The automatic doors slide open and a blast of arctic air catches my back. We stay quiet. An old lady with a cane ambles past us and through the second set of doors. Even when we're alone again Charlie keeps gazing at the floor. Which feels weird. What's he doing?

249

"For a long time I've wanted to tell you something," he says finally. "But, well, you were with Scott and then after that it just didn't happen. Besides, I wasn't sure how you felt about me and I didn't want to wreck anything. Plus there's Lemonade Mouth and all that. And so I thought maybe it'd be better if I just kept quiet. But the truth is I don't think I can keep my mouth shut anymore."

I fidget. He isn't making sense.

He takes a deep breath. "Thing is . . . I like you, Mo. And more than just as a friend, I mean. I always have. There. I've said it."

Now I'm having a weird flashback to last night's conversation with my dad, because Charlie's words sound confident but his eyes look scared. He waits for me to say something, but I feel a sudden, rising panic, along with a tsunami of other emotions. Part of me wants to jump for joy. Another part is terrified. I've been trying so hard to stay in charge of all the different pieces of my life, but now it feels like everything is spinning out of control. I need to keep my eyes on the big picture. Sweating and shivering in the cold, I suddenly need to get away. I want to run. Clear my head somehow.

Which is probably why, before I even know what I'm doing, I find myself biting Charlie's head off.

"Didn't we already talk about this?" I snap. "Didn't we already agree that you and I are going to be friends and nothing more? Oh, Charlie . . . you know about my grand plan. You know about my family. You know I can't. What are you trying to do? Ruin what we already have?"

I see the hurt look on his face, but the words are already out.

That's when I duck my head and storm past him, feeling

like the frontrunner in the contest for Heartless Dragonlady of the Year. And now my head is throbbing worse than ever and even my knees feel weak. But I remind myself that I have no choice. Right now I'm focusing on school and nothing else. Later I'll study medicine. Eventually, I'll marry another doctor or a lawyer or something like that—somebody as ambitious as me. I have my plans. And Charlie isn't part of them.

And I'm not about to start tiptoeing around my parents again. No way.

As I stagger over to the volunteer desk, my whole body is shaking. Behind the desk sits a tubby, bleached-blonde lady reading a magazine. She must be new because I don't recognize her.

"I'm Mo Banerjee," I say, trying to stop my teeth from chattering. "Do you have the sign-in sheet? I'm scheduled to volunteer this morning."

But she doesn't reach for the binder. Instead, she looks me over, one eyebrow raised.

"I don't think so," she drawls after a moment. "I think you better take a seat in the waiting area. Don't take this the wrong way, honey, but you look like death warmed over."

STELLA:
Last of the Fallen Heroes

There sat your Sista Stella, alone at the kitchen table only vaguely aware of the sounds of the step-monkeys watching their Saturday morning cartoons at the other end of the house. Staring listlessly at her dreary breakfast of a bran muffin and kiwi juice, she fought off a sudden desire to yank open the fridge, fry up the entire package of Canadian bacon she knew was in there, and then shove every juicy, meaty morsel of it into her mouth.

But fortunately, I got hold of myself.

It was just a brief moment of weakness. Still, who could blame me for feeling defeated? What *was* it with me? Why did everything I ever do go somehow awry?

But then I remembered the letter from the guidance counselor. It lay open on the nearby counter. After a long string of dismal grades, the school wanted to evaluate me to find out if I had a learning disability. But I didn't care to take any more stupidity tests. There was no point. I already knew what the problem was.

Eighty-four.

And that brought me back to the grim memory of the previous evening. *It's over,* I thought. *The final day of the revolution.*

"Don't take it so hard, Stella. It's only a band, not the end of the universe."

I looked up. I hadn't even noticed my mother coming into the kitchen but now suddenly there she was setting her newspaper and coffee cup on the table and pulling up a chair. Like me, she liked to sleep in on the weekends. Had I spoken my thoughts aloud? From the way she was wrinkling her forehead at me, I decided I must have.

"Really, I'm worried about you," she continued, her eyebrows pulling together. "Don't you think you've been taking this Lemonade Mouth thing a little too seriously? I'm concerned. You're obsessing about it. Maybe it's not such a bad thing if you and your friends set it aside for a while."

I glared at her. Of all people, how did my *mother* get off accusing *me* of obsessing?

The bathrobed scientist sat back and eyed me for a few moments. "Listen, I have an idea. Leonard wants to take everybody ice fishing this morning on Otis Cove. Doesn't that sound like fun? You should come with us."

"Ice fishing? You're kidding, right?" I had a hard time picturing my mother, the former sun queen of the southwest, spending hours in the freezing cold over a hole in the ice. My mom: Nanook of the North.

"Sure, why not?" she said, ignoring my look. "Clea's coming too. Why don't you join us? Try something new?"

"I can't, Mom. I have other plans today. In case you forgot." Not that I had any delusions about Catch A RI-Zing Star. I knew we'd be competing with the best of the best and that we'd probably get dropped in the early rounds. Still, my mother didn't have to act like it didn't matter.

I made sure to give her a hurt look but the woman hardly seemed to notice. "But didn't you tell me you don't have to be at the Civic Center until two o'clock? We can head out this morning and still be back in plenty of time."

And that was when she moved her arm to pick up her coffee, which is how the newspaper finally caught my eye. It was the *Opequonsett Gazette,* the weekly town rag that came out every Saturday. From where I sat it was upside down, but even so I noticed a small headline toward the bottom of the page. It said: NEW VENDING MACHINES SET FOR MIDDLE SCHOOL.

I pounced across the table. "No! I can't believe it!"

"What's the matter?" my mom asked, pulling her coffee back in surprise.

I spun the paper around and scanned the story. It was

short, only a couple of paragraphs. "Those *creeps*! How can they do this again? How can they just *ignore* us?"

"Ignore who? What is it?"

I kept reading until I'd finished the last sentence. "The twentieth?" I looked up. "That's *today*!"

"What is? Tell me what's going on."

I flipped the paper around again and slid it back across the table, jabbing my finger at the bottom of the page. "Take a look! They're pulling the same scam at the middle school now. Without any involvement from the students, somebody made a deal with the soda company just so they can put a stupid fountain in the school courtyard. Now they're going ahead and swapping out the lemonade machine. And they're doing it *this very morning*!"

For a few quiet moments she read it to herself. Then she looked up. "Stella, you're going overboard again. This is not a big deal."

"Not a big deal?" Wasn't she even a *little* offended about what was happening? But I was mad enough at the school board already and didn't want another fight with my mother just then, so I tried to stay as calm as I could. "Don't you see? They're exploiting kids. They even know that we know it. That's why they're sneaking the big corporate soda dispensers in on the weekend when they think nobody's paying attention. They must've kept it quiet, hoping to avoid a protest. But it won't work," I said, standing up. "I'm going to stop them."

"What? Where do you think you're going? And what exactly do you plan to do? March over to the middle school and chain yourself to the doors?"

"I don't know yet," I admitted. "Do you think that would work . . . ?"

She gaped at me like I was about to sprout a new nose. "No! And I advise you to clear any foolish ideas like that out of your head *right now*. Knowing you, you'll probably get yourself arrested or something. I think you've already made quite enough trouble for yourself lately, don't you? I just don't understand it. Why must you insist on pushing this lemonade issue?"

"It's *oppression*, Mom. It's about having choices and getting respect. How can I stand back and do nothing?"

For a moment she just stared. "Stella," she said finally, "it's okay to want to do the right thing, but you need to think things through first, make sure your goals are achievable." I couldn't stop the prickly annoyed feeling growing inside me. She was using her patented Voice of Wisdom again. "And even that doesn't guarantee anything. Wanting to change the world doesn't make it happen. Believe me, I should know."

I was about to argue back, but something in my mother's voice stopped me. "Why, Mom? What do you mean?"

She sighed. "I'm thinking about handing in my resignation from the lab."

I could hardly believe my ears. "You're kidding. Why would you do that?"

"The project is still having problems. Remember how I told you about the investor that was thinking about backing out? Well, he did. And now some of the others are threatening to do the same. I'm in charge, so they see our failures as my fault. They're right, too."

"So . . . you're just going to give up?"

"If I don't resign, they're probably going to fire me pretty soon anyway." She shrugged. "Maybe it's a good thing. Maybe we can move back to Arizona. I know you've wanted that for a long time."

I felt like all the air had been let out of my lungs. My mom was right, of course—this *was* what I'd wanted since we moved here. But now that it might actually happen, I wasn't happy at all. "But . . . how *could* you?" I said, amazed to hear myself arguing about this. "You really wanted this job. You were going to save the planet. And you always used to tell me *never* to quit, no matter what."

My mother was quiet for a few seconds. "Look," she said eventually, "I guess I'm finally realizing that one person can only do so much. Eventually I have to stand back and admit that I'm killing myself over a battle I can't win." She leaned forward significantly. "And you should too."

For a few seconds I couldn't even speak. This was the lady who once spent two nights in the branches of an ancient sycamore to prevent a construction crew from chopping it down.

My mother. My *hero*.

Only now she was breaking my heart.

"So . . . even though you know I believe this lemonade machine issue is about right and wrong, you're saying I should just drop it and go ice fishing?"

Her expression hardened. "There's no need to get sarcastic, Stella! I'm only saying that it doesn't make sense to keep fighting a lost cause!"

I could have swelled up and popped. I'd put up with a lot from my mother over the last few months, and believe it or not I'd kept my mouth shut plenty. But this took the proverbial cake. It was simply way too much to bear.

"I can't believe you, Mom! Who was it that always told me to stand up for what I think is right? That the people who make a difference are the ones with the courage to keep fighting even against the odds? Who used to keep me out of school just so I could go with her to protest rallies at wetland development sites? Well, you're not the only one who wants to change the world. In case you didn't notice, that's exactly what *I'm* trying to do *too*!"

"But you're being unrealistic! Don't you get it? Stop acting so stubborn! For once in your life, Stella, use your head!"

"Yeah? Well, maybe I'm *not* using my head. But even though I'm not brilliant like you, at least I'm *trying* to do something and not giving up! Unlike some people I know who throw in the towel just because of a setback! I'd rather be a dummy with a heart than a genius without a backbone!"

As soon as I'd said that, I felt terrible. What had come over me? But I couldn't bring myself to take it back.

My mother's face went pale.

And that's when I finally noticed my sister standing in the doorway. She was wearing her bathrobe, a towel wrapped around her head. I didn't even know Clea was home. "Nice going, Stella," she said, glaring at me. "What's your *problem*?"

I just stood there, unable to look my mother in the face. For a moment neither of us spoke. Finally I ducked my head, pushed past Clea and shot up the stairs. I slammed my bedroom door and started fishing through a pile of clothes like a madwoman. I threw on long underwear, jeans and a sweater. It was snowing pretty hard outside the window and I knew I'd need warm clothes if I was going to wait outside the middle school. I yanked on my comfortable boots and stormed back out of my room. My mom's cell phone was on the antique desk in the upstairs landing. I grabbed it.

I shot down the stairs and slipped out the side door. I didn't want to run into my mother again. And I knew better than to ask for a ride.

CHAPTER 8

*I put my heart and my soul into my work and
have lost my mind in the process.*
—Vincent van Gogh

CHARLIE:
The Curse of Ray Beech #1.
Thrashing into Oblivion

A drop of sweat trickled down my forehead to the bridge of my nose my hands slapped the congas again and again. I heard myself let out a grunt. My palms were already raw but I didn't stop I kept moving smacking the drums faster and faster every first and third downbeat hammering the timpani or one of the larger tom-toms.

BOOM shaka BOOM shaka BOOM BOOM BOOM!

After that horrendous conversation with Mo I'd trudged back home only to find the house empty. Shivering from the cold I grabbed the box of chai I'd bought at Mo's store all those months before. Last bag. I slammed the kettle onto the stove and charged down to the basement I needed to pound this feeling out to work the humiliation and frustration through my arms. The drums would absorb it all and transform it into a logical pattern. Order out of Chaos. That's the beauty of percussion. It's therapy.

Brother you are beyond hope. You are absolutely the biggest loser the world has ever known.

I closed my eyes and tried to block him out I felt the blood rush into my head my arms knew where to land and I let them wander wherever they chose and this time they chose the timbales and I shook the hair out of my face and another bead of sweat flew through the air.

WHAM a-bam-ba WHAM a-bam-ba WHAM WHAM WHAM!

What had come over me? What moronic impulse led me to the clinic this morning? Why did I have to go and ruin everything?

But I knew what it was.

Don't blame ME for this, Stammer Boy. If you'd done it my way and played it cool and casual everything would have turned out just fine I wasn't the one who stood there tongue-tied making a complete ass out of himself.

I gritted my teeth and concentrated on the rhythm that swelled and swirled around me like a hurricane that blocked out everything else and filled my ears and heated the cold basement with a power that didn't come from me but from someplace far away it centered my thoughts and tuned out everything but the sound.

BAM diddy-bop BAM BAM diddy-bop BAM BOOM chugga-chugga BAM BOOM!

Somewhere in the distance I thought I could hear a long steady note like a high-pitched whistle but it was only a secondary vibration from the cymbals and chimes a new thread in the fabric of sound it sent a fresh rush of Adrenaline and I kept pounding.

Balance. Every drummer knows how important it is. Like when you adjust a drumhead you need to crank the key just enough to keep it in tune or every time your stick lands only exactly the right amount of tension and relaxation in your wrist will produce the perfect tone and that's what I was counting on right now because if I came up with a rhythm complicated enough and if I could keep it growing and evolving without letting it get out of control it would block out everything else.

WHACK rata rata WHACK CRASH rata rata WHACK BOOM WHACK CRASH WHACK BOOM!

It was a relief not to think. I let myself disappear into the noise until I almost forgot who I was. Sweat whipped off my face but I kept going and going and burning and burning my hands stinging even worse than before. I was concentrating on the crash bang thud slam smash smash smash! It wasn't only in my ears it was all around I could feel it in my chest my blood my bones. It was everywhere.

My own personal cosmic connection to oblivion.

After a few minutes I pulled back a little and my hands hammered with a little less fury. That's when I noticed that whistle again. Only now it was different. Less urgent. Like a toy train running out of steam. Even as my palms continued to pummel the drums I guess a part of my brain was starting to come out of its trance and it gradually dawned on me that the sound wasn't just in my imagination after all. I wondered vaguely what it was.

And then all at once I remembered.

My hands stopped in midair.

In a panic I flew up the stairs. Idiot! I'd left the kettle on the stove so long that it probably boiled dry! I imagined it so hot that it melted to the coils or exploded all over the kitchen. What if I was burning the house down?

I charged through the doorway and toward the oven. Over the spout only a ghostly thin column of steam evaporated into the air. Without thinking it through I grabbed the kettle by the handle and pulled it off the stove but unfortunately ours was one of those kettles made entirely of metal and I didn't think to use the oven mitt. Pain shot up my arm. It felt like it took forever for my hand to let go but then the kettle crashed to the floor and the lid fell off and the tiny amount of water still left inside spilled onto my shoes.

I stared at the scalded fingers on my right hand. They still burned. I couldn't help screaming.

OLIVIA:
The Curse of Ray Beech #2.
Wailing at the Wind

Dear Ted,

I don't know what to do.

I'm so furious I can't even speak.

Brenda said it might help me calm down if I sat and wrote it all out, everything that happened. So here it is:

This morning I woke up already feeling like crap. Bruno's last night was an absolute catastrophe, and I had a feeling that today, Catch A RI-Zing Star day, keeping calm until the afternoon would be a struggle. And then around quarter to ten Wen phoned. Mo had called and told him she had a fever of a hundred and two. Charlie phoned him too, from the medical clinic. He'd hurt his hand somehow. Second degree burns. Neither of them could play the show.

"So that's it. A complete disaster," Wen said. "I guess we have to call the WRIZ people and let them know we're backing out. There goes any chance of a record deal."

I couldn't believe it. I felt terrible for Charlie and Mo, but at the same time a part of me felt a weight lifting at the thought of not having to play to such a giant crowd after all.

But I'd never heard Wen sound so miserable.

"Wait," I said. "Don't call just yet. Maybe we can think of a way through this."

But that's when I heard Norman, Wen's dad, in the background. Wen must have covered the receiver because for a few seconds all I heard were muffled voices. When he came back, Wen spoke in a whisper. "Listen, I can't talk right now. I gotta get out of here. Meet me at Paperback Joe's in about twenty minutes?"

Remember Paperback Joe's, that bookstore café place? Well, Wen and I met there a couple of times when we were planning out new songs. It's walking distance and more or less halfway between both our houses. I got there first but I ended up waiting for about twenty minutes before Wen showed up. When he finally did, he looked as pale as the snow that was already falling hard outside.

"Don't worry, we'll figure something out," I said. To tell the truth, I wasn't convinced about it myself but I hated to see him so upset.

But it turned out that Catch A RI-Zing Star wasn't the only problem on his mind anymore.

"No, it's not that," he said gloomily.

"It's not? What is it then?"

He sank into the seat opposite mine. "My dad."

And so he told me the whole story. Over the past few weeks, Wen's father and Sydney have been trying to include him in the wedding preparations, but he doesn't want any part of it. He's been finding excuses to stay out of the house. He told me his dad has been pushing especially hard in the last couple of days, though, making obvious attempts to have another man-to-man talk, something Wen's been trying to avoid at all costs. This morning as Wen headed out to meet me at the café, his dad trapped him. He asked for help moving some of Sydney's furniture up to the attic. It would only take a minute, he said. And while they worked they could talk. Wen tried to duck out of it. He told him sorry but he had to run because I was waiting at Paperback Joe's. But his dad insisted.

"I was cornered," Wen told me in the café. "And then as we were heaving this ten-ton stone-topped coffee table up the stairs he asked me to be part of the wedding. He wants me to be his best man."

I waited for the problem, but it didn't come. That was it. "But that's great news!"

"No, it's terrible," he said, fiddling with a napkin. "I'm not doing it."

"Why not?"

He raised his eyebrow at me. "You just don't get it, Olivia. You never do."

It's true, I _was_ having a hard time understanding him. "Being your dad's best man is an honor. What's the problem? This isn't about Sydney again, is it?"

"What do you think? Of course it's about Sydney. Just because she's leeching onto our family doesn't mean I have to be happy about it. And it doesn't mean I have to help."

I guess even then I really didn't fully understand how strongly he felt. I laughed. "That's ridiculous, Wen! You're overreacting."

But he didn't think it was funny. He looked hurt. A couple of seconds later he threw down the napkin, grabbed his coat and headed for the door.

"Wen? Where are you going?"

He didn't answer.

I snatched my own coat and followed him out the door. "Don't be like that." He didn't slow down at all. He kept walking through the snowy parking lot, his hands shoved deep in his pockets. "Come on," I called, trying to catch up. "We haven't even talked about Catch A RI-Zing Star. We need to figure out what to do."

"Nothing to figure," he said over his shoulder. "We can't play, so we're out."

Soon I was right behind him. "Maybe. But still, let's talk."

"Maybe?" he said bitterly, not looking at me. "You're the one who believes in omens. Did you ever consider that the fight last night might have been a sign? Don't you think maybe it's time for Lemonade Mouth to call it quits?"

"No," I said, shocked to hear him talk that way. All this time, he'd always been the one convincing _me_ not to drop out. It felt strange to suddenly be the one doing the convincing. "I don't know. I'd just hate for us to give up so easily. We've worked too hard. This can't be how it's supposed to end."

That was when he spun around. "No? Then what's supposed to happen? And why did Mo get sick? Why did Charlie burn his hand? Face it, Olivia. It's a lost cause."

The snow continued falling around us. I felt it on my face, and I watched it gather in Wen's hair and on his jacket. Eventually he turned away. I watched him traipse across the first two lanes of Wampanoag Road. A plow passed between us, a loud scraping against the asphalt. By then, Wen was on the narrow island halfway to the other side.

"So what are you saying?" I called over the noise. "You're giving up?"

"Yes!"

"And you won't even take a second to talk?"

"No!"

I couldn't believe it. He was being so unreasonable. At the same time, though, I felt like it was all my fault. I should have kept my mouth shut about Sydney. Another big vehicle rolled by, a noisy city bus, the hourly shuttle to Providence. After it passed, he was still on the median strip watching me. Then he turned and continued across the other two lanes.

"But you can't!" I called out finally. "What if this is our last chance?"

He was on the far side now. And that's when he shouted back. The wind picked up his voice, lifting and lowering it so it was hard to catch everything he said.

"I'm surprised to hear you say that, Olivia! You of all people I would have expected to be happy about this! It means you're off the hook! You don't have to go onstage. That's what you wanted all along, isn't it?"

That hit me like a punch, but I refused to let it

show. "What if Mo and Charlie decide they can still play tonight? It's only one song!"

"Even if they do, I'm done!"

We stood staring at each other for a few seconds. Another car went by. That's when I suddenly felt a hot rush of anger. I screamed into the wind and snow.

"This isn't about Lemonade Mouth and you know it, Wen! This is about your dad and Sydney!"

I could see in his face that I'd surprised him. He'd never heard me yell like that before. After a moment he called back, "Yeah? What do _you_ know?"

That's when I lost it. Everything came bursting out of me. All the frustration and sadness I'd been bottling up, all the words I hadn't said, it all came bubbling up from somewhere deep inside. And once it started pouring out, I couldn't stop it.

"More than you!" I shrieked at him. "You don't know anything! You don't even know what you have!" The wind blew my words back into my face, but that only made me shout louder. You should have heard me, Dad. Even you would have been surprised. "At least you have a father who's around! You even have Sydney, and she's terrific and really wants to be your friend even though you don't see

it! My mom's gone and I don't even know where
she is! My father's in prison! And you have the
nerve to feel sorry for yourself? You big baby!
You jerk!"

I'm not telling you this to hurt you, Dad, but
you already know how I feel. And of course I know
you would change the situation if you could. But
everything was rising up inside me. I couldn't help
letting it out.

"And now you're backing out on all of us? Well,
think about this: I've been showing up and
standing in front of that stupid microphone even
though every nerve in my body tells me to run
away! I've been doing it anyway! So go ahead!
Give up! See if I care! You're right, I wasn't
the one who wanted to be in a band in the
first place!"

"Then why did you do it?"

I could hardly believe he needed to ask. Was he
blind?

"For you! I did it for you! You jerk!"

I started to turn away but I realized I wasn't
done. There was one more thing I had to get off my
chest before I could go. I'd promised myself I'd
never mention it, but that wasn't going to stop me
now. I stepped back to the curb and yelled it at the
top of my lungs.

"She's too old for you, Wen!" I shouted into

the wind. <u>"And she's in love with your dad! Get over her!"</u>

And then I finally spun around and stomped away.

I knew I'd strained my voice with all that yelling. I guess I figured if he was really calling it quits, then it didn't matter. And anyway, he'd made me so mad, how could I help but scream? Wen could be so stubborn sometimes! Why couldn't he see how good he had it? Didn't he see that I would have given anything to have what he had?

I staggered home in an angry fog, barely feeling the cold as it filled my lungs. When I got to the house, Brenda was on the sofa reading one of her printing and graphics magazines. At the sound of the door she looked up.

"You're back early," she said. "You only left an hour ago."

Then she saw my face. She asked what happened. I wanted to tell her that it felt like I'd been gone for ages, that Wen and I weren't talking anymore, that Lemonade Mouth was over. But when I opened my mouth, what came out was only a little more than a whisper.

My voice was gone. 🐾

MOHINI:
The Curse of Ray Beech #3.
The Shivers

I've made up my mind. I'm not getting out of bed. Ever.

I won't take my exams. I'm going to drop debate, tournament or no tournament. Pre-calc too. It doesn't matter.

I sneeze again. I ended up having to call my dad to pick me up at the clinic and for the past hour and a half I've been shivering in my bed and feeling the room spin.

My Social Studies paper? I'll take the zero.

Biology? Who cares if I let that go? *I* certainly don't.

It's an immense relief, like I've finally figured out a way to wiggle out from under a sleeping elephant.

But no matter how I try, I can't stop my thoughts from drifting back to Lemonade Mouth. Not that I *need* to feel bad. Naomi called a little while ago and she was positive that everyone would understand. Even Wen agreed—it isn't my fault that I'm too sick to play. Still, the thought of letting everybody down makes me want to shove my face deep into my pillow.

And then there's Charlie. How can I ever face him again? How could I have been so heartless when he's never been anything but sweet to me? Why did I have to go and toss him away like an unwanted pair of jeans? The bizarre part is, I'm *crazy* about him. There's no pressure with Charlie. He listens. He makes me feel special. I'm *happiest* when we're together.

But that's gone now. Blown to smithereens.

I'm going to spend the rest of my life hiding in my room.

My dad appears at the door. "How are you feeling, Monu? Any better?"

I shrug as if to say, "Maybe a little." And then I realize it's actually kind of true. At least the room isn't rocking back and forth anymore.

He comes over, takes the thermometer out of my mouth, and holds it up to the light, squinting. Finally he kneels down close and runs his fingers through my hair. "One hundred point two. Much better. I believe the acetaminophen is working."

"Baba," I say. "I'm thinking of maybe dropping Precalc."

He stops stroking my hair.

"I know it's late in the semester, but I'm pretty sure they'll let me take an incomplete. It'd probably show on my record, but at least I can try it again next year."

"But I thought you enjoyed Pre-calculus. And your grades are good."

"I do sometimes," I say, already feeling yet another pang of guilt. "And my grades *are* fine. It's just . . . I don't think I can handle everything on my plate right now."

His bushy eyebrows pull together. I know this is a disappointment to him. I see his face redden but finally he says, "If that's what you want to do."

"It's not that I want to, exactly. I think I have to."

"Fine," he says again, not looking at me. "If you can't, you can't."

"I'm sorry to let you and Maa down."

Finally the lines around his eyes soften and he looks at me again. "Monu, I've been thinking about what you said last night, about how you're capable of making good choices. Really, I have. And, it's true. You are an intelligent girl. I know you'll do whatever you think is right."

"Really?" I can hardly trust what I'm hearing. What's going on? Is this my dad talking?

He nods. "I suppose it doesn't really matter to medical schools whether you take calculus next year or the year after." He looks at me apologetically. "You know all I want is for you to be happy. It's just that I'm always thinking about your future."

I feel my eyes heat up with grateful tears. "Thank you, Baba."

He leans down and kisses my forehead. Even long after he's gone I still feel the touch of his lips on my skin. For what seems like forever I lie in my bed, alone in my room, staring at the windowsill. It feels like my sleeping elephant just woke up and walked away on its own.

But the feeling doesn't last long.

Eventually the phone rings. It's Stella. I listen quietly as she tells me what's going on. After I hang up, I take a deep breath. There's no question about what I have to do. And there's no time to waste. I climb out of bed and start pulling my clothes back on.

"Why are you out of bed, Monu?" my dad asks, following me anxiously as I rush to the front door.

"I have to go."

"But where? You're sick."

"I'm fine," I lie. "I'm okay."

And just when I'm about to stop and explain everything to him, the concern on his face suddenly fades and is replaced with a furious scowl. "It's that Charlie boy again, isn't it? That was him on the phone! You're running off somewhere to see him! Admit it!"

Now I feel like I could scream. I can't believe him! I'm so tired of being treated like a child.

"Stop it, Baba! Lay off me!"

I run outside and he follows, but I'm way ahead of him. The snow's coming down fast now. As I run down the driveway I hear him shout, "Get back inside, foolish girl!"

All at once I decide I'm not playing along with any of his weird insecurities anymore. I might not be in control of my life right now, but neither is he. I spin around. "What if I *am* going to see Charlie? Would that really be the end of the world? Didn't you mean it when you said I make good decisions? Don't you trust me?"

A few yards away, he slows down and then stops. Suddenly I'm seeing that fear in his eyes again, that tightrope look. "Of course I trust you. You know that. But—"

"Then stop running my life! And stop trying to make me into something I'm not!"

"But Monu," he says. "Like I told you, you must understand—I'm just thinking about your happiness . . . your future."

"You keep saying that, but I'm not sure what you mean anymore because right here in the present you're making me very unhappy! At this moment I'm just about the un-happiest person I know! Because you're right, I *do* like Charlie!" I almost gasp at my own words. But they're out now, so I may as well keep going. "I like him a lot, Baba! He's sweet and kind and I want to be with him but I *can't*—and it's only because I know that just the idea of it makes *you* so miserable! And I don't want that either!"

My dad looks stunned. "Monu . . . I—"

But I cut him off. "*Let me go, Baba!* Stop pushing me! And stop trying to make me your perfect little Bengali girl! That's not what I am! It's not what I'll ever be!"

I can see that I've startled him, maybe even hurt him,

but right now I don't care. I glare at him. I've had enough. And I think he sees that it's no use arguing because he doesn't answer. Even though it's snowing and cold and my dad doesn't have his jacket and my head and throat are killing me, we stand there in the freezing air for a while, facing each other but not saying anything.

WEN:
The Curse of Ray Beech #4.
Sentimental Slam

I lumbered home, a dark cloud over my head as I hurried through the falling snow. I took the side streets, saving time by cutting through backyards and the wooded areas between neighborhoods. The snow, about an inch deep by now, hid the icy patches, and in my rush I slipped and fell backwards, landing hard on my butt.

Sure I was mad. Okay, so I'd never seen Olivia so pissed off, but she didn't know everything even if she thought she did. Sydney was a leech. She didn't belong in my house. Or in my family. And she was definitely wrong for my dad.

What did Olivia know about that?

I couldn't stop my father from marrying her, but that didn't mean I had to like it. Or to agree to be the best man. Even Olivia should have seen that this was just too much to ask. *Way* too much! And it wasn't like I didn't appreciate what I had. I *did*. I just didn't think about it that often.

Still, the fact that I'd needed her to point it out to me made me feel lower than a sea slug.

And what about Sydney? It made me squirm to think that Olivia had somehow guessed the truth. Of all people, how did Olivia see so clearly how I felt? I hated that it was so obvious to her.

The worst part, of course, the part I could barely get myself to think about, was what Olivia had said about why she agreed to go ahead with Lemonade Mouth. She did it for *me*? What was that supposed to mean? Was she saying what I thought she was saying?

Replaying her words in my head, I could feel my face redden again.

I wanted to flush my head down the toilet.

By the time I reached my street, the wind had died down. My lungs took in the cold air and blew it out again. There was an eerie, quiet feeling. During my entire walk back, I don't believe I saw a single person. I might as well have been on some far away planet, an empty world of ice-covered roofs, parked cars and trees. All this in a spooky universe of silent, falling snow as far as my squinting eyes could see.

Glancing up at the sky, I couldn't help thinking about Olivia's clouds—how they can take whatever shape you want, but they can also block the view. I had plenty I wanted to block out. I was still fuming and embarrassed, and I just wanted to go home. It wasn't fair that my dad was marrying a woman so beautiful it drove me crazy. It wasn't fair that Lemonade Mouth couldn't play tonight. I wanted to yell, shout at the top of my lungs just like Olivia, but what would be the point? Nobody would hear me.

Finally I came to my house. The truck was gone. I ran the last few yards up the driveway and to the front door. Inside, I bounded up the stairs.

Some people say this is where fate played a role again. I don't usually buy into that kind of stuff, but looking back at that morning I can't say I'm so sure either way. It certainly was weird how one thing led to another. Anyway, the truth was, the whole time I was walking home I had to pee. And now that I was in my house, I honestly thought I was alone. So when I came to the bathroom, I didn't think about knocking. I just turned the knob and pushed.

And that was why I happened to open the door on Sydney just as she stepped out from a shower.

Dripping wet and completely naked.

For a second I froze. The bathroom was a cloud of steam but even so, there wasn't much I couldn't see. Her body was like the sketches she'd drawn. Only real, and right in front of me. I was so mortified that I think it took a moment for my brain to fully register what was happening.

But then she screamed. In all the steam and surprise, I wondered if she even recognized me in the doorway.

"Aaaaaaa!"

The scream was so loud and sudden that it scared me, too. And then we were both screaming. *"Aaaaaaaaa!"*

She made a futile attempt to cover herself with one hand while her other one swiped for the towel hanging on the rack. Horrified, I averted my eyes. "Oh my God, Sydney. I'm so sorry!"

Then I turned and ran.

Unfortunately, I forgot about the heavy stone-topped coffee table my dad and I had heaved up the stairs only that morning. It was long and narrow, and even though it didn't fit anywhere in our house, Sydney said it had sentimental value and she couldn't part with it. We were going to store it in the attic, but my dad and I had only gotten as far as the upstairs hallway, where it still leaned against the wall, legs out.

And that's how I ended up charging into one of its thick wooden posts. It smacked into my upper lip like a punch to the mouth.

"Oof!"

The collision was swift and sharp. I screamed again, only this time in sudden, terrible pain.

A few minutes later I lay swearing on the sofa downstairs, holding an ice cube to my stinging mouth. Every now and then I put a finger to my lip to see if it was still bleeding.

"Is it any better?" Sydney asked. In her bathrobe and slippers, she was standing over me, her forehead wrinkled in concern. "Maybe we should bring you to the emergency room."

"No, I'm fine."

"Are you sure?" She tried to brush my fingers aside to get a better look but I swatted her hand away. The truth was, my lip still felt warm. I was lucky I hadn't dislodged a tooth.

"Come on. Let me see," she said sympathetically. She tried again to move my hand and this time I let her. She came in close and squinted. Eventually she said, "Doesn't look good, Wen. It's still swelling. Better keep the ice on there a while longer. Your dad'll be home in a half hour or so. Should I call him now anyway?"

I shook my head. To be honest, I was surprised at the fuss she was making. She was being so nice to me and seemed genuinely worried. I hadn't expected her to care so much.

I have to admit I even felt a little embarrassed about it.

"Weren't you heading out somewhere, Sydney?" I asked even though it hurt to move my mouth.

She shrugged. "Just to the hair dresser, but I can make another appointment. Your lip is more important. Listen, I'll be right back. I'm going upstairs to find you some anti-biotic cream. We don't want an infection."

And then she shot out of the room. My fingers numb with the ice, I found myself staring at the place where she'd turned the corner at the end of the hallway. I was still feeling the dizzying aftershock of seeing her naked. It wasn't just the surprise of walking in on her; even more than that, it was the unexpected effect it'd had on me. And now all I felt was confusion. I'd thought I knew myself, but now I wasn't so sure.

What a morning.

Soon after that the phone rang. A minute later Sydney came back with a tube of cream in one hand, the phone in the other.

"It's for you," she said, holding out the receiver. "It's Stella."

STELLA:
The Curse of Ray Beech #5.
The Unwitting Vehicle of Cruel Fate

It was too icy to bike, so our shivering subversive slogged the mile or so on foot through the snow and biting wind to the middle school. I was glad I'd grabbed my mom's cell. As I walked I dialed my friends, each time crossing my fingers that they'd be around. All the while, I half-expected my mother's green Volvo to pull up beside me and for her to roll down the window, still furious. But it didn't happen. Eventually I arrived at the middle school parking lot. My pulse sped up when, at the rear of the building, I spotted the long white truck backed onto the loading area.

I ran over to look inside.

Nobody in the driver's cab. The cargo door was open, so I checked that too. It was empty except for one item: A Mel's Organic Frozen Lemonade machine.

My heart sank. I was too late.

But just then, your downhearted protagonist heard voices calling her name. Charlie, Olivia, Mo and Wen were approaching from four different directions. As each of them scrambled across the snowy field or slogged along the icy parking lot, I couldn't help noticing the bandage on Charlie's right hand. Or that there was something wrong with Wen's lip. It looked like somebody had clocked him.

"Holy crap!" I called out. "What *happened* to you guys?"

Neither of them answered right away. They seemed embarrassed. And even when their stories did come out, it all sounded kind of sketchy. I wondered how Charlie was supposed to play his drums tonight with only one good hand. And could Wen even blow into his trumpet with a lip like that? But I decided not to push them about it right then.

One crisis at a time.

"Well, thanks for coming," I said.

By then Mo and Olivia had reached us too. Then followed what I can only describe as an awkward silence. The four of them just kind of stood around, staring at their feet. Now, I may not have been the most perceptive person when it came to these kinds of things, but I could have sworn I felt a strange vibe in the air. Why weren't any of them looking at each other?

"What's going on?" I asked.

"Nothing," said Mo. But that's when I noticed that her face was an odd gray color.

"Really?" I asked. "Everybody *sure* they're okay?"

More quiet nods. More staring at the ground.

Luckily, whatever it was, it didn't last long. "Look," I said, pointing at the cargo area of the truck. "I'm sorry to say this now that you're all here and everything, but they've already moved the lemonade machine. I'm pretty sure we're too late."

And that's when everybody sprang back to life and seemed to put aside whatever cloud was in the air. They stepped around the back and peered in.

"The machine's still here," Charlie said, "so the driver must be around somewhere, right? Possibly inside setting up the new dispensers?" He looked back at us. "Maybe we could talk to him about not taking this one away."

"I doubt it'd be that easy," I said. But I thought about it. Charlie was right about the driver still being here somewhere.

Which gave me an idea.

Five minutes later two beefy men stood at the edge of the loading dock. One of them wore an oversized orange sweater that made him look like a giant pumpkin with glasses. "What's going on down there?" he called. "What do you kids think you're doing?"

The five of us were laid out spread-eagle in the snow, directly in front of the truck. I could feel my heart pounding in my chest.

"We're protesting the removal of the Mel's Organic Frozen Lemonade machine!"

His forehead wrinkled. "You're doing what?"

"You heard her!" Wen said. "We're not budging until you put it back. In order to move this truck you'll have to run us over!"

The two men glanced at each other.

A minute later they climbed down from the dock. Their boots crunched in the snow. Soon they were standing over us, staring quietly down into our faces. From where I lay, they looked upside down.

"A protest, huh?" the pumpkin asked. "How long you plan on sticking it out down there in the cold?"

"As long as it takes," I said.

The other guy had kind eyes, shaggy black hair and a stubbly beard. He looked kind of like a male Sista Slash on steroids. He chuckled. "Jesus, of all the crazy things . . ."

There was another silence as I watched their breath shoot out in long, puffy clouds. Soon I had to brush the snow from my eyes. It was coming down hard.

"Okay, have it your way," the pumpkin finally said. "We'll wait inside until you guys are ready."

And then they walked away, leaving us lying there on the ground. The two men climbed back onto the dock and disappeared through the door at the back, into the warmth of the school.

The wind picked up. I shivered again. "They're trying to break our will. Are you sure you guys are okay?"

That's when Mo coughed. A sinister, phlegmy cough that came from deep inside her lungs. "Jesus, Mo," I said. "That doesn't sound too good."

"I'm fine."

But that's when it came out that she'd practically dragged herself out of her deathbed. The rest of us tried to talk some sense into her but it was no use. "Mo, you can't do this if you're sick. It's not worth catching pneumonia or something. You should go home, back to bed."

"No," she said. "I'm feeling better. Maybe it's the excitement. Anyway, I don't care. I'm not getting up."

What could anybody do?

About ten minutes later the guys came out again. Looking down at us once more, the pumpkin blew into his cupped hands. By then the snow was freezing my back even through several layers of clothing.

Brother Slash squatted down. "Come on, kids. I gotta get this truck back. I'm on a schedule."

"Nope," Wen said. "We already told you the deal."

"And we don't care about your schedule," added Charlie. "We're not changing our minds."

Brother Slash rubbed his eyes. "And it doesn't matter that we don't have anything to do with . . . whatever it is you're trying to protest here? I just deliver the machines, and he's just the custodian. Why don't you wait until Monday so you can take this up with the principal or something?"

I had to fight to stop my teeth from chattering. "No."

Of course I understood that these two weren't the decision makers here. But they were all we had, and through them I was pretty sure the message would eventually rise up the ladder. And there was no way we could wait until Monday. By then the machine swap would already be history.

The pumpkin took a step forward. The way he was looking at my arm, I had the sudden feeling he was about to reach down, grab me and force me away. But I squirmed. Even though he was at least twice my size, I gave him the most threatening glare I could muster. "Don't you *dare*!"

283

He froze, his eyes wide. He looked unsure for a moment, but he backed off.

After that, they used scare tactics. The pumpkin sneered at us while Brother Slash hopped into the truck and started the engine. He revved it for a while. Perhaps he imagined that this would be enough to send the inconvenient anarchists scurrying out of his way. But it wasn't. Eventually he gave up and came grimacing out of the cab.

"Dammit, Phil," the disappointed pumpkin called to him. "I can't wait here all day."

Brother Slash, whose real name apparently was Phil, narrowed his eyes. "Okay, kiddies. Enough playing around. You better move your butts away from this truck right now or I'm calling the cops."

I have to admit that until that moment, I sort of liked Phil. Not anymore. At the thought of the police, I considered jumping up and running away. How far did we really want to let this go?

But that's when I heard Olivia's voice, so raspy and tortured it was more of a series of croaks than the already breathy voice I was familiar with.

"I'M . . . NOT . . . GETTING . . . UP."

My God! What had happened to her? She sounded like a crank call! Sure, she'd been quiet the whole time, but Olivia was *always* quiet. And what about when we'd spoken on the phone? Had I done all the talking? Now that I thought about it, perhaps I had.

And then Mo said, "I'm not moving either." Wen and Charlie were quick to follow. "Not a chance," they said. "No way."

Picture it. Five supine agitators shivering in the snow, four of them in bad shape, and yet none of them agreeing to move out of the cold. Your prone protagonist could hardly believe what was happening. I could barely take in the full significance of the situation. These were the same kids that hardly cared to speak with me that first afternoon in Mrs. Reznik's detention. And even though your formerly ostracized heroine knew each of them felt strongly about the lemonade machine, I also sensed that the true reason they were sticking by me was that they really were my friends.

Needless to say, I felt a rush of emotion.

Suddenly I had a little more confidence. Maybe I could take the pressure after all. Maybe those guys were bluffing about the police. And even if they weren't, I thought, it didn't matter. What mattered was that my friends and I were sticking together. And even if the lemonade machine ended up going away, nobody was getting us up off the ground without a fight.

"Go ahead," I said finally. "Call the cops."

As it turned out, they weren't bluffing. A few minutes later a police cruiser pulled up and a youngish guy with cropped blond hair ambled out. His boots crunched through the snow. Finally, he stood over us. I read the upside-down name on his blue jacket. Officer Schumacher.

"What seems to be the problem here?"

So, from my position in the snow I told Officer Schumacher the whole story, how the Powers That Be at the school, together with big business, were manipulating the students, how we never had any say in the decision to take the beloved machine away. It was unfair, I explained, to disregard one group of people in favor of another. In fact, if you really thought about it, the soda machine situation was actually symbolic of a much larger issue—rampant tyranny, the callous oppression of the powerful over the voiceless.

Officer Schumacher had a kind face, which I saw as a good sign. He listened patiently until I was done, but after that he didn't seem as sympathetic.

"That's all well and good," he said, "but now you need to get up. You kids can't stay where you are."

I couldn't help feeling disappointed in him, even irritated. After I'd given such a long, heartfelt speech, how could he give such an indifferent response? Wasn't he listening?

I folded my arms across my chest. "I'm not moving."

Phil and the pumpkin waited behind him, their hands in their pockets. Frowning, Officer Schumacher stepped a little closer. It was an impressive view, this red-faced policeman towering over us, the other two peering over his shoulders. Even in the cold, I felt the heat rise in my chest.

"Technically, guys, you're trespassing," he said, obviously trying to sound reasonable. "And causing a public disturbance. Now, I don't want to have to do it, but unless you move aside and let this truck through, I'm afraid I'm going to have to arrest you."

"Arrest us?"

He nodded.

It's not easy to admit, but I nearly panicked. I forced myself to stay put, though. "If anybody wants to get up," I called out to my friends, "go ahead. Everyone will understand."

But by then I knew. Nobody was giving in.

All five of us stayed where we were.

By the time my mom picked me up at the station, it was a quarter to two in the afternoon. I was the last of us to get sprung out of there. The frigid air of the parking lot stung my face even worse than before. I slid onto the Volvo's passenger seat and closed the door. I couldn't even look at my mother.

Finally, I couldn't stand the tension anymore. "Mom," I said. "I'm sorry."

My mother didn't answer. She started the engine and let the wipers clear the snow off the windshield. She stared straight ahead.

"Did you hear me? I just apologized. You probably want to ground me for the rest of my life now."

She sighed as we backed out of our spot. "Look, Stella. They're only giving you a warning, nothing that stays on your record. So let's leave it at that, okay?"

"Mom, my friends and I got *arrested* today."

"Don't remind me," she said quietly. We pulled into the street. She didn't say anything else until we came to the light at Rumstick Road. Even when she did, she still didn't turn her head. "But on the other hand, you weren't hurting anybody, and it wasn't as if you were doing drugs, or destroying property or beating people up. You and your friends were just standing up for what you believed was right. If you *had* to get arrested, I guess that isn't such a terrible reason."

At first I didn't think I'd heard right. "Wait . . . you're not mad?"

She gave a noncommittal shrug. "If you truly feel that strongly about this lemonade thing, I guess I can't really fault you."

This was too weird. I didn't know what to say.

At last she turned to face me. "I guess I've been doing some thinking after our conversation this morning, Stella. You were right. Maybe I just needed reminding about backbones, and that some lost causes *are* worth fighting for."

The light changed. I couldn't believe my ears. But I knew enough not to say anything else. If this was really how my mother felt, I wasn't going to ruin it by opening my stupid mouth.

Now I was anxious to get home and grab my uke. But instead of turning left on Rumstick toward the house, my mother took a right.

"Where are we going?"

She pointed her thumb over her shoulder. I looked around. My ukulele was resting in the backseat. "I hear there's a revolution going on," she said. "You don't want to miss it, do you?"

The five of us agreed. It didn't matter that we weren't going to win. It didn't matter how terrible we might sound. Even if we had to drag our broken bodies up onto that stage, we weren't going to let anything stop us from playing Catch A RI-Zing Star.

Now, ten minutes before we were scheduled to go on, I sat backstage listening to the crowd. They screamed and cheered. Desirée Crane, this year's emcee, announced the next band and then Jelly Belly, an electro-pop trio from Cranston, kicked into their song. The Civic Center, seating over fourteen thousand people, was almost full, both in the audience and in the dimly lit backstage area where we waited on fold-up chairs. Other musicians, most of them older, milled around. Some of them wore shiny, matching outfits, some had fifties pompadours or other mousse-dependent hairdos. Even here I felt like my band didn't quite fit in. Instead of feeling nervous, though, I was experiencing an unexpected calm. I carefully set my uke on the fold-up chair beside me, closed my eyes, and grinned. I was enjoying the moment. Okay, so there was no telling whether we would be able to manage even one good song considering our various wounds and illnesses. But at least we were all here. I know it sounds crazy, but even then I thought we might somehow pull it off. After all that had happened, I was beginning to believe that together the five of us could do almost anything.

And it wasn't as if our string of bad luck could get any *worse*, right?

Wrong.

That's when your pensive protagonist heard the squeaking of metal wheels rolling past. Someone was pushing yet another cart full of equipment through the backstage area. The sound came closer and then stopped.

I opened my eyes, but it was too late.

A very fat, sweaty roadie was about to take the seat beside me. His butt, large enough for an IMAX double feature, was already making its ominous way downward. Before it registered in my brain what was happing, before I could even cry out, "No! Stop!" I heard an evil crunch, along with the twang of a snapping string. The guy heard it too. He immediately shot back up and spun around to look at the seat.

"Oh . . . my . . . God . . ." he said, bending over to examine the ukulele. Even the darkness couldn't hide his blanching face. "I am *so* sorry."

Wen, whose lip still looked about the size of a goose egg, was only a few feet away. "What was *that*?"

But I couldn't speak. I gently picked up my instrument, the ukulele that, until now, I'd kept in perfect condition. Two of the strings were gone, and the neck hung at an unnatural angle. I gaped at the mortified klutz, the blood suddenly rising into my head. But even before I could choke any words out of my mouth, that idiot, the unwitting vehicle of cruel fate, must have realized how serious the situation was. He turned around and high-tailed it out of there, leaving his cart behind.

But I was out of time. That's when one of the WRIZ clipboard guys appeared in the doorway. "Lemonade Mouth!" he called out. "Come with me. You guys are on in two minutes."

The next thing I knew, he was leading us out to the stage.

CHAPTER 9

Neither a lofty degree of intelligence nor
imagination nor both together go to
the making of genius. Love, love, love,
that is the soul of genius.
—Wolfgang Amadeus Mozart

MRS. REZNIK:
Something Dreadfully Amiss

Desirée Crane, silicone enhanced and poofy-haired as ever,
bounded back onto center stage. I couldn't help laughing.
The famous teen sensation wore a billowy purple strapless
that didn't suit her and a giant glittery tiara with stars and
moons that wobbled at the ends of what appeared to be
springs. She looked like a contestant in a beauty pageant on
Mars.

Even as she theatrically waved to the cameras and the
band that had just finished, all around me kids were already
holding up signs and screaming for Lemonade Mouth.

"Thank you! That was wonderful!" she beamed. "Let's
hear it for Jelly Belly!"

Jelly Belly had been good but not great. The audience
seemed to enjoy them but frankly, to me the band relied a

little too heavily on synthetic sound and not enough on melody. But maybe I was biased.

There were quite a few Opequonsett High School students back here in the upper stands where I sat. The Civic Center was packed. This event, it seemed, brought together an eclectic mix of people. Pot-bellied bikers clad in leather, long-haired twenty-somethings in baggy pants, silver-headed grandmothers, buttoned-down men shouting into cell phones, middle-aged couples in tight tank tops, even a few families with young children. And all of them cheering alongside hordes of screaming teenagers.

But it was the Lemonade Mouth fans that stood out. I could see them sprinkled throughout the arena. It was our costumes. I have to admit, I was enjoying the attention I was getting as a Renaissance Minstrel. I'd borrowed the outfit from a friend affiliated with the Newport Shakespeare Society. I wore a red and green velvet hat, a jerkin with puffy, striped shoulders and frilled cuffs, velvet leggings and soft leather boots. I even carried a lute. Every time I moved, the bells on my ankles jangled.

So what if I was a little caught up in the spirit of it all? Since Lemonade Mouth, my school had felt like a different place. In the past few months some of the usual apathy and cynicism had been replaced with passion and a renewed energy. And the music—well it spoke for itself. It was original and exciting and somehow gave off a feeling of promise and possibility. I was a true fan.

Desirée Crane's smiling face was gigantic on the overhead screen. Finally, she stared back into the TelePrompTer and the crowd settled down. I couldn't help feeling butterflies. And I wasn't alone. At least in my section of the stadium, I could almost feel that I wasn't the only one with sweaty palms.

Frankly, I was dying for a cigarette but I'd be damned if I was moving from my seat just then.

When Desirée spoke, her voice echoed through the sound system. "The next band is made up of five high school freshmen from Opequonsett."

A spontaneous round of hooting and hollering drowned her out, so she paused and flashed her big, toothy grin until, a few moments later, it quieted again.

"Unknown to WRIZ's staff only a few weeks ago," she continued, "this group's last-minute addition to our set list was the direct result of a passionate appeal from more than two thousand fans—" Another thunderous whoop, this time even longer than before. Desirée smiled again. "A group that has recently become one of the most intensely requested bands that *Local Emissions,* WRIZ's new music show, has ever had, let's give a warm welcome for . . ." She paused and squinted at the TelePrompTer. ". . . *Lemon Mouth!*"

She got the name wrong, but that didn't stop the costumed masses from jumping to their feet. Including me. At last, it was here, Lemonade Mouth's moment to shine. As I cheered, I couldn't help feeling a tiny burst of pride when I recalled the small part I'd played in their story. And in that instant—and even up until a few moments later—I honestly believed that Mohini and her friends had a reasonable chance of making it to the Catch A RI-Zing Star finals. Maybe even winning the whole shebang.

Our cheering continued. I expected them to step out from behind the curtain, but it took longer than I thought it would. Soon I realized something must be wrong.

Twenty or thirty seconds after they were announced, they still hadn't walked onto the stage.

At last they appeared. Even from this distance I didn't need the overhead screen to see that there was something dreadfully amiss. There was an audible gasp from the crowd. Charlie's hand was wrapped in a cumbersome white bandage. And there was something wrong with Wen's lip. And then there was Stella's ukulele. As she plugged it into her amplifier, the entire neck momentarily teetered to one side. What on earth had happened? I watched her scramble to set it back in place. Was she trying to tune it? A ukulele with a broken neck? Was that even possible?

Uh oh, I thought.

The five of them soon took their positions and then Charlie called out the time. I held my breath.

DELILA CZERWINSKI:
The Plaintive Cry of an Injured Moose

Dina, Veronica and I came as belly dancers, with colorful skimpy outfits and bright transparent veils over our heads. We even painted each other's eyes to look exotic and mysterious. We worked ourselves into a sweat twisting and slithering around as each of the first bands played. But when Desirée Crane finally announced Lemonade Mouth, Veronica started calling out, "Oh God oh God I love him! Oh God oh God!" By now, her early infatuation with Charlie had bloomed into all-out worship.

But the truth was, I was screaming too.

We'd been looking forward to this since we first found

out that Lemonade Mouth made it into Catch A RI-Zing Star. Veronica had bagged all her classes one afternoon just so she could call into WRIZ. They were giving away tickets every half hour, and she kept hitting redial until she won. Which is why we were so close to the stage. And now we had our lemonades ready, along with a giant cardboard sign that said WE LOVE YOU, CHARLIE!

When we finally saw the band stagger out from behind the curtain, though, our screaming petered out pretty quickly. Dina shot me a puzzled glance. What was going on here? Why did they look like they'd just climbed out of a bus accident? Charlie and Wen looked beat up, and Mo had big gray suitcases under her eyes. For a second I wondered if this was some kind of onstage joke.

When they finally began, it took me a while to recognize the song. It was "Back Among the Walls," but it didn't sound right at all. Wen seemed to wince in pain with each sad blat that came out of his horn. Charlie whacked at his drums, but with only one hand it just wasn't the same. Mo looked like she didn't have enough energy to even hold her bow, let alone play it. And there was something up with Stella's ukulele. She strummed it but the sound wasn't right, like it was only a cheap plastic toy or something. Standing at the microphone, Olivia looked around in panic. I got the feeling this wasn't a joke after all. Her face went red as a strawberry, but then she grabbed the microphone as if she wasn't going to let this setback stop her. Unfortunately, when she opened her mouth to sing what came out was a God-awful screech—like a seal barking maybe, or the cry of an injured moose. If it wasn't so horrible to see my band this way, I would have thought it was funny.

What was happening? This was not the way this was supposed to turn out. Lemonade Mouth was supposed to blow the other bands away. They weren't supposed to suck.

My heart sank into my shoes.

We were close enough to see them start to sweat. But for a while they pressed on anyway. I guess they were determined to make it through this against all odds. But it was pointless. It didn't work. The harder they pushed, the worse it got. The noise was hideous. Finally, even Lemonade Mouth realized they couldn't go on. They stopped playing less than a minute after they started.

My hand rose to my mouth to stifle another gasp.

For a moment they were still. I watched them glance around at each other, their faces red and shiny. And then they stared out at us. I could see it in their desperate eyes. They knew.

It was over.

RICHIE BENEDETTI:
The Center of an Earthquake

For a moment, the entire Civic Center was quiet. Fifty-three rows back from the stage, my buddies and I sat in our seats, stunned into silence.

How could this have happened? This was Lemonade Mouth's biggest gig so far. Look how many people showed up in costume! And I knew for an absolute fact that a lot of them weren't even from Opequonsett High School! Everything had lined up perfectly. This was supposed to be the beginning of even bigger things. Epiphany Records. National radio airplay. Maybe even a tour.

How could they have blown it all? And so horribly? Somehow, it didn't seem fair.

My throat choked. And it wasn't just because of the performance or even the recording contract. I just felt bad for those guys. As they started unplugging their instruments and backing away from the microphones, I thought what a shame it was that there were people in this audience who would never know what this band meant to so many of us. I couldn't help remembering what my school was like back in September. Back then, Pete and I were like second-class nothings, shunned and cut off in our own lonely little world in the fringes. I didn't feel like a Parking Lot Flea anymore. Look at the row of kids here with us: Terry, Digby, Leslie, Kate, Manny, Cynthia, all of us dressed as paper cups of Mel's Lemonade. If it weren't for Lemonade Mouth, Pete and I might never have hooked up with these guys. But then I looked around and realized there were people in this arena who never would understand that to us this was more than just a little high school band. To my friends and me, Lemonade Mouth was the center of an earthquake.

Desirée Crane's face hesitantly poked around the curtain. She seemed uncertain what to do or say. I'm sure the short performance must have thrown the timing completely off. For all I knew, the next band wasn't even ready yet. After a moment of hesitation, her shoulder appeared on the stage, and then the rest of her. A big, fake-looking smile grew on her mouth and then she started the long journey across the stage. In the quiet, the microphones picked up the clip-clop of her shoes.

Faces pale and embarrassed, Mo, Stella, Wen, Olivia and Charlie were already creeping to the back of the platform and would soon slip out of sight. I suddenly wished there

297

was some way to help them. If only there was something I could do to show my support.

That's when my buddy Terry Cabeleira—little nervous Terry who hardly ever spoke—stood up. For a second I thought he was just getting up to go to the bathroom or something, but he didn't move. He just stood there. I was about to ask him what he was up to but I didn't get the chance.

That's when he started singing.

At first I just sat there and listened. What was he doing?

Lonely day
After the storm has come and gone
There will never be another tomorrow like today

It was "Back Among the Walls," one of Lemonade Mouth's slower tunes but just the same, one of our favorites. And as I listened, I started to understand. Now, I have the worst voice ever and I would normally never sing in front of anybody, but watching my band heading toward the curtain I suddenly had the urge to join Terry.

So I stood up beside him. Now there were two of us belting out the words:

In my own way
I wait for the light of dawn
I look for a sign of things to come and change to stay

I may be back among the walls
I may be back among the walls
I may be back among the walls
But I am not alone

By the end of the verse, Pete, Digby, Kate, Leslie, Cynthia and even Manny were on their feet. But in this huge stadium, even with all of us singing I wondered if our voices would even reach the stage.

RAY BEECH:
The Ultimate Insult

Believe me, it wasn't *my* idea to sit through Catch A RI-Zing Star. Adding my own special twist to the previous night's show at Bruno's had been a blast and everything, but why did I need to see that freshman band ever again? But my buddy Scott said he was going and I didn't have anything better to do so I said what the hell? Why not? Maybe they'll bomb.

Okay, I admit that when I said that I was just talking. I didn't honestly think it'd *happen*. But then it *did*—oh, and how! Their act was a complete train wreck. As far as I could see, there was no way anybody could ever overcome a humiliation like *that*. It was an absolute meltdown! When they finally stopped embarrassing themselves, there was this weird silence. Eventually I heard some polite applause. But I couldn't help laughing. It was just *too good*!

Finally, maybe this would put a long overdue end to the cult of Lemonade Mouth!

But that was before those kids in the lemonade outfits down near the front stood up and started singing that damn song. When that happened, it seemed like everyone craned their necks to see what was going on. It wasn't long before a couple more losers rose to their feet too. First one, then another, then another. Soon there were bigger groups getting up to sing, some in costume and some not. It started off kind of spreading out from the center, but before long they were popping up all over the arena.

I couldn't believe this was happening.

And I couldn't believe how many people seemed to *know* that stupid song!

That Desirée Crane chick reached for the microphone and opened her mouth like she was about to say something. Maybe announce the next band or maybe tell Lemonade Mouth how sorry she was about their pathetic act. Oh, wouldn't that have been just *perfect!* But we'll never know because her mouth closed up again. I guess she was waiting for the voices to settle down. She stood there smiling, probably thinking the song would just peter out.

But it didn't. It kept growing.

I could have screamed.

And then the ultimate insult was when this string bean stood up in front of me. He was a pointy-nosed runt of a kid, probably about my age but with a neck like a straw. To have to listen to him warbling that damn tune right in front of my face—well, it was just too much to take.

I guess Scott could tell I was getting pissed because he shot me a look like I should leave him alone. But I ignored him. I leaned forward, put my hand on the kid's scrawny little shoulder and gritted my teeth. "Sit down, choirboy," I growled at him. "You're blocking my view."

When the kid turned I expected to see fear in his eyes. But instead, he only looked me over and then tapped the shoulder of his buddy sitting next to him.

Now, I hadn't noticed his friend before, but when the guy stood up I saw that he was as big as a bear. His feet were a row below me, but still he towered over me, his eyes squinting like he was ready to kick my butt.

I felt all the blood rush from my face.

What could I do? I backed down.

JANE SEISEKI:
An Electric Charge

The song kept spreading. As soon as we realized what was happening, our whole section jumped to our feet. Naomi, Seth, Wendy, Lyle, Rodney—all of us. Andrea Beckham waved her arms and sang at the top of her voice.

With a giant cardboard box wrapped around me (Andrea and I had come as a pair of dice) it wasn't easy to climb up onto my chair but somehow I managed it. I wanted to see the stage better. By then, Lemonade Mouth had turned back around to see what was going on. It was incredible. It seemed like half the place was singing, swaying and clapping their hands. I saw Desirée try to interrupt a couple of times, but the song wouldn't let her. It got louder and louder. After a while, all she could do was step back and chuckle.

Just behind me, Mrs. Reznik stood on her chair too, moving her arms and belting out the words like I never would have expected.

In some bright place
There may be another choice
But for now we're here, and you I can't replace

So in this space
I will listen closely to your voice
Someday I will scale these walls and you will see my face

It felt like there was an electrical charge in the air. As we sang out the "Back Among the Walls" part again I thought about how much had changed since that first time I'd heard Lemonade Mouth at the Bash. Back then, I'd still been stuck in the same old rut about Seth Levine. Not anymore. I'd done a lot of soul-searching since then and I realized now that he was a great guy and all, but he wasn't right for me. Hanging out with Andrea and Rodney and seeing how sweet they were together had made a big difference. I set my sights higher now. Andrea and I had become especially close too. We talked a lot about life—and about music. As a matter of fact, we'd written a few songs together. I'd even bought an acoustic guitar and started taking lessons. These days, I had a whole new focus.

Andrea and I held up the signs we'd made. Mine said, I'M A FREAK AND I'M PROUD! Hers said, LEMONADE MOUTH FOR PRESIDENT! The song was very loud now. While some of us clapped and stomped the drumbeat, I heard others sing out Wen's trumpet part. *Ba ba baaa—! Ba ba-ba baaa—!* It may sound weird, but if you were there you would understand. It was all pretty emotional.

No wonder the *Barking Clam* later dubbed this the Second Lemonade Mouth Miracle.

Stella and the others stood at the edge of the stage, their mouths practically hanging open in amazement. I realized that their song hadn't been such a disaster after all. This *was* their song. Except that now we were Lemonade Mouth and those five freshmen were the audience.

It was a beautiful feeling, like I was giving back something for all they'd done for me.

MR. BRENIGAN:
Petunias

I wouldn't have come to the competition at all except, as it happened, I was in charge of my nephews for the weekend and they absolutely insisted. At age ten and eleven, they were avid WRIZ listeners and, unfortunately, devout fans of Lemonade Mouth. My brother-in-law had already bought the tickets. There really was no getting out of it.

From where we sat high up in the nosebleed area I had a panoramic view of the whole stadium. I had a hard time believing my eyes. Or my ears. People sitting on each other's shoulders, a sea of waving arms and singing voices. How could this have happened?

My nephews had been momentarily deflated by the unexpected failure of their heroes, but they suddenly perked up again at the impromptu swell of support. And now they were both on their feet, gleefully singing and stomping their feet to the rhythm. My own nephews.

I couldn't have stopped them even if I tried.

I have to admit that when Stella and her friends had blown their song I didn't feel particularly sorry for them. Not after all the trouble they'd given me, especially putting me in such an uncomfortable position with regard to the finance committee. I'd been told in no uncertain terms to put a stop to any and all student pressure concerning the Barkley deal or it would be my head. There was nothing *illegal* about the deal, of course, but no one wanted a spotlight shined on it.

Which was why it was so frustrating how every time I tried to hush those freshmen, somehow they always had their say. And came out smelling like petunias too.

By now so many voices had joined the chorus that my ears rang. The total effect of all those people singing and clapping the same song together was impressive. And loud. It was as if those kids held some spell over the place. They'd bombed miserably, but still the crowd was with them.

But even when the mass of people finally finished the song and the arena erupted into one giant, elated cheer, I felt a rising dread. I sensed it wasn't over.

Somehow I knew what was coming next.

And then it did. Desirée Crane stepped back to the microphone yet again but once more she was overwhelmed by the will of the multitude. Somewhere, a new chorus had started up, and the other voices were only too eager to join in. Soon, even the metal supports of the stadium seemed to vibrate with it.

I WANT LEMONADE IN MY CUP!
Hmmmmm, Hmmmmm
HOLD IT HIGH! RAISE IT UP!
Hmmmmm, Hmmmmm

They chanted it over and over. My nephews squealed with pleasure. As they joined the refrain, their little round faces beamed up at me.

Oh no, I thought with a sinking heart.

Those freshmen did it again.

CHAPTER 10

Gray skies are just clouds passing over.
—Duke Ellington

MOHINI:
A Foggy Notion

Funny how things happen. The next day a reporter from the *Providence Journal* calls. She says she heard how, in the hours before the show, we were all arrested for protesting the removal of a lemonade machine. Her name is Carolyn Brussat and she wants to interview each of us. The following morning the East Bay section of the paper has a giant color shot of the five of us standing at the edge of the Civic Center stage. The headline reads:

STUDENTS HOPE DETERMINATION
CAN TURN LEMONS INTO LEMONADE

Beneath that is a full-page story all about my friends and me, the soda controversy and what happened at Catch A

RI-Zing Star. In the article it hardly seems to matter that we weren't able to stop the school from taking the lemonade machine away or that we lost Catch A RI-Zing Star— we didn't even make it past the first round.

For a few days, WRIZ-TV keeps showing a ten-second clip of us up onstage at the contest. They repeat it over and over again for comic value. At the event it felt horrible and embarrassing, but now that I see it on TV I realize it *is* kind of funny, with Stella, Charlie, Wen and me frantically struggling with our instruments, and poor Olivia sweating it out, screeching into the microphone like an antelope in heat.

But I'm just relieved that the contest is behind us.

It's four whole days after Catch A RI-Zing Star before I'm well enough to get out of bed, and even after I go back to school it still takes me a while to fully recover from my cold. But by the middle of March I'm feeling much better.

On a Friday afternoon I stay late talking with Mrs. Reznik about a Mozart piece she wants me to play at the May recital. After that I have a few minutes to kill on the floor of the school lobby as I wait for the late bus home. At first I figure I'll make use of the time by reading ahead in Biology, but as I put my hand into my backpack I change my mind. Instead, I pull out a paperback that Olivia loaned me. "P. G. Wodehouse isn't deep reading or anything," was what she said, "but it's fun."

I've made up my mind. There's no point in trying to be Supergirl.

I'm a few pages into it when somebody sits down next to me. By that time I'm so involved in the story that I don't pay much attention. But I guess a part of me feels somebody watching, hovering over me, so eventually I look up.

"Hiya, Mo," grins Scott.

I wonder only vaguely why he's here. He and I have hardly spoken since forever. But my mind is still in a London cab with a donkey.

"Hello."

He looks like he has something to say so I wait. "I'm an idiot," he says finally. "I screwed everything up and I know it."

"Then why did you break up with me?"

"I don't know. Insanity, I guess. And that whole thing with Lynn Westerberg, well . . . that was yet another stupid mistake. I guess I'm not the sharpest guy around when it comes to figuring out what I really want."

I'm not sure how to react. "Why are you telling me this, Scott?"

He flashes me his trademark half-smile. "Listen, I've been thinking. It's been a long, crazy year, and you and me, well, we went through a rough patch, but that's all behind us now. But I still like you, and I think you still like me. So I was wondering . . . why don't we get back together?"

All I can do is blink at him.

Thing is, a part of me used to secretly hope for this. In my weaker moments I dreamed that Scott would come back and everything would be happy. And now here he is. But instead of feeling elated—or even amused or angry— I'm surprised at what I feel. Nothing. Nothing at all. And that's when all at once my new reality hits me.

I don't care about Scott anymore.

How did it happen? Exactly when over the past few months did he turn into just some guy I know? Some boy I used to like? It feels strange to realize such a gigantic tidal shift can happen without my even noticing.

Thankfully, that's when the bus pulls up and kids begin shuffling through the glass double doors into the cold. But I don't stand up right away. I don't want to seem cruel.

"I'm sorry," I say as kindly as I can. "I'm not interested."

He looks surprised, even a little hurt. I can't help feeling sorry for him. But there isn't anything else to say so I gather my things and head out to the bus.

That night Naomi comes over and we all watch *Kaise Kahoon Ke Pyaar Hai,* an Amit Hingorani musical about a college student living a split life as a part-time thief. And for some reason that makes me look around and realize that I'm living a split life too. On the one hand I'm an ordinary American girl going to school with regular American friends. On the other I'm part of a Bengali family, one that goes to a Hindu temple, eats a lot of curried fish, with parents that grew up in a world completely separate from the one we live in now. I'm a two-sided coin, a walking contradiction.

Suddenly I have the urge to tell Charlie. I want to share my revelation. I know he'll get it. With his quarter flipping and his theories about twins and balance in the universe, if anybody understands about duality and paradox it's Charlie.

But I also know I can't really have that conversation. Not the way I want to, anyway. Even though Charlie and I still talk, there's been a wall between us ever since that awful morning at the clinic. My cheeks still burn whenever I think about it. Not only because of the terrible way I treated him, but also because of the emptiness I still feel whenever he and I catch each other's glance.

The next morning before I go to school I find my dad

praying in our pooja room. I stop what I'm doing. For a while I stand in the doorway, just watching and listening. I'm reminded of what Mrs. Reznik is always saying about beauty and honesty. After a minute or so I feel the urge to pray too, so I walk over and kneel down beside him.

"Baba?" I ask him later when we're eating breakfast together. "When you told me all you want is for me to be happy, did you really mean it?"

He looks up from his paper at me, his forehead suddenly wrinkled with concern. This is the first time either of us have mentioned the argument he and I had the morning of the contest. In the days after that blow up, I happened to overhear my mom and dad on the phone a couple of times having long conversations with Selena's parents. I couldn't hear what they were saying, exactly, but I suspected they were looking for advice about how to deal with wild Americanized daughters. But since then I've been trying to be on my best behavior—and I've been noticing that my dad has too.

"Yes," he says. "You know I did."

I'm nervous to be talking about this, but I keep going. "And you trust my judgment?"

He glances over at my mother, but she suddenly seems deeply interested in her breakfast. I think they both understand what I'm getting at. When he looks back at me, that tightrope panic flickers across his eyes again. But then he looks down at his paper. He sighs. When he finally answers, his voice doesn't sound so much eager as resigned to the inevitable.

"Yes, Monu. I trust your judgment." From his stiff expression, I'm positive that we understand each other.

I wrap my arms around his neck and give him a giant hug.

I have the beginnings of a new idea. Not exactly a grand plan, more of a feeling really, a foggy notion. And anyway, I realize now that grand plans can change. I'm not sure of any details of my idea yet, but that's okay. For now, a foggy notion is enough. 🖋

CHARLIE:
Forgetting to Breathe

After killing an hour or 2 downstairs with the A.V. Club I finally stepped out of the school Lobby into a surprisingly warm afternoon. The sky was cloudy but most of the recent snow had melted into puddles on the pavement there was even a bird chirping somewhere.

Don't let the sunshine and tweety-birds fool you bro whispered my cynical twin *it's only 1 of those March teaser-days—an aberration that'll end up raising your spirits and making you feel like Spring is right around the corner only to send you crashing back down to Earth with more freezing New England Winter in a day or so. 1 of nature's cruel jokes.*

I tried to ignore him. I considered whether I should take advantage of the mild weather and walk home instead of taking the bus. After so much cold it would feel good to walk outside with my coat unzipped on the other hand some of the clouds did look kind of gray and the late bus was right there waiting by the curb.

Unable to make up my mind I reached into my pocket and fingered my lucky quarter. I tossed it into the air. Heads I'd hoof it, tails I'd take the ride.

It spun as it rose and just after it started back down I

snatched it into my hand. Which had pretty much healed by then. I uncurled my fingers. The familiar silver eagle holding its wings wide like a flasher.

Tails.

OK buddy. The bus it is.

The verdict was clear but somehow unsatisfying. I decided to toss the quarter again only this time I let it fall to the walkway. I bent over to inspect it. Tails again.

Come on brother get hopping or our ride's going to leave without us!

I glanced back at the bus. Its engine revved into life. I still had time to catch it but suddenly I felt tired of listening to Aaron. Whether it was him or my own lack of confidence or even just the shifting whims of the Universe, why should I let anything make my choices for me like I'm just some powerless leaf twisting and spinning in the wind? Sure I was sorry he was dead and everything. But still.

Fair or not, my brother was gone and I was here.

And I had my own ideas.

All at once I made up my mind. I turned my back on the bus and left the quarter on the pavement. I walked away.

Goodbye Aaron Jacob. From here on in I'm going it solo.

My boots squelched through the muddy field behind the gym I couldn't help smiling. On a day like today it wasn't hard to picture what would of been nearly impossible to imagine only days before. The pounding of fists into leather gloves. The crack of baseball bats.

Unfortunately my premature Spring glow didn't last. Before I even reached the main road I felt the 1st raindrop on my ear and within seconds I found myself in the middle of a sudden cold downpour.

Just my luck.

But soon I noticed her. A girl with a wide red umbrella watching me from the sidewalk. I stopped.

"What are you doing here Mo?"

"Walking." She held her umbrella out. "Offering to keep the rain off you."

"But you don't live in this direction."

She shrugged.

Whatever was left of my good mood disappeared. After all, I was still stinging from the way she'd treated me at the clinic. Since then I'd been comfortable enough around her when we were with other people but I'd avoided being alone with her. And right now it was just her and me.

Plus something about this unexpected meeting felt a little too coincidental.

"How did you know I was going to walk home today?"

"I didn't I saw you coming across the field and decided to meet you."

Hmmm. I wondered what she was up to. But then again, Naomi lived in this direction only a few blocks away so maybe it wasn't so strange.

There was nothing I could do but join her we started down the street together with Mo holding the umbrella over both our heads and for a long time I didn't say a word and we walked in an awkward silence. But then eventually she came out with "How's English Comp?" as if everything else was perfectly fine.

"Great" I said keeping my eyes on the sidewalk. Why did she even bother to ask? She knew it was my worst subject. "Except of course that I'm practically failing."

After that we both went back to not saying anything but I could tell there was something weird going on. Some unfamiliar weight. She was definitely up to something.

Finally we reached the turnoff for Naomi's street. "Here we are" I said quickly. "This is where we part ways see you tomorrow."

I walked on. For a moment she stayed where she was but soon I heard footsteps running up behind me. "Wait Charlie don't go! You don't have an umbrella I'll walk you a little farther!"

I could see on her face that there was something on her mind. I thought of just coming out and asking her what it was but I decided against it. You never knew with Mo. Whatever it was I figured I'd find out soon enough. A block later we passed the Post Office. That was when I 1st felt her fingers brush against my hand. It happened quickly but I noticed it. I didn't say anything in case it was unintentional. But my senses were on red alert.

A little while after that our hands touched again only this time I knew it was no accident because her fingers wrapped around mine.

I stopped walking. "What are you doing?"

"Holding your hand."

My heart was suddenly in my throat but I made an effort to stay cool. "Yes I realize that. I'm just surprised. Especially since you already made it perfectly clear you don't want anything to do with me."

She was biting her lip and looking really nervous. "I know I did I'm sorry I'm so so sorry but at the time I was messed up and confused and I didn't know what I wanted but you're truly the best thing that's ever happened to me and I love being around you and I really do want to be with you I've wanted to tell you that for so long but I didn't know how to do it because I've already made such a mess of things."

The rain had picked up by then and it was falling hard all around us and I was having a hard time making sense of this.

"I don't get it Mo. What about everything you said about us being too different?"

"I was wrong I'm sorry" she said again. "I screwed up."

"What about your parents? I thought you didn't want to sneak around anymore. Like you did with Scott?"

She shrugged. "My parents already know. We worked it out. They want me to be happy and they trust my judgment."

They worked it out? Huh? Did I miss something? Were we talking about the same parents she always said would hit the roof if she even hinted she was dating anybody? Was she serious?

I wondered if I would ever understand this girl. Who did she think I was? A toy she could play with? Some robot with no feelings? I pulled my hand away remembering what she'd said to me.

"Well you're too late Mo. I'm not interested. I have my own grand plan now and you're not in it."

She bit her lip again and it looked like she might even cry. "I never meant to hurt you Charlie . . . I hope you can at least forgive me."

I felt a wave of heat and I was about to tell her what she could do with her apologies but that's when she took my hand again and stepped even closer. The way she peered up at me all anxious it put the brakes on whatever I was about to say.

All I could manage was "What are you doing?"

"Remember that time you poked fun at me because I never do anything on impulse? Anything reckless just because I'm dying to know what it feels like? Well get ready. I'm about to do something reckless."

She suddenly raised herself on her toes. She must of lost track of how she was holding the umbrella because I felt the rain pelt down on my neck and the back of my jeans but I hardly paid any attention to that.

Because that's when she kissed me.

It was quick and soft and so unexpected I nearly fell over.

"Oh God I'm sorry!" she said seconds later as she re-adjusted the angle of the umbrella. "You're all wet!"

"What was *that*?" I asked. I was too surprised to be angry. The truth was that even though I didn't want to admit it I still liked this girl just as much as ever. I never stopped thinking about her. Part of me wanted to find a way to get over my hurt feelings so we could be together only I didn't know how.

"It was a kiss" she said. Like that wasn't obvious. "And you want me to tell you how it felt?"

What could I say? My brain was on overload.

"Right. It felt . . . right. Tell me you didn't feel the same thing."

But I wasn't ready to give up being angry yet. After all, she'd totally crushed me back at the clinic.

"You're out of your mind" I said.

I started to pull away but she wouldn't let go. She grabbed my hand tight and came in close again. Then for what seemed like a long time we both just stood there. Me fuming and Mo still squeezing my hand. Neither of us saying a word and the rain pelting down on the umbrella.

And that's when she stood on her toes again. And kissed me for the 2nd time only this one was even softer. And longer.

OK so now let me tell you something I learned about the Universe. It doesn't make any sense at all. For weeks I'd been licking my wounds over this girl. Practically pulling my hair out over her. And yet now here I was standing under an umbrella kissing her. And even the kiss didn't make sense because in my mind I'd always pictured (when I'd dared to anyway) that if Mo and I ever did kiss (and I mean a real kiss) it would be exotic and wild the kind that leaves you on your knees. But in real life it wasn't like that at all. The genuine article was quiet and much more comfortable than I'd ever imagined. And to be honest, much better.

When it was over the calves of my jeans were soaked and I realized I'd forgotten to breathe.

WEN:
Green Specks and Suspicious-Looking Sea Creatures

George was watching TV, but he kept wandering into the kitchen to steal pieces of dark chocolate off the counter, leftover ingredients from the concoction Sydney was working on. It was in the oven now, a complicated wonder she called a Doberge cake. Right now she and my father were too busy staring anxiously into a pot on the stove to notice George's hand shoot out, grab a few loose chunks and pop them into his mouth.

It was a Saturday in late March and my fat lip was only a memory. Sydney and my dad were taking a Creole cooking course once a week and today they were attempting some of the recipes they'd learned. Gumbo, jambalaya and God only knew what else. They'd spent the afternoon peeling shrimp and slicing vegetables. That's why my friends were coming to dinner. Tonight would be an experiment with Lemonade Mouth as the guinea pig.

"Okay, try it now," my father said to Sydney, his voice a little anxious.

She dipped a spoon into the pot and tasted the creamy goop. After a moment's consideration her frown softened. "A little better, I guess. What do you think, more Worcestershire? I'm not sure."

My dad turned to me. "Wen, how are you doing out there, kiddo? Want to tell me what you think of this meunière sauce?"

"Not especially," I called from the sofa. "I'm reading."

It was weird to see him so enthusiastic in the kitchen. Not that my father never cooked before, but tuna noodle casserole and green beans mixed with canned cream of mushroom soup was about as adventurous as he ever got.

Dubious as this culinary episode seemed, I had to admit that the spicy smells wafting into the living room weren't awful.

As I leaned back with my book, my legs automatically stretched out to rest on the black wooden trunk we'd kept for weeks in front of the sofa for lack of anywhere else to put it. Only when my feet landed on the floor was I reminded that we'd finally moved the massive thing along with most of Sydney's other old furniture to a storage place in Warren. Besides her graphic design plans, Sydney was now also talking about starting up a part-time antiques business. I still wasn't used to having so much space.

On my lap was *Shakespeare's Complete Works*, a thick volume I'd found on top of a box in Olivia's room. I'd asked to borrow it. Olivia had agreed without seeming to give it much thought. When I brought it home and flipped through the pages, though, I found notes scribbled all over the margins in slanted black pen. In the same handwriting, the name printed on the inside back cover caught my attention.

Ted Whitehead.

Holding the book more gingerly now that I knew it once belonged to Olivia's father, I opened to *Twelfth Night,* the play Olivia said her name came from. I spent an hour or so trying to plow through it, but the ancient, flowery language was like Swahili to me. I struggled with all the "perchances," "know'st thous" and head-scratchers like "she hath abjured the company and sight of men." But from what I could make out, it was this crazy love story where everybody is miserable from being in love with somebody who loves someone else. Olivia is this beautiful, rich countess with all kinds of servants and clowns milling around her house. This other guy, Duke Orsinio, lies around all day and listens to music. I forced myself to plod ahead, but to be honest there was a lot I didn't get.

"Are you ready to be astounded and amazed?"

I looked up. My dad and Sydney stood over me grinning. Sydney held out a spoon and a small cup of lumpy brown liquid. "Come on," she beamed. "Try this."

"What is it, exactly?"

"Crawfish bisque."

I peered into the cup. Green specks and suspicious looking sea creatures floated at the top. I considered trying to postpone the inevitable until dinner, but they seemed so proud of themselves that I didn't have the heart. I took the cup and the spoon and put a tiny dab of the stuff in my mouth.

Not so terrible. Pretty okay, actually.

I gave them a thumbs-up and they scurried back to the

kitchen. From all the high-fives, you would have thought they'd just found a cure for cancer.

It was then that it suddenly dawned on me that I hadn't dreamt about Sydney in ages. I tried to remember the last time. Weeks ago, I guessed. Not since before the morning I'd seen her naked. In the days that followed that supremely awkward moment, I'd spent a lot of time thinking. What was it about that bathroom incident that had left me feeling so confused? It took me a while, but finally I figured out what it was.

Seeing Sydney's body hadn't felt exciting at all. I'd gotten no thrill out of it, no secret lust. Nada.

Instead, walking in on Sydney without her clothes had felt more like mistakenly walking in on an older cousin. Or maybe an aunt. Somebody I didn't feel any desire for. It wasn't at all what I'd expected.

I'd felt nothing but embarrassment.

And it'd made it even worse when Sydney had fussed over my fat lip like a mother hen.

Still, I was okay with it now. After so much shame, it felt liberating to realize that I didn't burn with guilt around her anymore.

George shut off the TV and switched on the computer. Pretty soon he was exploring some noisy underground cave full of angry trolls and vials of poisonous potions. I went back to my reading but soon felt myself losing interest. Finally I gave up. I flipped back through the pages, marveling at all the indecipherable scribbles Olivia's father had made. My eyes fell on a passage he'd drawn a thick box around and marked with asterisks. I hadn't understood it the first time, but I looked at it again. The clown in Olivia's house was singing a song that went:

What is love? 'tis not hereafter;
Present mirth hath present laughter;
What's to come is still unsure:
In delay there lies no plenty;
Then come kiss me, sweet and twenty,
Youth's a stuff will not endure.

There was a tap at the window. I looked up. Olivia's face peered in at me, her Scooby-Doo backpack over her shoulder. Recently, Mo had quietly taken me aside and warned me to be careful with Olivia. "Don't hurt her, Wen," she'd said. "I've seen the way she looks at you." But now, looking at Olivia through the window, I finally recognized the warm rush I felt whenever she was around. It was a rush I could never feel for an aunt or a cousin. I suddenly understood why I'd been hoping she might show up early.

Back in the kitchen, my dad and Sydney wore expressions of deep concentration, both of them busy chopping and stirring the ingredients of their weird, fishy food. For the first time, I realized that they looked kind of sweet together.

That's when I had a sudden idea what the passage might have meant. And it occurred to me that maybe Shakespeare was onto something.

It'd been my idea to invite Mrs. Reznik. I was happy when she'd actually agreed to come. We had to pull the table away from the wall so everybody could fit. There were nine of us, including George, my dad, Sydney, my friends and me. I was surprised how fancy everything looked. Sydney laid out a tablecloth, dimmed the lights and lit candles to set the mood. My dad brought out the cloth napkins and the good china. Zydeco music bounced quietly from the stereo. There was so much food it was like a restaurant. Some of it was pretty spicy, and to be honest I'm not a big oyster fan so I could take or leave the chowder, but the gumbo was amazing and I ended up taking two helpings. There were even special meat-free versions of just about everything especially for Stella. Everybody gobbled it up.

Well, maybe not everybody. George eyed the cake, which loomed on the counter like a monument, a champion chocolate dessert on steroids, but other than that I don't think my little brother was much of a Creole fan. He picked at the jambalaya and had a few bites of a crabcake, but mostly he just sat there listening to everyone else talking and laughing.

Mrs. Reznik told a hilarious story about how she once got locked out of the house in her bathrobe and shower cap one morning because she thought she saw a lame bird in a tree. She can be a hoot when she gets going. Sydney was laughing so hard I thought her ice tea might come shooting out her nose.

But then toward the end of the meal, the mood completely changed.

"Listen, everybody," Stella said in the middle of a rare lull in the conversation. "I . . . uh . . . got some news today. Serious news, actually."

Of course, I didn't have any idea what Stella's news would be, and it didn't occur to me at first that there might be anything to worry about. Sure, she'd been a little quieter than usual today, but it hadn't seemed like a big deal. Plus, at that moment my attention was on Sydney. She'd just set the Doberge cake on the table and I was watching greedily as she began to cut it into slices. But when I finally glanced over at Stella and noticed her somber, unsmiling expression and the way she was waiting for everybody's attention, I pretty much forgot about the cake.

Something was clearly up. Something serious.

It was obvious that everybody else sensed the same thing. Everyone got quiet. Sydney stopped slicing and even George looked up from the stack of breadsticks he'd been arranging as a fortress around his napkin. We all looked over at Stella and waited for her to tell us whatever it was.

She looked down at the tablecloth.

"I'm not exactly sure how to say this. My mother . . . well, she only told me this afternoon so it's still something I'm getting used to myself."

"What is it?" Sydney asked anxiously, setting aside her cake knife and sitting back down. "Tell us."

Stella took a deep breath and then started into her story. Apparently her mother had taken her out to lunch, just the two of them. In the middle of the meal she'd reached into her purse and pulled out a long, white envelope.

"We need to talk," she'd said softly. Which of course made Stella kind of nervous. And it got even worse when her mother had put her hand over hers and said, "Now, I don't want you to get upset about this, honey. It's going to be okay."

"It was bad enough that I've had so much on my mind lately anyway," Stella said to us now. "But the way my mom was acting was completely freaking me out."

"Go on," Mrs. Reznik said with concern in her eyes. "What happened?"

Her mother told her that the envelope had arrived a couple days earlier, but she hadn't said anything to Stella about it until now because she was waiting for the right moment. She said she figured Stella was going to take it hard. She set the envelope on the table.

"So as you can imagine, by then I was sweating estuaries. I looked down at the letter. It was from the high school guidance department."

Mrs. Reznik's eyebrows pulled together.

"Remember I told you all about how they made me take all those stupid tests? How my mother had to come in and later I had to spend a whole Thursday afternoon stuck in that little green room in the guidance area? Well, I'd almost forgotten all about that. It was just a bad memory I preferred not to relive. But here it was back to haunt me. Now, I didn't really want to know what was inside the envelope, but my mom was waiting so I picked it up off the table and pulled out the letter. I could feel my heart thumping. Before I even started reading the thing I looked over again at my mom's face and knew that whatever news this piece of paper had, it wouldn't be anything good. Something was obviously out of whack."

At this point in Stella's story she reached into her pocket and pulled out an envelope that I guessed, rightly, was the same one as in her story. As we all leaned forward, waiting anxiously to hear what she was going to say next, she slowly and dramatically pulled out the letter.

Then she read aloud.

"The Opequonsett Public School system recently completed a full core evaluation of your daughter Stella and testing resulted in a finding of dyslexia. After reviewing input from her teachers and mother, Stella's physician reports a diagnosis of Attention Deficit Disorder. These problems would negatively influence Stella's ability to read and fully comprehend written material as well as maintain focus in class."

I suddenly felt terrible for Stella. After all, we all knew what an issue this stuff was for her. She was always so sensitive about her bad grades, and if anybody ever kidded her about something she said, any innocent comment she could wrongly interpret as being a jibe at her intelligence, she went all moody. Somewhere she'd gotten the crazy idea that she was dumb. It wasn't true, of course, but that was Stella. Once a notion found its way into her head, it wasn't easy for anybody to argue it out of her.

Mo and Olivia started to open their mouths, probably to say something consoling, something to let her know that this really was okay and not such an awful thing. But Stella held up a finger to stop them. She continued reading.

"The school has developed a plan for accommodating Stella's needs. Going forward, Stella will be given individual and small group help from our Resource teacher who will supplement and support her regular classroom work as well as work with her on an alternative reading method. Stella will also be given preferred seating where she is closer to the classroom teacher and away from hallway disruptions. In addition, for written tests, Stella will be allowed to complete her work in a quiet, comfortable area without any distractions or time restrictions."

She lowered the letter. I was surprised to see the expression on her face.

She was grinning.

"You should have heard my mom," she said, laughing. "She kept saying stuff like, 'This is not the end of the world,' and 'a lot of people have these kinds of problems.' She didn't understand that this was the best news I'd heard in a long time!"

But I still didn't follow. I struggled to understand how this was good news.

"Don't you get it?" she said to our confused faces as if we were missing the obvious. "*This* is the reason I've been having such a hard time in school! This is why there's always so much stuff I don't get! Why my grades are so crappy! You know, I even failed an IQ test at my old school, but now I know the reason." She jabbed her finger up and down at the letter. "*This* explains a *lot*!"

Charlie and I exchanged glances. He looked as puzzled as I was. And after a quick glimpse around the table I saw that we weren't the only ones.

But Stella only laughed again, beaming at us like a convict relieved of a death sentence. "Don't you see? It's like I just had the idiot-stamp removed from my forehead! I'm not a moron after all, I'm just *easily distracted*!"

It seemed like a weird thing to be so ecstatic about, but there it was. And however odd the reason, I felt glad for her. It wasn't long before everybody was laughing along with her, and giving her our congratulations. Sydney cut us each a celebratory slice of her Doberge cake, and Mrs. Reznik even made a toast:

"To friends, family, food and taking exams in comfortable, quiet areas without distractions or time restrictions!"

Everybody clinked glasses. Stella practically glowed.

OLIVIA:
A Great and Mysterious Design

Dear Naomi,

Of course, you already know how it all played out that spring, how that first Providence Journal article led to a flood of letters of support for us and our lemonade cause. And that led to more articles and even an interview on the local news. And with the continued radio play, and with WRIZ-TV never seeming to tire of showing that clip of our disastrous performance at Catch A RI-Zing Star, interest in Lemonade Mouth kind of snowballed. People seemed to think we were hilarious. It even got to the point where complete strangers would sometimes come up and ask me if I was one of those funny kids they'd seen on TV or read about in the paper. For a few weeks there, we were almost like celebrities.

It was a weird time. My grandmother kept a scrapbook.

One day a columnist at the <u>Providence Phoenix</u> wrote an opinion piece that even called us "icons of their generation." "You don't have to be in high school to sympathize with their plight," the writer said. "In a way, Lemonade Mouth is like Everyman. We can all relate to the difficulty of finding ourselves in over our heads, trying to maintain our dignity and sense of humor while undertaking tasks that sometimes seem out of our grasp." After Stella read that one aloud at the Freak Table I still remember all the puzzled faces.

It was all pretty overwhelming.

Needless to say, with so much media coverage,

the pressure on Mr. Brenigan and the finance committee to bring back the lemonade machines eventually got pretty bad. So bad that they eventually had no choice but to give in. The administration tried to play it all down—they didn't even make an announcement about their change of heart. But somebody must have tipped someone off because word not only got out that the machines were coming back, but we even found out ahead of time which day the delivery truck was coming.

I'm sure you remember that Saturday in early April, the morning we all waited in the high school parking lot. After all, you were there too, along with what seemed like half the school. Despite the cool temperature, a bunch of kids set up lawn furniture, others ran around throwing Frisbees or playing guitars while we waited. It was a blast. There were reporters there, too, including Carolyn Brussat from the _Providence Journal,_ the lady who'd written that first article about us. There were even camera crews from a couple of local TV stations.

Terry Cabeleira stood lookout at the corner of the street so he could spot the truck before anybody else. Finally he shouted, "I can see it! Here it comes!"

As the truck backed up to the loading dock everybody cheered and waved, and some kids held up signs. Along with the usual HOLD IT HIGH! RAISE IT UP! were others like VICTORY FOR THE UNHEARD! and WHEN LEMONADE MOUTH SPEAKS, THE WORLD LISTENS!

Turned out, I recognized one of the delivery people. It was Phil, one of the two guys who'd ended up calling the cops on us that day we'd all lain in the snow in front of his truck. But today he was in a much better mood. He seemed to eat up the attention. He grinned and waved to the crowd, and after wheeling the machine out of the cargo area he tipped his cap and bowed to the cameras. Which made us all cheer even louder. The TV crews loved it.

I wish I could have somehow recorded the giddy grins I saw the following Monday on the faces of so many kids—and some of the teachers, too. Sure, the school would have to return some of the scoreboard money to the soda company, but word was already out that the sports teams were going to make up the difference by selling chocolates.

At lunch Stella barely said a word. I knew she was trying not to gloat, but she looked like she might burst.

So now, Naomi, I'm grappling with a question: Where to end my part of the story? It's a tough decision for me because, like I said before, I don't think of stories as having any precise moment you can point to and say "right there is exactly when it all began" or "this is where everything finished." Especially in real life, it doesn't work like that. But I guess there's no getting away from it, because wherever I happen to stop writing becomes, by definition, the end of the story, or at least my part in its telling.

So where to set down my pencil?

I suppose I could end with Mrs. Reznik, how after pressure from students and parents, she was eventually moved back to her old, quieter classroom, which was on the first floor but still not too far from the lemonade machine. When I asked her if she ever missed the symphony she just laughed. "It's still there. Anytime I want to visit, I can. But I'm a music teacher now, and despite what certain people may want, they'll have to drag me out kicking and screaming before I'll retire!"

Or maybe I could write about Ray Beech, how with Dean about to graduate and move to Ohio for college, and with Scott Pickett uninterested in continuing Mudslide Crush, Ray decided to form his own band called the Vicious Circles, which featured Ray on the electric ukulele and Patty Norris on the timbales. They didn't last long, though, because Patty quit in a huff after Ray told her she wasn't keeping a steady beat and why doesn't she at least take a couple lessons for godsakes? Patty Keane followed her out the door since she only agreed to sing because the other Patty was in the band.

But if I <u>have</u> to pick a single moment to end on, I guess I'll choose a day that happened before any of that, one Sunday afternoon in mid-April that Brenda and I spent selling shell ashtrays at the church fair. In a fit of energy my grandmother had painted about fifty of them and we wheeled them all into town in our little red wagon. A bunch of people I didn't even know stopped by our table only because they recognized me from the TV clip. And every one of our ashtrays sold.

On our way back home this grizzly old guy in a black coat, some random person on the street, walked right up to me, stuck his unshaven face directly in mine and growled, "You're that plump girl with the voice like a brake problem."

Now, another person might have been taken aback, insulted even, but I'm a reformed Virgo working hard to go with the flow, so I chose to see it as a compliment. This was merely one stranger expressing his brotherhood with another, a kind of hello. I smiled and then he smiled and we both continued on our separate ways.

Weird but okay.

Brenda and I rolled our empty wagon up our driveway and had just rounded the corner to our house when I noticed somebody sitting on the front step. It was Wen.

"Hey," he called out.

"Hey yourself," I called back. "What are you doing here?"

"Waiting for you. Hello, Brenda."

As we came closer I noticed that he was holding something on his lap. Something small, furry and orange. I got near enough to see what it was.

It was a kitten.

"I brought this for you," he said, stroking its head. "A present."

I blinked at it. It was a little tabby, probably eight or ten weeks old. It flopped on Wen's lap and peered back at me, sleepy and content.

"Where did it come from?"

"One of Sydney's friends found her under a tree in her backyard. She asked around but nobody seems to know how she got there or where she belongs. She can't keep her, though, and neither can we because Sydney's allergic. If you don't want her, I can figure something else out."

I looked behind at Brenda and saw in her expression that the kitten had already won her heart. Then I crouched down low to get a better look. When our eyes met, her tiny face perked up. She was only a baby. She rolled onto her back and wiggled playfully.

"Of course we want her," I said, watching her bat at some invisible object in the air. "Thank you, Wen. She's lovely."

I held out my hand and the kitten let me scratch behind her ears. Her body vibrated under my fingers. I already knew what to name her. She reminded me of Daisy Buchanan in <u>The Great Gatsby,</u> careless and charming, a beautiful fool.

Wen grinned and I felt a warm glow and an odd dizzy sensation. And then I remembered something my dad once wrote me about falling in love. He said the phrase was apt because falling is exactly what it can feel like, as if you've finally allowed yourself to let go of some safety bar you didn't even know you were clinging to, and suddenly you find yourself tumbling towards the exciting unknown.

I picked up Daisy and stared into her face. I recognized at once that I'd found another kindred spirit. And I thought about all the people that had contributed, one way or another, to the events that led her to Brenda and me. Not just Sydney and her nameless friend, but also Charlie, Stella, Mo and of course Wen. And so many more, too—some that I knew and some that I would never know. I believe in a great and mysterious design. There's no telling what's ahead for any of us, but it feels right to be reminded that our lives are all connected, and *that whether we realize it or not we are each playing an important part in some larger plan. Nothing happens without a reason.*

And as I already mentioned, I don't believe in accidents. 🐾

STELLA:
A Pomegranate in the Throat

Leonard maneuvered the Volvo between the cars that lined the street and finally brought your Sista Stella and her family to a stop near Wen's long driveway. It was a May afternoon, clear and warm. A beautiful day for a wedding.

My mom turned around. "Need help carrying anything, Stella?"

"No," I said, popping open the door and grabbing my stuff. "It's only my new uke and a little amp. Plus, you're already late. Don't worry, I got it."

"Are you sure?" asked Leonard. "It's no trouble."

"I'll be fine."

My mother had decided to stay with the lab after all. Some of its initial investors had indeed backed out of the project, but following a round of frantic phone calls and a few all-nighters, my mom had been able to organize an impressive presentation that managed to win over a new batch of investors. So the quest for the perfect, world-saving Frankenstein plant would continue, at least for a few more months. Today, in fact, the company was having an open house for families. I would have gone too if I hadn't had this other commitment. But it was great to see my mother busily doing what made her happy.

"Well, okay . . ." the biochemical crusader said, checking her watch. "Good luck and have fun, sweetie. And give Sydney and Norman our congratulations."

Through the open backseat window, my brothers looked bored. Clea eyed me skeptically. "Wait, don't go yet, Leonard," she said. "That's a long, pebble driveway Stella has to navigate, and it's her first time in heels. *This* I gotta see."

I ignored her. As I headed toward the house, Leonard called out to me before he pulled away. "Hold it high, Stella!" he said. "Raise it up!"

I smiled and waved again. Leonard was all right.

By that time the song "Everyday Monsters" was starting to get pretty regular airplay on WRIZ radio. Crazy as it sounds, the manager of Results May Vary, a local band successful enough to go on tour every now and then, called to ask if Lemonade Mouth wanted to open for them when they played the Waterplace Park amphitheater in July. You should have seen the look on Olivia's face at the thought of *that*—the poor kid practically needed oxygen. After several long discussions the five of us finally agreed that we wouldn't give in to any pressure to do anything unless *everybody* wanted to. And as far as Results May Vary went, well, Olivia was still thinking about it.

But of course, when Sydney and Wen's dad asked if we would perform at their reception, how could anyone say no?

Before I even reached the top of the driveway (and despite Clea's taunting, your firm-footed phenom was able to keep the wobbling down to a minimum), a blue Subaru pulled up and Mo and Charlie stepped onto the sidewalk. It'd felt weird at first that the two of them were going out, but now I was getting used to it. Mo's parents, waving stoically at them from the front seats, seemed to be going through their own adjustment process, but I admired them for making the effort.

"Oh my God, Stella! Look at you!" called Mo, her jaw dropping.

I couldn't help grinning. I wasn't usually a dress person, but the previous day I'd suddenly decided to wear one. My mom had helped me pick it out—a shiny black, knee-length spaghetti-strap thing. Plus I was growing my hair out a little longer and only the night before had dyed it black, almost my natural color, to go with my outfit.

But even though my mother had rolled her eyes, I'd insisted on wearing a matching black Sista Slash dog collar too. I didn't want anybody to think I'd sold out.

Still, it was a whole new look for me. And from the amazed expression on Mo's and Charlie's faces, and the sideways glances I was getting from the two young khaki-and-tie *GQ* guys whose eyes had followed me up the driveway, you would have thought nobody ever noticed I was a girl before.

All I could think to say was, "Thanks. You both look great too." And they did. They looked glamorous together, like they stepped out of a magazine.

Mo's dad honked goodbye before driving away. Then we all headed around the house to the big tent that was set up in the side yard. Clea had been right about one thing— those shoes weren't exactly designed for comfort.

We sat in fold-up chairs arranged in rows in the grass. The ceremony was short and sweet. Sydney wore a simple white dress and sandals, with wildflowers in her hair. I couldn't stop staring at Wen standing next to his dad, fidgeting nervously with the rings. With his glasses and his new blue suit, I could almost imagine him someday working at a bank, or maybe a government office—some real job. Scary.

A couple of people read poems and then Sydney and Norman recited their vows. They wrote their own. Even before they started talking, I could already sense Mrs. Reznik beginning to choke up to my left, but when Norman shed a tear in the middle of his speech, that was enough to send the old music teacher over the edge. I felt her shake quietly beside me. Mo reached out for Charlie's hand, but I pretended not to notice that either. When Sydney made her speech about how lucky she felt that she'd finally found the love of her life, though, it must be admitted that even your dyslexic diva, normally the poster girl of self-control, may have succumbed just a little to the pomegranate she felt in her throat.

Not that I was about to admit it to anybody.

After the meal, a DJ played pop tunes for a while and the five of us went out on the dance floor together. It wasn't my kind of music and I'm not much of a dancer, but in my new dress I felt like a different kind of girl, the kind that goes out there no matter what tune is playing. Still, there was no way I was attempting any fast moves in those heels, which by that time were killing me. I threw them off and danced in my bare feet. Moving around in my new dress, I sensed that it wasn't only the two *GQ* guys who had their eyes on me now.

I had to admit I was having a great time.

When the cake came out, everybody went back to their seats. I hadn't yet caught my breath when two giant bearded muscle guys who looked like they knew their way around a Harley Davidson leaned over from the next table.

"Oy, you're Lemonade Mouth then, right?" asked one of them in an accent I couldn't place. He was a fearsome fellow with a grizzled beard and two missing teeth.

"Uh . . . yes," Mo said.

"I knew it!" He gave a broad, hairy grin and slapped Charlie hard on the shoulder. "Chuffed to meet you. Spank and I are ape-nuts about you guys!"

His friend, an even larger specimen with a shaved head and an alarming scar across his left cheek, held a little flowered teacup in his thick fingers. He nodded bashfully. "Can we get you lot to autograph a napkin?"

So our heroes started up a conversation with them. Turned out, they were Spank and Dave, friends of Sydney's who'd flown all the way from Australia to come to the wedding. She'd sent them a CD and, at least according to them, they were big fans.

"We play *Live at the Bash!* all the time at home, don't we, Spank? What's the name of that one that always brings tears to your eyes?"

"Nancy," his friend said solemnly as he skewered his cake with a tiny fork. "Skinny Nancy."

"Right, mate! That's the one. Bonzer, that is. Lovely."

I couldn't help smiling. It was nice to be appreciated.

After the cake part was over, Mrs. Reznik went away to chat with Wen's dad. Sydney strolled over and told us we could start playing any time we wanted. Almost immediately, somebody called her away and then it was just the five of us again. And that's when I looked at the faces around the table and suddenly felt as if everything about each of us was changing right before my eyes. Maybe it was just the novelty that we were all dressed up and at a wedding together. Maybe it was Mo, the way she'd spent the afternoon sitting back and laughing with the rest of us. I'd never seen her so relaxed. Or maybe it was the way Olivia and Wen kept looking at each other like they shared a secret. Whatever it was, I felt like we were on a rollercoaster ride and there was no getting off.

We made our way to the corner of the dance floor where our instruments already waited. I grabbed my ukulele and took my position. I looked out at the audience and felt the thrill of their applause. And then we started playing. Soon I felt calm again. I knew I was exactly where I belonged, up there with my friends making the music we all loved.

And I was reminded once again how a song really can change the world.

About the Author

Mark Peter Hughes was born in Liverpool, England, and grew up in Barrington, Rhode Island. Mark's obsession with music has led to many ups and downs. Setbacks included getting ejected from eighth-grade music class for throwing a spitball and the heartbreak of learning that the accordion has no place on a thrash-metal stage. Success came later when he fronted an alternative-rock band. He owns a pennywhistle, a broken violin, and a boxful of other musical instruments of mass destruction. He now lives and often hums quietly in Massachusetts.

Lemonade Mouth is Mark Peter Hughes's second novel. His first, *I Am the Wallpaper*, was a BookSense Children's Summer Pick and a New York Public Library Book for the Teen Age.

Visit Mark's Web site at www.markpeterhughes.com.